THE MIDNIGHT KNOCK

ALSO BY JOHN FRAM

No Road Home
The Bright Lands

THE
MIDNIGHT
KNOCK

A NOVEL

JOHN FRAM

ATRIA BOOKS

NEW YORK AMSTERDAM/ANTWERP LONDON
TORONTO SYDNEY/MELBOURNE NEW DELHI

ATRIA
BOOKS

An Imprint of Simon & Schuster, LLC
1230 Avenue of the Americas
New York, NY 10020

For more than 100 years, Simon & Schuster has championed authors and the stories they create. By respecting the copyright of an author's intellectual property, you enable Simon & Schuster and the author to continue publishing exceptional books for years to come. We thank you for supporting the author's copyright by purchasing an authorized edition of this book.

This book is a work of fiction. Any references to historical events, real people, or real places are used fictitiously. Other names, characters, places, and events are products of the author's imagination, and any resemblance to actual events or places or persons, living or dead, is entirely coincidental.

First Atria Books hardcover edition October 2025

ATRIA BOOKS and colophon are trademarks of Simon & Schuster, LLC

Simon & Schuster strongly believes in freedom of expression and stands against censorship in all its forms. For more information, visit BooksBelong.com.

For information about special discounts for bulk purchases, please contact Simon & Schuster Special Sales at 1-866-506-1949 or business@simonandschuster.com.

The Simon & Schuster Speakers Bureau can bring authors to your live event. For more information or to book an event, contact the Simon & Schuster Speakers Bureau at 1-866-248-3049 or visit our website at www.simonspeakers.com.

Manufactured in the United States of America

1   3   5   7   9   10   8   6   4   2

Library of Congress Control Number: 2025026689

ISBN 978-1-6680-6942-4
ISBN 978-1-6680-6944-8 (ebook)

This book is for Melissa,
the Queen of Second Chances

I ain't seen you with the lights on
Two nights in a row.
BARBARA MANDRELL, "Standing Room Only"

The land is always stalking people.
ANNIE PEACHES, Western Apache

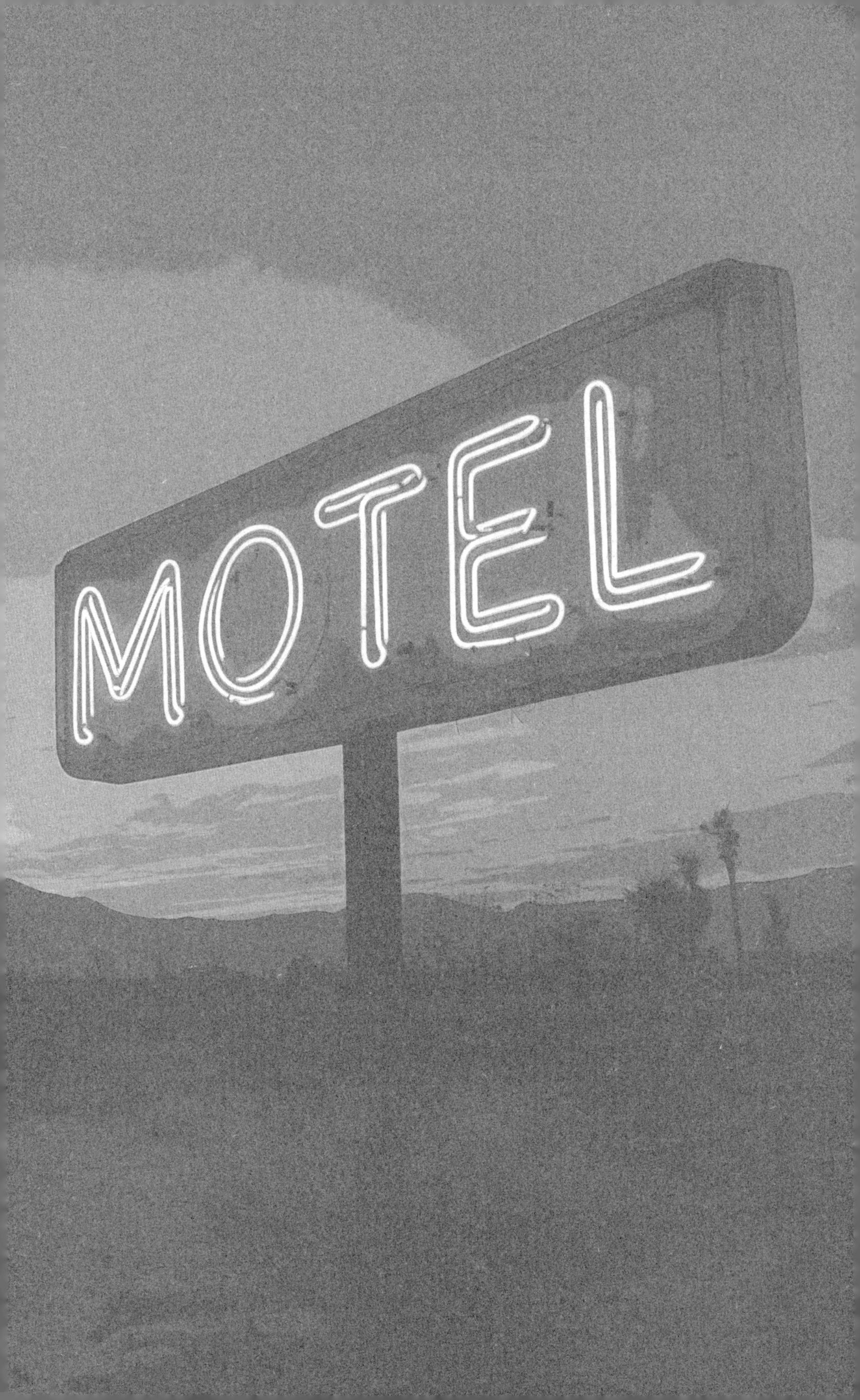
MOTEL

Part I

DÉJÀ VU

LEAVING

They left town at dawn. They left behind a corpse sprawled on a couch in the spare room upstairs and a string of fires burning in the engine bays. They left behind the apartment, the shop, the street where Ethan and his brother had once played Cowboys and Indians until well after dark. They left behind Ethan's brother. They were heading west, into the rising sun, and as they slipped onto the highway a cloud of smoke rose in the rearview mirror: Ethan's whole life, going up in flames.

No turning back now.

Ethan was behind the wheel, exhausted from the night's work and numb with shock. Hunter brooded on the other end of the truck's long seat, watching the sunrise, quiet as a knife.

Six weeks ago, just after Christmas, Hunter had wandered into the little east Texas town of Ellersby like a man from nowhere. No driver's license, no social security number, no phone. Nothing but a backpack with a change of clothes that didn't fit him and the most remarkable pair of hazel eyes Ethan had ever seen. All Ethan had going for him was an auto shop he'd inherited from his mother. His mother's shop, and her mountain of debt.

Hunter had wandered in off the street. Taken a look around the shop. Asked for a job.

Ethan had almost laughed out of despair. His hometown of Ellersby had somehow been dying for a decade, and it was trying to take the shop with it. Ethan ran sales and promotions. He turned on the lights every morning. He survived, because what else was there to do? He didn't have the money to pay this handsome stranger a regular wage—some days, Ethan barely had the money to eat after the bank took their cut of the pie—but he said Hunter was welcome to hang around, help with odd jobs when they came up. Hunter said that would be fine.

Hunter asked if there was anywhere cheap around town he could sleep. Ethan said there was a couch in the spare room upstairs.

Ethan would always remember the moment that came next. A pile of tires, gaskets discounted for two years, dust turning in the pale winter light. Hunter meeting Ethan's eyes. Ethan had always been good with people, the same way he was good with engines. The flicker of an eyelid, the twitch of a half-formed smile—they were the clicks and rumbles of an engine, all betraying the motor of the heart.

But for a long, long moment, Hunter's face betrayed nothing, absolute zero, and Ethan realized this might have been the first man he couldn't understand. Hunter's heart was impossible to read, his desires utterly opaque. This was thrilling to Ethan. Uncharted territory.

It never occurred to Ethan that a man so skilled in hiding himself might have something dangerous to conceal.

That day six weeks ago, after a long, long hesitation, Hunter smiled. Both men knew, in that moment, that Hunter wasn't going to sleep a night on that couch in the spare room upstairs. Not with Ethan's bed just down the hall.

What they didn't know was how sick Hunter would become after he moved in, or how fast, or how hard it would be to get any decent medical attention in the wooded abyss of east Texas. The world was only a few years into a new millennium. Progress was still miles away. Ethan hadn't known how many nights he would lie awake watching Hunter sleep, watching the scars on Hunter's chest glow and shiver in the moonlight as the man struggled to breathe, his lungs making a sound like a clogged carburetor gasping for air.

So last night, when Ethan and Hunter heard the shotgun go off, they knew their opportunity had come. Hunter laid out a plan. Ethan listened. Gasoline, socks, documents. A prayer to anyone listening. Before he left, Ethan risked a single glimpse at the horror in the spare room. He started to practice the lie he would have to tell for the rest of his life.

The shirt on Ethan's back wasn't his own. The old Ford truck, the wallet in his pocket, the ID inside—they weren't his. His name wasn't even Ethan Cross.

They were driving to California. Everyone started their lives over in California.

Ethan still believed, then, that it was possible to start your life over.

THE SILVER GLARE

THE TWINS

4:00 p.m.

The end of the day is just the beginning. That was the only thing their father had taught them about running a motel. Would he have taught them more if he'd known it would turn out like this? Taught them more about this place? More about tonight? In the end, a single letter was all he left them. *Nothing matters more than this.*

This: Thomas and Tabitha at the empty edge of the west Texas desert, marooned in the shadow of a mountain no one ever hiked, halfway down a road no one ever traveled. Thomas and Tabitha ran a nine-room establishment complete with gas pump, cafe, and bar. A motel with a ludicrous name. A legend from another age.

Thomas and Tabitha were the twin stewards of a place they'd never asked for and could never leave.

Remember: death sustains it.

They split their duties around the motel. Tabitha cleaned the floors and changed the linens. Thomas handled the common areas, the bathrooms, scrubbed the blood in the bathtub left over from last night. Every afternoon, the same routine. The motel returned to perfect condition. You would think, being this far from civilization, that they would never receive enough business to justify all this work.

You would be wrong. The night's guests were already on their way.

The day things finally changed, Tabitha was in room 5. She was standing next to the room's second bed, stuffing pillows into fresh cases, when she looked out the front window. The old gas pump in the parking lot. The tarnished gold haze of the desert scrub. A translucent sheet of blue sky, its horizon so infinitely far it felt like they'd been set adrift in a great uncharted sea.

A sudden flare of light passed over that pale sky. The light was strange and quick and brilliant, like the glare off a tilting mirror. The light was everywhere; it was almost blinding—and then it was gone.

Tabitha never did get used to that light.

There was a soft *tick*, and the clock on the room's nightstand flipped over from 3:59 to 4:00. It was a familiar sound, so common she'd almost forgotten to hear it. With long practice, she tossed the pillows onto the bed, where they landed with a soft *thwump* at precisely the right angle to look dense and inviting. Her rag whispered along the headboard.

And then a noise came that she wasn't used to. A noise that neither of the twins had ever heard before.

There was a faint, high *tink* from the bathroom, like the sound of a tooth chipping the rim of a shot glass. A few quick steps and Tabitha stood in the bathroom doorway. Thomas was frozen over the bathtub, blood dripping from the sponge in his hand, face turned to stare over his shoulder. He was just as shocked as her.

A fine crack had appeared in the bathroom's mirror. It ran from the top edge of the mirror's frame to the bottom, bending with a subtle arc on the way down.

Somewhere outside, a door slammed shut. Somewhere down the road, the night's guests were fast approaching.

Here in the bathroom of room 5, Tabitha and Thomas stared at the cracked mirror with a mounting horror.

"That . . . that . . ."

"That's never happened before."

ETHAN

His mother always warned him to avoid west Texas. *Life had a way of falling apart in the desert*, she said. But what did his mother know? Ethan's life had already fallen apart long before he left home.

It couldn't get any worse, he thought.

At Hunter's suggestion they took the back roads out of Ellersby, spent their morning on the drowsy highways. "Just in case our exit wasn't as clean as we think." The boys would be wanted for arson now. The cops would probably have some questions about the corpse they'd left behind while they were at it.

After eight hours of driving, those back roads ended in the cracked parking lot of a diner in a little desert town called Turner. There were no trees in Turner, no hills, no beauty. Nothing but a few faded buildings, a broken windmill, a great gold-brown emptiness.

And this diner. Lola's Den. The sign out front advertised DEEP-FRIED HAPPINESS.

Ethan didn't want to stop. He was desperate to get out of Texas; the state was so vast it seemed determined to hold on to him. Hunter said he was starving. They hadn't eaten breakfast.

The boys crossed the diner's parking lot at a jog. It was two in the afternoon, the sun well up in the sky, but the temperature was barely above freezing. It was February, the dead of winter. Pity they hadn't packed any cold-weather gear. Maybe it would have been worth the risk. Ethan had never felt a cold like this.

Inside, Lola's Den was like a lot of Texas: it must have been charming, once. A few booths, a few tables, a bar running in front of the short-order window that opened to the kitchen. Faded and scuffed, all of it, but the diner was warm and smelled like biscuits and was probably the closest thing to home Ethan would find for a long, long time.

A tall man in a gray gabardine suit was the only other customer. He sat at the bar with a cup of coffee, his eyes fixed on the wall, a matching gray hat perched on the stool beside him. The man didn't look their way. Instead, a scrawny fry cook with a hard face studied Ethan and Hunter through the kitchen window. Their presence clearly displeased him. He stared.

Hunter stared back. Hunter never blinked from a fight.

The fry cook turned away, pretending to be busy. Hunter stifled one of his nasty coughs. Thumping his chest, nodding to the bathroom, Hunter said, "I need a piss."

Ethan stood near the cash register at the closed end of the bar. He never knew, in places like this, if he was supposed to seat himself. A long lull: Ethan alone with the man in the gray suit, both of them watching the clock on the wall. 2:02.

"How old are you, son?"

The man in the gabardine suit had a smooth voice. It was smooth and level—like a preacher, a statesman—but with a hum coursing along under the words, a faint tremor. It almost sounded like he was holding down a laugh.

But a laugh at what?

"Twenty-four, sir," Ethan said.

The man nodded. "Old enough to know better, then."

"Pardon?"

"This your first time in the borderlands?"

"The border of what? Mexico's miles away." Ethan hesitated. "Ain't it?"

"I didn't say Mexico."

Ethan shot a look at the bathroom door. It was childish of him, but he didn't want to be alone right now.

The gabardine man turned on his stool to study Ethan. The man had a square, handsome face, but it was a shifty kind of handsome. He was in his mid-forties, if Ethan had to guess, gray hair sprouting along the temples, but when Ethan looked at the man's eyes, he wondered if he might not be drastically underestimating his age. They were the eyes of someone well past his forties. They were the eyes of a man who'd seen more of life than he'd ever cared to see.

The man gave Ethan a wide, wide smile. The smile was so tight, Ethan would swear he heard the teeth grind together with a faint crunch, like stones under the heel of a boot.

"Let me show you something, son."

Turning again on his stool, the man pointed out the diner's front window, and Ethan noticed the way the man's index finger ended early, just past the second knuckle. A mass of scar tissue was all that remained of the rest of the finger. Whatever had removed the joint from the gabardine man's hand, it hadn't been pleasant.

"Notice, if you will," continued the man, "that three roads lead from this humble parking lot. One goes back the way you came. One goes north. The other goes south. Do you see?"

Ethan struggled to pin down what this man was thinking, where this was going, why it all felt like some sort of trap. Ethan felt his frustration rise, and along with it, anger. This was a new emotion, or maybe just newly indulged. "So what?"

"So this humble parking lot is, in fact, the border of many places. A liminal space, if you will. An outpost of solid ground in a very dangerous corner of Texas."

"Why are you telling me this?"

The man ignored the question. "The road to the left, to the north, will take you to Fort Stockton. It's the largest settlement around here, and also the base of operations for a very dangerous man named Franklin O'Shea. Everyone calls him Frank. Have you heard of him?"

"No."

"Count yourself lucky." The gabardine man grinned at Ethan. There was no joy in those old eyes. "Frank O'Shea runs all the country around Fort Stockton. He controls the mayors, he controls the law, he controls all commerce coming and going. He's a bad man with his fingers in a lot of pies. Eyes in every corner. The little rat-faced fuck who works the kitchen here—he's one of Frank's. That cook makes a tidy side income telling Frank about any interesting customers coming or going. Isn't that something?"

Ethan looked at the bathroom door again. His temper rose. What was taking Hunter so long in there? But the temper was a cover, of course. If Ethan weren't angry, he knew he'd be scared. That grinding smile, those blank old eyes: Ethan wondered if this man in the gabardine suit might be a little insane.

Ethan kept his voice level. "I really don't want to hear about none of this, sir. We're just passing through."

The gabardine man ignored him again. He pointed out the window once more. "What's funny is that Frank O'Shea never sends his men down that road to the right. That road *there*. The road to the south. No one goes down *that* road if they can help it. That road leads to Mexico eventually, in a roundabout way, but there's quicker ways to the Rio. No. Folks call that southern route the Dust Road, on account of how little it's disturbed. Do you know why no one goes that way?"

"I'm just going to grab a booth. You have a good day, sir."

"*Wait.*"

That tremor in the man's voice grew stronger, became almost a steady hum. Ethan paused. The man stared at Ethan, dead in the eye. Never blinking. Never looking away.

"That road to the south, the Dust Road, they say there's a curse on it. They say that road gets *hungry*. That it captures people sometimes. They say that sometimes the road just goes on forever, miles and miles of driving that leads to nothing but more desert, more blacktop, more nothing. The road goes on until your car runs out of gas and the cold creeps in. The night falls fast out there. You wouldn't believe how dark it gets." The man smiled wider. "I wouldn't want to be alone out there when the dark rolls in. I wouldn't want to see what was waiting for me in all that nothing."

Ethan wanted to leave, wanted to say something, wanted just to turn his head. All of it felt impossible. It was as if the hook of the man's smile had run straight through Ethan's mind. He couldn't move. Couldn't speak. Could only stare back into the man's old, old eyes. Could only listen.

"You know what you might find down that southern road, young man? You know what might be your only salvation? A little motel in the shadow of a big, lonely mountain. The motel is abandoned, of course, but it would be shelter, of a sort."

Ethan found himself able to speak, though he didn't say what he wanted to say. "Abandoned?"

"Long empty, yes. Twelve people vanished from that motel in 1955, the owners included. No one ever wanted to take it on again. 'The Brake Inn Motel,' the place was called. I'm sure someone thought that was clever."

Ethan suddenly felt very cold.

"See, one frigid night in February—almost fifty years ago to the *day*, come to think of it—a group of strangers checked into the Brake Inn Motel for a little night's solace. The next morning, a delivery truck found the place empty. Utterly deserted. There was blood in one of the bathtubs—a lot of it—but no other sign of violence. None of the windows were broken. None of the doors showed any signs of burglary. Several were even locked from the inside. Think about it. Just think about it. Nine empty rooms. Twelve cold beds. Not a scrap of evidence to say what happened. The legend says that if you drive past the motel at twilight—just as the sun starts to sink behind the mountain—you can sometimes see the twins who run the place still going about their duties. Washing the windows. Changing the linens. It's almost like they're expecting guests for the evening."

The gabardine man finally looked away, turning his eye to the clock. His smile flattened. The hook the man had run through Ethan's brain slipped free. Ethan's body was his own again.

Ethan took a step back. His limbs felt heavy, his thoughts sluggish.

His anger was long gone: nothing but cold fear now, from scalp to toes. "Who *are* you?"

"Me? Maybe I'm a nice guy trying to give you a sporting chance." The gabardine man climbed from his stool. "Or maybe I'm just an insurance salesman killing time before my next appointment. Telling tall tales. My daughter used to love them."

The man lifted his gray hat and settled it, just so, on his head. He rose all the way up to Ethan's six foot three. He stuck out a hand, the one with the scarred finger, and Ethan found himself shaking it.

"Name's Jack Allen," the man said. "Be careful with your friend in the bathroom there. Your boy has a railroad spike where his heart ought to be. But maybe a monster is exactly the sort of person you need by your side, considering your circumstances."

"He's not a monster."

Jack Allen didn't deign to answer. He crossed to the front door, tipped his hat. "Be seeing you, Mister Cross."

How did the man know his name?

How did the man know his name?

Outside, Jack Allen climbed into a vintage black Buick that Ethan had somehow failed to notice in the parking lot until this very moment. Like everything else about Jack Allen, from the gabardine suit to the matching hat to the old, old eyes, the car was strangely antiquated, or like something out of time entirely.

Jack Allen gunned the engine. Headed north. Toward Fort Stockton. Away from the route he called the Dust Road.

Ethan envied him that luxury, later.

The diner's back door opened near Ethan's end of the bar. It let in a flinty older woman and a lingering cloud of cigarette smoke. She wore a black apron, the kind with pockets for pens and order pads. "Sit anywhere, hun," she said. She didn't sound thrilled at the idea.

A radio behind the bar had come back to life: Barbara Mandrell, burning the midnight oil. Ethan hadn't realized the radio had been silent. The clock on the wall said it was 2:03, but it must have been broken. There was no way only a single minute could have passed during that conversation with the gabardine man.

Be seeing you, Mister Cross.

Hunter emerged from the bathroom a moment later, swiping his hands on the seat of his jeans. The rat-faced fry cook emerged from his distant corner of the kitchen, arriving at the short-order window just in time to see Hunter touch Ethan's elbow.

"You all right?" Hunter said. "You look scared."

The fry cook sneered. When Ethan said, "I'm fine, I think," the cook let out a snicker loud enough to be heard over the hiss of the kitchen's grease.

What a mistake.

There had been times, before they left Ellersby, when Hunter's opaqueness had split open to reveal a sharp edge, a ruthlessness he'd directed at anyone who didn't mind their own business. It had gotten tense, once or twice. Sheriff Powell had even pulled Ethan over when he was returning from Walmart alone. *Wanted to give you a chance to talk one-on-one*, the sheriff said. *Just in case you've got yourself in a bind with a man you can't handle.*

Ethan had waved this away. It's not like Hunter ever actually came to blows with anyone. He didn't start fights. He just ended them.

Was there anything sexier?

Ethan narrowed his eyes at the fry cook. "What's funny?"

The cook turned up the temperature on the kitchen's deep fryer, chuckling to himself, ignoring Ethan.

Never raising his voice, Hunter said, "My friend asked you a question."

"We don't get a lot of people like y'all out here, stud," the cook said. "I guess we ain't used to it."

The waitress sighed. "Ignore Cleveland. I've fired him for worse and he keeps turning up for work."

Hunter didn't even glance at her. A dark light had started burning behind his hazel eyes, something Ethan had never seen before. It was like the first flicker of a black fire.

"What do you mean?" Hunter said. "'People like us'?"

"You really need me to spell it out for you?" the cook said.

"I guess so. I'm not understanding."

The rat-faced man looked up from his work. "Then you're an idiot *and* a fairy and if I weren't so busy I'd kick your ass."

"Christ alive, Cleveland," the waitress said. "What business is that of yours?"

Hunter stepped away from the bar, murmuring something in Ethan's ear as he walked by. He proceeded outside.

The fry cook snickered again. "I scare him off that easy?"

Hunter was at their truck, rooting through the bags in the bed, his back to them.

The waitress looked sincerely mortified. She said to Ethan, "Whatever y'all want, it's on the house. It'll be the last meals he makes here. I don't— Oh, sweet Jesus."

Outside, Hunter found what he was looking for. He turned around. He returned to the restaurant.

He was holding Ethan's old 12-gauge Remington pump-action shotgun.

Movement snapped Ethan to his senses. The old waitress hustled past him, making for the open end of the bar. Ethan understood what Hunter had murmured in his ear on the way outside.

Watch her—she probably has a piece.

Ethan didn't think. When the waitress started running, Ethan hiked his boot onto a stool and heaved himself across the bar. He scanned the shelves beneath the cash register—trash can, a box of pens, a pocketbook.

There, glinting atop a small safe, was a Colt .357 Python.

Ethan grabbed the gun and raised it as the waitress reached the open end of the bar.

She froze, mouth wide, hands up.

Hunter strode inside, the shogun braced in both hands. He walked behind the waitress, kicked open the door of the kitchen, raised the shotgun to his shoulder as Cleveland spun on his heel.

The shotgun was in the fry cook's face. Hunter said, "Turn around. Now."

A long moment of horror for all involved. A frozen gasp in time. Ethan's stomach lurched. A cold sweat, a TNT heart.

He felt a terrible pressure in his jeans, shameful and wild.

In the kitchen, the fry cook turned around as Hunter instructed. The cook stared at Ethan through the window. No more spite. No more snickers. Every strand of hair trembling with fear. "I'm sorry, man, I just say shit sometimes, I—"

"Did I ask you to *talk*?" Hunter said. He never raised his voice. He never had to.

The fry cook went silent.

"Go back to what you were doing. Go on."

"I—I was just heating the grease, man, I wasn't—"

"Did I ask you to talk?" Hunter said again. He came up behind the cook and pressed the mouth of the shotgun against the back of the man's skull. "Take a step forward."

"There ain't nowhere to go."

"Do it."

Terrified, bewildered, the cook took a step closer to the kitchen's window. The Python still raised at the waitress, Ethan risked a glance down through the window. But at what? There was nothing in front of the cook except the long range of sizzling deep fryers.

Oh God.

"Tell me something, Cleveland." Hunter's voice still level. The eyes still burning with ruthless black fire. They landed on his name tag. "What hand do you use?"

"What?"

"What hand do you touch yourself with?"

The fry cook started to turn around, shocked, but Hunter pressed the shotgun into his scalp.

"I asked you a question, Cleveland."

"You're fucking sick. Who asks—"

Hunter pumped a round into the shotgun's barrel: *chunk-SHUNK*. "Last chance."

The waitress was rooted to her spot at the end of the bar. Her eyes were fixed on Ethan. Not on the gun in his hand. On Ethan.

"Dear God," she said. "You're enjoying this."

Ethan ignored her.

Cleveland murmured, "M-my left."

"Your what?"

"My left hand, you crazy fuck!"

"Then do it."

Another silence.

"Do what?" the cook said.

"You know what. Do it."

Cleveland was bewildered, then curious, then aghast. His eyes settled where Ethan's had: the vats of amber grease roiling in the deep fryer.

Ethan finally felt reality catching up to him. "Hunter, you scared him fine. Let's—"

"Don't worry. It won't take long. The best lessons never do."

The grease let out a hot *pop*. Ethan could feel the heat from this side of the kitchen's window. Those fryers must have been running at three-hundred-fifty degrees. Maybe four hundred. Maybe more.

The waitress spoke. "Oh, son. You have no idea what you're dealing with, do you?"

Ethan turned. The waitress was shaking her head. She didn't look scared anymore.

She looked sad, the frown so similar to his own mother's that Ethan almost pulled the trigger of the Python just to make it stop.

"You poor, poor boy," the waitress said. "Mark my words. This man is going to get you into the sort of trouble you cain't never get out of."

"Quiet," Hunter said from the kitchen. He tapped the cook's head with the shotgun. "Do it."

"Please, man, anything. I swear to God, I'll do anything but—"

"Do it, or it'll be your brains in that grease instead."

With a horrible feeling—vertigo, or maybe the thrill of a bullfight—Ethan watched as the cook extended his left hand over the grease. The waitress closed her eyes. She made a low groan in her throat: resignation, horror, defeat.

Ethan looked at Hunter. At the black fire burning in those eyes.

Ethan said nothing. For a long time after, he'd wonder why.

Hunter said to the fry cook, "Do it."

Cleveland let out a croak of horror. He lowered his shaking hand closer to the hot grease. Lowered it by an inch. Another.

And there it stopped, just above the grease, shaking.

"I can't do it." The cook was sobbing. "I can't, man, I—"

Hunter took one hand off the shotgun. Wrapped it around the cook's left elbow. Thrust the cook's arm into the sizzling oil.

Ethan had never heard such a scream.

The grease seethed and hissed as it cooked Cleveland's flesh. The cook started to fight. Hunter struck him with the butt of the shotgun and stepped away. Cleveland fell, stunned, to the floor. Curled around his hissing hand. Watched the steam rising off his red fingers. Cleveland made a noise somewhere between a sob and a scream.

Hunter knelt down, very close to his ear. He spoke in a tone that was almost loving.

"Now every time you touch yourself, you'll think of me."

Ethan didn't think. Didn't breathe. They piled into the truck and tore out of the parking lot, heading south. Headed down the route the gabardine man had called the Dust Road.

They didn't have a choice. When Hunter had stepped out of the diner's kitchen and the older waitress fell straight on her ass, scrambling to get away from him, and Ethan followed his man outside, the fry cook had shouted after them.

"Frank is going to kill you faggots! He's going to fucking butcher you!"

According to Jack Allen, the man Ethan had met in the gabardine suit, the road to the north led to Fort Stockton, base of operations for a bad man named Frank O'Shea. According to the same Jack Allen, the fry cook at the diner *worked* for Frank. If Frank was as bad as Jack Allen said, logic dictated that Ethan and Hunter had just made a dangerous enemy to the north. No going that way.

It went without saying they couldn't head east either. That would just take them back toward Ellersby and all the problems they'd left burning there.

No choice, then. The southern road. The Dust Road. Fast as the truck could carry them.

Too fast, as it turned out. A few miles outside of Turner, Ethan heard a faint high whine from the engine that he realized, later, was the fuel line cracking. Hunter probably didn't understand the sound, but it must have triggered alarm bells. He laid a hand on Ethan's shoulder. "Easy there. Easy."

As if he were talking to a horse.

Ethan shot a glance at Hunter. The black fire in his eyes was gone, but a dangerous tremor remained in the man's voice. A vein pulsed dangerously along the jaw. "Do you think what I did was wrong?"

Oh, son. You have no idea what you're dealing with, do you?

After a long, long silence, Ethan said, "No. That guy had it coming."

"Good answer."

Mark my words—

Ethan tightened his grip on the wheel.

This man is going to get you into the sort of trouble—

Ethan didn't slow down. He drove.

Almost two hours later the road hadn't changed at all. Same gold-brown desert. Same weathered blacktop. A kingdom of sky and air, empty of everything but them.

No animals. No birds. No sound but the rumble of the old Ford's engine.

The longer this went on, the more Ethan had to fight memories of the gabardine man back at the diner.

They say that sometimes the road just goes on forever.

Why worry about old stories? There was more immediate danger inside the truck. The fuel line had indeed cracked when they'd sped out of Turner. Ethan could see a thin ribbon of gasoline in the rear-view mirror, dribbling behind them like a blood trail. They'd reached that town with most of a tank. Even with the old truck's awful mileage, the needle should not be this low.

Ethan had spent most of the last hour debating whether to tell Hunter. What to say. Hunter himself hadn't said a word in ages, but he'd watched their mirrors plenty. Surely, he saw that black line on the asphalt. Surely, he knew what it meant.

The road goes on until your car runs out of gas and the cold creeps in.

The fuel gauge sank into the red. Ethan would have to say something. But what?

Outside, something finally changed. A hand-painted sign appeared on the side of the road.

BRAKE INN MOTEL
GAS—FOOD—WARM BEDS
HIKE SCENIC MT APACHE
5 MI THIS WAY

Past the sign, in the distance, the shape of a tall black mountain came into view.

It was like the sight was too much for the truck. The engine seized up. There wasn't enough fuel left in the tank to overcome the loss of pressure from the broken line, and all of it choked and stalled. Kicked once. Twice. Died.

Ethan was just able to steer the truck onto the shoulder. They rolled to a stop right at the foot of the motel's sign.

"'Gas. Food. Warm beds,'" Hunter read aloud, slowly. He'd never been the best reader. Ethan sometimes wondered just what sort of education the man had received as a child. What sort of childhood the man had endured, period.

Hunter added, "I'll take all three."

He grinned at Ethan, probably expecting Ethan to grin back, but Ethan was too busy telling himself he wasn't afraid.

Nine empty rooms. Twelve cold beds.

Already the desert's chill was creeping into the cab. *The night falls fast out there.*

"Ethan?"

Something strange happened in that moment. Light passed over the sky, a bright silver flash like the glare off an enormous mirror. The light was brilliant, unnerving, unlike anything Ethan had ever seen. It only lasted a second, maybe two, but its afterglow shimmered for ages at the edges of his vision.

The light almost hurt his eyes, but it seemed to jolt Ethan out of a daze. His body felt like his own again. He glanced at his watch. It was four o'clock. Time was moving.

Hunter stifled a nasty cough. He rubbed his head like he was fighting off a headache. "I'll carry the duffel bag. You get the gas can. Hold on to the Python while you're at it."

Ethan said, "What about the cops?"

"I don't think the cops are our problem."

"What do you mean? The waitress must have seen us take this road. Where else would they go to look for us?"

"If they were coming, they would have caught up to us by now." Hunter hesitated, clearly more to say, but a cold wind struck the truck, moaning its way through the door seal. The temperature in the cab had already fallen five degrees.

"We need to worry about sunset," Hunter said. "If we get stuck out here after dark, we'll freeze to death before dawn."

Ethan said, "I wouldn't want to be alone out there when the dark rolls in," and realized he'd heard those exact same words before.

KYLA

Up the road, a girl named Kyla Hewitt walked the silver streets of a dead city.

The city had once been grand. Long buildings rose with curved limestone walls. The walls had no seams, no grout, no cracks, just an endless pattern of whorling grooves that made Kyla think of an ocean's waves. Quiet plazas were studded with dead fountains. Vast gardens had taken centuries to go to seed. In the distance, tall spires of white stone reached toward a permanent night that had never known a star.

There was no one here. No one left. Just a labyrinth of looping silver streets, streets that spiraled in and in and in, inward to the city's waiting heart.

Kyla was going deeper. Kyla must go deeper.

The air thrummed with energy. A tingle of heat singed her nostrils. She smelled hot ozone. It was like she'd stepped near a fallen power line, like the whole city was dangerously unstable. Too much more of that power and even the grooved stone walls might ignite in flames.

Kyla couldn't stay here for long.

But still she went deeper. She must go deeper.

She was awaited.

Except when she arrived at her destination, Kyla realized she wasn't alone. The last of the silver streets ended at a tall stone archway, past which there rose a column of silver light that Kyla knew, in the way of dreams, was the source of all this unstable power. This was the heart of the city. The light was coming up, up, from deep in the earth, and so Kyla must go deeper still.

But a man stood between her and the light. A tall man in a faded gray suit, the kind no one ever wore anymore. The man was staring at the light, a hand outstretched like he wanted to hold it.

The man's index finger ended at the second knuckle. Something had seared the rest of it away.

In his other hand, the man held a long, long knife. Its blade dripped with blood. With a shivery rush of fear, Kyla knew that this man was dangerous. That he had done things more horrible than Kyla could ever imagine. She eased herself back the way she'd come, as silent as she knew how, but it was no good. The man in the gray suit knew she was there. He had always known, because she was always here.

The man turned to give Kyla a wide, wide smile. His teeth ground together like stones.

His face was coated with blood.

"Oh no, Miss Hewitt," the man said. How did he know her name?

How did he know her name?

"It is I who shall have audience once more."

Kyla jerked awake in the passenger seat of a Chevy Malibu at four o'clock sharp, just in time to see the glare of silver light pass over the desert sky. She wondered if she was still dreaming. That silver light: it looked almost identical to the column of energy she'd seen rising from the dead city's heart.

Her mind was still cloudy. A word came to her lips. A word, or maybe a name.

Te'lo'hi.

And then reality returned. Kyla remembered why she was in this Malibu, where she was going, who she was with. She remembered who the car belonged to. She remembered what had happened this afternoon at Fort Stockton. She reached for the gun resting in the pocket of her door. She wished she could go back to sleep. Even if it meant seeing that horrible man with the grinding smile—

How did he know her name?

—Kyla wanted to be dreaming again. Kyla wanted to be anywhere but here.

"You are awake," Fernanda said.

Fernanda was driving the car. She was tall, sharp-boned, in her early twenties, a little younger than Kyla. And yet unlike Kyla, Fernanda possessed the dignity of a much older lady, a classy hauteur that made other women jealous and turned most men into simpering fools. Kyla had never done either, which was probably why Fernanda liked her. The feeling was mutual. Usually.

In spite of the circumstances, in spite of the afternoon the girls had endured, Fernanda still looked poised and restrained at the Malibu's wheel: chin up, eyes wide, long hair falling to either side of her face in two perfect black sheets. Fernanda was from Mexico—she'd arrived in Fort Stockton last year in very unpleasant circumstances—and somewhere in Monterey she'd picked up a cool, precise English. No contractions, no split infinitives, no swearing. Fernanda's English, like her poise, always made Kyla feel vaguely ashamed of the way Dallas had raised her.

Fernanda said, "Are you feeling any better?"

Kyla said, "Are you fucking kidding?"

They were still in the desert. Still driving this same endless road. Still exposed from every angle. There was too much sky overhead, too much horizon. Kyla turned to peer out her window at the empty nothing behind them, her eyes searching the sky for drones, planes, even a fucking hot-air balloon (yes, really). Franklin O'Shea had all the toys a bad man could ever desire.

Kyla had no doubt he'd deployed them all by now.

"I think we are safe," Fernanda said. "Frank never sends his men down this road. He told me so himself."

"We won't be safe until we're in Mexico. Not with this."

Kyla toed a bright green backpack that rested at her feet. Their future was in that backpack. Their death sentence, too, at least while they were stateside.

"I do not think you need to be so scared," Fernanda said. "We would have seen trouble by now."

Kyla gave her naive friend a long look. She shook her head. "You don't know what trouble is."

Fernanda glanced her way. She tried to smile. "Have you heard the story of the rabbit who met the pirate king?"

"No stories. I feel like I'm already living in one of the awful ones."

Fernanda winced. That had stung, but Kyla was in a stinging mood. Fernanda was part of the reason they were in this mess in the first place.

(If Kyla was honest, of course, she'd had her own part to play, but thank God she was seldom honest. At least not with herself.)

Fernanda, however, was honest to a fault. "In that case, I should tell you that our fuel is falling very low. We will run dry in thirty miles. Maybe less."

Kyla sat straight up. "You're shitting me."

"No. You have been asleep for some time. I thought we would be closer to Mexico by now." Fernanda shrugged, chewed her cheek. "I had hoped to fuel up in Turner, but of course that was out of the question."

Fernanda was right. They'd passed through the town of Turner shortly after two o'clock this afternoon, though it was a miracle they'd made it through at all. When the girls had reached town, the parking lot of the diner that served as the little town's main juncture had been ablaze with flashing lights, cops everywhere. The girls had thought it was a roadblock set up just for them, but then they'd seen the color of the SUVs, the department names printed on their side panels, and realized that something must have happened at the diner itself. Something the girls wanted no part of.

Kyla had told Fernanda exactly what to do. *Don't avoid looking at the cops, but don't look at them for too long. Stay well to the edge of the big parking lot. Slow down, but not too much. Keep breathing.*

They'd reached the southern road without drawing so much as a second glance.

They'd been driving ever since.

Now, a little after four fifteen, something finally changed. A mountain appeared to the south: sharp peak, dark sides, an air of menace Kyla told herself she was imagining.

A much more welcome sight appeared by the side of the road. Above an abandoned old Ford truck, a hand-painted sign read:

BRAKE INN MOTEL
GAS—FOOD—WARM BEDS
HIKE SCENIC MT APACHE
5 MI THIS WAY

There was a ping from the dashboard: the Malibu's little fuel icon springing to life. Kyla said, "Perfect timing."

She expected Fernanda to be relieved, but the woman studied the sign with a frown as it passed by. Something was poised on the tip of her tongue.

It passed, like the sign. Fernanda shook back her hair. She said simply, "Yes. Very fortunate."

Not a mile past the sign, two figures appeared up ahead on the side of the road. Two men. One carried a brown duffel bag. The other a red gas can. One was tall and lithe, the other short and muscular. They turned at the sound of the approaching Malibu. The shorter one stuck out his thumb.

Kyla said, "They're armed."

Fernanda said, "How can you tell?"

Kyla said again, "They're armed."

She sat very still, her fingers wrapped around the gun in her door's pocket. Kyla was hardly a marksman, but her boyfriend had taken her to the range a few times, taught her enough to be dangerous.

Dangerous for him, as it turned out.

Fernanda reached one hand into her own door's pocket, touched her own pistol there. She said, "You are sure?"

Kyla looked at the two men again. They both looked like trouble, but for different reasons. The taller one seemed shifty, angry at something, but it was all a little much, a little strong. He was forcing himself to be angry so he couldn't feel something else. He was probably dangerous, but not in the way that he wanted to think. Men like that could be unpredictable in the worst ways.

But it was the shorter of the men that frightened Kyla, the muscled one with the darker hair. He had a flat, impassive look, hard hazel eyes, an unreadable face. He looked strong, lethally capable.

He looked exactly like the sort of man Frank O'Shea hired to do his dirtiest work. Kyla would know the type. Until this afternoon, she'd been a waitress at the best steakhouse in Fort Stockton. She'd spent much of the last six months serving rib eyes to men just like this short bruiser with the hard, inscrutable face.

"Is it an ambush?" Fernanda's voice was low, barely a whisper, like she thought the men could hear her.

"Maybe."

"But if they were chasing us from Stockton, how did they get up the road without passing us?"

Kyla almost rolled her eyes. Her friend lacked imagination sometimes, which was ironic when you knew how she'd survived this long. "They could have come from the border. They could have come cross-country over the desert."

"Or they could just be travelers running low on gas. Like ourselves."

The men were getting closer. Fernanda had a point: these two men might explain the rusted Ford pickup they'd seen abandoned near the sign for the motel.

"They are not dressed for this weather," Fernanda said.

"That ain't our problem."

"I did not say it was."

The men were thirty yards away. Twenty. The taller of them stuck out the gas can. Kyla saw it trembling.

"Do you recognize them?" Fernanda said.

Kyla looked from one face to the other, her mind rolling back through all the faces she'd served at Stockton Steaks. "I don't think so."

"So they might not work for Frank."

"The man hires contractors. If they came from the border, there's no telling who they are."

"You know they will die in the cold."

"I don't know that."

"We have already killed one man today," Fernanda said.

Kyla said, "What's two more?"

The men were ten yards away. If they were going to try something, they would try it now. Kyla's fingers tightened around the gun in her hand.

Fernanda said, "You do not mean that."

The Malibu pulled level with the boys. The shorter one was already turning away: he knew the score.

The taller boy, the one trying so hard to look hard, met Kyla's eye. She saw a flash of something on his face. Saw an honest emotion break free from all that fake anger.

Kyla saw a deep, roiling fear inside the boy. She knew that fear.

She felt it herself.

And then the boys were gone, behind them, the Malibu racing onward. Already, Kyla regretted their decision. Fernanda must have caught something in the air. She said, "We can still go back."

Kyla eased back into her seat. She released the gun, shook her head, patted down her hair. She forced herself to stare straight ahead.

If she started feeling regret now—regret, shame, horror at all that had happened this afternoon—she'd never stop. She'd never make it to Mexico. She'd never survive.

"Keep driving," she said. "We need to get to that motel before the gas runs out."

PENELOPE

Down the Dust Road, coming from the other direction, was a bland gray minivan, a Honda Odyssey, driven by a bland man with a bland name. In the back of the van, on the floor, hidden well out of sight, was a sixteen-year-old girl wearing new clothes, a new haircut, and all her old rage. She was not riding in this van willingly. Her name was Penelope Holiday. The man up front was her grandfather. His name was Stanley. Penelope hated Stanley, and not just because she was sixteen.

Stanley was driving her back to Fort Stockton, a place that would be terrible even if it *weren't* run by Penelope's Uncle Frank.

Three days ago in Mexico City, Penelope had realized she was getting the wrong kind of looks. At the time she'd been with a different man, a man who was the opposite of bland, and the gap between her age and the man's was clearly drawing attention, even in the shadier parts of town. She'd felt a strange nagging sensation, like someone was perched behind her, digging their nails into the back of her scalp, and after long experience, Penelope knew that this was usually a sign she was missing something, that she was in trouble, that she needed to watch out.

There had been times in the last three years—ever since The Bad Night—when this itch on her scalp had grown so irritating (so painful) Penelope had asked her doctors about it. They'd done scans. Run tests. In the end, they told her it was just residual nerve damage left behind from the surgery that had removed the bullet from Penelope's brain. *But if you feel like it's telling you something useful,* her surgeon had said, *no harm in listening.*

Penelope had listened, down in Mexico City. She was a slim girl who'd never felt safe in her own body, and thus had never worn anything to flatter it. Time for a reinvention. The man who'd taken her to Mexico had money (she didn't ask from where), and in a department store in La Colonia Centro, Penelope had found some tight sweaters and skinny jeans that made her look five years older. She'd gotten her hair cut short and dyed blond. The man with her had been impressed. *A whole new girl.*

Not that it had done much good, in the end. Yesterday morning, that itch on the back of Penelope's scalp had been so vivid it had dragged her from a sound sleep. Looking out the hotel window, she'd seen this bland Honda Odyssey double-park on the street outside, watched as her grandfather Stanley heaved himself from the driver's seat like a bear on a mission. Even before she saw the gun on Stanley's hip, Penelope had known the jig was up.

That furious itch went wild, long fingernails of dread scraping across her scalp, her skull, her mind. The pain almost sounded like it was saying, *I told you so.*

Penelope had been on the floor of the Honda Odyssey ever since. She thought she was going to lose her mind from boredom. She liked to read, but of course Stanley hadn't brought any books (*I'm a numbers guy, what can I say?*). She liked to draw, to paint, to dance. She could run a quick mile, arm wrestle with the boys, hold her own on an Xbox. She'd tortured her grandfather for a while with The Game, but it had never been the same since her sister died. She'd spent the last several hours counting the notches on the zippers of the seat cushions above her. Stanley had said it would help her fall asleep.

Now, for the first time in hours, her grandfather spoke, if only to himself. "The hell is that?"

Penelope propped herself off the floor in time to watch Stanley adjust his rearview mirror. Turning to look over the back seat, Penelope saw nothing behind the van but the big gold-brown bowl of the desert everywhere, the empty thread of highway that had been unspooling since forever.

"Get down, Penn," Stanley said. "We're still in no-man's-land."

Penelope ignored him. She squinted down the highway, curious and bored, and blinked when she saw a small glint of light at the limit of her vision. It almost looked like the sun reflecting off something small and metallic. The handlebars of a motorcycle, maybe.

Ryan drove a motorcycle. It's what he'd been driving last week, when he'd pulled up unannounced outside Penelope's school and caught her eye through the window of her biology class and patted the back of his seat. He'd raised a spare helmet in her direction, like a question. By the time anyone realized Penelope was gone, she and Ryan were across the border. Penelope could be sneaky when she needed to be.

She'd ridden on that motorcycle across the entire length of Mexico. Some people would find that scary, but not Penelope. Not much can scare you after you've survived getting shot in the head.

Now, for instance, Penelope wasn't afraid when Stanley said, "I told you to get *down*." Penelope just watched the highway, waiting for another glint of metal. Waiting for Ryan's bike to come back into view.

Instead, the next light she saw was a sudden silver glare that washed over the entire sky. The silver light was brilliant, it was everywhere— and for the first time in years, Penelope was afraid.

She'd seen that silver light before, three years ago, in her old house, in her old room, moments after she'd awoken in the middle of the night and discovered a strange man standing next to her bed with a gun pressed to her temple.

She'd locked eyes with the man. He'd pulled the trigger, and Penelope's whole world had gone silver.

It was the same exact silver she saw now. Penelope had no idea what it meant, had no idea why she'd seen it the first time, let alone why she was seeing it now, but she knew this: that itch on the back of her scalp was suddenly more painful than it had ever been before. Those long fingernails were practically burrowing into her brain. The pain was so intense, Penelope screwed up her eyes, but even in the darkness, she saw stars.

Brilliant silver stars.

And now, as the nails dug and dug and dug into her brain, Penelope heard a voice, clear as day, whispering from just behind her ear. It was a voice she hadn't heard in years.

Three years, to be precise.

"It's four o'clock, Polly," the voice said. "Time to get busy."

WHAT ARE THE ODDS?

ETHAN

5:15 p.m.

He'd never feel warm again.

Ethan couldn't feel his hands, his face, his clothes. His feet were so numb the boots they wore seemed to clop along of their own volition. The empty gas can thumped at his side, the fingers around the handle frozen to stone. The heavy Colt Python he'd stolen from the diner in Turner dug at the small of his back. He'd stuck it down the waistband of his jeans before they'd left the truck. *Better than nothing*, Hunter had said, but what good would a gun do if a man couldn't use his hands?

The boys were walking toward the only break in the landscape anywhere around: the dark mountain up ahead, its peak a knife aimed at the great belly of sky.

For a while as they walked, Hunter had talked, but never about what had happened at the diner. What he'd done to that fry cook. "It's good the Malibu didn't stop for us. Those girls were armed."

The Malibu that had whisked past them on the road. The two girls—one Mexican, one Black—who'd studied them from inside like cops. Ethan's lips were so numb, words sounded stupid coming out of his mouth. "What?"

"They had guns. You saw the way they were reaching for the pockets of their doors. They were waiting for us to make a wrong move."

Ethan thought of the Black girl in the Malibu's passenger seat. For a moment when she whisked by, he'd imagined he saw a trace of regret in her eye. A flash, there and gone. Ethan said, "They didn't seem so bad."

Hunter opened his mouth to reply but broke off when a stab of pain passed through him. He shut his eyes, rubbed his temples, scowled. Ethan didn't have to be a genius of empathy to see the man was in the grip of an awful headache.

And typical of Hunter, he didn't say a word about himself. When Ethan shivered, Hunter said, "It's good you're still cold. If you start feeling warm, the hypothermia is setting in."

Might not be such a bad thing.

A sign appeared on the road up ahead: BRAKE INN MOTEL, NEXT RIGHT.

Ethan's eyes followed the arrow painted at the bottom of the sign. A quarter mile away, at the foot of the black mountain, he saw the outline of a building: horseshoe shape, unlit neon sign, another taller building in the distance behind it.

Nine empty rooms. Twelve cold beds.

"Hunter?" Ethan said.

"Yes?"

"What if the motel's abandoned?"

Hunter glanced back, puzzled by the question. "Then we kick down a door and make you a fire."

A gravel drive split off from the main road up ahead, but the boys didn't bother walking that far. They crossed the open desert at a diagonal, faces screwed up against the wind pouring down the mountain. The sun had neared the mountain's peak—trembling at the tip, threatening to slip down the other side—and the cold world had somehow become colder. By the time they arrived at a gravel parking lot, Ethan was so desperate for warmth he would have gladly walked through the gates of hell.

The Brake Inn Motel didn't look nearly so grand.

Like he'd seen earlier, the main body of the motel was a squat horseshoe: long middle section, two arms stretching toward the road and framing this parking lot. A raised porch with a metal overhang ran around the motel, its roof studded every few yards with heavy-duty mercury bulbs, all of them currently dark.

The motel's walls were sided with dark wooden shingles. The doors were painted a bright turquoise, the same color as the chevroned metal bars welded over the windows of each room. All of it looked clean. Practically new. As they drew nearer, Ethan could see that a third, shorter arm extended backward on the left-hand side of the motel, so that the building looked more like an incomplete *H*. This shorter arm appeared to hold some sort of dormant restaurant, its lights all dead.

Ethan counted doors. The Brake Inn Motel had nine rooms.

And twelve cold—

Twenty yards behind the motel—or maybe it was thirty, the distance was strangely difficult to gauge—an old two-story house stood right at the foot of the mountain. In contrast to the bright colors and clean lines of the motel, the house seemed like a product of another age, if not another part of the world altogether. Ethan didn't know the first thing about architecture, but he was pretty sure all of the house's peaked roofs and gables and fussy trimmings probably meant it was a Victorian. The place must have once been lavish; it had a front porch so wide you could have fit half of Ethan's old shop inside, but why would anyone have built something so grand in the middle of absolute nowhere?

After a few steps, Ethan realized something stranger: he couldn't seem to take his eyes from the house, and yet the longer he looked at it, the more anxious he began to feel. Something was *off* about the old house behind the motel. It seemed to have too many windows, too many doors. Its angles all felt slightly out of true, as if it hadn't been built completely square. Even the building's dimensions seemed to shift and adjust themselves with every step Ethan took. The porch suddenly looked smaller than it had a moment before, yet the front wall looked somehow wider. He noticed a window in the middle of the house's second floor that he would swear hadn't been there a moment ago. Ethan blinked, half expecting the window to be gone when he opened his eyes again.

The window was still there. Ethan saw a small glint of light behind the glass, maybe the reflection off a mirror, but the longer he stared, the less certain he became that he'd seen anything at all.

"Look," Hunter said, finally drawing Ethan's attention free from the house. "Someone beat us to that fire."

A small chimney jutted from the end of the motel's left-hand arm, rising up from a room that was clearly the office. A trail of smoke curled away into the fading sky. Ethan smelled burning wood. He realized that the man in the gabardine suit back in Turner must have just been toying with him—the story the man had told about an abandoned motel and its mysterious disappearances had just been something to pass the time, a little petty torture—but Ethan couldn't bring himself to feel entirely relieved.

Hunter wasn't happy either. After a few steps across the gravel parking lot, he slowed down, stopped. "The cars. Look."

There were two cars already parked here. One was a bright red Range Rover parked outside room 4. The other was a white sedan parked at the motel's sole gas pump.

A Chevy Malibu.

"That car passed us an hour ago," Hunter said. "Those girls were in a hell of a rush. Why are they still here?"

The boys took two more cautious steps across the parking lot, and now Ethan could get a clearer view of the gas pump next to the Malibu. He stopped. He stared.

The pump was an ancient model, a relic. Its body was a metal rectangle with a brilliant aquamarine paint job and a glass dome on top of the rectangle, the word GULF painted on the side in bold white letters. The pump had no credit card slot, not even a meter. The words CONTAINS LEAD were printed clearly near its handle.

"Who still sells leaded gas?" Hunter said. "How old do you think this pump is?"

Ethan knew the answer to that second question, though it still didn't make much sense. Why would something this out-of-date be standing outside a motel that looked so new?

He swallowed. "A gas pump like this—it's from the fifties."

KYLA

She hadn't seen the white boys arrive. If she had, she wouldn't have left her room, more out of shame than anything. Ever since she and Fernanda had left the two men out in the cold on the side of the road, Kyla had seen the eyes of the older boy haunting her everywhere she looked. Back in the car, she'd seen the way that tall boy was clearly into some mess that went way over his head. She'd seen the way he was acting tough, callous, so he wouldn't be scared.

She knew the feeling. Kyla had known that leaving those boys on the road had been the smart thing to do. The safe thing to do. But it hadn't felt like the *right* thing to do.

Once she and Fernanda had reached the motel, of course, they'd discovered they had much bigger problems than a little guilt.

Now, almost an hour later, Kyla stepped out of room 5 and made her way down the covered porch to the office. After a moment, Fernanda slipped out of their room after her and locked up. "You should not go anywhere alone," she murmured. "Frank's men might come at any moment." Kyla was almost disappointed Fernanda had followed her. If anyone had a right to be paranoid, it was Fernanda, but that didn't mean the woman wasn't exhausting company.

If you were looking at the motel from the parking lot, the office was behind the first door of the building's left-hand arm, on the end that faced the road. Stepping inside, Kyla came into a room that was longer than it was wide, a rectangle that held a glossy wooden desk along one wall and a crackling fireplace in the other. There were a few chairs, a cowskin rug, a side table with a pot of coffee and a few porcelain mugs. Knickknacks on the fire's mantel. Windows on either side of the fireplace: desert, sky, the main road in the far distance.

A walnut door stood in the back wall of the office. Closed.

The two boys from the road turned to watch Kyla come inside. The taller one was warming his hands at the fire. The shorter one— the one who would have looked right at home working in Frank

O'Shea's outfit—stood at the desk, frowning at the motel's propri-
etors. Kyla couldn't blame him. The motel was run by a pair of twins,
a man and a woman, and they might have been two of the strangest
people Kyla had ever met.

The twins didn't look like they'd moved an inch since the last
time Kyla had been in this office. They still stood behind the main
desk, clad in simple red shirts and black pants that didn't flatter them
in the slightest. They were well-tanned, tall, with thick dark hair
and identical embarrassed frowns. The twins were in their early thirties, maybe younger, but with their bland haircuts—a sort of crew
cut for him, an old maid's bob for her—they looked decades older.
Out-of-date.

The man's name was Thomas. The woman was Tabitha.

Judging by the way they spoke, the twins had clearly spent way
too long in each other's company.

"I'm afraid we're out of gas," Thomas was saying to the shorter
boy.

His sister Tabitha said, "We've been waiting on a delivery for
days—"

"Almost a week," Thomas said. "But—

The twins had given Kyla and Fernanda the same exact speech
when the girls had arrived an hour ago:

But we've been promised fuel will come in the morning.

Tomorrow.

Finally.

At last.

Now, however, when Kyla stepped back into the office, the twins'
shared brain seemed to glitch out. Thomas and Tabitha both turned
to stare at Kyla and Fernanda, clearly aghast, like this was some absurd interruption. Unfathomable. Absolutely unprecedented. Kyla
had the strangest feeling she was an actress who'd missed her cue
and stumbled onstage during a production that had been rehearsed a
hundred times without her.

Kyla blinked. She knew she'd never get used to these people.
"Sorry. I just came to see if we could get some towels."

Thomas turned to Tabitha. Tabitha frowned at Thomas.

Thomas said, "Towels?"

"Yes," Kyla said. "Towels. There's none in our bathroom."

"Oh," Thomas said.

"I see," Tabitha said.

"We must have been—"

"Distracted," Tabitha said. "When we were cleaning your room."

Thomas nodded. "Right. Distracted."

"We'll take some to your room."

"It was our mistake."

"Our pleasure to make it right," Tabitha said.

"Yes. Our pleasure," Thomas said.

Now it was Kyla and Fernanda's turn to trade concerned frowns. The green backpack—the biggest reason the girls had gotten into this mess in the first place—was in their room. It was hidden under a mattress, sure, but that didn't mean much.

"That's all right," Kyla said. "Just bring them here. We'll wait."

Even if that means sharing an office with two boys who have every right to hate us, Kyla thought. It was safer than letting anyone anywhere near room 5.

"Of course," Thomas said.

"One moment," Tabitha said.

The twins came around the desk in unison, making for the door, filing between Kyla and Fernanda and leaving a smell of fusty soap in their wake. Frosted glass stood on either side of the office's door. The pair's blurry silhouettes hurried past the glass, moving with a purpose, their heads bowed together like they were locked in some furtive conversation.

Kyla raised an eyebrow at Fernanda. Fernanda nodded, clearly just as confused by the twins' gravitas. "They are only towels."

The white boys from the side of the road didn't seem to care about any of this. The shorter one leaned his weight against the desk, toed the duffel bag at his feet. "Thanks for the ride."

There was a hard flatness in his voice. A dangerous edge.

Kyla said nothing. What was there to say?

The shorter boy went on. "I'm surprised to still see y'all here. You were in an awful fucking hurry."

Kyla bristled. Fernanda was more contrite. "I apologize. We were dangerously low on fuel. We were afraid the car might not even make it this far."

"And look at all the good *that* did you."

The shorter boy looked ready to say more, but the taller one turned from where he stood by the fire. He looked at Kyla. He studied her the same way he had by the side of the road. Kyla saw, again, that flicker of fear in him.

She was probably imagining things, but she thought he saw the same thing in her.

"I get it," the taller boy said. "It's dangerous out here. There's no telling what kind of people could be looking for a ride."

When Kyla heard the boy speak, she realized what was going on between the pair. The taller boy's voice was high and soft. Obvious. The shorter one was watching him with an intensity no one would give a mere friend. Something protective about him. Something adoring.

The boys were an item. Way out here. Maybe the new millennium *was* bringing progress. Imagine.

Kyla said, "For what it's worth, I felt bad about it. I'm sorry."

The taller boy gave her a smile, just a little twitch of the mouth, before his face darkened again with whatever had him so scared. Kyla went to warm herself with him near the fire. Her eye glanced over the bric-a-brac arranged on the mantelpiece: a deer's antler, a framed photograph of the mountain out back, a pair of grooved white rocks the size and shape of chicken eggs.

The shorter boy spoke. "Are they telling the truth? Is the motel really out of gas?"

"Yes," Kyla said. "I checked it myself. That pump is bone-dry."

The shorter man had turned to fix Kyla with a curious stare. "Why didn't you believe them?"

"I . . ." Kyla hesitated. "I'm not sure. I guess I didn't *want* to believe them."

"You didn't want to be stuck here either. Just like us." The taller boy studied her, and Kyla had the uncanny feeling he understood something about her—saw something decent in her—that she'd never seen within herself.

She wondered if she'd ever find it.

The taller boy said, "So y'all paid for a room?"

"The twins gave us one," Kyla said. "Free of charge. They were upset we were stranded here. They'll probably do the same thing for y'all."

The shorter boy said, "Does that strike anyone else as strange?"

Fernanda said, "It is better than freezing to death in our car."

"Fair point." The shorter boy let out a rough bark of a cough, covered his mouth, thumped his chest. It sounded like he had something gnarly in his lungs.

Kyla said, "You sick?"

The shorter boy wiped his lips with the back of his hand, rubbed his temples like he had a headache. "Not with anything you can catch."

"It sounds like we're all going to be stuck here together for the night." The taller boy was clearly eager to change the subject.

Kyla said, "Looks that way."

"Well, I'm Ethan," the taller boy said. "This is Hunter."

"Kyla," she said. "And Fernanda."

The boy called Hunter frowned. Kyla suspected he didn't like having his name in the picture. Judging by the way Fernanda twitched, she was probably feeling the same thing.

"For what it's worth, we're not the only guests here," Kyla said. "Whoever drives that Range Rover is staying in the room next to us."

Hunter said, "Five guests in one night? No wonder the twins forgot your towels. This is probably the busiest they've been in years."

Ethan said, "That Rover doesn't belong to the twins?"

Kyla said, "I doubt it. Room four is definitely occupied. The twins mentioned it when we got here."

Ethan frowned deeper. "So where's *their* car? There's no way the twins could survive way out here without a vehicle."

Hunter said, "Maybe they have it parked at the old house out back. Right along with their horse and buggy."

Despite the warmth of the fire, Ethan and Kyla both shivered at the same exact time. Kyla didn't know why, but the thought of going anywhere near that old house filled her with a dread she could neither name nor explain.

What was taking the twins so long with those towels?

A creak from the porch outside dragged them all from their thoughts. A woman in her late thirties stepped into the office. She had olive skin and very black hair tied up in a ponytail. She wore the kind of comfortable outerwear a well-off traveler would take on a camping trip: tall brown leather riding boots, gray cashmere sweater, black vest trimmed with fox fur. A camera hung around her neck. It looked expensive.

A large knife in a leather sheath rode on the woman's hip.

At the sight of the woman, Kyla had to clench her jaw, otherwise it would have fallen open in shock. *What are the fucking odds?* She knew this chick. The woman's name was Sarah Powers, and she'd lately become great friends with none other than Frank O'Shea, the great and the terrible.

This could be bad. This could be very bad.

For her part, Sarah Powers showed no sign of recognizing Kyla (thank God). The woman turned a polite smile on them all. "Afternoon. Y'all out of gas too?"

Only Ethan replied. With a slow nod, he said, "That's your Rover?"

"It is. I can't believe I ran dry. I thought I'd left Stockton with a full tank."

Kyla turned away, looking at Fernanda, wondering if maybe they should forget about the towels and get back to their room. Fernanda, for her part, seemed unbothered, which made sense. She would have never met Sarah Powers, seeing as Sarah had only ever come to the steakhouse. In all the time she'd lived in America, Fernanda had never been allowed to leave Frank's *house*.

Sarah Powers herself still showed no interest in either of the girls. She took a few steps toward the coffee maker in the corner of the office, rubbing her hands like everyone else, only to hesitate mid-step when she neared Ethan. She looked at the boy, looked at him again.

"I'm sorry," Sarah said. "But is your last name Cross?"

Ethan went stiff, his eyes widening in surprise. A few steps behind

Sarah, still standing at the desk, Hunter's face tightened, and he eased a hand behind his back. Kyla had spent enough time serving steaks to men like this to know what that meant.

Hunter was reaching for a gun.

Sarah Powers noticed none of this. Staring at Ethan with an expression of mounting surprise, she said, "This is going to sound crazy, but I think I knew your mother."

HUNTER

His father had taught him well. *Always watch your angles. Keep your back to a solid wall. Never let anyone get the drop on you. Never even let them think it.* Growing up, his father used to cuff Hunter behind the ear if the boy ever forgot one of the golden rules. Even when the two of them were alone at home. Even when the only danger around was the big man himself.

Hunter still had a mass of scar tissue behind his ear from all the times his father had beat the forgetfulness out of him.

Still had the scar on his chest from when he'd killed him, too.

His old man had been a beast, but his rules had stuck. The moment Hunter and Ethan had stepped into the motel's office, Hunter had positioned himself at the far end of the desk, his back facing the corner. It gave him a clear view of all points of egress: the front door and the frosted glass, the wide windows framing the fireplace, the walnut door in the back of the office.

Hunter had watched the way Ethan and this Kyla girl had made nice. Hunter wished Ethan hadn't given Kyla their names, but it wasn't like Hunter could expect otherwise. Ethan was a decent man, empathetic to an uncanny degree. Ethan was scared and angry, but who wouldn't be angry if they'd spent their whole life getting kicked around in a shithole like Ellersby, Texas? Who wouldn't be scared, trying to start their whole life over? With a man like Hunter, no less.

Do I scare you, boy? his father used to say.

No. But sometimes Hunter scared himself.

Hunter hadn't expected to see the girls from the Malibu here. Kyla and Fernanda. The girls were clearly on edge, clearly on the run from their own mess. They didn't seem aware they were doing it, but they were constantly looking at the doors and windows, shooting glances out at the road like they were waiting for an army to come rolling in after them. Hunter didn't want Ethan to spend much more time in the girls' company. The boys had enough trouble of their own without getting tangled up in anyone else's.

Or maybe Hunter just wanted them to stop talking so his head could get a break. He rubbed his temples. Ever since that weird silver light had passed over the sky earlier, he'd had a migraine that would kill a dog.

But when the door of the office opened, Hunter realized his head was the least of his worries. He knew this new woman who stepped inside. Sarah Powers.

Six weeks ago, Hunter had met this woman in the visitor's center of the Huntsville state prison.

What were the fucking odds?

Tell Sarah—

Tell Sarah, the mountain—

Before he could stop himself, Hunter blinked in surprise. He regained his composure quick. He stood very still, very calm, at the end of the desk. He could become practically invisible when he wanted to. He watched. He waited to see what Sarah Powers would do.

He hoped, for her sake, that she didn't recognize him.

But no, of course the day was just going to get weirder. Because instead of looking at Hunter, Sarah Powers fixed her attention on Ethan and said, of all fucking things, "I'm sorry, but is your last name Cross? This is going to sound crazy, but I think I knew your mother."

Silence in the office, a startled hush. Hunter saw the way the girl Kyla was studying Sarah Powers, the recognition in her eyes. Unless he was much mistaken, *she* knew Sarah too.

What was going on here?

But then Ethan had a surprise of his own. After a moment's consideration, he said, "I doubt it. My mom didn't know a lot of people out this way. She moved out of west Texas when she was a kid."

Hunter tilted his head. Ethan's mother used to live in this neck of the woods?

Sarah must have heard the caution in Ethan's voice. "Sorry, that sounded weird. It's just . . . an impression I had. You look like her. In a good way, I mean. My car died when I was driving through east Texas, maybe ten years back. Your mom fixed it up for a song."

Ethan still didn't relax. Hunter didn't either.

"What kind of car?" Ethan said.

"A Taurus. An '87 Taurus. One of the originals. It was an old hand-me-down that no one in the family had taken care of. The thing overheated when I was driving back from a conference, and when the tow truck finally came, the driver said the only town nearby with a decent mechanic was a little place called Ellersby. I'd barely started teaching courses and your mom must have seen *broke* written all over my face. She had the problem fixed in ten seconds and hardly charged me a dime. I've never left a mechanic feeling like I owed them *more*."

"What was the problem?" Ethan said.

"Something with the radiator fan, I think? Apparently, those early models had an issue with their fan motors. By the time I was driving mine, they'd started to fail left and right."

"I see."

"Your mom was a good person," Sarah said. "How's she doing? How's the shop?"

Hunter tensed, curious how Ethan would handle this. They were skirting very close to the lie the boys had spent all morning rehearsing. It would be the first time Ethan would have to tell it.

Hunter might have to do some damage control.

Ethan shrugged. "I don't know. My brother Carter runs the shop now that mom's dead. I haven't been home in years."

"I'm sorry for your loss," Sarah said.

"It's all right. We weren't close," Ethan said.

Hunter was so relieved he could have kissed the man then and there.

"I apologize," a voice cut in. Fernanda, the imperious Mexican chick who'd been driving the Malibu. She nodded now, at the camera around Sarah's neck. Fernanda said, "Is that a Nikon F3?"

Sarah looked surprised. "You have a good eye."

"My family used to own a camera store. That model is . . . quite valuable."

"They ran a camera store?" Sarah's surprise brightened. "You must know something about a good picture."

"I am not so sure of that."

"I'll be developing the film this evening—I have a little lab set up in my bathroom and everything."

Fernanda smiled but said nothing.

"I'd love your feedback on some of these shots," Sarah went on. "I'm trying to get better. Maybe make it more than a hobby."

"I doubt I could help you much. It has been some time since I had anything to do with photography."

Sarah hesitated, finally reading the room. She shrugged. "Well, stop by if you change your mind. If you knock and I don't answer, I'm probably developing film in the bathroom. Just let yourself in. It's not like I need to lock the doors around here, right?"

Hunter tilted his head. He couldn't quite put his finger on it, but all these speeches of Sarah's seemed forced and awkward, like she was trying to perform some rehearsed lines but couldn't quite sell them. He was getting tired of it, fast.

Or maybe he just wanted to get out of here before Sarah had the chance to get a good look at his face.

Kyla said, "Why wouldn't you lock your doors?"

A flash of movement in the window pulled Hunter's attention away. There was a vehicle up on the main road. It was driving from the south, from Mexico, but now it slowed, slowed, slowed. The vehicle was a minivan, a Kia or a Honda, plain and dowdy. The sort of car no one ever paid much attention to. Perfect for moving contraband in this part of the country.

The vehicle took a lazy left and started down the motel's long drive. For somewhere so remote, the Brake Inn Motel seemed to stay awfully busy.

Kyla and Fernanda froze at the sight of the van, fear printed in their eyes. Fernanda murmured to Kyla, "That is one of Frank's."

Sarah's face lit up. "Do you know Frank?"

Everyone in the room, even Ethan, stared at her.

Fernanda said, "Do *you*?"

"Of course. What are your names? I'll tell him you said hi."

Kyla tensed. "You'll do what?"

"Tell Frank you said hi. I'm working on a little project for him, actually. Research." Sarah tapped a finger to her lips: *mum's the word.* "I have a call set with him this evening, after dinner."

"A call?" Kyla said. "I don't see any phone lines around here."

"Frank gave me one of his satellite phones. He wants nightly reports. You know how he is."

Whether they did or not, Kyla and Fernanda were gone. No more words: the two girls booked it out of the office without looking back.

The gray minivan was twenty yards away.

Sarah glanced between Ethan and Hunter. "Was it something I said?"

When Ethan didn't reply, her eyes finally turned to Hunter. They lingered on his face just a second too long.

Hunter turned away, quick, and let himself behind the motel's desk. A hook board loaded with keys was mounted to the wall, and after a moment to consider the layout of the motel, Hunter helped himself to the key to room 9. He came back around the desk, hefted their heavy duffel bag. Metal rattled inside: the Remington shotgun they'd brought from Ellersby.

Glancing to Ethan, registering the boy's surprise at the key in his hand, Hunter said, "The twins were going to give us a room anyway, right?"

He didn't wait for a response. Hunter stepped outside, heard Ethan mumble some sort of goodbye to Sarah Powers. The gray minivan had nearly reached the parking lot. Hunter ignored it. He made his way around the motel's covered porch, up the building's left arm and across the main body and then down the right. At the very last door, directly across the parking lot from the office, he unlocked room 9 and let himself inside.

He found the switches for an overhead light, for an old-time grille heater. The room was exactly what he'd expected: a queen bed, a long armoire, a wardrobe, a little table with an easy chair in the corner. Straight across from the front door was a hall that led to a bathroom and another door that let onto the back porch. There was a turquoise coverlet on the bed. Bland brown carpet on the floors.

It would do.

Behind him, Hunter heard the minivan pull to a stop outside the office. One of its doors opened, but before the driver could even step out, Sarah Powers exclaimed from the porch. "Stanley! What a surprise!"

Oh Christ, Hunter thought. As if his headache couldn't get any worse, he glanced around in time to see Sarah Powers snap a photograph of Stanley Holiday, Frank O'Shea's right-hand man. What was *he* doing here?

But then Hunter froze. Really, truly clenched up.

He froze because there was a face watching him from the back of the van. A young face. A girl's face. The face of a teenage girl with a terrible round scar on her forehead. The scar was a round white disc, the size of a quarter. Even from this distance, he recognized it. He would know it anywhere.

Charon's coin, his father used to call scars like that. *From when death sends you back with a refund.*

There was no way this teenage girl in the back of Stan Holiday's minivan could have survived the damage that had caused that scar. Hunter knew it for a fact.

Yet here she was, staring at Hunter, looking just as frozen with fear as him.

And then Ethan finally made his way along the motel's porch, breaking Hunter's gaze. The boy stepped past Hunter into room 9, looked around, then frowned as Hunter closed the door and locked it and crossed the room to check the lock on the back door as well. Ethan turned on the brass lamp on one of the bed's nightstands. He looked at an old alarm clock and checked the time against his watch. 5:47.

"How do you know her?" Ethan finally said, and for a long, sickening moment, Hunter thought he meant the teenage girl in the van.

"Know who?"

"The lady from the office—Sarah—how do you know her?"

This wasn't much more of a relief. Hunter tossed the duffel bag on the bed. "Who says I know her?"

"Your eyes. They got real wide for a second when she came inside. They never do that."

Hunter closed the curtains of the room's sole window. "Never seen her in my life."

"You sure? Now you seem nervous."

"Aren't *you* nervous? Something's wrong with this place. Can't you feel it?"

Ethan ran his thumb over the coarse fabric that upholstered the easy chair in the corner. "You're upset by more than just the motel."

"I already said I don't know her."

"Fine. Fine." Ethan shook his head, puzzled. "It's just . . . she was full of crap. That Sarah woman—she was lying through her teeth from the moment she stepped into the office."

THE WOMAN IN ROOM FOUR

KYLA

7:30 p.m.

Kyla awoke to the sound of a toilet flushing. Her heart was in her throat, a chill on her skin: she'd dreamed of the dead city again, and the man in the gabardine suit, and his horrible smile: those teeth, grinding together like stones.

Oh no, Miss Hewitt. It is I who shall have audience once more.

Fernanda stepped out from the bathroom, wiping her hands clumsily on her jeans. "I do not mean to worry you, but I believe the motel might be running out of water."

Kyla sat up on the edge of the bed, hardly hearing. She looked at the alarm clock. The time was pushing seven thirty. She'd slept with her shoes on. Ready to run.

She stood and risked a quick peek through the curtain of their front window. Night had fallen hard in the time she'd slept. A great ring of light surrounded the motel, past which the darkness of the desert was so dense it seemed almost like a living force, the maw of a void.

A neon sign burned in the parking lot.

Brake Inn Motel
Vacancy

Kyla didn't feel rested, not in the slightest, but she'd awoken with clarity about one problem that had been nagging at her before she'd drifted off. She would need to go to dinner. There was no getting around it.

Not that Kyla wanted to eat; that was never going to happen on a day like today. It wasn't to get the fresh air, either, because if Kyla could have her way, she and Fernanda would barricade the doors and windows and not leave this room until sunrise.

Kyla said in a low voice, "I need to talk to her."

"Who?" Fernanda had settled herself at an easy chair near the corner table and tilted her head back against the wall. She closed her eyes, and Kyla realized this was the first time she'd ever seen the woman look tired.

"Sarah Powers." Kyla murmured the name softly, nodding to the wall that divided their room from room 4 next door. "I'm going to make sure she doesn't mention us to Frank. It would be very bad if he found out we were here."

That was an understatement. Returning to her bed, shoving back her mattress, Kyla found the green backpack resting right where she'd left it before she dozed off. She unzipped the bag, poked through its contents, as if anyone could have disturbed the bag while she slept. She found everything exactly as she'd left it.

Frank would do anything to get this bag back. And there was no telling what he would do to the girls in the process.

Kyla jerked the mattress back into place and started pacing. Thinking. Room 5 was much like any other room at any other motel. It was clean, well-maintained, but more than a little dated, even by the faded standards of west Texas. There were two twin beds with heavy carved-wood headboards. There was a nightstand with a brass lamp wearing an accordion shade. The window in the bathroom wasn't a window, but a glass block set straight into the wall, the kind of thing that had probably seemed so modern fifty years ago. It all felt fusty and old, and yet it had been kept in perfect condition. These headboards must have been antiques, for instance, but they didn't have a scratch on them.

Kyla gave herself a little shake. She was wasting time.

Plucking up their key from where it rested on the room's nightstand, she held its wooden fob to the light. On one side, it read ROOM 5. On the other, someone had printed

7:30 DINNER

DRINKS TIL 9:00

12:00 LIGHTS OUT

Lights out. Like they were at some sort of summer camp.

"Dinner is coming up any minute," Kyla said.

Fernanda's eyes were still closed. "I agree that this Sarah woman is a concern. But would it not be suspicious to say, 'Please, ma'am, when you talk to Mister Frank, do not mention our names'?"

"I have an idea for that. I think I can play it off."

Kyla paced: back door, bathroom, front door. She turned. She started again. As she neared the back door a second time, a creak of wood from the porch outside made her pause. Slowing her step, treading softly, she held her eye to the door's peephole and saw the two boys, Ethan and Hunter, making their way to dinner. To the left, she could see the glowing windows of the motel's cafe. A neon sign burned in its window.

Hot Food
Cold Drinks

"But why should we go all the way to dinner? The woman is right there." Fernanda opened her eyes, nodded at the adjoining wall. "We could go next door and speak with her now. She said she would leave her doors unlocked."

Kyla resumed her pacing. "Going to Sarah's room would draw too much attention. If we talk to her in public, then she won't think we have anything to hide."

"But Stan Holiday is here. You saw him arrive in the van, same as me. What happens when *he* comes to dinner? He will be awfully surprised to see me here, so far from Frank's house, without any sign of Frank. There is nothing you can say that would not make *him* suspicious."

"Isn't Stanley in some kind of trouble? He went off to Mexico against Frank's direct orders. I heard it from . . . well."

Kyla had heard this from a man named Lance, but the thought of Lance brought the smell of gunpowder to Kyla's nose, brought back the sound of a bullet burying itself in a man's stomach. *You live by the sword, you die by the sword,* Fernanda had said this afternoon, when it was all over—when they'd been taking Lance's keys, Lance's guns—but Kyla had taken one look at her boyfriend's dead face and tasted bile in her mouth.

Dying by the sword sounded more pleasant than what they'd done to Lance.

Now, in the motel, Fernanda only nodded. "I believe you are right. I heard Frank arguing with Stanley on the phone the day before yesterday. 'You will be passing through enemy territory. You will just make the situation worse. Do not dare go after her.' I remember that clearly."

"So there you go. Whatever Stanley's doing, he's probably not in a hurry to get hold of Frank."

"No." Fernanda chewed her lip. "If Stanley *is* in hot water with Frank and sees us here, delivering us back to Frank would be the perfect opportunity to return to his good graces."

Kyla paced: front door, bathroom, back door. Every time she passed their bathroom, she saw herself reflected in the mirror above the sink. It was the only furnishing in this room that wasn't in perfect condition. A long crack bisected the mirror from top to bottom, so that for a few seconds on every trip, Kyla appeared to be two subtly different women. There was probably a lesson in there somewhere. Not that she had the patience to learn it.

"It doesn't matter if Stanley sees us here. There's no landline here, and Frank only gives out the satellite phones to people on official business, which Stanley definitely is not. I've never seen Stan with a cell, but the only tower is in El Paso, and that barely works in Stockton. He would never have a signal this far away."

Fernanda looked at their nightstand, as if to confirm what Kyla had noticed the moment they arrived: there was no telephone in the room. "The twins must have some way to communicate with civilization. First they have no car, now they have no phone?"

"Who cares? We just need to survive the night here. The second that gas delivery comes in the morning, we're gone."

"Do you really believe the twins, though? That gas will come tomorrow?"

"Why would they lie about that?"

"I do not know." Fernanda rubbed her arms. "But nothing about this place feels right. Frank used to say that this road was cursed. There used to be another motel—"

A noise from room 4 cut her off. Kyla heard it too: a woman was speaking next door, talking to a man. She didn't sound happy. Kyla paused her pacing and inched her way over to the adjoining wall. She pressed her ear to the wood, held her breath.

Someone was with Sarah Powers in her room. They didn't sound pleased about it.

Kyla heard a man say something. It sounded curt and brusque, but he spoke too low for her to make out the words. Sarah Powers replied with something equally unhappy. The man responded, now even quieter than before. Kyla strained her ears, struggling to make out the conversation—struggling even to identify the speaker—but it was no good. They were practically whispering by now.

In a whisper of her own, Fernanda said, "Is that Stanley?"

Kyla turned away from the wall. She shrugged. "I can't tell. But who else would it be?"

Fernanda said nothing.

Kyla didn't do well with too much advance planning. She was a girl of action, decisive sometimes to a fault (just ask Lance). She made her way to the nightstand between the room's twin beds and opened the top drawer and found both their guns still inside. Both of Lance's guns, that is, not that he would be needing them anymore. Checking the magazine and the barrel just like Lance had taught her to do, Kyla handed one to Fernanda, tucked the other down the back of her jeans.

The frozen metal bit into her skin. Good. A little pain was exactly what she needed to get moving.

"I'm going to go to dinner. I'll go armed and wait for Sarah. You can stay here if you want. Maybe it would be best if you stayed out of sight."

Fernanda considered the gun. She shook her head. "I would rather not be alone."

Kyla nodded. She wasn't sure if Fernanda was afraid of solitude or afraid that Kyla might somehow throw her to the wolves to save her own skin—the girls weren't exactly the closest of friends, whatever Frank might think—but she didn't see a point in arguing. It was going to be a difficult night whatever they did.

And Fernanda was right about something else: everything about this motel felt *off*. Somewhere deep, deep down in the base of her brain, Kyla wondered if Stanley and Frank and all the horrors of Fort Stockton might not be the least of their worries.

The girls secured their jackets and their firearms. They headed for the back door. Stepping out into the cold, Kyla risked a glance at the strange house behind the motel and would have sworn—just for a moment—she saw a glimmer of light in the upstairs window.

A silver light.

As Kyla made to lock their back door, the sound of footsteps came from around the corner of the motel. The sound came from the right, the direction of Stan Holiday's room, and so Kyla hesitated, the room key in her hand, wondering if they should duck back inside. If maybe it would be safer to try to avoid the big man after all.

But it wasn't Stanley who appeared around the corner. Of all people, it was Penelope, Stanley's teenage granddaughter, the strange kid with the awful scar on her forehead. Kyla hesitated. As far as she knew, she had no reason to be afraid of Penelope.

The girl looked ill at ease, so distracted by her own thoughts she hardly noticed Kyla and Fernanda until she almost collided with them on the porch. "Oh. Hi. What are y'all doing here?"

"I could ask you the same question," Kyla said. "Did you come with Stanley?"

"No. He's sleeping." The girl blinked. "Oh, you mean to here. Yes. He took me from Mexico."

"What were you doing in Mexico?"

Before Penelope could reply, Fernanda's face went pale. Plucking the key from Kyla's hand, she stepped back into their room. "I need the restroom again. I will catch up with you at dinner."

And without another word, Fernanda vanished, leaving Kyla alone with the desert and Penelope Holiday and the strange house in the distance and the towering black mountain behind it.

A hard wind blew over the porch. Penelope whispered, almost to herself, "It's not really an *if* question. It's more a *who* question."

Kyla shivered. "What?"

"It's something my sister said." The girl started down the porch. "When you consider all the people stuck here tonight and all the trouble we're in, it's not really a question of *if* someone is going to get hurt. It's *who*."

ETHAN

The motel's cafe was a long bowling alley of a room. A few wooden booths at one end, a well-stocked bar at the other. A steaming silver buffet waited, empty, against the wall opposite the doors and windows.

Ethan and Hunter arrived a few minutes before seven thirty and were greeted by a crash of dishes from around a cornered hallway. Thomas the twin stood behind the wooden bar, seemingly oblivious to the commotion. He polished a glass with a spotless white rag and nodded to the wall of liquors behind him, looking for all the world like the proprietor of an Old West saloon. "What'll it be, sirs?"

Without hesitating, Ethan said, "Whiskey. Ice. Water."

Hunter proceeded to a corner booth in the back of the bar. He didn't drink.

A few minutes ago, back in their room, Hunter had awoken from a doze and dressed and said, "We should get something to eat. It's been a long day." He'd given Ethan a small, sad smile. "No thanks to me."

Hunter had been different all night. Shortly after they got to their room, Ethan had needed space, the chance to think—whatever the man might say, Ethan knew for a fact that Hunter had recognized Sarah Powers when she'd walked into the office with the camera around her neck—and so Ethan had climbed into the shower, losing himself in a cloud of steam, and tried to work out what it could all mean.

Because he was certain about something else: Sarah Powers had never gotten her car repaired in Ellersby, Texas. The story she'd told about needing a new engine fan for her Ford Taurus was horse crap.

But in that case, how had Sarah recognized Ethan in the first place?

He hadn't come to any conclusions by the time Hunter had shouted through the bathroom door, "I'm going out for a smoke." Ethan had rolled his eyes. He'd thought he'd broken Hunter of that habit.

Clearly not. The man must have smoked half a pack. Around six forty-five he'd come back to their room, where Ethan had been sitting on their bed, clad in the only change of clothes they'd dared to bring from Ellersby, still trying to work through what all of this could mean.

Trying to work out what the hell kind of mess Hunter had gotten them into, and how they were going to get out of it.

But then Ethan had seen the look on Hunter's face. Hunter poked his head around the corner of the room's short back hall, his shirt already off and bundled up in his hands. He looked at Ethan with an expression of absolute tenderness—a gentle sort of concern so vulnerable it almost bordered on fear—and sniffed the shirt and said, "Sorry about the smell. At least it fixed my headache."

"Glad to hear it. Where'd you get the cigarettes?"

"Just on the road. Want me to rinse off any of your clothes?"

The question had been surprising. Hunter was tidy enough, always cleaned up after himself around the house, but in the six weeks they'd been together the man had never volunteered to do something as banal as laundry. "Don't sweat it."

That gentle concern still hadn't left Hunter's face. His hazel eyes had practically sparkled with it. "Are you sure?"

Ethan nodded, baffled by this change in such a hard, hard man. For all his powers of empathy, he had absolutely no idea what to make of it.

"All right, then," Hunter said. "Don't go anywhere. I want to ask you something."

And then he'd stepped into the shower, leaving a whiff of menthol smoke in his wake. Ethan had listened as Hunter scrubbed himself down, shook out his hair, scrubbed his clothes and twisted them dry. He'd listened to Hunter cough and cough and cough. Ethan rolled his eyes again. The cigarette might have helped Hunter's headache, but had the man stopped to ask what it would do for his lungs?

As Hunter finished up in the shower, Ethan had heard a soft choking noise from the pipes of the bathroom, heard the spray of the shower's jets dribble down to nothing. *God*, he thought. Don't tell him the motel was running low on water.

When Hunter had stepped out of the bathroom he'd been wearing nothing, not even a towel. The scars on his muscled chest seemed to have grown deeper in his absence. That tenderness in his eyes—so close to pain, or the fear of pain—hadn't left him. It still churned there, right under the surface, almost like the man was about to weep. As if Hunter could ever weep.

The man had crossed the room, naked, with a wary care, arched up on the balls of his feet, as if he was worried Ethan would send him away if he made too much noise. Hunter settled at the edge of the bed. Gently, he'd turned Ethan onto his side and climbed onto the coverlet and pressed himself against the boy and said, "I'm sorry."

Again, Ethan was almost too stunned for words. Hunter, sorry? "For what?"

"For getting you into this shit."

"What are we going to do when that Frank guy comes looking for us? Or the police?"

"We'll figure it out. We have so far."

"What was it you wanted to ask me?"

Hunter had wrapped an arm around Ethan's chest. "Can I hold you for a minute? Just like this?"

Now, in the motel's cafe, Ethan was watching Thomas mix his drink—something about the bottles along the back wall had caught Ethan's eye, but he couldn't say quite why—when a bell chimed over the door. Kyla stepped inside, joined by a teenage girl Ethan had seen in the back seat of the gray minivan earlier this afternoon.

The younger girl hardly seemed to notice him now. She shot one look at Ethan, risked a rapid glance at Hunter, and then settled herself alone in the booth closest to the silver buffet. She flinched at something, frowning, shaking her head, as if she was engaged in a deeply unpleasant conversation here in the silent bar. Ethan couldn't help but stare.

The girl had a round scar on her forehead that gave him all sorts of willies.

He said to the girl, "Are you all right?"

"My grandfather abducted me from Mexico City. He's taking me back to Fort Stockton against my will. Does that sound all right to you?"

"Abducted you?" Ethan said, stiffening.

The girl twitched again, seemed to shrug off some comment he hadn't heard. "I'm fine. I'm just angry. Aren't teenagers always angry?"

"I don't know many teenagers who call themselves teenagers."

Thomas said, "Your drink, sir," and pushed a frosty glass across the bar atop a thick paper napkin. Kyla joined Ethan at the bar, gave him a gentle bump with her elbow. She murmured, "Just leave her be."

To Thomas, Kyla said, "I'll have what he's having. How long until food is ready?"

Thomas plucked up a fresh glass. "Any minute."

Ethan looked from Kyla to the teenage girl to Hunter. The man was too distracted looking from the hall to the doors and back again. He was back to his usual self: watching all his angles.

Kyla was watching the front door. Ethan said, "Where's your friend?"

"The restroom, apparently." As if making up her mind about something, Kyla turned to catch Ethan's eye. To hold it. "I need to ask you something."

"Shoot."

"Are y'all part of the outfit?"

"What outfit?"

"Frank O'Shea's crew."

Ethan shook his head. "I keep hearing that name today. Who even is this guy?"

"That's a good enough answer for me." Kyla turned back to Thomas. "Are we talking five minutes on the food? Ten?"

Thomas said, "Not long. It's been some time since my sister had to cook for so many people."

"You could go help her," Kyla said.

The man chuckled like she'd told a great joke. He poured her whiskey with a smile.

An eerie sound reached them from the desert. It was a faint, high SHRIEK like the cry of an owl, but judging by the volume, it sounded like a larger owl than one Ethan had ever seen. His eyes drifted to the cafe's windows, to the endless dark past the motel's lights.

He said to Thomas, "Y'all have some big birds out this way?"

The man unscrewed a glass bottle to pour water into Kyla's drink.

"We have some unusual wildlife in this corner of the desert. Some specimens you won't find anywhere else."

From the kitchen there came another great clatter of dishes. His eyes following the sound, Ethan saw that the teenage girl was watching him again.

"My name's Penelope," she said. "My sister says it'll save time if you know that."

Ethan looked around the cafe. He was almost tempted to look under the booths, behind the bar. "Where's your sister?"

Penelope said, "I've been trying to figure that out all night."

KYLA

A few minutes before seven forty-five, the bell above the door chimed, and Fernanda stepped inside, looking wan and ill at ease, totally unlike her usual poised self. She settled into a booth next to Kyla, wincing as the gun tucked in her waistband bit into her back.

"Sorry," she said. "Today has been . . . difficult on my stomach."

"Can't blame you."

Fernanda glanced around the room—at the boys in the next booth over, at Penelope sitting alone and staring into space—and murmured to Kyla, "Sarah has not come yet?"

"No."

Instead, at 7:52, the bell chimed again. The door didn't open so much as it crashed into the cafe, snapping everyone to attention. Kyla and Fernanda both fumbled for their guns, but if they'd been in any real danger, they'd already be dead.

Stan Holiday was inside, red and angry and ready to crack heads.

And he had a massive Desert Eagle magnum riding on his hip.

Stan looked worse than he had a few hours ago, when Kyla had watched through her curtains as the man led Penelope into room 7. Sometime between six o'clock and now, Stanley had gotten into some kind of fight. His lip was busted and barely scabbed over, his jaw swollen and starting to bruise.

Who the hell had worked him over like that?

Kyla sat very still, as if maybe, just maybe, Frank's right-hand man wouldn't notice her if she made herself as inconspicuous as possible.

It didn't work, of course. Stanley looked right at her—right at Kyla and Fernanda both—and then just kept on walking like they were the least of his concerns. Hardly seemed to register them. Hardly seemed to care. He made his way to Penelope's booth, thumped the table, and said, "Get up. You're coming back to the room."

"Back?" the girl said.

"To the room. Now."

"Why?"

"To keep you safe."

"Safe from what?"

Stanley hesitated, just a moment. "That bastard's here. He cut our tires."

That got everyone in the cafe sitting up a little straighter.

"Who did?" Penelope said.

"Ryan. Ryan Fucking Phan."

Tabitha appeared at that moment, wheeling in a metal trolley loaded down with serving dishes. The woman looked exhausted: her cheeks red, her hair damp, flecks of grease spattered on her sleeves. She started loading up the buffet, breathing hard from the strain.

Thomas, her brother, did nothing to help her. "Don't forget, Miss Powers asked that you bring her a plate. She will be eating dinner in her room tonight."

Tabitha gave him a tired nod. She started to fill a plate with food.

Kyla shot a look at Fernanda. *Shit.* So much for trying to speak with Sarah casually in public before the woman's phone call with Frank O'Shea.

"How could Ryan be here?" Penelope said. "You stole his passport back in Mexico. You nearly killed him."

"I saw him. I saw him sneaking around the side of the motel."

"And did you go look for him?" Penelope said.

Stanley's red face grew redder. "Of *course* I went to look for him. He's gone to ground somewhere. It's the only thing he's good at. But he's trying to steal you again. I don't know how much the cartel is paying him but I'm not going to let it happen."

Penelope appeared thoroughly unbothered by her grandfather's bluster. She rolled her eyes, God help her. "We were in Mexico for days. If Ryan was trying to sell me to the cartel, don't you think it would have happened by the time you got down there?"

At the end of the buffet line, Tabitha finished loading a plate with food. She grabbed a knife and fork and napkin and headed for the doors. She clearly had no interest in dealing with whatever was about to happen, and Kyla thought that sounded like a *great* idea. She shot a glance at Fernanda. She mouthed, *Let's go.*

But Fernanda, strangely enough, seemed riveted to this conversation between Stanley and Penelope. Her hand was in her lap. Look-ing down, Kyla saw she had her gun out and ready.

Oh Jesus.

Stanley was clearly near the end of his rope. He was so angry he was spitting, and his busted lip sent a fine mist of blood across Penelope's booth. "Frank can deal with Ryan when he gets here. You're coming with me. *Now.*"

When he what? Kyla thought.

Penelope said, "Adeline wants to know who busted your lip."

That was the last straw. With a furious grunt from deep in his chest, Stanley wrapped a massive hand around Penelope's arm and wrenched her from the booth. Her knees struck the table on the way up with a loud *crack*. The girl yelped in surprise. In pain.

"You're hurting me," she said, sounding genuinely afraid at last. "*You're hurting me.*"

From the booth behind Kyla and Fernanda, Ethan was up on his feet. "Let go of her."

Stanley froze. He turned his red face very, very slowly toward Ethan's booth. He studied the boy with a look of such profound fury, Kyla felt her own heart quail.

"What did you say to me?"

Ethan, to his credit, didn't back down. "I said you can't touch a child like that. Are you crazy?"

"Am *I* crazy?" A lethal smile spread over Stanley's bleeding mouth. "A fucking fruit like you, telling me how I can operate in my own territory?"

Hunter was still seated next to Ethan. It didn't look like he'd moved a muscle this whole time. He hardly moved now. He only tilted his head to say, "You're going to stop talking like that. Now."

Stanley's smile didn't waver. "And why is that?"

"Because I don't want your granddaughter to see what would happen next."

Kyla swallowed. In any other man, she would have taken this as bravado, but not in Hunter. It was right there in his voice: the man sounded like he knew how to do terrible things. Men like this could make a fortune in Frank's outfit. Tough, quiet bastards fueled by violence. Danger in the blood. She'd served a few of them at the steakhouse over the last year, seen the way even Frank's toughest sons of bitches gave them a wide berth.

Specialists, Lance used to call them.

Specialists in what? Kyla asked.

If you have to ask, you're already dead.

Even Stanley, idiot as he was, seemed to register that this was no mere tough guy. The fury in his face flickered, just a moment, but he didn't let go of Penelope. He said, "Have I seen you around somewhere?"

Before this could sink in, a faint noise came from outside: a thin, high whine, sharp and abrupt, like the sound of a hinge straining past its breaking point.

Except that wasn't right. The sound was human. Subtle as it was, the sound made everyone in the cafe freeze. Stanley let go of Penelope's arm. Ethan crouched down a little, like he might need to take off at a run. Hunter sat up in his booth.

Fernanda tightened her grip on the gun in her lap. Kyla strained her ears.

The sound came again, louder, and this time there was no mistaking it.

Tabitha was out there, screaming and screaming and screaming in the night.

ETHAN

They found her in room 4. Hunter was the first to arrive, barreling through the open back door and down the short hall. Ethan was right behind him. Tabitha stood near the end of the hall, a plate of food fallen at her feet. She was staring at the bed. She was screaming like the world had come to an end.

Ethan couldn't blame her.

A jumble of papers and junk rested on the room's corner table. A backpack and a suitcase were on the floor: both open, their contents tossed everywhere. The drawers of the nightstands stood open. Cash was tossed across the long dresser, at least a few hundred bucks in twenties and tens.

The room had a solitary queen bed, like the room Ethan shared with Hunter. Unlike the bed in the boys' room, this one was burdened by a corpse.

Sarah Powers was sprawled over the coverlet, face down. Her boots were still on, same as her shirt, but her pants and underwear had been pulled to her knees, revealing the pale flesh of her backside and a glimpse of the private hair between her legs.

As Ethan's eyes moved up the bed, from Sarah's boots to her backside to her neck, he found two bright red pillows resting where her head should be.

The pillows covered Sarah's head and neck. They were soaked with blood.

Tabitha finally stopped screaming, only to lapse into a silence that somehow felt worse. Her brother, Thomas, made his way into the room and stopped at her side. He stared at the room, at the bed, at his sister. He put a hand on Tabitha's arm. The twins began to tremble.

Staring at the corpse on the bed, Thomas said, "She was our cousin."

Ethan breathed, very slowly, behind Hunter. Kyla and Fernanda had come in behind him. They stood near the wardrobe, both women studying the scene with revulsion, but maybe not as much revulsion as might be expected.

Ethan knew, in the way he could sometimes intuit things, that this wasn't the first corpse the girls had seen today.

Stan Holiday blundered into the room. He came down the hall, pushed past Ethan and Hunter, and sank to his knees right beside the bed. His every movement was slow and bewildered, like a man in a nightmare. He shook Sarah's shoulder as if he could wake her.

"No," he said. "Not after all this."

Ethan looked back, expecting Penelope to follow her grandfather inside, but there was no sign of the girl. Instead, at the end of the room's hall, Ethan suffered some sort of hallucination. For a moment—just for an instant—he saw a man's face watching him from the back door. A man he'd never met before. A man who looked like trouble.

A blink, and the man was gone.

Kyla and Fernanda had clearly had enough. The two girls headed for the back hallway, no doubt on the way to their room. Ethan touched Hunter's shoulder. The man nodded, turned away.

Whatever was going on here, they wanted nothing to do with it.

Not that any of them made it far.

"No," Thomas said.

"We will not let this stand," Tabitha said.

The girls paused on their way down the back hall, Ethan right behind them. Kyla turned back. "Excuse me?"

"Come to the office," Thomas said.

"All of you," Tabitha said.

Fernanda said, "Why should we do that?"

"It's your choice," Thomas said.

"Stay out here and die," Tabitha said.

"Or come to the office, and maybe survive."

Hunter went very still.

Ethan said, "Survive?"

The twins turned a frown in his direction.

"Survive what's coming," Thomas said.

"What's already on the way," Tabitha said.

Thomas said, "Whoever did this will suffer."

"We will see to it," Tabitha said.

"An eye for an eye."

"Blood for blood."

"The old law."

"The law of the desert."

Together, the twins said, "Justice will be done."

THE ULTIMATUM

ETHAN

8:15 p.m.

The office was cold, the air clotted with shadows. The fire in the grate had burned down to embers. A single gold lamp with a green glass shade glowed on the front desk, barely bright enough to illuminate the walls around it. The windows looked out on nothing but the ring of light surrounding the motel, the vast desert blackness beyond.

The walnut door, set into the room's far wall, was little more than an outline in the dark.

Five of them filed inside: Hunter and Ethan, Kyla and Fernanda, Stanley alone. Penelope was still nowhere to be seen. Kyla and Fernanda stood very near the office's front door, looking like a pair of rabbits ready to bolt. Stanley collapsed into one of the office's easy chairs. He shivered, his lip trembling: a big, frightened child. A child with a very large gun on his hip.

Hunter went all the way to the back of the office and settled against the wall near the walnut door. He vanished into the shadows, his eyes a pair of hazel jewels in the gloom.

Ethan looked at them all. He thought of the exposed flesh he'd seen in Sarah Powers's room. The bloody pillows where her head should be.

Who in this office would have a reason to do *that*?

And where on earth was that teenaged girl, Penelope?

The twins stepped inside as Ethan tossed a spare log onto the fire, and in the long shadows of the sudden flame, Thomas and Tabitha looked far, far older than they had all evening. Older than should be possible. The pair walked in unison, made their way around the front desk, stood very still for a long, long moment.

Finally, Thomas said, "A grave crime has been committed on our land."

"Against our family," Tabitha said.

"Against our blood."

"We will see justice done," Tabitha said.

"Even if it means watching all of you die."

Kyla reached a hand around her back. For a gun, no doubt. She said, "I'd like to see you try."

"It's not us you have to fear," Thomas said.

"We won't be the ones to see the guilty punished," Tabitha said.

"We're just the stewards of the mountain."

"We're just the ones who know what's coming next."

Fernanda spoke up, trying to sound confident, scornful. "And what would that be?"

Thomas returned her stare. He let out the smallest sliver of a smile, and the temperature in the room fell five degrees.

"At midnight," he said, "three things will happen."

"The door will open," Tabitha said.

"The lights will go out."

"And anyone who's not with us will die."

Another long, long silence filled the office, broken only by the crackle of the fire. On the fireplace's mantel, the deer's antler and the carved white rocks shivered in the weak firelight. The clock's hands inched forward. 8:18.

Ethan said, "What are y'all talking about?"

In response, a terrible *BANG* shook the room. Everyone, even Hunter, jumped and stumbled away from the noise. There was another *BANG*, and Ethan realized it was coming from the other side of the walnut door in the back of the office.

A furious scratching sound. Claws on wood. Like talons. Whatever was in there, it released a piercing *SHRIEK* that raised every hair on Ethan's body, momentarily shut down every nerve in his mind. It sounded like the cry of the owl he'd heard earlier in the night, but when his brain came online, he asked himself again: How could any bird be big enough to make a noise that *loud*?

Stan Holiday had half fallen from his chair. "What the fuck is in there?"

Thomas shrugged. "The same thing as what's out there."

Tabitha raised a finger to the desert through the window. Like the flick of a conductor's stick, the motion seemed to set a chorus of *SHRIEKS* echoing through the night. Out the windows, Ethan saw motion in the shadows at the edge of the motel's lights, flickers of a deeper black against the dark. He saw a glint of yellow, another, here and gone.

He felt an uncanny certainty that those were eyes. Dozens and dozens of yellow eyes. Watching him. Staring right back.

Thomas said, "At midnight, when the lights die, there will be nothing to stop those creatures from coming inside."

Tabitha said, "They are the Guardians of this place."

"The Guardians of this night."

"They are terrible and fierce."

More *SHRIEKS* tore through the air, the sounds seeming to come from everywhere. The motel, Ethan realized, was surrounded.

Thomas said, "We have a hiding place. Somewhere safe from the creatures of the dark."

"A place we use, on nights like this," Tabitha said.

"This happens a lot?" Kyla said. "Why the hell do you even live out here?"

Hunter asked the smarter question. "What's the catch?"

"We'll make you a deal," Thomas said.

"An ultimatum," Tabitha said.

"Prove to us who killed our cousin," Thomas said. "By midnight, tonight."

Tabitha said, "We will then take the innocent to safety."

"And leave the guilty to die," Thomas said.

The twins spoke so simply, it took Ethan a moment to realize what they were saying. "You want us to solve a murder?"

"Yes, Mister Cross," Thomas said. "That is exactly what we want."

Ethan hesitated. Had Thomas ever heard his last name?

Kyla said, "You're idiots. We're not cops. We don't have, like, forensics and shit. Just call the police in the morning. It's not like any of us can go anywhere."

Tabitha said, "At the rate you're going, Miss Hewitt, there won't be a morning for you."

Kyla went very still.

"But she is right. This is absurd. Like something from a cheap novel," Fernanda said. "We are not detectives. Crimes are not so easily solved."

Hunter nodded. "And how do we know this safe room of y'all's even exists in the first place?"

"You can believe us or not," Thomas said.

"We will be safe," Tabitha said.

"If you wish to join us, bring us proof of who killed our cousin."

Tabitha said, "Strong, incontrovertible proof."

"But how the fuck are we supposed to *do* that?" Kyla said.

"We don't care," Thomas said.

"You have until midnight," Tabitha said.

"That's our offer."

"There's no negotiating."

"Learn who killed our cousin and live," Thomas said.

"Or die screaming in the cold," Tabitha said.

Stanley was up on his feet, spitting and furious. "You people are insane, aren't you? This is some kind of game for you. How do we know it wasn't y'all who killed her in the first place?"

"It is absurd," Fernanda said again. "All of it, absurd."

Stanley's hand rested on his Desert Eagle. He said to the twins, "You crazy fucks know we're armed, don't you? If we wanted to, we could get you to open this safe room of yours. It wouldn't be too difficult."

The twins didn't blink. Thomas said, "You wouldn't be the first to try."

Tabitha said, "Or the first to fail."

Ethan leaned back a little at that.

Kyla was clearly done with this. She turned on her heel, grabbed Fernanda by the arm, said, "We're going to our room. Now."

But as she started for the office's front door, someone opened it from the outside. Someone new. A man stepped in, a man with a face Ethan had seen for just a moment, watching him from the back door of Sarah Powers's room. The man was in his forties, Asian, with dark hair, a broken nose, a bright sneer. He wore black leather boots and a motorcycle jacket. A tattoo of a dragon crawled up his neck and peeked up from his collar. He smelled of menthol cigarettes.

Who the hell is this? Ethan thought.

"I think we can clear all of this up right now," the man said, his bright sneer widening. "Can't we, Stanley?"

KYLA

She stumbled back from the door, reaching for her gun. "Where the fuck did you come from?"

"The road. Where else?" The new man smiled at her, revealing a cracked front tooth. He extended his hand. "Ryan Phan, nice to meet you."

Kyla backed away from the hand. "Have you been here this entire time?"

"I got here just before sundown. The twins were kind enough to give me a room."

Stanley was getting red again. "I knew I'd seen you skulking around. I *knew* it."

"I'm not sure how—I fell asleep just about the second I got here. I didn't wake up until I heard all the screaming." This Ryan fellow didn't miss a beat. "It wore me out, chasing you and Polly back across Mexico. Where is she, by the way? I'd like to get her somewhere safe."

"She's—" Stanley hesitated, grew redder. "She's not coming anywhere near you. Not now. Not ever again."

"That would be a shame. I was all set to make you an offer of my own, Mister Holiday."

Kyla interjected. "I'm sorry, but you're weirding me the fuck out. How could you get here without any of us noticing?"

"*I* noticed! I told all of y'all—"

"Can you ever just shut the fuck up?" Kyla hadn't realized, after six months of dealing with him at the steakhouse, just how tired she was of Stanley Holiday. The big man, for his part, seemed so stunned by her disrespect he couldn't speak. She'd take it.

Kyla looked at Ryan again. "I don't get it. Why are you even here?"

"I'm here to get my stepdaughter away from this asshole. Away from the whole fucking outfit. I did it once already, and Stanley went all the way to Mexico to get her back. He gave me this in the process." Ryan gestured to his splinted nose with a flourish.

Ethan said, "Penelope is your stepdaughter?"

"No," Stanley said. "No, she is not. She—"

"She would have been, if I'd had the chance to marry her mother. Stanley made sure that couldn't happen." Ryan's swagger faltered for just a moment, a memory flickering behind his eyes. He seemed to push it away with a physical effort. "But we don't have time for the past. What matters is right now, Stan. You give me Penelope and I won't tell this office why you butchered the lovely Miss Powers."

Stanley looked briefly, genuinely, astonished. "Are you insane? I'd never met the woman in my life."

Kyla arched an eyebrow. "Are *you* an idiot? You've spent the last six weeks having dinner with her. I served the two of you a pair of T-bones not five days ago."

Stanley spun on Kyla, but Ethan was the first to speak. "You served Sarah dinner?"

"Many times," Kyla said.

"But she didn't recognize you earlier, here in the office."

"I'm not surprised. She was just there for Stanley and Frank. They—"

"Stanley and Sarah were an item," Ryan Phan cut in. "Penelope told me about it while we were in Mexico—all about the woman Stanley had fallen for."

"You think I was in *love* with Sarah Powers?" Stanley looked almost ready to laugh. "We were working with her, you idiot. She was doing a job for the outfit."

"Five seconds ago you said you'd never met her," Ethan said.

Ryan said to Stanley, "Exactly what kind of work was she doing for y'all?"

"You think I need to explain myself to you?" Stanley said.

"You might want to. Because Penelope told me plenty more than just that."

Kyla's eyebrow arched higher; this all felt a little too easy. "Like what?"

"Enough for Stanley to be very worried. Let's just say it wouldn't be the first time he let his temper get out of hand with a woman. I heard about a little something that occurred in a motel closer to Stockton. The Terra Vista. Ring a bell?"

Stanley, to Kyla's surprise, said nothing. The only sign he was listening was a vein in his throat that started to pulse, very fast, beneath the skin.

Ryan appeared to take this as a good sign. "The good news for Stanley is that if he gives me my stepdaughter, no one has to know about any of that. I'll get Penelope to safety. We'll be halfway back to Mexico City by dawn."

Ethan said, "You realize that information could be life or death for the rest of us?"

"I'm sorry, kid, but that's really not my problem. Y'all seem smart. Tough." The man's eyes drifted over the room. They lingered, just a moment, on Hunter. "I bet you'll figure something out."

The vein in Stanley's throat throbbed faster.

From out in the dark, one of those terrible SHRIEKS sent adrenaline tingling on Kyla's skin. Fernanda seemed to feel it too. In a quiet voice, she said, "Do you really believe you can simply *leave* this place?"

"I don't see why not. I don't see—"

What happened next only took a few seconds.

Stan Holiday started marching toward the office's door, that vein *thump-thump-thump*ing in his throat. The guy was over this. Beyond over it.

Kyla took a long step sideways, well out of his way, because she knew that even though Stan Holiday was a thug and a bully and an overgrown child, he also had a gun on his hip, two hundred pounds of a white man's entitlement and a dangerously short fuse. Her father had always warned her to give a person like this a wide, wide berth.

Maybe Ryan hadn't gotten the same lesson. Maybe he just wasn't thinking. He stepped into Stanley's path. "Where do you think you're going?"

Stanley pushed the man back with his left hand.

Ryan came right back, fists up now, looking like he was ready to coldcock a man fifty pounds heavier and a good four inches taller. Kyla had to give him credit: whoever this guy was, Ryan Phan would've probably been a hell of a drinking buddy.

Stanley didn't seem to think so. With his right hand, the big man raised the Desert Eagle from the holster on his hip. "Out of my fuck-ing *way*."

And then it happened.

Stan didn't appear to aim. He fired twice, and between the flashes of the gun's massive barrel and the deafening *crack-crack* of the powder, Kyla didn't realize Ryan was dead until well after his body landed on the floor.

No one moved. No one screamed. They just stared, dumb-founded, at the way this man, Ryan Phan, was suddenly missing half of his head and a decent chunk of his face. A thick coating of blood and brain matter coated the office's front door. It plastered itself onto the narrow windows. It steamed on the cold glass.

When someone started screaming, it was Stanley. Before anyone else could even register what had happened, Stanley was running—out of the office, into the parking lot, screaming and screaming like no one was more horrified by this turn of events than Stan Holiday himself.

STANLEY

He hadn't planned to hurt anyone. Hadn't come to the motel, hadn't come to the office, hadn't started moving for the goddamn *door* wanting to hurt anyone. It was Ryan Fucking Phan and his fat fucking sneer that had done that. Ryan Fucking Phan and all his fucking chatter.

You want to know the craziest part? All his life, Stanley Holiday had been a terrible shot. When he pulled the Desert Eagle from his hip, he hadn't actually planned to *hit* Ryan Phan: he'd just wanted to scare the little man. Warn him. Send a couple rounds whizzing past his glib fucking face to get Ryan out of his goddamn fucking way.

But tonight, for once in his life, Stanley hit his target. Twice. Ryan's head split open, and a great hot wash of blood doused Stanley's face, and Stanley was suddenly running—running and running and running—out the door and into the parking lot and up into his van. Stanley didn't realize, until he buried his key in the ignition, that the person he heard screaming was himself.

He hadn't meant to do it. *He hadn't meant to do it.*

Just like he hadn't meant to do what he'd done at that other motel back in Stockton. The Terra Vista. It had been an accident. Both times. He would swear it on his life. He—

Stanley heard a gunshot from the office. A bullet struck the van's driver's-side window, a few inches from Stanley's ear, and buried itself in the reinforced plexiglass. The Honda Odyssey was tougher than it looked. It was one of Frank's transport vehicles, designed to move difficult cargo through dangerous places. It was the same reason the van was going to keep rolling even though someone had slashed its tires earlier in the night. It was equipped with run-flat tires. They'd get him a few miles. They'd get him out of here. They'd get him at least as far as Turner, and in Turner Stanley would call Frank and figure out why the man wasn't fucking *here*.

Because Frank was supposed to be here tonight. *Frank was supposed to be here.*

Another bullet struck the window, and this time the plexiglass started to crack. Stanley saw the short, muscled man with the hazel eyes was standing on the porch outside the office, a massive revolver in his hand.

Where had Stanley seen that man before tonight?

Stanley threw the van into reverse, gunned the engine, slewed out of his parking space, and tossed it in drive and went bounding toward the road. Through the passenger window Stanley saw that the other guests—the surviving guests, God in heaven—had come out to the front porch to watch. Someone was missing, he registered that, but Stanley was such a fundamentally self-interested man it didn't occur to him for several seconds that he was abandoning his granddaughter to this awful place.

Penelope would be fine until the cavalry arrived. That's what Stan told himself. Just until the cavalry arrived.

Stan pounded on the gas and the van rocked and bucked on the run-flats, but it kept him going, kept him moving, kept him fucking *zooming* away from this clown show.

A ring of light surrounded the motel, a halo of illumination almost like the glow of a campfire in the wilderness, and as Stanley neared the edge of the parking lot—the edge of that light—he felt something that might have been instinct or his guardian angel or some sort of inherited primal fear start to whisper just behind the ear.

"Think about this," the little voice seemed to say.

"Think."

Stanley told himself he was imaging this, just like he'd imagined the man in the mirror earlier. He kept driving. Driving and driving and driving even as every instinct, every nerve ending in his body said this was a terrible, no good, very fucking bad idea.

The edge of light was twenty feet away. Ten. Five. A cold sweat had broken out on Stanley's arms. That awful whispering voice wouldn't quit. "You really sure about this, Stanley? Are you really sure you want to go out there?"

Stanley wasn't a coward. He gunned the gas and sent the Odyssey rocketing over the gravel.

He reached the edge of the motel's lights. He crossed it.

He drove into the dark.

Stanley was going to Fort Stockton. He was going to Frank, the man who had protected him his entire life. He was going to get revenge. He was going to get answers.

He didn't make it thirty feet.

It was a struggle to keep the run-flats driving straight on the gravel drive, a full two-handed operation, but Stan risked a second's loss of control to take one hand off the wheel and fumble for the headlights. He found the toggle, twisted them on.

In the sudden light, he saw something very big and very dark and very strange—Were those feathers that caught the light? Scales?—whisk across the road ahead. The thing moved on two legs. It was almost seven feet tall.

It moved *fast*.

The thing vanished into the blackness of the desert to the left, but not before it let out a *SHRIEK* that sent the flesh crawling on Stanley's thighs, sent his balls clambering into his stomach. The same sound came again, somewhere behind him. Was it an echo, he wondered, or—

A great blow struck the side of the van, sent it slewing off the gravel. Stanley let out a scream, fighting with both hands to keep the wheel straight, but another blow came and whipped Stanley's head against the doorpost. He wasn't wearing his seat belt. Why had he forgotten to put on his seat belt?

The blow to the head dazed him, but Stanley kept his foot on the gas. It occurred to him that he was armed, that he should get hold of his gun, but when he risked another hand coming off the wheel, risked pulling his eyes off the dark road, he found the passenger seat was empty. The Desert Eagle must have gotten knocked to the floor somewhere. To retrieve it, he would have to stop the van and bend over and look. All of which seemed like very bad ideas, because when Stanley's eyes returned to the windshield, he realized he was surrounded.

Dots of yellow were watching him from the dark. Yellow eyes. Dozens of them. Everywhere.

In that moment, something strange occured to Stanley. He realized that once, long ago, the human race had been just like any other animal. That it had been stalked. Chased. That it had been eaten by things that used to live outside the edge of the campfire's light, things with names long forgotten. Stanley, in that moment, recalled a fear so old it almost didn't have a name.

Stanley had discovered the fear of being hunted.

Panic washed through him. He floored the gas. At that exact moment, a third blow struck the van. In the corner of his vision, Stanley saw the passenger door buckle and curve inward. He heard the reinforced metal creak and squeal.

And then he felt the van lift off the ground.

With a lurch in his stomach, Stanley found himself suspended in the air, the van balancing on the driver's-side wheels. The world tilted; his heart stopped—the angle of repose.

The van tipped over, and took Stanley with it.

He fell, hard, against the driver's window. Pain screamed through his body, but Stanley didn't have time for pain. He didn't even have time to catch his breath. There was a furious scratching above him, a high squeal of shredded metal, and the passenger door—reinforced frame and all—was wrenched free from the body of the van. Up, up, and away.

A rush of cold air flooded into the cab. It brought the stench of carrion.

Stanley looked up. He saw what awaited him—what awaited all of them—out here in the dark.

The sight was so horrible, Stanley couldn't even scream. Not yet.

He didn't start until the windshield exploded and a *SHRIEK* fried every synapse in Stanley's brain and a long claw buried itself in the flesh of his arm and dragged him, wailing, into the dark.

ETHAN

They couldn't see much from the porch. A massive black shape darted through Stanley's headlights, followed a moment later by another slamming against the van. Then came a second blow. A third. The van's taillights flipped from horizontal to vertical.

None of the other guests was stupid enough to think they could help Stanley. They listened as glass shattered, as a dozen *SHRIEKS* ripped through the night.

They listened as claws dug into flesh. As bone was ripped from bone. As Stanley screamed.

And screamed.

And screamed.

Stanley screamed for longer than Ethan would have thought possible. Those things in the dark—whatever they were—they weren't just eating him. They were keeping him alive. They were letting him suffer. It was almost like they were making an example of the man.

Or toying with him.

The screams stopped, all at once, cut off by a wet, guttural gasp. A final *SHRIEK* rang out, long and shrill.

Silence fell over the motel. Stillness. The awful frozen silence of the void.

And then slowly, gradually, a great low sighing sound rose from the west. Ethan turned, staring over the motel. An uncanny sensation crept over him. Had the mountain behind them grown larger since they'd checked in? Was he crazy, or had its silhouette grown to eat more of the night's stars?

And there, past the motel, Ethan saw the strangest sight of all: a pale silver light glowing in the upstairs window of the old Victorian house that stood at the foot of the mountain.

Where had Ethan seen that light before?

"Let this be a lesson," said Thomas.

"For anyone stupid enough to leave the ring of light," Tabitha said.

The twins stood in the door of the office, side by side, their faces blank. They didn't even glance at the corpse of the man named Ryan Phan—whoever the hell he'd been—sprawled on the floor behind them. Ryan's one remaining eye lolled from its shattered socket, frozen in a permanent expression of surprise.

Ethan thought of his own brother, spread across the spare room above the shop back in Ellersby.

"You have until midnight to find who killed our cousin," Thomas said.

"Or what happened to Stanley will happen to you," Tabitha said.

Hunter said coolly, "What do you expect us to do? The two most obvious suspects just died."

Fernanda said, "How do we even know you have a place of safety? That you will protect us from those things?"

"We don't care how you do it," Thomas said.

"We don't care if you believe us," Tabitha said.

"We will be safe either way."

"You, on the other hand . . ." Tabitha let the sentence trail off.

Ethan was shaking, but not from the cold. He wanted to weep, to vomit, to scream the way Stanley had screamed when the man discovered monsters are real. *We have some unusual wildlife in this corner of the desert.*

Fool that he was, Ethan used to think he knew what fear felt like. No. This dead hand around his guts, the frozen electricity scaling his nerves—*this* was fear, true horror, raw and primal.

Something came flying out of the dark. Stanley's head, ripped clean from the neck, struck the porch, and rolled to rest near Kyla's feet. The slick whisper of flesh on wood sent a fresh jolt of nausea through Ethan. Blood coated the cheeks like stage paint. The mouth was still open in a scream.

A *SHRIEK* tore through the night. It almost sounded like a laugh.

"You're wasting time," Thomas said.

Tabitha watched them, silent, long enough for Thomas to glance at her.

Whatever her brother expected Tabitha to say, it wasn't this:

"You're asking the wrong questions," she finally said. "Just like the last guests."

Thomas blinked, incredulous.

"The last guests?" Ethan stared at her. It took everything in him to say, "Y'all . . . y'all have done this before? To other people?"

Tabitha said, "Yes, Mister Cross. Many, many times."

She held out a pair of keys. Ethan took them numbly, barely registering their numbers.

"I hope you're luckier than the last ones," Tabitha said.

She shut the door.

A bolt slid into place.

Then silence.

TIME FLIES

ETHAN

9:00 p.m.

Ethan followed Hunter down the front porch. He was freezing. He was hungry. He was frightened to the root of his soul.

And yet when they passed the open door of room 4, Ethan hesitated. Sarah's room. The scene of the crime.

Hunter just kept walking, and Ethan's first instinct—his second, third, his twentieth—was to follow the man, go to their room, hide under the covers or under the bed or maybe just take himself out with the help of a firearm before whatever was waiting in the desert could tear him, very slowly, from limb to limb. Ethan wasn't cut out for whatever this night had in store for them. He wasn't built for this.

But still: he hesitated at room 4.

Hunter looked back. "We need to get busy. If we start now, we can have our room barricaded by midnight. Whatever the twins have planned, we can deal with it."

In the direction of the road, Ethan could still hear the soft wet whispers of flesh being eaten. "Do you really think we have a shot of surviving those things if the lights go out?"

Fernanda and Kyla had joined them on the porch. Kyla leaned against a wall, looking like she was barely keeping herself upright. "Who says the lights will even go out at midnight? If the twins are just planning to flip a switch somewhere, we can stop them, we can—"

As if the motel itself was laughing at her, the ring of lights flickered. It was a soft stutter, so subtle Ethan was tempted to tell himself he'd imagined it. All night long, the distant rumble of a generator's engine had made up the texture of the motel's ambience, part of the background noise Ethan had quickly stopped hearing, but when those lights stuttered, there was a change in the distant engine's sound. It hitched, ever so slightly.

Ethan knew engines. He knew what that noise meant. "The generator's running out of fuel."

Kyla said, "Oh God."

Fernanda stepped past Ethan, pushing open the door of room 5— it registered as strange, way down in his brain, that the girls' door would be unlocked—and gestured for Kyla. "I do not know what is happening. I do not know what is coming. But we are not safe outside."

Hunter nodded his agreement. He coughed, thumped his chest, took another step down the porch. Spitting out a mouthful of bloody phlegm, he said, "Let's go."

Kyla said, "Shouldn't we at least *try* to figure out what happened to Sarah?"

"Why?" Hunter said. "Why should we have any reason to think the twins plan to help us? You heard Tabitha—this isn't the first time they've done this. They're playing some sort of game. Even *if* they have some kind of bunker, and even *if* they have a way to keep us safe, we could still bring Sarah's killer to them on a silver platter, and they could still leave us out in the cold. First rule of survival: don't play by other people's rules."

Ethan thought back over the strange ultimatum the twins had made in the office. Had it felt . . . off? Yes. Staged. Performative. Like everything else about them. But did that necessarily mean they were lying?

Ethan said, "You heard what those things did to Stanley's van. Do you really think our rooms will be any safer?"

Hunter took a third step down the porch. He was getting irritated. He was getting *scared*.

Imagine.

"Come on, Ethan. Now."

But Ethan didn't look at Hunter. He looked at Kyla, who appeared just as terrified, just as lost, as him.

On any other night, in any other life, that would have probably been the end of it. No one here was qualified to solve a crime. There was no reason to think there was even any point in trying. Ethan checked his watch. Nine o'clock. It would be midnight before they knew it, one way or the other.

And yet on this night, in this life, Ethan met Kyla's gaze and held it.

He had no obvious reason to be friends with this girl, no good reason to think they could work together. That would have required trust, and Kyla and Fernanda had left him and Hunter to freeze on the side of the road.

But Kyla had apologized. She'd come to the office to find some towels and found Ethan and Hunter instead. Dumb luck. Funny timing. It had given Ethan and Kyla a chance to speak, if just for a moment. For Ethan to see the tremor in her eyes, the way she couldn't quite stand still, like she was afraid she might need to bolt at any moment. It had given Ethan the chance to see that Kyla was terrified and in over her head and fighting to keep it all together, just like him.

It wasn't much, but it was enough to feel a faint connection with this girl. A little mutual understanding. Maybe the first flicker of trust.

Kyla held Ethan's gaze. She didn't look away.

Ethan gestured to room 4. "No harm in us just poking around for a couple minutes, right?"

Kyla gave the door of her own room a dubious kick, tugged at one of the metal bars on the window. She didn't look impressed. She ignored Fernanda's stare. Hunter's anger. She looked out at the ring of light and the black desert and the dozens of yellow eyes that flickered in the dark.

She swallowed. "Beats the shit out of waiting to die."

KYLA

Kyla stepped past Ethan and straight into room 4 before she could talk herself out of it. It was crazy to try to figure out what had happened here tonight, but hell, they'd already passed crazy twenty miles back. Like it or not, the four of them were driving very fast into a very dangerous unknown.

If Kyla had learned one thing from her last six months in Fort Stockton, it was this: better to get on top of a problem than to let a problem get on top of you.

Room 4 was in even worse shape than she remembered. The air was frigid; in all the confusion earlier, no one had thought to close its doors. Sarah's body was still sprawled across the bed, her pants still pulled down, a pair of bloody pillows still stacked over her head and neck. At least, Kyla assumed the woman's head was still there. With a lurch in her gut, she realized she was going to have to check.

Who on earth *was* this woman? Six weeks ago, Sarah Powers had breezed into Stockton Steaks like a glamorous cloud, drifted straight over to Frank O'Shea's booth, and said something in a low voice that Kyla, a few tables over, hadn't caught.

Whatever Sarah had said, it had certainly gotten Frank's attention.

Now, to Kyla's surprise, Fernanda was the first to follow her inside room 4, followed a moment later by the two boys. Kyla said, "Anyone ever investigate a murder?"

"I've covered up a few," Hunter said. When the other three turned to stare at him, Hunter shrugged. "It's a joke."

Ethan edged away from Hunter very slightly, joke or not. "I guess we could start by looking around. Maybe the killer left something behind, right? Or we could figure out the motive for wanting to kill her in the first place. That might help eliminate suspects, right?"

Hunter said, "Our two most obvious suspects are dead. Stanley was definitely afraid of that Ryan person revealing *something* back in the office. He—"

"I'm not sure Stanley was such an obvious suspect," Ethan said.

He gestured to the spot by the side of Sarah's bed where the big man, earlier in the night, had crouched next to her corpse in total shock. "The guy seemed stunned to find her like this. That's hard to fake."

"Not as hard you think," Hunter said. "But sure. Say it wasn't Stanley. That leaves this Ryan person, a man who spent all night hiding from us until he decided to make a big entrance and start throwing accusations around. If that's not suspicious, I don't know what is."

Ethan said, "So what do we do?"

Hunter scowled. "We go barricade our doors and pray for the best. Just like I've been saying. Most crimes are solved from interviews, not evidence. Cops spend days getting people to say shit they shouldn't. Without that or a forensics team here to dust for fingerprints and look for stray hairs, there isn't much we're going to turn up just poking around this room."

Kyla said, "Are you done?"

Hunter scowled. "Fine. You want to find a motive? Look at the way Sarah's pants are pulled down. That seems pretty unambiguous."

Kyla supposed he had a point. Leaving the front door cracked (cold as the room was, she also had a feeling it was probably keeping the body from starting to smell), she took a long breath, went to the side of the bed, forced herself to look. Sarah Powers's jeans had been pulled down halfway to the knees. It certainly looked sexual, maybe even nonconsensual, but when Kyla hefted the room's chunky brass lamp and brought the light closer, she said, "I don't see any stains."

"Maybe the killer didn't finish," Hunter said. "Maybe he got interrupted. Sarah started to wiggle free, so he killed her."

"But wouldn't there be blood between her legs if it was rape?" Kyla said.

Ethan looked at Hunter.

Hunter looked at Ethan.

Ethan said, "You expect us to know?"

Fair point.

While Kyla replaced the lamp, Ethan took his time gazing around the room. His eyes passed over the money scattered across the long dresser, the mess of junk on the corner table, the suitcase and purse on the floor with their contents spilled everywhere. "Was Sarah really messy, or did someone toss this place? Did the killer come here to take something and Sarah just got in the way?"

"How would we know the difference?" Kyla said.

"I don't know," the boy said, but he got on his knees and started sifting through the woman's luggage.

Kyla said, "Is there any way to figure out when exactly she died?"

Hunter frowned. "The doors to this room were open for an hour. The temperature's been below freezing the whole time. Touch her. She's probably stone-cold."

Kyla really, really didn't want to do that, but she supposed there was no way around it. She reached down and plucked up Sarah's stiff arm from where it was stretched over the coverlet. A flood of goose bumps washed over her. Sarah was so cold she didn't even feel human anymore.

"You're right."

"Meaning she could have been killed at any point between— what—six o'clock, when we all go to our rooms, and eight o'clock, when Tabitha finds the body. Two hours is a long time. It'd be hard to narrow down suspects with such a wide window."

Kyla was inclined to agree with him, only for something to occur to her. "No. It's actually not that wide. Me and Fernanda heard Sarah talking to someone in this room at seven thirty. A man. It sounded like an argument."

"A man?" Ethan said, looking up from the suitcase.

"An argument?" Hunter said.

"Yes, it was definitely a man's voice, but the man and Sarah were talking too quiet for me to hear much through the wall," Kyla said. "But they were having an argument. That was pretty easy to tell."

"Was that argument so bad it could have come to blows?" Ethan said.

Kyla thought of Stan Holiday's busted lip, the restless rage that had filled him when he'd come into the motel's cafe shortly before the body was discovered. "Maybe. The important thing is that Sarah was still alive by seven thirty. Meaning the murder actually happened in a very narrow window of time."

Hunter leaned back against the long dresser, folding his arms, looking curious almost despite himself. "Alive at seven thirty, dead by eight o'clock. You're right. That is manageable."

Ethan said, "It stands to reason the killer is the man she was arguing with, right?"

"Not necessarily. We don't know how long that conversation lasted," Hunter said. "The mystery man could have left at 7:35 and the killer come right in after him. It wouldn't have taken *that* long to do this. Especially if . . ."

He drifted off.

Kyla, for her part, couldn't stop staring at the corpse. "Why would the killer put pillows over her face? Were they, like, ashamed of what they'd done? They didn't want to see her?"

"No." Fernanda finally spoke. The woman had spent the last few minutes in her thoughts, standing very near the room's door like she hoped to slip back out the moment she could. Now, however, she took a few steps closer to the bed, squinted at the bloody pillows, nodded.

"This is a cartel trick. You place one pillow over the victim's head to cover any screams, then place another over the neck to control the spray of blood. Look at that one, the pillow over Sarah's neck. It has a hole in the side. That is where the knife went in."

Fernanda wasn't wrong. Looking closer, Kyla saw that the pillow over Sarah's neck had a clump of something small and red frozen next to it on the coverlet. On closer inspection, she realized they were feathers—small down feathers—that had spilled from a gash in the side of the pillow. The hole in the pillow looked like it went straight through one side and out the other: a through-and-through stab. The hole shimmered, bright and crusted with blood, like a geode grown from a grave.

Steeling herself, Kyla lifted the pillow away. Hunter looked at the wound in the neck Kyla had revealed. "That's definitely a knife puncture. And a big one, too. You could fit a letter through that hole."

He wasn't exaggerating. Kyla shot a glance at Fernanda. How did the woman know a trick like this?

"You might as well lift up the other one," Hunter said, gesturing to the pillow over Sarah's face. "We should make sure it's actually her. Just a formality, though."

Kyla nodded. The blood in the pillow had frozen to Sarah's long black hair, and as Kyla lifted it free, she heard strands of hair crackling like cold grass underfoot. They found a head staring straight down into the coverlet.

Hunter came to Kyla's side. With a little grunt of effort, he grabbed hold of the dead woman's shoulders and flipped her over, though they didn't learn much. This was, indeed, Sarah Powers. Now that they could see her face, Kyla thought the woman looked like she'd died in the grip of some awful insomnia, staring at the ceiling with an expression of absolute dread.

But Fernanda had been wrong about one thing. The woman had died with her mouth closed. That second pillow hadn't muffled any screams.

From where he was seated on the floor, something caught Ethan's eye. After lowering himself to his stomach and reaching his arm under the bed, he emerged with a long knife in one hand and a brown leather sheath in the other.

The knife's blade was crusted with blood.

Ethan dropped the knife onto the frozen pillow. "Sarah was wearing this knife in the office."

Kyla looked up, nodded. "I remember."

Hunter frowned, running his tongue along his teeth. "They killed her with her own weapon."

Before this could settle in, Fernanda made a discovery of her own. Stepping down the short hallway at the back of the room, she flipped the switch in the bathroom. A moment later, an infernal red glow washed over her.

Fernanda took a sharp step back. She gestured to Kyla. "You must see this."

Sarah Powers had replaced the plain light bulb above her sink with a red one. A piece of black paper had been taped over the glass block that served as the room's only window. The tub was filled with a thin layer of water, in which sat three glass bottles with handwritten labels bearing the names of chemicals Kyla didn't recognize. A toiletries bag and pair of nail scissors rested on the vanity. Sarah's camera—the one Fernanda had been so enraptured with back in the office—was perched beside them.

Next to the camera were a pair of tweezers and two plastic cylinders, one big and one small. The small cylinder was a yellow roll of film—Kodak 400 Gold—the sight of which sent a thrill of déjà vu through Kyla, considering the reason they'd had to leave Fort Stockton in such a hurry this afternoon. What were the odds?

The other cylinder on the counter was much stranger. It was black, and when she picked it up Kyla found that the cylinder was made of thick plastic, bulky enough to need two hands. It had a screw-on top, at the center of which was a wide mouth that tapered inward like a funnel. The lid felt loose.

Fernanda practically snatched the cylinder out of Kyla's hand. Bringing the black cylinder to her ear, she gave it a soft shake. "Close that door. We cannot risk any light coming inside."

"Is that what I think it is?" Kyla said.

"Yes. Sarah was not lying about one thing. This is a development tank for exposing photo negatives." Fernanda gave it another shake. "And there is still film inside."

ETHAN

When the girls closed the door of the bathroom, Ethan turned his attention to the junk on Sarah's corner table. Most of it looked like the sort of trash he assumed people accumulated on road trips: granola wrappers, water bottles, receipts, fast-food napkins. A pair of bifocal glasses, a plain watch. A small brass coin with a Roman numeral *I* and the words *To Thine Own Self Be True*. He almost smiled. After the mess his brother had made of his own life, Ethan knew an AA chip when he saw it.

"Sarah was in recovery," Ethan said to Hunter.

From where he stood near the corpse, Hunter said, "Not much temptation left for her now."

Ethan refocused on the clutter. He found a book of matches printed with the Brake Inn's name, one of its matches missing. He found a porcelain dinner plate that Sarah had used as an ashtray. But something was off.

The plate was full of ash, but the room didn't smell like any sort of smoke. Instead of cigarette filters or burned stubs, the only things he saw mixed in with the ash were a few bits of darkened plastic, their edges perforated with tiny squares.

A glint of silver caught Ethan's eye.

He tipped the ash onto the table. A strange, metallic substance had hardened in the center of the plate, almost like liquid chrome frozen mid-pour. Ethan wiped away the ash and saw that while the substance was charred around the edges, its center was still polished and reflective. As he lifted the plate, the metal caught the light, sent a bright silver glare across the wall.

His breath hitched.

Where had Ethan seen a glare like that before?

Hunter appeared beside him and glanced curiously at the plate before poking through the junk on the table. He knocked an empty water bottle to the floor, a greasy take-out bag, before his hand flinched away from a strange object concealed near the edge of the table.

It looked like some kind of stone ornament. After plucking it up cautiously, turning it to the light, Hunter passed the object to Ethan. "Careful. It's heavier than it looks."

He wasn't kidding. The stone was small, about the size and shape of a chicken egg, but it settled into Ethan's palm with the weight of a rock twice its size. The stone was pale white, almost the color of limestone, but far denser than any limestone Ethan had ever encountered.

A whorl of fine grooves was carved into the egg. The grooves turned and turned around the stone, seemingly with no beginning or end. The handiwork was so good Ethan couldn't find a single chink in the carving, an uneven groove, a seam. He wondered what sort of machine could carve a rock this dense in such fine detail, but in a way, he doubted it could have been machined at all.

The rock felt *old*, somehow. Almost prehistoric.

Ethan realized he'd seen a stone like this somewhere before. Two of them, to be precise, on the mantel of the fireplace in the motel's office.

Hunter closed Ethan's fingers around the stone.

"Hold on to that," Hunter murmured. "It might be important."

Hunter crossed back around the bed and opened the tall armoire, then poked through the pocket of a jacket Sarah had hung inside, shook his head. "You know what I can't find anywhere? The satellite phone. Didn't she say that Frank person had given her one? That he expected a call after dinner?"

"She did. Could it be in her Rover?" Ethan said.

"I guess it's possible. I found her keys on her dresser. I could double-check."

"But she'd have probably wanted to keep it nearby, wouldn't she?" Ethan said. He opened the drawers of the dresser: all empty. "A cold night like this, you wouldn't want to have to go back outside and get it."

"Precisely. So where did it go?"

Ethan chewed his lip.

Hunter looked at something on the floor of the armoire. After pulling loose a spare blanket the twins had left folded up on the armoire's bottom shelf—Ethan had seen one just like it in the armoire of their own room—Hunter shook the blanket open and draped it over Sarah's corpse. Ethan was surprised how relieved he felt when the woman's face was finally shrouded. When he didn't have to see the woman's dark eyes, staring in horror at whatever fate had come for her.

For the millionth time, Ethan wondered who could have done *that* to this woman.

The door to the bathroom opened. Fernanda emerged with a roll of film in her hand and a disappointed frown on her face.

"Sarah developed this before she died," Kyla said. "But someone's beaten us to the good stuff."

Ethan saw that the end of the film had been neatly snipped off. Fernanda said, "There are only thirty frames here. A roll this length would hold thirty-six."

"The killer cut off the final six shots?" Hunter said.

"They might have taken them somewhere," Kyla said, looking almost excited at the prospect of a lead. "We should check Ryan's body. We should check the rooms."

Ethan almost felt bad to disappoint her. "I don't think they were hidden anywhere. Look."

He returned to the corner table and plucked the pieces of burned plastic from the ash he'd spilled out of the dinner plate. Returning to Fernanda, he held one of the scraps near the film in her hand. There was no mistaking it: the burned scrap had the same even square holes along its edge as the border of the film.

"Someone burned those last six shots," Ethan said. "Whatever Sarah photographed, they wanted to be sure we never saw it."

KYLA

"Well, shit," she said. "Just when I thought we were getting somewhere."

The four of them lapsed into silence. Fernanda pinched the length of the surviving film between finger and thumb, held it to the light, pulled it from frame to frame to study the negative. After a moment, Hunter asked, "Anything good?"

"Desert shots. The mountain. The motel. Nothing interesting. Yet."

Kyla took the charred scraps of film from Ethan's hand. She said again, "Shit."

A soft *click* drew her attention to the nightstand.

Kyla dropped the film to the floor. She couldn't contain a gasp. The time was 9:52.

"Please tell me that's wrong," Kyla said.

Ethan followed her eyes. He looked at the clock, the watch on his wrist. He shook his head in surprise. "It's not wrong."

"How is that possible?" Kyla said, "It was barely nine o'clock when we came in here. That was twenty minutes ago. A half hour, tops."

Fernanda lowered the roll of film, very slowly, from the light. "Time has felt strange all evening. I thought . . . I thought it was just me."

Hunter said, "I told you this game was rigged. It'll be midnight any second."

"*Rigged?*" Kyla said. "You think the twins are cranking up the speed of time itself?"

"After everything else we've seen tonight? Would it really surprise you?" Hunter said.

"Oh, please," Kyla said.

Ethan said, "That sounds ridiculous, Hunter. You have to know that."

"Ridiculous?" Hunter said. "It means we have even less time to get ready than we thought."

"Get ready?" Kyla said. "If the twins are so fucking power-ful they can break the rules of Newtonian physics, do you really think that hiding in our rooms is going to protect us from whatever they've got planned?"

"I keep trying to tell you: they're playing a game." Hunter scowled. "They've just never played against me before."

From any other man, a line like this would have made Kyla snort, but Hunter was clearly not like most other men.

It was Ethan who shook his head. "No. We're getting some-where. Maybe the killer didn't burn *all* of those photographs. Maybe they saved a few, hid them. And there's the missing satellite phone: the killer could have stolen it. If we track *that* down, wouldn't that be the proof the twins needed?"

"That's circumstantial," Hunter said. "It wouldn't prove much."

Kyla said, "There's someone we're forgetting."

Ethan nodded. "Penelope."

"I haven't seen her since dinner. It's like the girl vanished the minute the body was discovered. That's a hell of a coincidence."

Hunter gestured at the shrouded shape of Sarah Powers. "You think a teenage girl could do *that*?"

Kyla shuddered. She sincerely hoped not. "Even if she didn't kill Sarah, Penelope might have seen something she shouldn't have. Might have heard it. She grew up around some very bad people. She probably knows when it would be safer to disappear."

Ethan said, "And she could be in danger. Who knows what other tricks the twins haven't played yet?"

"I'm sorry, but is that really our problem?" Hunter said.

"That a sixteen-year-old girl is alone on a night like this? In a place like this?" Ethan said. "Yes, I think that's everyone's problem."

Kyla said, "So that's three things we can look for. The missing pho-tographs from this roll of film. The satellite phone. And Penelope."

Ethan pulled a pair of room keys from his pocket. They were, Kyla realized, the keys Tabitha had given him back on the office's porch. One key was marked *3*. The other, *7*.

Kyla said, "Stanley and Penelope were staying in number seven. It seems safe to assume that Ryan was in three."

"And what happens when you don't find anything in those rooms?" Hunter said.

"We search everywhere. We saw a big maintenance closet earlier, and who knows what's behind the cafe," Kyla said.

"And there's the old house behind the motel. We could search there," Ethan said, although judging by the way he said it, the boy was just as unenthusiastic about the idea of visiting that old house as Kyla felt.

She couldn't put her finger on why, exactly, but just the thought of that grand old two-story Victorian—so out of place way out here—filled her with a dread she couldn't quite name.

Fernanda was still looking at the film pinched between her fingers. "I do not think Penelope could be hiding in that house. I do not think anyone could have concealed anything there tonight."

"Why's that?" Kyla said.

"Because they would have to leave the ring of light to reach the house. They would have to pass through the dark," Fernanda said. "Those creatures are out there. We would have heard the screams."

Kyla swallowed. The woman had a point. "So Penelope's somewhere in the motel. Penelope, and everything else. We just need to get busy."

"But with what time?" Hunter said. "It just hit ten o'clock. The next two hours will be gone before you know it."

He had a point. Kyla looked at Ethan. Ethan looked at Kyla.

Ethan nodded, as if he knew what she was thinking.

Kyla nodded back. "We'll split up."

NOT LIKE THE LAST ONES
THE TWINS

10:00 p.m.

They sat in the dark, lit only by the embers of the dying fire. No lights on, no heat: it wouldn't have been fair. There wasn't much fuel left in the generator. If the guests weren't mindful of the power, it might not even last until midnight.

The corpse of Ryan Phan was still sprawled near the door of the office, exactly where it had fallen after Stanley shot him. Phan's brains still clung to the wall. His blood had congealed around him, crusty as spilled sugar.

This would all be over before the body really started to smell.

"They're not like the last ones," Thomas said, speaking of tonight's guests. "They didn't go back to their rooms. They still haven't."

"Is that really the best way to describe them?" Tabitha said. " 'The last ones'?"

"Don't start."

"How can I not?"

In the back of the office, the thing behind the walnut door was getting restless. It clicked and scratched across the wooden floors of its room. Clawed at the walls. Rustled its great feathers. Hissed its long tongue.

It let out a *SHRIEK* so loud even the twins flinched.

From where they sat, they could just make out the dim shape of Stan Holiday's overturned van. They weren't surprised he'd come to a bad end. The man had been doomed almost from the moment he arrived. When he'd checked in earlier, Stanley had thought he was making polite conversation. *The two of you live in that old house out back?*

No matter how many times the twins heard questions like this, they still shivered.

Live *there*. Imagine.

Now Thomas said, "You know he'll still come tonight."

"Maybe he won't," Tabitha said. "We've never had a night like this before."

"That crack in the mirror won't save anyone."

"It seems to have gotten them out of their rooms. Like you said."

"You don't know that's because of the mirror."

"You don't know that it wasn't."

For the second time that night, the generator stuttered and stalled. This time, it stalled properly. For a few seconds, the lamps outside burned down to little more than a wisp.

It looked like they might go out entirely. That would be unfortunate.

The generator kicked back to life, but it took a moment for the lamps outside to return to their full brightness. A dim twilight reigned around the motel, a gloaming of mercury vapor.

And then it cleared, the lamps brightened, if not quite back to their old strength. The generator was getting weaker. The lamps' light didn't extend as far as it had a moment ago.

The circle of light around the motel had shrunk.

In the office, Thomas shook his head. "Did you see that?"

"I was watching the desert."

"Maybe a mercy."

"You sound scared." This was also new. She turned, surprised. "What happened?"

Thomas's eyes were trained on the windows to either side of the office's front door. Watching the parking lot. "He'll come tonight."

"You keep saying that."

"I'm starting to think he never really leaves."

ETHAN

A moment before the generator stalled, he hesitated outside the back door to room 3, the key in his hand, watching Hunter and Fernanda make their way around the far corner of the porch. Fernanda had really, really not wanted to split up—"Do they not screen horror movies in Dallas?" she'd asked Kyla. "You never, ever split up."—but in the end, Kyla had persuaded her with some simple logic.

"We saw Ethan and Hunter heading to dinner five minutes before we heard Sarah talking with someone in her room." Kyla had looked at Ethan. "Y'all stayed together that entire time, right?"

"Yes," Ethan had said, which was the truth. Hunter hadn't left his side since he'd returned from his smoke break, almost an hour before Sarah's death. "You can ask Thomas. He was with us in the cafe from the minute we arrived."

Kyla looked at Fernanda. "So you don't have any reason to be afraid of going to search Stan's room with Hunter. He couldn't have killed Sarah. Neither of them could."

Hunter had given Kyla a small smile at that. He looked almost abashed. For his part, Ethan could only think of the fry cook at the diner in Turner and the smell of flesh swimming in hot grease. Ethan wasn't sure if anyone could ever be entirely safe from Hunter, but Kyla was correct about one thing: the man was one of the few people at the motel with a solid alibi.

Unlike others still here.

Hunter had said simply, "We meet back here, room four, at eleven thirty. No questions. Okay?"

Ethan had said, "Okay."

Now, as Hunter and Fernanda stepped out of view, Ethan heard a strange sound rolling in from the desert. It wasn't another *SHRIEK*, but a murmur. It sounded like a man was out there, talking to himself in the dark.

Kyla heard it too. "That almost sounds like Stanley."

And then the generator stuttered, the lights flickered, and Ethan unlocked room 3 as fast as he could. "Get inside. Quick."

Room 3 was laid out like all the others: a short back hallway, a bathroom to the right, the main room up ahead. The curtains on the room's front window were open, giving Ethan an unobstructed view of the parking lot.

And there, in the moment's half-light—in the eerie gloaming of mercury vapor as the lamps flicked back to full strength—Ethan saw a man standing at the parking lot's far edge, watching him through the chevroned bars of the room's window. The man stood near the motel's neon sign with his hat in his hand, looking for all the world like he'd wandered in off the road after a long day of travel. Ethan couldn't be certain, but in the weak half-light it almost looked like the man was wearing a suit. A gray gabardine suit. The kind no one ever wore anymore.

The man was staring at Ethan. Straight at Ethan. He raised a hand in greeting, and Ethan saw that there was something wrong with his index finger. It was too short. It ended at the second knuckle.

The man's face broke out in a tight, tight smile.

Be seeing you, Mister Cross.

The lights came up fully. The man dissipated like smoke on a breeze—here one second, gone the next. Ethan stared and stared and saw nothing in the parking lot but the deep treads Stan Holiday's tires had made as they went slewing toward the road.

And yet Ethan would swear he could still hear the sound of the gabardine man's tight smile hanging in the air, the teeth grinding together like stones.

"Did you see that?"

Kyla was too busy locking the back door. "See what?"

"Never mind."

Turning her attention to the parking lot, she pointed out something so obvious Ethan had missed it entirely. "The lights are weaker than they were a second ago. The circle's getting smaller."

"Then let's get busy."

Ryan Phan hadn't left much of a footprint in his room. There wasn't a single wrinkle in the coverlet. The pillows looked undisturbed. A

motorcycle helmet rested on the floor near the bed, next to a pair
of leather saddlebags. Ethan flipped on the nightstand's lamp, toed
the saddlebags. He said, "I think Ryan was telling the truth before
he died. He probably did sleep here, on the floor. These bags are
situated just right for it."

Kyla said, "Out of sight of the window. Whoever he was, he knew
how to keep a low profile."

The saddlebags were practically empty. One held a fistful of
Mexican pesos, a large band of American cash, and a bag of Fritos with
Spanish on the back.

The other saddlebag held an American passport, but it didn't
belong to Ryan Phan. An Asian man who vaguely resembled him
stared back at Ethan from the photograph inside. The name on the
passport was "Trent Ly."

Ethan showed this to Kyla. "Do we think Ryan Phan's name was
actually Trent Ly?"

"Hardly. He must have gotten hold of the guy's passport somehow."

"Is that hard to do?"

Kyla took the passport, flipped to the stamps in the back. "There's
a whole network of documentation floating around if you know
who to ask."

Ethan considered this. "You worked at the steakhouse in Fort
Stockton, right? You served dinner to Frank O'Shea and his whole
crew. Had you ever heard of this Ryan guy?"

"No," Kyla said. "But I've only lived around here for six months.
The way Ryan was talking to Stanley, it sounded like they had ancient history."

"Ryan said he was Penelope's stepfather. Or he would have been,
if he'd been able to marry Penelope's mother. What did that mean?
And could it have anything to do with Sarah Powers?"

"I know that Penelope's mom died in a burglary a few years back.
At least, it went down as a burglary, but no one can think of anyone stupid enough to rob Frank's goddaughter. I guess the results
were about the same. Some goons broke into the house and killed
Penelope's mom and her sister and shot Penelope in her sleep. It's

kind of a legend around town. A miracle, you know, that the girl survived. She's always been a little weird since."

"God," Ethan said. "That explains the scar on her forehead."

"Exactly. But does it have anything to do with Sarah Powers?" Kyla shrugged. "Sarah certainly seemed connected to everyone else around here. She and Penelope met at dinner one time, I remember that, but it was just for a few minutes while Penelope dropped by to see Stanley. But maybe Sarah and Penelope met other times. Maybe they connected somewhere else."

Ethan followed Kyla to room 3's bathroom. A little pyramid of rolled towels rested on the vanity, an untouched bar of soap.

Something nagged at Ethan. "So Stanley really was having a lot of dinners with Sarah Powers?"

Kyla glanced at him. "I wasn't lying. She'd been coming at least once a week."

"Since when?"

"About six weeks, I guess."

Ethan opened his mouth, hesitated.

Hunter had turned up in Ellersby six weeks ago.

"Did these dinners seem . . . romantic?" Ethan finally said. "Back in the office, Ryan made it sound like Stanley was in love with Sarah."

"I've served dinner to a lot of lovebirds. I'm inclined to believe Stanley's version of the story."

"That Sarah Powers was working for the outfit?"

"Yes. But doing what, I have no idea."

Ethan and Kyla stepped out of the bathroom. Ethan heaved up the room's mattress, stripped the sheets, found nothing concealed underneath. Studying the dresser, the pattern of the carpet, the carving of the furniture, Ethan was struck again with just how outdated everything at the motel was, and yet how it was in such good condition.

He flipped on the nightstand's lamp, turned it off. Even the way the switch clicked felt unlike any of the electronics he'd grown up with.

Yet for some reason it felt almost familiar.

Ethan said, "So Sarah's dinners with Stanley were business. Meaning Sarah was telling the truth about being here, at the motel, on a mission for Frank."

"I think so, yes."

"She said she was doing research for him. Any idea what sort of research the outfit would need done?"

"Beats the shit out of me. I don't know if you've figured it out yet, but Frank's a thug. Guns. Drugs. People. He moves things across the border and sells them down the river. Sarah also mentioned something about a being a teacher, but I have no fucking clue what kind of classes Frank O'Shea would want to take."

"I wonder what her field was."

"And why it would bring her way out here." Kyla pulled out all the drawers of the dresser, the nightstand, tugged open the door of the armoire. "Maybe it was something to do with the mountain. Like a geologist or something?"

Or the motel, Ethan thought. That brief sight of the man he'd imagined in the parking lot a moment ago—the man in the gray gabardine suit—made Ethan remember the diner in Turner. The story he'd been told there.

Nine empty rooms.

Twelve cold beds.

"Were there . . ." Ethan faltered, almost afraid to hear the answer to what he was about to ask. "Were there any legends about this place, back in Fort Stockton?"

Kyla said, "Legends? About the Brake Inn Motel? Not that I ever heard. But again, I've only been there since August. Why?"

Ethan didn't know where to begin. "I was just wondering. What about the other motel Ryan mentioned in the office? The Terra Vista? He said that Stanley had a secret about that place."

"The Terra Vista? It's a hot sheet place. Stanley takes girls over there plenty. He roughs them up."

Ethan stared at her. "You say that really casually."

"He pays them well and he's the second-biggest cheese in town. People don't really talk about it, but it's hardly a secret. If that's what Ryan was going to say in the office, it wasn't much of a bombshell. Everyone knows Stanley's beat up girls in the past. He put his ex-wife in the hospital. But most men are bastards. It doesn't mean that he killed Sarah."

"Doesn't mean he wouldn't have some practice, though."

Kyla shrugged. "Frank's outfit is dirty, but it's loyal to its operators. If Sarah was working for them, Stanley wouldn't have treated her like a piece of merchandise he could slap around. He could have killed her, sure, but if he did, then he just pulled down her pants to make it look like rape. They're bastards, Frank and Stanley both, but one time a freelancer having dinner gave me a slap on the ass. Frank had his hand broken in twelve places, and I don't even *work* for those guys."

"I don't know how you lasted so long around people like that."

"I kept my head down."

The pair were silent a moment, surveying the room. It was clear there was nothing here to get excited about. Whoever Ryan Phan was, what exactly he'd been doing between the time he arrived at the motel and the moment Tabitha started screaming, he hadn't left any trace of it here.

And even though it hadn't felt like more than a few minutes since they stepped inside, the time was already 10:35.

Kyla said, "You feel like ripping up the carpet?"

"No. But something's been nagging at me all night."

"Care to share?"

Ethan didn't quite know where to begin. The moment Sarah Powers had walked into the office, Hunter's face had betrayed a rare moment of genuine surprise. Surprise and recognition and unease. Hunter's face had closed up tight again in a second, his eyes had hardened, but whatever the man might say to the contrary, Ethan was still certain Hunter had met Sarah Powers at least once in his life.

And he hadn't been happy to see her here now.

But he hadn't killed her. Sarah had been alive at seven thirty, and Hunter had been in the cafe with Ethan. So if he hadn't killed her, maybe this flash of recognition didn't really matter.

Instead, Ethan told Kyla the same thing he told Hunter when they first got to their room: "Sarah Powers lied about knowing my mother. That story she told about her car breaking down out east and Mom fixing it up for a song—it was all bull. The failing fan motors she talked about were happening to GMCs at that time, not Fords. Even if Sarah *did* have a broken fan engine and even *if* she had to come to Mom's shop, those repairs aren't quick and they aren't cheap, however much Mom liked to run a fair deal."

"But then how did Sarah recognize you?"

Ethan held in a shiver. "I've been trying to figure that out for ages."

HUNTER

A few minutes earlier, Hunter followed Fernanda into room 7 as the generator stuttered. Darkness closed over the motel. Every nerve in his body started firing. His hand was behind his back, wrapped around the Python, before Fernanda even appeared to realize what had happened. Hunter twisted the lock of the back door and leaned against it, hard, in case any of those things out in the desert decided to get too close.

He waited.

The generator sputtered back on—or tried to. A weak half-light reigned over the motel, a gloaming of mercury vapor, and from beside him Hunter heard Fernanda let out a startled gasp. She was pressed against the wall, staring at the room's bed, her body stiff with fear.

Hunter followed her gaze. He, too, went very tense.

They weren't alone.

Two women lay on the bed. One was wearing nothing but an old-fashioned garter belt. The other woman was completely naked. Their hairstyles were out-of-date: a bob for one, a short beehive for the other. The two women were kissing, madly. Touching each other. Breathing hard, but they didn't appear to make a sound.

The woman with the beehive opened her eyes. It was just a little blink, like she was coming up for air. She closed them.

She opened them again, wide. She stared over her companion's shoulder at Hunter and Fernanda with the same shock with which they were staring at her. The other woman turned, saw them for herself, scrambled to pull the blanket over her bare body.

The woman screamed, but her open mouth remained silent as a cry in a nightmare.

The lights came back up. The women dissipated like smoke.

Hunter said nothing.

Fernanda shuddered. The roll of Sarah's film, draped over her neck, whispered against her long hair. "You saw them too."

Hunter said nothing.

Fernanda said, "Are we losing our minds?"

"I hope not," Hunter said. "We don't have time."

Hunter had his doubts about Fernanda. He wasn't sure he could count on this girl if trouble hit the fan. (Case in point: in all the chaos of the last couple minutes, she'd never once reached for her gun.) Fernanda seemed strung out on adrenaline, wrecked by a very long day.

The good news was that Hunter didn't exactly need her help. For most of the night, he'd had a pretty clear idea of everything that had happened at the motel since he and Ethan had arrived. He knew who had killed Sarah Powers, and how, and why.

He also knew that the odds of anyone finding conclusive proof of the killer's guilt would be next to impossible, meaning all of this was a waste of time.

"Go search the bathroom," Hunter told Fernanda, mostly to keep her out of his hair. "The toilet. Under the vanity. Everywhere."

"For what?"

"Anything that might have been stolen out of Sarah's room. Guns. Money." He hesitated. "The satellite phone. Or just anything out of the ordinary."

"You are not afraid of what we just saw?"

"I've seen weirder."

"Weirder than *that*?"

Hunter frowned, if only to himself. He thought about one of his last nights in Huntsville, listening to the horrors being whispered about in the cell next door. The last night of The Chief.

Tell Sarah—

Tell Sarah, the mountain—

Hunter said to Fernanda, "You'd be surprised."

He took stock of room 7. Stanley and Penelope had made themselves at home. There were two full beds, only one of which had been slept in. The room had the same wardrobe and long dresser and brass lamps as all the other rooms. The same reddish-brown carpet and turquoise coverlets and chevroned bars on the front window.

There were two pieces of luggage in sight. A brown overnight bag stood on the corner table. The bag was stodgy and less impressive than it wanted to appear, like Stanley. A muted pink backpack rested on the easy chair. Penelope's, no doubt.

Penelope's backpack held only a sports bra and a pair of athletic shorts, like the girl had been packing for a PE class, not a trip to Mexico. Stanley's bag didn't have much more in the way of clothes: a few shirts, some socks, a couple pairs of underwear.

Hunter called to the bathroom, "The Holidays weren't packing for a long trip."

"I do not believe Penelope packed for a trip at all," Fernanda said. "I heard a little about it at Frank's house. Ryan Phan picked the girl up from school three days ago. They were in Mexico by the time anyone thought to miss her. It all sounded rather unplanned, at least on her part."

"You were at Frank's house?"

Silence.

"Any idea what sort of work Sarah Powers was doing for Frank?"

"No."

Hunter ran a thumb along the seams of Penelope's bag, then Stanley's. Sure enough, he found a false pocket in the lining of Stan's overnight case. Hunter pinched the fabric and tugged it open, revealing a cache of cash: five hundred-dollar bills. An emergency travel fund, typical for people at risk of mugging. No real surprise.

He thought of the cash spilled across Sarah Powers's dresser. He put Stan's money away.

His eye caught something on the floor, over near the bed. Looking up, he saw a few fine dots on the nightstand, a mist of red-brown stains. He cocked his head. He hadn't expected this.

But before he could take a closer look, Fernanda poked her head out from the bathroom.

"You call him Frank. Not Frank O'Shea."

Hunter met her eye. "So?"

"Have you met him?"

"No." This was a lie, but the truth would be too much of a headache to explain. "Why?"

"Their mothers disappeared from this area. Frank's mother, and Stanley's. Both on the same night. Perhaps even from this motel."

Fernanda pushed back her hair. "There is a legend about this place. That twelve people vanished without a trace one night, many years ago."

"Do we really have time for legends?"

Hunter said it dismissively, but he remembered the morning he'd met Sarah Powers. He remembered the awful things he'd heard in Huntsville the night before. Terrified whispers in the dark. The last night of The Chief.

Tell Sarah, the mountain is getting restless.

Fernanda said, "There is great power in a story. Even if you do not believe it."

"Where are you going with this?"

"The women on the bed just now. One of them had Frank's jaw. The other had Stanley's hair."

Hunter looked from Fernanda to the bed and back again. His lungs were starting to burn from the room's dry air. He thumped his chest. "I'll keep that in mind."

Fernanda didn't let it go. "Something much stranger is happening here than a simple murder. I have felt it all night. Those things in the desert, the time running fast, now these shades on the bed—we are dealing with something we do not understand."

"Then let's get busy figuring it out."

Still—still—Fernanda didn't move. "You do not care about Sarah's murder. You are just killing time until you can get back to your room."

Hunter said nothing.

"I do not think you killed Sarah, but I think you know many things you are not saying. Things you do not want Ethan to know about you. Things that might complicate his picture of you. You are hiding something."

Hunter rose very slowly from the floor, and Fernanda drew away, clearly frightened of him. He almost wanted to tell her she had nothing to be afraid of—if he wanted to hurt her, she'd never know it was coming.

No. It was just time to play hardball.

"Takes one to know one, ma'am."

With a few quick steps, Hunter reached the side of the room's rumpled bed. Crouching down, he plucked up the curious item that had caught his eye a moment ago: a glossy black hair, long enough to reach a woman's waist.

He held the hair where Fernanda could see it.

"Stanley had short red hair. Penelope has long blond hair. These rooms were all immaculate when we checked in, all the carpets vacuumed. So if this black hair wasn't left by a previous guest and if it wasn't left by the room's occupants, that begs certain questions."

Now it was Fernanda's turn to be silent.

Hunter watched her. Fernanda was right: he wasn't terribly interested in trying to solve Sarah Powers's murder, but now he was curious. This single thread of hair looked poised to complicate the picture he'd had of the evening. To answer questions he hadn't even thought to ask.

Hunter said to Fernanda, "There are only two people at this motel who have black hair this long. So tell me—was it you who came here to see Stanley tonight, or the dead woman in room four?"

KYLA

Heading out the front door of Ryan's room, Kyla looked to the right. Down the arm of the motel, the door to the office was closed, the windows dark. She could almost feel the twins inside, watching her. Let them.

There were three more doors along that wing of the motel. Up the wall from the office were the doors to rooms 1 and 2. Room 2 looked unoccupied: the curtain open, the bed made, the lamps unlit.

Room 1 was also dark, but the curtain was drawn. She tested the door. Locked.

"Have you seen anyone come or go from this room tonight?" Kyla asked Ethan. "Seen the lights on?"

A hard wind was blowing down off the mountain. Ethan's teeth started chattering. "Pr-pr-probably where the t-twins sleep."

"We'll get the key from them in a minute. It's only fair they let us search every room."

Ethan looked at his watch. "It's al-al-almost ten forty-five."

"Fuck me. There just isn't time, is there?"

Ethan shook his head. There was clearly something he wanted to say, but his lips were turning blue. The guy didn't have a jacket, and this frozen wind wasn't letting up. The ring of lights around the motel flickered. Out in the desert, a warning *SHRIEK*, like some primal alarm, cut through the night.

"Let's get inside," Kyla said.

Past room 2, sheltered by the roof of the walkway that ran between the motel's northern arm and its main body, Kyla found an unlocked door she'd noticed when they'd checked in. Inside was a wide, windowless supply room stocked with cleaners, linens, tools, spare dinner plates. The room wasn't exactly warm, but it was shelter from the wind.

Kyla was still thinking about what Ethan had told her a moment ago, the way Sarah Powers had been lying through her teeth when they'd first met the woman in the office. "Was it true what you told her? That your mom died?"

Ethan rubbed his arms. He nodded.

"Same thing with my dad," Kyla said.

"When?"

"Six months back. Feels like yesterday."

"Is that why you moved out this way?" Ethan said.

Kyla was surprised. He wasn't far off the mark. "It's a little more complicated than that. But I guess not by much."

"What got him? Your dad, I mean."

"Car accident," Kyla said.

"Cancer," Ethan said.

"Same thing. Just slower."

Ethan's body seemed to warm up enough for him to start walking again. He took a few steps around the supply closet, his hands tucked into his armpits, deep in thought. "Does your friend Fernanda have stomach issues?"

The question was so strange Kyla took it seriously. *Did* she? Kyla wasn't entirely sure. The girls weren't especially close. After a few months of her working at the steakhouse, Frank had hired Kyla to help cater one of the massive barbecues he threw for his men at his big compound outside of town. It had been hard for Kyla not to notice the imperious, beautiful Mexican woman standing alone in the corner of Frank's house like a piece of furniture. Kyla had said hello to her. Frank had been delighted. *Swing by tomorrow, keep her company*, he'd said, as if Fernanda were some kind of restless animal.

Frank had added, *Ask her to tell you a story.*

Here, in the motel's supply room, Kyla said honestly, "I'm not sure. We don't know each other all that well."

"She said she was late coming to dinner because she needed to use the restroom," Ethan said. "But it seemed a little long for a bathroom break, if you don't mind me saying. You and Penelope got to dinner around, what, 7:35? It was ten, maybe fifteen minutes before Fernanda turned up. Do you think she was in y'all's room that whole time?"

Kyla narrowed her eyes, if only because she'd tried to avoid asking herself this same question all night. "I don't think Fernanda could have killed Sarah. She isn't that type of girl."

"But you just said you don't know her very well."

"She wouldn't have done *that*. You saw the way Sarah's pants were pulled down. I feel pretty confident my friend isn't a rapist."

"We don't know that Sarah Powers was raped." Ethan looked almost pained to be asking these questions—pained on Kyla's behalf—but he didn't stop. "The way her pants were pulled down could just be a smoke screen, something the killer did after the fact to confuse us, just like you said a few minutes ago. Fernanda knew the cartel trick with the pillows. She knew that Sarah was going to talk to Frank after dinner. She knew that Sarah had a satellite phone. She knew that Stanley was here, too, and if he didn't have one of those phones, he might want to use Sarah's if he ever found out she had it."

"Why would Fernanda care about the satellite phone?"

A little smile came over Ethan's face. "Please. It's obvious y'all are on the run from Frank's outfit. It would be very, very bad if either Stanley or Sarah told Mister O'Shea that y'all were here. I don't know the details of y'all's trouble—respectfully, I don't *want* to know—but you ain't exactly being subtle about it. That satellite phone could really complicate your lives. Making sure Sarah didn't have it would be good. Making sure she never got the chance to tell anyone she saw y'all here could be even better."

"I don't . . . ," but Kyla trailed off. She wasn't stupid. She'd considered this angle for herself already, many times, and never come to a satisfying answer. It wasn't like she could ask Fernanda to admit to murder and leave the woman out in the cold when the lights died.

Could she?

"What about your man?" Kyla said to Ethan, desperate for a change of subject. "Was he with you all night?"

"He was with me well before seven thirty."

"That's a rather lawyerly answer." Kyla turned from a shelf full of laundry detergent to arch an eyebrow. "I asked if he was with you *all* night."

Ethan examined shelves of his own. He held up a white plastic bottle and said, "Look at this label. Doesn't the logo look old, like the sort of thing you see in old commercials?"

"You're avoiding the question."

"Because there ain't much to say. Hunter just took a smoke break, is all. Got back to the room around six forty-five and took a nap with me. I couldn't sleep, though. I just stayed awake with him until he got up and we went to dinner."

Kyla said, "Six forty-five. You're sure on that time?"

"I am."

"Why, though? Were you watching the clock? Were you waiting for him to come back?"

"Of course I was waiting for him to come back. We're in a strange motel in the middle of nowhere and—" Ethan broke off, clearly debating whether to tell her something. "Y'all aren't the only people who'd like to steer clear of Frank O'Shea. Back when we passed through Turner, Hunter did something pretty awful to a man who works for Frank. I was worried the guy's goons were sure to come looking for us."

"Was it Cleveland, the fry cook with the little rat face?"

"You know him?"

"Little shit came to dinner on Frank's dime once a month. Always found some excuse to look down my shirt." Kyla almost smiled at the idea of that particular fucker having a run-in with Hunter. "Whatever your man did to him, the boy had it coming."

"I don't think anyone deserves what Hunter did to that guy."

Yes. Well. Kyla sure wasn't one to talk about unintended acts of violence.

She and Ethan lapsed into an uneasy silence. They were poking through the contents of the maintenance room, but what were they even looking for? That mythical satellite phone? Penelope Holiday? The girl certainly wasn't here—there was nowhere for a sixteen-year-old girl to hide in a room this size—and the other junk seemed just as gone.

Why were they even bothering? Kyla could practically feel time slipping away from them, vanishing underfoot like a highway under the wheels of a speeding car. She was genuinely afraid to ask Ethan to check his watch. Judging by the way the light of the room was flickering, the motel's generator hadn't discovered a surprise second wind.

The lights were going to die, sooner or later. Kyla couldn't accept that the same would happen to her, but it was getting harder and harder to believe otherwise.

Ethan looked just as unnerved. "What do you think Tabitha meant after Stanley died? She said she and Thomas had done this before, done this with other guests, but how is that possible? It would draw attention. That's probably the last thing someone like Frank O'Shea would tolerate in his backyard."

"Unless the twins work for Frank," Kyla said. "I say we give this five more minutes and then we go find the others. We take matters into our own hands. We've all got guns. It's four on two. Whatever game they're playing, I'm not going to end like anyone else they stuck here."

"Do you really think that will work?"

"It beats the shit out of this." But then something occurred to Kyla. "Your man went for a smoke break earlier this evening, right?"

Ethan didn't seem thrilled at this new line of questioning. "Yes."

"He's sick in the lungs. Why would he do that?"

"Old habits die hard. I thought I'd convinced him to quit, but I realized today I can't convince that man of anything."

"What kind of cigarettes?"

"I don't know the brand. I didn't even know he still had a pack."

"No, no." Kyla shook her head. "When he came back inside, did he smell like menthols?"

Ethan glanced over from a corner in the back of the supply room. "How did you know that?"

"Lucky guess," Kyla said. "But don't you remember who else smelled like menthols tonight?"

Whether he did or not, Ethan didn't get the chance to say. A new noise rolled over the motel, a sound unlike anything Kyla had ever heard before. She thought at first it was the cry of a whale in pain, the moan of a massive animal in agony, but there was something inorganic about it, like a massive piece of metal being bent out of shape, stone shearing from stone.

And yet stone or not, the moaning noise still sounded *alive*. Alive and afraid and in pain.

The sound sent a tremor through the earth, subtle but unmistakable. It made the lights flicker, warped the air of the supply room, sent a wave of *SHRIEKS* spreading across the desert. The creatures outside: call Kyla crazy, but they almost sounded afraid.

Ethan said, "That noise came from the mountain."

But Kyla was distracted by something else. When the lights had flickered, they'd briefly grown brighter, bright enough for her to see something that had been too murky to notice a moment before. The concrete floor of the supply room was coated with a thin layer of dust. No doubt the twins never bothered to clean in here. Why would they? The guest rooms must have kept them plenty busy.

Which was a good thing for Kyla and Ethan. There was a mess of footprints near the door and around the shelves that must have seen the most activity: the sheets, the glass cleaner, the plates.

But there was only one set of prints that weren't like the others. They were boot prints. Not a large boot, no more than a size nine, with a rounded toe and grooved soles. The boots had walked from the door of the supply room to the furthest corner, ending at a shelf full of paint supplies.

Kyla looked at Ethan's feet. They were big, easily an eleven or twelve, and shod in cowboy boots with pointed toes. Not a match.

She could only think of one other person who'd worn boots tonight.

Kyla followed the steps in parallel, careful not to disturb them. She stopped at the can of paint supplies and surveyed its contents. Cans, brushes, acetone, a folded tarp.

And tucked away on the edge of the shelf she found an empty paint can with its lid removed. It held a few wooden stirrers, a screwdriver, a weathered pencil. Shaking the can under the light, Kyla found something else squirreled away in the clutter. Something small and round and yellow.

Fishing her fingers into the can, Kyla plucked out a plastic cylinder with a yellow case. Even without reading the letters on the side, Kyla knew what the little cylinder contained. She'd seen plenty of ones just like it today.

On the side of the cylinder were the words KODAK GOLD 400.

35 MM NEGATIVE FILM.

36 EXPOSURES.

A small tab of orange celluloid jutted from the side of the roll. Kyla wasn't a professional photographer, but she was pretty sure that meant there was raw film inside. Maybe even a full roll.

"Do you think this is from Sarah's camera?" Ethan said.

"I can't think of anywhere else it would have come from," Kyla said, though her mind was suddenly moving too quickly for her to really consider such a statement. "Sarah had a bathtub full of development chemicals in her room. Fernanda knows how to expose film."

Ethan looked at his watch. "I hope she can work fast. It's already eleven thirty."

ETHAN

He almost collided with Hunter as he rounded the corner of the back porch. The man looked strange, both furtive and weirdly triumphant, like he'd learned something he wasn't eager to share. Before Ethan could say a word, Hunter wrapped a hand around his arm. "You ready?"

Ethan said, "We found something."

Kyla raised the yellow roll of film. "It was in the supply room. Ryan Phan hid it there—he's the only person whose boots would fit the tracks on the floor."

Fernanda came up behind Hunter, her hair flying in the hard wind, her face pale. "The mountain. Look."

Ethan followed her finger. It was easy to see what had her so spooked.

The silhouette of the mountain had grown larger since Ethan had seen it last. He didn't know how it was possible, didn't know what new laws of physics this corner of the desert was subject to, but there was no mistaking it: the mountain had blacked out most of the night sky. It looked like it had devoured the stars.

And there, in the upstairs window of the distant house, Ethan saw a silver light blazing in the dark.

That light sent a strange sensation running through him, from his eyes to his toes.

Without thinking, he said, "Something wants us to go there."

"Good luck with that," Hunter said. "It's a twenty-yard dash through the dark. You wouldn't make it ten feet."

Kyla pushed the roll of film they'd discovered into Fernanda's hand. "How long would it take you to develop this with the chemicals in Sarah's room?"

Fernanda tilted the canister toward the light. "It would be an hour at least. And with time running so strangely, the exposure to the chemicals would be difficult to gauge. Easy to ruin whatever is here."

"You've got to be shitting me," Kyla said. "We have one lucky break, and we can't do anything with it?"

Hunter hadn't released Ethan's arm. He tried pulling Ethan down the porch, in the direction of their room. "We gave it our best shot. Time for plan B."

Ethan held firm. "No."

"No?"

"No."

Ethan wrenched himself free. He looked, again, at the silver light spilling through the window of the old house. He could finally name the strange sensation the light gave him.

Déjà vu. Ethan had seen that light before. It had passed over the sky at four o'clock sharp, and nothing had ever felt the same since. The moment Ethan realized this, a million fragmentary observations suddenly clicked into place. He thought about the labels on the bottles in the maintenance closet and the liquor behind the bar, the furniture of the rooms, the switches of the bulbs. He thought of the story the gabardine man had told him in Turner. He thought about nine empty rooms. Twelve cold beds.

Y'all have done this before?

Yes, Mister Cross. Many, many times.

Ethan understood what was going on here. It had been staring at him from the moment they arrived.

A gas pump like this—it's from the fifties.

He turned toward the office. He started back down the porch. Another of those awful, bellowing moans—part stone, part animal—rolled down from the mountain, shaking the earth under their feet. Ethan just kept walking.

Hunter grabbed for him again. "Where the hell are you going?"

"The office. The twins."

"Why bother? We don't have anything to tell them."

"No. They have something to tell *us*." Ethan swallowed. He couldn't believe what he was about to say, and yet he knew, somehow, that it was true. "They've trapped us here. Just like they trapped the people in 1955."

ENDGAME
ETHAN

11:40 p.m.

The twins had unbolted the door of the office. They were ready for him. Ethan found Thomas and Tabitha already standing behind the desk, lit only by a dim lamp with a green glass shade. The fire had died. The room was freezing.

As Ethan walked, he felt something gummy cling to the soles of his boots. It was Ryan Phan's blood.

Ethan looked at Tabitha. "How did y'all do it?"

She tilted her head. "Do what, Mister Cross?"

"The same thing y'all did to those folks in the fifties."

The twins exchanged a look of raw, unvarnished surprise. Tabitha almost looked proud. "You've never figured that out before."

Before.

Kyla shuffled into the office looking, as always, like she desperately did not want to be here. Hunter and Fernanda followed a few steps behind her. If Ethan was crazy, he'd have said that Hunter looked afraid.

The time was 11:42.

Ethan felt a sudden, new cold spread up his spine at Tabitha's words. "What do you mean, 'before'? I've never been out this way in my life."

The twins traded one of their mute shrugs. Thomas said. "We are in some disagreement on this."

"Like much in philosophy, it hinges on the question of the soul," Tabitha said.

"Does it exist?"

"In what form?"

"Does it survive death?"

The lamp on the desk sputtered and whined. The generator was struggling to keep the motel lit. Standing at the window by the fire, Fernanda said, "One of the lights outside just died."

With a flurry of scratches and bangs, the thing in the back of the office *SHRIEKED* behind its walnut door. The creatures outside answered.

There was no hiding it now: Hunter was frightened. "Ethan, come with me. Come *on*."

Ethan didn't budge. He didn't turn away from the twins. "What does a soul have to do with any of this?"

"Everything, Mister Cross." Tabitha looked almost astonished by the question. "The soul—or whatever exists within the human form—is a source of immense power. A catalyst waiting to be sparked."

"What the hell is that supposed to mean?" Ethan said.

"I'm inclined to believe that the soul persists after death," Thomas said. "One permanent soul. That's what the people in the city seemed to believe."

"I was always the stricter scientist," Tabitha said. "I'm not sure it's the same souls every night. I'm not even sure it's the same *guests* every night. Not in the strictest sense."

Another moan from the mountain shook the earth. Time took a giant step forward. 11:47.

Thomas said, "If I am correct, it would imply that you're wrong, Mister Cross. That you *have* been here before."

Tabitha said, "On the other hand, I'm inclined to believe that you are correct. You—this you, speaking with us right now, tonight— have never been here before."

Ethan stared.

"I was hoping that tonight might be different," Tabitha said.

"A relief it wasn't, when you realize what's at stake," Thomas said sourly.

11:51.

Kyla said, "Why is time moving so fast?"

Tabitha said, "You should have asked Sarah when you had the chance. She was the physicist."

Thomas said, "We are but humble archaeologists."

11:54.

Fernanda said, "Another light just died outside. There are eyes everywhere."

Ethan said to the twins, "Why us?"

"Because the ceremony seeks repair," Thomas said. "Without it—"

"It's an evil thing we've done," Tabitha said.

Thomas's head snapped around to study his sister. She wasn't supposed to say this. "Be quiet."

11:58.

"We've been doing this for so long," Tabitha said. "It isn't working. It can't survive."

A wave of *SHRIEKS* rose up from the desert and didn't stop. The creature behind the walnut door grew wild. A savage wind buffeted the motel, shook the windows, moaned through the roof.

"What is this?" Ethan said. "What have you done to us?"

"There's no time to explain," Tabitha said. "It's almost midnight."

Ethan said, "Then take us to your safe place. Explain what the hell is going on."

"There is no safe place. Did you ever really believe there was?" Tabitha said.

"You aren't supposed to say that," Thomas said.

"I never agreed to those terms," Tabitha said.

11:59.

Tabitha looked at Ethan. At Kyla. She looked desperate. "Please, tomorrow—find a way to remember."

Thomas held up a hand to stop her.

Tabitha ignored him. "We've been trapped for so long."

"Be *quiet*!" Thomas said.

"We've been trapped here," Tabitha said. "Just like you."

The clock struck twelve. The noise cut out. All of it, at once, just like that: the moaning from the mountain, the *SHRIEKS* from the desert, even the clamor behind the walnut door. The wind died down to a mournful breeze. It played across the porch and the parking lot like the last gasps of the past.

In the silence, in the cold, they heard a new sound from the desert.

It was the whisper of tires on a gravel road.

Tabitha went pale. Thomas looked at her, almost triumphant.

"I told you he'd still come."

THE MIDNIGHT KNOCK

ETHAN

12:00 a.m.

Headlights washed through the office's windows. In the glow, Ethan saw the scene around him with a startling new clarity. Kyla and Fernanda stood near the dead fire. Hunter was beside Ethan, his hand still clasped around Ethan's arm. Through the windows near the fireplace, a sea of yellow eyes watched them from the dark.

Thomas and Tabitha stared at the front door: him looking smug, her resigned to whatever was coming.

The car outside, this new arrival, pulled to a slow stop. The engine cut out. The headlights went dark.

A metal door whined open.

At the edge of his vision, Ethan saw Kyla take an instinctive step away from the noise. Her shoulder brushed the mantel above the fire and sent something falling to the floor. It landed with a loud crack: a warning shot.

Ethan's eyes followed Kyla's to the floor to see what could make such a noise. It was one of the grooved stone eggs.

A foot stepped onto the gravel outside. Another joined it. The metal door swung closed. Those feet crunched across the parking lot, thumped up the steps of the porch, creaked across the wooden boards. They came to a stop on the other side of the office's door. A tall shadow stood on the other side of the frosted windows. For a moment, it didn't move.

A long, long silence stretched.

And then, there was a *knock*

Knock

Knock.

. . .

No one moved to answer the door. Ethan didn't think any of them would dare. But after a polite pause, the door opened regardless, and a man stepped inside. A tall, slim man dressed in a pale gray gabardine suit with a matching hat in his hand. No one wore suits like that anymore. It was a little faded, a little worn around the edges, utterly unmistakable.

The man had small, cool eyes. A faint hook of a smile that looked like it would try to sell you something at the slightest provocation. The index finger of the man's right hand ended at the second knuckle. A mass of scar tissue was seared to the joint.

The new arrival spoke with a soft twang. An eerie formality.

"Evening, folks," the man said. "Room for one more?"

It was the man from the diner in Turner. The man who'd told Ethan the story of the Dust Road and the Brake Inn Motel. The man who'd warned him that sometimes the road gets *hungry*.

The man Ethan had seen in the gloaming of the mercury lamps an hour ago, waving to him from the edge of the parking lot.

He wasn't a ghost. He wasn't a hallucination. When the man stepped into the office, his shoes made the floorboards creak. He threw a shadow from the lamp on the desk. It made no sense how the man could be here—if nothing else, how had he made it safely past the horde of creatures outside?—but there was no denying that he *was* here. In the flesh.

Smiling so tight his teeth ground against each other like stones.

The man made his way across the room. He stepped over Ryan Phan's corpse, hardly blinking at the carnage. He gave Ethan a nod, pure Texas courtesy. "Good seeing you again, Mister Cross."

In his wake, the gabardine man left a strange odor, a blend of stale cologne and staleness itself, like he'd spent years gathering dust in an unused room.

The gabardine man rested his hat on the front desk, pulled over the motel's leather-bound register. He plucked up the thick fountain pen that rested on a little tray beside it. Unscrewed the cap. Balanced the pen's weight in his hand. Even with his mangled finger he seemed able to write just fine.

The gabardine man smiled to the twins. "Been an age since they've all been together in one place like this."

That awful silence persisted, broken only by the *scritch-scratch* of the fountain pen across the register's paper. Just as he had in the diner in Turner, Ethan felt himself slackening in the gabardine man's aura, almost mesmerized, as if something about the man was simply so strange, Ethan's mind couldn't function in his presence.

What was the name the man had given himself at the diner?

What was his name?

Hunter didn't seem so afflicted. He gave Ethan's arm a hard jerk, and Ethan stumbled backward, toward the door.

Without looking back, the gabardine man said, "Leaving so soon, Mister Cross?"

The words rooted Ethan to the spot. He barely found it in himself to say, "Who *are* you?"

"The wiser question would be to ask, 'Who is *he?*'" The gabardine man turned to point the sharp golden nib of the fountain pen at Hunter. "Your tarnished warrior. The bruiser with the beautiful eyes. This strange man you've lashed your fortunes to. I warned you about him, didn't I, back in the diner? Told you he had a railroad spike where his heart ought to be."

Ethan felt panic coursing through Hunter's palm. Who would have thought such a thing was possible?

The gabardine man smiled. "Has your man told you his old nickname? They used to call him 'The Hunter of Huntsville,' back in the penitentiary. He had a savage reputation around those parts. It's where he met poor Mister Ryan Phan here. The two men shared a cell together."

Hunter gave Ethan another pull.

"You knew him?" Ethan jerked his arm free. He looked from the corpse on the floor to Hunter and back again. "You were in *Huntsville?*"

"The maximum-security unit, even," the gabardine man went on. "Everyone wondered, of course, how Hunter wasn't on death row, considering the way your man used to make a living."

Ethan only said again, "Huntsville?"

Hunter stared back.

"He killed families, Mister Cross," the gabardine man said. "Whole households. Mothers, fathers, children, even the pets. It was a specialty for Hunter, and a very lucrative one at that. If you were a criminal who wanted to wipe out the competition in the most efficient way possible, you called this fellow right here. I even believe Franklin O'Shea had a cause to hire him, once or twice. Did Hunter really never tell you?"

Ethan wasn't entirely stupid. He'd always suspected that a man as skilled at violence as Hunter—a man with a past he never discussed—had probably endured a few brushes with the law. You don't deep-fry a person's hand without a little practice at brutality.

But Ethan could have never imagined Hunter capable of what the gabardine man was describing.

Or maybe he *could* imagine it, and that was the worst part of all.

Mark my words. This man is going to get you into the sort of trouble you cain't never get out of.

The gabardine man just kept talking with the same courteous twang. "Of course, you have secrets of your own, don't you, Mister Cross? Your name isn't even Ethan. You used to be named Carter, but after your brother's suicide you took on his life to escape your own. The clothes on your back are your brother's. The truck you drove here. Your wallet and the ID inside—all his."

Ethan turned to stare at the gabardine man. "How do you—"

He didn't get the chance to finish. Hunter wrapped an arm around Ethan's chest. The other slammed something heavy into the back of Ethan's head.

The room swirled. The lamp went dark. Ethan was suddenly moving, though not of his own volition. From very far away, Kyla shouted, "Wait!"

And then he was out.

KYLA

Things moved too fast.

Hunter withdrew the heavy magnum from the back of his jeans and brought the butt of the gun down on Ethan's skull. Ethan slumped backward, against Hunter's chest, and Hunter hooked his arms under Ethan's shoulders and dragged him out of the office, kicking open the door, letting it slam behind him.

"Wait!" Kyla shouted, but Hunter was already gone.

"Oh, let him go, Miss Hewitt. You'll see them again soon enough. Unless, of course . . ." He shot her a cunning look. "Y'all haven't found where Penelope is hiding, have you?"

She could only stare at the man: his gray suit, his mangled finger. His empty black eyes.

"You were in my dream," Kyla said. "The dream of the dead city."

His smile tightened. "Ah. So you finally remembered."

On no, Miss Hewitt. It is I who shall have audience once more.

Here, in the office, the man touched his scarred knuckle to his temple. "My name is Jack Allen. Lovely to make your acquaintance again."

Still standing near the window next to Kyla, Fernanda finally spoke. Her voice sounded slow, heavy, just like Kyla's mind. "How did you drive through the dark? How did you make it past the creatures outside?"

"That is a wise question, ma'am."

Leaving his hat on the desk, the man named Jack Allen ambled toward the back of the office, the fountain pen twirling back and forth between his fingers. Back and forth. Back and forth. He nodded at the grooved stone egg that rested on the floor between the two girls, the one Kyla had knocked from the fireplace's mantel. "It's been ages since anyone has touched one of those. Have y'all not figured out what they're for?"

Fernanda said, "What do you mean? I have never been here before. I have never seen you."

"You always are the slowest to believe. Ironic, considering the way you've kept yourself alive for so long at Frank O'Shea's house. I'd imagine that you—you of all people—would understand the world doesn't quite function the way we think it should."

Kyla found herself unable to move in Jack Allen's presence. Every nerve in her body was urging her to move to *run* to fucking *GO*—

But she couldn't. Even though Jack Allen felt like some horror out of one of Fernanda's stories, a lethal trickster from the realm of the dead, Kyla found herself unable to move an inch. She only watched, mesmerized, as Jack Allen twirled that fountain pen: back and forth, back and forth, the sharp gold nib winking in the light.

"You want to know something funny, ladies? The mountain behind this motel is known as Mount Apache, but the Lipan Apache never dared come near this place. When they arrived in Texas a few hundred years ago, they heard warnings from the local tribes about a terrible curse that had been put on this mountain. The locals said that it had once been a sacred place, a place of great power, but it became corrupted when a great being fell from the sky and crashed into the mountain's heart. A fell god. The Lake That Travels. The local tribes said that after the great being's arrival, the mountain was haunted by long nights and terrible beasts, creatures out of a nightmare. Monsters that bore the features of everything a man could fear."

Outside, in the dark, a creature *SHRIEKED*.

"There's a legend about a party of Apache braves that came to scout the mountain for themselves, to see if perhaps the local tribes were simply trying to scare them away with these purported horrors. The legend of the Apache braves has several variations, but the results are always the same. As night came, as darkness rolled over the mountain, the braves died, one by one, until only a single young man was left behind to warn his tribe of the hell he'd seen. No one came here after that. Even the white men waited a long time to settle out this way. It wasn't until the tribes were finally broken, the old legends long buried, that some fool finally built this motel."

Jack Allen paused, considering.

"You want to know the definition of madness, ladies? Even though there was no record of anyone ever having lived here, when

our erstwhile motelier arrived to survey the land he'd purchased—
sight unseen, I might add—he discovered a vacant two-story house
siting right at the foot of the mountain. He said—and this is the
God's honest truth—that that old house seemed like it had always
been here. 'Since the beginning of time,' apparently. You'd think the
man would have taken that as a warning, but fools are fools." Jack
Allen's hooked smile widened. "Tell me, Miss Hewitt—have you
figured out how to reach the house? Without being torn to shreds,
of course."

Kyla found herself shaking her head.

"Pity. This motel is just a distraction, really. A way station. The
house—the *house* is what matters. Or, to be more precise, what the
motelier discovered in the basement of the house, back in 1955."

One of those great, bellowing moans echoed from the mountain.
Jack Allen chuckled. "It's getting restless."

He arrived, at last, at the back of the office. With a slow, effortless
grace, he reached a hand into the pocket of his gray suit and removed
a simple brass key. He slid the key into the walnut door. He smiled.

It was only as the man began to turn the key in the door's lock
that Kyla and Fernanda, at the same time, remembered what waited
on the other side of that door. The warning that the twins had given
them after Sarah's death.

At midnight, three things will happen.

The door will open.

The lights will go out.

And anyone who's not with us will die.

Kyla reached for her gun.

Fernanda seemed to jerk back to life. She held out a hand. "Stop!
Don't open—"

Jack Allen hardly acknowledged her. The man half turned in her
direction, made a flinging motion with his hand like he wanted to
shoo her away, and Kyla didn't realize anything was amiss until she
heard a wet squelching noise, like a finger pressing into ripe fruit,
and twisted on her heel to see the black barrel of that heavy fountain
pen jutting from the socket of Fernanda's left eye.

Jack Allen had flung the pen with such force—such practice—
that golden nib had buried itself in her skull.

With a great, heaving twitch that overwhelmed her entire body, Fernanda fell to her knees. She raised a hand to grab at the pen. She missed. Tried again. Couldn't close her hand. Fernanda's mind and her fingers seemed to have separated, never to return. The woman made a noise in her throat, a delayed grunt of shock or pain. A brilliant thread of blood curled from the corner of her eye and into her open mouth. The arc of the blood's course reminded Kyla, of all things, of the curve of the crack in her bathroom mirror.

Fernanda fell, face-first, to the floor. The pen dug deeper with another wet squelch.

Fernanda went still.

Kyla was too horrified to even scream.

Jack Allen turned again toward the walnut door in the back of the office. He turned the brass key. He shrugged his narrow shoulders. "Here we go again."

Finally, one of the twins spoke. It was Tabitha.

She whispered, "Run."

Kyla regained the use of her feet as the walnut door eased open. As a great towering shape loomed up out of the darkness inside. As a piercing *SHRIEK* echoed off the walls of the office.

Kyla didn't realize she'd dropped her gun until she was outside, in the cold, and looked over her shoulder in time to see Tabitha's head crash against the narrow front window with a damp thud. Thomas screamed. Screamed.

Stopped.

And Jack Allen called after Kyla, all courtesy. "See you shortly, Miss Hewitt."

ETHAN

He awoke on the floor of his room.

For a moment, mercy: Ethan had no idea why his head hurt, why he was on the carpet, why Hunter was heaving the mattress off their bed. For a moment, Ethan wasn't afraid of Hunter. No: on the contrary, he was afraid *for* Hunter. Hunter's chest was heaving, the air thick and heavy on its way out of his lungs. The man was sweaty, pale, clearly exhausted. Hunter had overexerted himself somehow, and his illness was punishing him for it.

Ethan realized, all over again, just how sick Hunter was.

And then Ethan remembered what happened in the office.

He went scrambling backward across the floor, away from Hunter, tried to stand.

"Ethan!"

Hunter dropped the mattress and leapt across the room, wrapping a hand around Ethan's ankle. Ethan kicked him with the other foot. Hunter grabbed it too.

"Let go of me!" Ethan shouted. "Get away!"

"Ethan, please, listen—"

Ethan fought to pull himself free. "Who *are* you?"

"Listen. Please." Hunter didn't let go. "There isn't much time. That man, the man in the suit—he's dangerous. He's the most dangerous man you will ever meet."

That made Ethan pause. "How do you know that?"

"Because I've met him before." Hunter swallowed. "I'd tell you the full story if we had time, I would, but we don't. Between Jack Allen and those things in the desert, we're dead if you don't do exactly what I say."

Ethan's head was still swimming from the blow Hunter had struck in the office. There was only one thing he knew for sure. Something he'd long suspected. Maybe even known and refused to see.

Now, finally, he could admit it.

"You're a monster."

"I *was* a monster, Ethan. I was the worst man a man could be."
Hunter still didn't let go of Ethan's ankles, but his grip was weakening. Those same two tears Ethan had seen earlier stood, again, in the corners of Hunter's eyes. "I was a monster. And then I met you."

"You met me six weeks ago. People don't change in six weeks."

Hunter smiled. Ethan realized it might have been only the second time he'd ever seen him truly smile. "You'd be surprised how much a guy can change, knowing a guy like you."

A sudden bout of coughing made Hunter choke. He released Ethan's ankles, thumped his chest, covered his mouth. He gasped for air.

Freed, Ethan pushed himself a few feet away, only to freeze when the room's lights flickered. A wave of *SHRIEKS* washed over the hotel, sounding closer than ever. Hunter caught his breath. He wiped his palm on the carpet. Ethan saw blood on the man's lips.

"Please, Ethan," Hunter said. "Help me get the bed over the window. We can barricade the doors with the nightstands and the dresser."

When Ethan still didn't move, Hunter pointed to something on the floor nearby. Carefully, Ethan followed his finger and saw their guns resting not a foot away.

"You can have whichever one you want. Take both, I don't care. We just need to get busy. If he's smart, Jack Allen's going to take out the generator, and then where will we be?"

Ethan hesitated a moment longer. He looked from the guns to the tears in Hunter's eyes to the mattress half slewed to the floor. He wondered if he could ever trust Hunter. He wondered if he could ever trust *himself* after being such a fool.

This man is going to get you into the sort of trouble you cain't never get out of.

Hunter never looked away from Ethan's face, even as he spat a wad of blood and phlegm toward the trash can. "Maybe I *am* a monster, Ethan. But have you considered that could be exactly what you need right now?"

Ethan dragged himself to his feet. He didn't like their odds, he didn't like Hunter, but his mother hadn't raised a quitter. "Where do we start?"

KYLA

She, too, was on the floor of her room, curled into a ball, alone. *It'll pass*, she tried to tell herself. *It's just another dream.*

But of course it wasn't. Kyla wasn't asleep. The night wasn't that kind.

Fernanda was dead. Again and again, Kyla heard that wet squelch as the fountain pen buried itself in Fernanda's brain. It didn't feel possible. It didn't feel *fair*. Fernanda was too calm and poised to die. Too careful. She couldn't be dead.

She couldn't have left Kyla to handle this alone.

Kyla rose to her feet, barely thinking. She started for the front door, thinking that she should go find Ethan—he was the closest thing she had left to a friend here—but then she remembered that Ethan would be with Hunter, and Kyla had been right about that man from the start: Hunter was exactly the sort of specialist Frank O'Shea liked to hire.

Going to find Ethan would also involve going outside. When the lamp on Kyla's nightstand flickered and a chorus of *SHRIEKS* echoed around the motel, Kyla knew that going outside was a very bad idea.

Think, Kyla. Think.

She took an inventory of her situation. She hadn't thought to grab Fernanda's gun off the woman's corpse back in the office. Like an idiot, she'd even dropped her own weapon in the scramble to escape the thing behind the walnut door. Kyla was four foot nine, weighed barely a hundred pounds, and she was unarmed. She didn't like her chances.

As she turned to look at the heavy lamp on her nightstand, her eyes passed over the room's tall armoire. Stopped. Moved back. She approached the armoire, studied it from several angles, gave the soffit at the bottom a soft kick.

She might not have liked her chances, but maybe being small had its advantages.

ETHAN

The power died right as they got the long dresser pushed against the front door. There wasn't time to barricade the back. With a hiss and a click, the lamp on their nightstand went out, followed an instant later by the lights outside. This time, it all felt final. There was no faint half-light. No gloaming.

Darkness came over the motel, thick and permanent.

"He killed the generator," Hunter whispered. As if Ethan couldn't guess.

Hunter pressed something cold and metal into Ethan's hand. The Python he'd stolen from the diner in Turner. Hunter held the shotgun they'd brought from Ellersby. He was wheezing hard.

He whispered, "Watch the back door."

Ethan had expected the darkness to bring a new wave of SHRIEKS, but when the lights went out for good, he heard instead something far worse: a soft rush of feet, a great rustle of many wings, a strange animal hiss that started in the parking lot and echoed around the motel. The hiss felt coordinated, steady, almost rhythmic. It made Ethan think of the pulse of sonar, or the whistle of deer hunters circling their prey.

His eyes had adjusted well enough to the dark for Ethan to make out the shape of the back door. Hunter pressed his back to Ethan's. He was barely breathing.

Ethan heard a creak of wood behind him, directly outside their front door. He heard a long, sustained hiss. It was echoed by another hiss, a third.

At least three of those things were here, right outside their room.

A long talon tapped the wood of the door. Another tapped at the bars on the window.

Hiss.

Instinct told Ethan what was happening: those things were debating if their prey might be inside.

He heard another tap, this one against the wood of the back door.

There hadn't been time to barricade that door. Nothing held it closed but a dead bolt and chain.

The creature outside tapped again.

Again.

Again.

Ethan didn't breathe. Didn't move. Didn't make a sound. Hunter was just as silent. They waited, their ears straining. Ethan's senses had become so sharp he could count every fiber of his denim sleeve just from touch, feel the weight of the atmosphere on his every individual hair.

The taps stopped. The hissing. Ethan heard steps move up the porch. When there was another hiss, it sounded like it came from outside room 8 next door.

The creatures were moving on. Ethan almost—almost—risked a sigh of relief.

And then he heard a new noise, much closer. It was a wet rattle, a warning: a carburetor gasping for air. With a rush of cold sweat, Ethan knew what that sound was. It was coming from Hunter's lungs.

Hunter tensed against Ethan's back. As softly as he could, he took one hand off the shotgun and thumped his chest.

The hissing outside stopped.

A creak of wood from the porch, another: they were coming back.

Hunter tried to hold his breath. Ethan felt the man thump his chest again, desperate now.

A hiss, directly outside the door.

Hunter coughed.

SHRIEKS came up from every direction, so loud Ethan's mind clenched up.

And then, through the cough, he heard Hunter say, "Run."

KYLA

She was freezing. It had taken every ounce of willpower in her body, but Kyla had opened the room's back door. She'd cracked the front door, too, left it ajar. If her plan was going to work, she needed her room to look empty. Needed it to look like she'd flown through the front door and gone straight out the back.

It was a long shot, but it seemed smarter than bolting both doors from the inside. If she did that, she might as well put a sign out front: HIDING, COME FIND ME.

Kyla didn't understand who this Jack Allen was—she certainly didn't understand what in the fuck he'd been talking about when he spoke of a cursed mountain and Apache braves and a wandering lake—but it seemed pretty obvious that whatever he wanted with Kyla and the rest of the guests, it wasn't good.

At least she'd figured out a decent hiding spot. Kyla had realized, a moment ago, that although the soffit paneling around the base of the armoire made it look like the armoire's interior should run straight to the floor, the bottom shelf actually rested several feet off the ground. When she'd pulled the armoire away from the wall— easier said than done; the thing seemed to weigh about as much as Kyla herself—she'd found a cavity in the paneling, a gap between the bottom shelf and the floor that was barely big enough to hide inside, provided she curled her body into the tiniest possible ball.

By pressing out with her arms and lifting with her back, she was just able to muscle the armoire over herself a moment before the lights around the motel died. She got the armoire most of the way to the wall. Close enough to look convincing. Hopefully.

When the generator cut out, she heard a soft rush of feet outside, an eerie rhythmic hiss. The darkness of the armoire's cavity became darker. It was far, far tighter than she'd expected. Wood penned her in from all sides. Kyla hadn't thought, until this moment, that she could ever be claustrophobic, but as the panels of the armoire dug into her elbows and the shelf crushed her back, she almost convinced herself that the space was growing smaller, that it was running out of oxygen, that she couldn't breathe. She almost convinced herself—

Footsteps creaked on the porch outside, coming from the direction of the motel's cafe. The steps were calm, thoroughly unhurried. So calm, indeed, they could only belong to one man. The man from the office. The man from her dream.

Jack Allen, who would have audience once more.

His footsteps stopped on the back porch. They stopped right behind Kyla's room.

After a moment, Kyla heard more steps, these muffled by carpet as they came down the room's back hall.

Kyla's claustrophobia left her in a hurry. Her heart thundered in her chest, the sound so loud she was certain the man in the room must be able to hear it reverberate in the wood of the armoire.

The carpeted steps came closer. Kyla caught a familiar smell: old stone, old cologne, staleness itself. His steps passed inches from Kyla's head. In that thoroughly polite twang, he called out, "Miss Hewitt?"

Kyla heard a rustle of fabric as he lifted the skirt of her bed. He opened the door of the armoire above her. Through the narrow crack between the soffit paneling and the floor, she could see slivers of Jack Allen's shoes, a shiny blackness in the dark.

She didn't move. Didn't breathe.

The door of the armoire closed. Jack Allen's footsteps moved away. They returned to the hall and on to the back door. There was silence, punctuated only by the scratches and hisses of the creatures in the desert.

Kyla let herself exhale. She shifted her weight, struggling to get comfortable in the narrow confines under the armoire, and wondered when she could risk a few moments to come out and stretch her legs.

But then, with a cold stab of panic, she realized there was a sound she hadn't heard: she hadn't heard the creak of wood from the back porch. She hadn't heard any indication that Jack Allen had really left her room.

She also didn't hear him coming back down the hall, silent as a cat, until he dragged the armoire away from the wall.

Air rushed over her. His stench flooded her nose. Outside, a wave of *SHRIEKS* rose from the direction of Ethan's room.

"Hello, Miss Hewitt," Jack Allen said. "I don't think you've ever tried hiding here before."

ETHAN

Outside, Ethan heard one of those creatures rip a metal bar off their window. The metal let out a squeal and a twang, like a mangled engine fan. Another bar came away. Glass shattered. Fabric was shredded as a talon tore into the mattress they'd barricaded over the window. One of the things outside slammed against their front door with a heavy thud. The bolt creaked in the frame.

These barricades weren't going to hold for long. If the boys were lucky, they might have a few seconds.

Hunter said again, "Run."

Ethan was already moving. He didn't have much of a plan, but he knew that staying in this room was a death sentence.

Ethan hadn't taken two steps down the hall before one of the night creatures heaved itself against the back door. The door's bolt shattered and swung open, a bloom of sawdust in a shaft of starlight. A massive figure stood on the porch, silhouetted against the night. The creature raised its wings. It *SHRIEKED*.

Ethan brought up the revolver in his hand. He fired. In the flash of the muzzle, he caught stray glimpses of the thing in the dark: bright talons, black feathers, black scales.

He saw the shape of the thing's head. In his gut, he felt another squeeze of that ancient primal terror that had gripped him all night.

But the revolver's rounds hit home. The creature stumbled backward with a startled wail, a furious hiss. Whatever the hell it was, it wasn't immune to bullets.

The thing fell off the porch, twitching and prone. Hunter slammed against Ethan's shoulder, the shotgun still in his hands. "Go!"

Ethan was overclocked with adrenaline. He felt like he could see further, clearer, than a normal man. He could absorb every detail around him. He saw time collapse into a series of frozen, vivid moments:

The porch, empty and cold.

Black clouds, faint reflections of starlight.

The creatures of the desert everywhere: a feathered darkness in the cosmic afterglow.

Ethan was running. Hunter was behind him. They were running up the porch, toward the rear of the motel. Toward the mountain? Not exactly.

They rounded the corner of the porch and there it was: the two-story house at the foot of the mountain, its upstairs window shining with silver light. It was calling to them. Ethan knew, way down deep in his soul, that something in that old house was waiting for him.

Ethan said to Hunter, "It's our best shot."

Hunter made a grunt. Whether it was another *yes* or another wad of phlegm, they just kept running.

A creature rounded the corner of the porch, raised its wings.

Before it could finish its *SHRIEK*, Ethan fired.

The bullet hit. The creature staggered sideways.

Hunter said through a cough. "You've got one shot left."

The boys were off the porch. The old house was twenty yards away, maybe a hair less, but in the dark the distance seemed to last forever. Dead ahead, the mountain loomed over them, larger than it had ever been before.

The mountain moaned. The earth shook so violently Ethan feared he'd lose his balance.

A *SHRIEK* came, right beside him.

"Son of a bitch," Hunter said. The shotgun went off with a deafening boom. Ethan kept running. He felt a strange sensation somewhere along his right leg. It felt like a twitching nerve, a second pulse. He ignored it.

The old house was getting closer. Was Ethan crazy, or did its front door look wider than it had a moment ago? Had the wooden porch somehow grown shorter? Had the house's walls been brick when they'd arrived at the motel, or had they always been clad in this gray wooden siding?

It was like every time Ethan looked away from the house, it changed.

A creature whisked past Ethan, all feathers and yellow eyes. Ethan's foot caught a stone and he went sprawling forward. He fired as he fell. The last bullet in the revolver hit nothing.

When he landed, the gun tumbled from his hand and went skittering away into the dark.

In that moment, the clouds parted, bathing the desert in stark starlight. When Ethan looked up, he saw a dozen of the night creatures watching him from all directions. He finally saw clearly what they were made of. He saw horror made flesh.

He felt another pulse in his pocket.

One of those things stood between the boys and the house's front porch. It was a creature like the others, but it was taller than its companions. A towering thing, eight feet high, standing on two long legs like a man. It had long arms, with hands that ended in gleaming black talons. Its limbs and chest were blanketed with black feathers, the same feathers that coated the enormous pair of wings that sprouted from its back.

Where the thing's head should be—where one might have imagined the beak and eyes of an enormous bird—Ethan instead saw scales, a long curving neck, and the head of a great black serpent with yellow eyes and bared white fangs.

They were all like that, all the creatures around them: the arms and legs of men, the bodies of birds, the heads of snakes, like something out of some old legend. They had Ethan and Hunter surrounded. They were circling, coming closer.

The massive creature before Ethan raised its black wings in a glorious display. It opened its serpent mouth wide and released a SHRIEK that stopped Ethan's heart.

"Stay down!" Hunter shouted. He fired the shotgun over Ethan's head.

Its boom was so loud that all Ethan could hear for a moment was a high, tinny whine in his ear. He saw the massive creature skitter sideways, a great chunk of its wing and arm blasted away.

Ethan felt a hand on the back of his shirt, hoisting him to his feet. Hunter shouted, "Go!"

Ethan didn't think. The massive thing had stumbled out of the way of the door and so he was running, running, running up to the house. He clambered up a short flight of stone steps (hadn't they been wooden a moment ago?) and over the stone porch and threw himself against the front door. It was unlocked. Ethan shoved it open.

He turned back, expecting to see Hunter directly behind him.

Instead, as he turned, Ethan heard a wet squelch. He heard two choked words. They might have been, "Thank you."

Ethan looked back in time to see Hunter staring at him from the porch's steps, the man appearing almost normal until a bubble of blood burst from his mouth and the talons buried in his neck wrenched him backward into the desert. Hunter's eyes widened in surprise. He pointed toward the house. He tried to speak, but the massive creature with the shattered wing flung Hunter to the ground and buried two serpent teeth into Hunter's eyes.

KYLA

A few minutes earlier, Kyla was on the floor of her room, gasping in shock as Jack Allen wrenched the armoire away from the wall. Air rushed over her: air and the man's ancient smell and the realization that she was about to die.

Jack Allen smiled down at her. "Hello, Miss Hewitt. I don't think you've ever tried hiding here before."

With a scream, Kyla played the only trick she had left. She pulled her arm free of the armoire's compartment and slammed her hand into Jack Allen's calf. It held the light bulb from her room's heavy brass lamp clasped socket first in Kyla's palm.

It worked.

The glass of the bulb shattered, burying itself in Jack Allen's leg. The man let out a startled roar of pain and stumbled backward. It gave Kyla space. She bounded to her feet and pushed past him and flew into the hall—

Just in time to see one of those creatures outside, through the open back door, as it sprinted down the porch in the direction of Ethan and Hunter's room. Kyla heard gunfire, shouting. Another creature passed her door. They were everywhere. Outside was a no go.

Kyla skidded sideways, into the bathroom. It seemed like her only option. She slammed the door behind her.

The force of the slam made the glass of her mirror let out a *chink* of dismay. For a single, suspended moment, Kyla saw a man reflected in her cracked mirror, staring back at her. It wasn't Jack Allen. For a moment, in the mirror, Kyla saw a short Black man she'd never met and yet who felt oddly familiar. The man was watching her with an expression of profound sadness. It made her think of her father.

Jack Allen struck the door behind Kyla. The crack in the mirror widened, the man on the other side vanished.

Kyla pressed her back to the door, reached a hand backward to fumble for the lock.

Jack Allen kicked the door, and the glass of the mirror trembled.

Kyla turned the lock.

Jack Allen kicked the door again.

The cracked mirror shattered.

A great rush of hot air washed through the bathroom. Shards of glass chimed like bells as they fell into the sink.

And on the other side of the shattered mirror, Kyla saw the dead city of her dreams.

As if the frame of the mirror had become the frame of a window, Kyla found herself staring out from one of those curved stone buildings. She saw the silver streets, a faceless monument, trees and grass growing slowly in a pale light. Hot air rushed over her face.

In the distance, Kyla saw a great column of silver energy rising toward the city's everblack sky. The silver column seemed to scream, and a moment later, the mountain behind the motel let out one of its awful bellowing moans.

Of course, Kyla thought. *Of course.*

A shotgun boomed outside the motel. Closer to hand, she heard two loud pops and felt a searing pain in her back. Two bullets passed through the door and crashed into the porcelain of the sink.

They passed through Kyla's chest too.

Without wanting to, Kyla sank to the floor. Blood was suddenly everywhere. With a final sharp kick, Jack Allen got the door open. It smacked against Kyla's heel, though she didn't feel the blow. She struggled to crawl away, but her limbs were heavier than her body could handle. Darkness was already closing in the edges of her vision. A terrible sadness seemed to be slowing her heart, though that was probably just all the blood loss.

Kyla realized there was so much she didn't understand about tonight. What was on the film Ryan had stolen from Sarah's room? Why had Stanley turned up to dinner with a busted lip? Where had Fernanda disappeared to in those few minutes before dinner? Where was Penelope?

Where was Penelope?

Kyla saw herself reflected in her blood on the tile. Maybe she deserved this. Retribution for what she'd done to Lance this afternoon. Retribution for all the people she hadn't saved these last six months. For the shambles she'd made of her life.

In her last moments, at least, Kyla had one satisfaction. As Jack Allen stepped into the bathroom, Kyla's own gun smoking in his hand, the man hesitated at the sight of the mirror. A look of absolute shock came over his face, a profound awe. He reached out his hand, the one with the mangled finger, looking for a moment like he hoped to reach through the mirror and climb through to the city on the other side.

A brilliant flash of silver light burned through the room. Jack Allen recoiled with a grunt of pain. From where she lay on the cold tile, she could see a sliver of the mirror. It was simply a piece of shattered glass again. Nothing waited inside its frame but a cinder block wall.

Outside, a second shotgun blast tore through the night.

Jack Allen was still staring at the place the city had been. "That . . . that's never happened before."

With the last of her strength, Kyla asked the most obvious question of all. "Why . . . are you . . . hurting us?"

"I told you, Miss Hewitt. I will have audience once more. I will commune again with Te'lo'hi. With The Lake That Travels. The silver god that fell from the stars." Jack Allen's old self was returning to him: his grinding smile, his lethal courtesy. He turned to her with a banal little shrug. "And you people are standing in my way."

"H-how?"

"I'll make this last part painless, Miss Hewitt. It's the least I can do. Your grandfather was always kind to me."

"You knew—my grand—"

Almost like an afterthought, Jack Allen raised the gun and fired a bullet into Kyla's face.

ETHAN

The angles of the old house were all wrong. It was the only way Ethan could describe it. None of the doors hung completely square, none of the hallways ran entirely true. The front room was bare of furniture or windows—there were no lamps, no lit fires, no starlight—and yet the air seemed to glow with its own faint silver illumination. Ethan saw plain wood floors opening onto a hallway to the left and another to the right.

He chose a hallway at random. It was a long straight tunnel of plain wooden paneling. It stretched on and on and on, far longer than the bounds of the house should have been able to contain, and yet when Ethan reached the end of the tunnel, he realized it must have curved back on itself without his noticing. The hallway deposited Ethan right back where he'd started, in the bare front room.

What was this place?

Ethan tried the other hallway. This one had a corner every ten feet or so: left, right, right, left. Once, twice, as he came around one of the hall's endless corners, he caught sight, up ahead, of someone vanishing around the next. It was a challenge to make out many details in the soft light, but Ethan thought he saw Hunter rounding one corner. The next time he saw someone, they looked like Fernanda.

Once, Ethan saw someone who looked like himself.

And then the hallway deposited him again back where he'd started, in the bare front room, only now it wasn't so bare. Where the other hallway had been, Ethan now found a solid wall. On the wall hung a large black-and-white photograph in a stark wooden frame.

It was a picture of the mountain. Beneath the photograph was a small brass plaque that read:

IT SLEEPS

The hall he'd just come from was gone, replaced by another wall with another photograph, but it took him longer to make out what he was seeing in this picture. The image looked like it had been taken from a satellite somewhere at the edge of the solar system. There were stars, and planets, and with a little patience Ethan could identify Neptune and Jupiter.

Where the Earth should be, however, Ethan saw a small blue orb exploding around a column of silver light. The light seemed to pierce the planet from one side to the other, like a stick through a ripe berry, and as he watched he saw the silver light in the photograph grow brighter. Brighter.

The light vanished, leaving behind nothing but a terrible void—darker than any black he had seen before—where the earth and the moon should be. The void expanded. It would consume the rest of the planets sooner than later.

Another plaque rested under the photograph. The plaque read:

IT WAKES

The air of the front room shifted. To his right, opposite the house's main entrance, he now found a door set into the wall. Ethan hadn't seen that door when he'd stepped inside, and yet somehow he knew it had always been there, waiting for him. The door was simple: varnished oak, brass hinges, a pattern of six even squares lathed into its surface. It had a brass knob, but above the knob was a latch held shut by a massive silver padlock. Ethan gave the lock a tug, gave the door a kick, but it was no good. The latch was shut solid. The door would not open tonight.

When Ethan stepped away from the door, he found his final surprise. A plain wooden staircase was waiting for him, going up.

It sleeps.

It wakes.

Upstairs, Ethan found another plain hallway, and in this hallway, there was another door. A dull silver light glowed around the door's frame. A distant rush of sound—like the whisper of a hundred voices—leaked through the air.

The upstairs door was unlocked.

Jack Allen found him eventually. When the man came at last into the upstairs room, Ethan didn't try to run. He'd been sitting, for as long as he could remember, on the room's bare floor, staring at what he'd found inside.

The hem of Jack Allen's sleeve brushed the back of Ethan's neck.

Ethan said, "How long have we been trapped here?"

Jack Allen stared, too, at what had been hidden beneath the sheet. Almost reverently, the man said, "I lost count around night fifty. And that was a long time ago."

"And it's the same every night? Over and over, we keep coming back to the motel?"

"More or less. You've never come *here* before."

"That's what Tabitha meant by 'the others.' She was talking about us. About the versions of us that died here on all those other nights."

"I have no idea." A rustle of fabric: a shrug. "Tonight's been different. Normally Hunter breaks your neck when it's obvious the Guardians of the mountain are going to get into your room. You never feel a thing. He's a master of his art."

It took a while for that to sink in.

"What about Sarah Powers?" Ethan said. "Does she die every time?"

"Of course. None of this would work if she didn't. Everything proceeds from her death. Like a river from a wound in the earth."

It sleeps.

It wakes.

They watched shapes and faces, time and space. They watched something that neither of them, not even Jack Allen, could quite comprehend.

Ethan finally found the shape of a possibility. "So if we keep Sarah from dying, we can stop it. Stop all of it."

"You might want to be careful with that, son. You have no idea the powers at work here." Jack Allen smiled: those teeth grinding together like stones. "Just like you don't understand the rewards that can be won. I tell you, Mister Cross—I will be granted audience once more. I will ascend to a purer form. I will make a purer world."

"You're insane, aren't you?"

"No. I am a totem of unbounded potential. I will drink of the source."

Ethan swallowed. He had no idea what this could mean, but he doubted it was a good idea for a man this crazy to be granted any kind of power. "No. We're going to stop you. We're going to find a way."

"You want to know the truth of it? When you wake up tomorrow, you won't remember a thing."

Jack Allen moved so fast, Ethan hardly felt the fingers in his hair, the knife move along his throat. Ethan felt a great warmth running down his chest.

"See you tomorrow, Mister Cross."

PENELOPE

It was dark in Penelope's hiding spot, dark and colder and smaller than you might think, but thanks to Adeline it was mostly dry, and Penelope had brought her sweaters, a cushion, snacks. "We won't be down here for long," Adeline had whispered, but that had been hours ago, back when Tabitha had started screaming at dinner and everyone had gone running and left Penelope alone in the motel's cafe.

Except, she hadn't been alone. Adeline had still been there with her in the cafe, practically perched on Penelope's shoulder, whispering in Penelope's ear like she'd been doing since the weird silver light had passed over the desert at four o'clock sharp.

Not that Penelope had a clue why any of this was happening. Or how any of it was possible.

"We're trapped in a time loop," Adeline had whispered, back in the van as Stanley's Odyssey had barreled toward the motel.

Penelope had whispered all the usual things you would think—"This can't be real, you're dead, I'm hallucinating your voice, I have brain damage"—but after a while Stanley had called from the driver's seat, "Why are you talking to yourself, Penelope?" and the weird Adeline presence nestled against Penelope's back had said, "Hush, Polly, or he'll make things more complicated than they need to be. Just listen."

So Penelope had listened, even though she didn't believe a word of what she heard. At least not at first. Adeline kept talking about "a time loop" and "we've been doing this over and over" and "if you want to survive you need to do exactly what I say."

"Survive?" Penelope said. "If I'm just going to wake up again tomorrow, why should I worry about surviving?"

"Because you're the most important part, dummy," Adeline said. "If *you* die too soon—if we *all* die—then it's over. For good."

"What's over?"

"Everything. Literally everything."

Obviously, Penelope had believed she was just going crazy in the back of Stanley's minivan, that the weird silver light in the sky had done something to make her brain snap, but then things started happening exactly like this weird Adeline presence had said they would.

Adeline had said, "Stanley is only a couple hours' away from home, but he's going to stop at a little motel on this road. He says he's going to need gas, but if you look at the meter, he doesn't. He's stopping here for some other reason. The place is called the Brake Inn Motel. Just watch."

Adeline had said, "As Stanley pulls in, he's going to see a car that belongs to a guy named Lance. He's going to see two girls leaving the office and say out loud, 'That looks like Fernanda and the waitress from the steakhouse.'"

Adeline had said, "When Stanley parks, look to the right. There's going to be a man watching you from the door of room nine. It's the man from The Bad Night. Whatever you do, don't try to talk to him."

Talk to him? Adeline must have been the crazy one, because even though things proceeded exactly the way her sister had told her they would, nothing could have prepared Penelope for the face of the man watching her from room 9 of the Brake Inn Motel. He was a muscled man with hard hazel eyes, and at the sight of him Penelope's whole body had squeezed up, from her toes to her eyes. Only her bladder seemed loose. For the first time since she was Adeline's age, Penelope had thought she was going to wet her pants.

The last time Penelope had seen that man with the hard hazel eyes, he'd been standing beside her bed in her mom's house with a gun pressed to Penelope's forehead. They'd watched each other, Penelope and the man with the hazel eyes, and somehow, even before he pulled the trigger, she'd known that her mother and her sister were already dead.

Back then, on The Bad Night, the man hadn't said a word. He'd pulled the trigger, and Penelope had seen bright silver.

"Now do you see why you need to be so careful?" Adeline had whispered in Penelope's ear in the back of Stanley's van. "You need to do what I say. You have no idea how important it is."

Penelope had swallowed. It was crazy, but it was hard to argue with a girl who clearly wasn't lying. "What do I need to do?"

. . .

There had been a lot of screaming tonight. First Tabitha, and then what sounded like Stanley getting eaten by a bear (scary, of course, but Penelope hadn't been as upset as she would have thought to realize her grandfather was dead). There had been some weird *SHRIEKS* that had made Penelope think of nails on a chalkboard, and some weird moans that sounded like a massive animal getting crushed under a big rock.

"What the heck *is* that?" Penelope had whispered.

"Trust me," Adeline said. "You really don't want to know."

She'd gotten bored (who wouldn't), and for old times' sake she thought they could play The Game, but Adeline hadn't gone along with it for long. "You have to stay quiet. Please. You have no idea."

"What are you so afraid of?" Penelope said. "Aren't you, like, dead?"

"Not as long as you're alive."

Fair enough, she guessed. But the silence left Penelope with nothing to do but think about all the strange things Adeline had made her do today. It made Penelope think of the shower, and sneaking out of Stanley's room, and the things they'd done in room 4.

Penelope really, really did not want to think about room 4.

Dark as their hiding place was, Penelope had known when the motel's lights had died. There was a wave of *SHRIEKS* and screams and some weird hisses and gunshots and more screams and then— silence. The desert was quiet. Penelope understood, in a way that was hard to understand, that everyone was dead.

Now Penelope was scared.

"You're the last one standing," Adeline said. "And you need to keep it that way until it's too late. Don't move a freaking muscle."

Overhead, Penelope had heard footsteps. They sounded close. A man called her name even though Penelope was certain she'd never met him before. She would know. She was good with voices.

"It's not too late, Penelope!" the strange man shouted.

Adeline hissed in her ear, "Don't make a sound. It's almost over."

"The ritual is failing!" the man shouted outside.

There was another moan from the direction of the mountain. The man had to shout over it.

"We can't keep doing this forever, Penelope. One way or another, the seal is going to break."

Panic was rising in Penelope. She didn't like this voice. How did he know her name?

How did he know her name?

"Just come out, Penelope. I won't hurt you. I just need to know where you are."

Another moan came from the mountain, louder than the any of the others, and this one didn't stop. A tremor shook the earth so hard it threw Penelope from her seat and slewed her sideways. Her head hit the wall of her hiding place. Hit it hard.

Her shoulders sank into cold.

The tremor, like the loud noise from the mountain, didn't stop. It seemed to be growing stronger and stronger, an earthquake, but didn't earthquakes stop at some point? Penelope stopped trying to be sneaky. She was too scared for it.

"What is this?" she said. "What's happening?"

"Relax, Polly," Adeline said. "It's just the end of the world."

A new sound came, a great crash of breaking stone. It was the last sound the planet would ever know.

All sound stopped, then. In the final silence—in this new, absolute hush—a great flash of silver light flooded the world over Penelope's head, followed by an explosion so powerful it flattened her against the wall of her hiding place. She was about to die. The entire world, she realized, was about to die.

Penelope started to scream, even though there was no one left to hear.

And then, between one moment and the next

THE
MIDNIGHT
KNOCK

A NOVEL

JOHN FRAM

ATRIA BOOKS

NEW YORK AMSTERDAM/ANTWERP LONDON
TORONTO SYDNEY/MELBOURNE NEW DELHI

Ooh, and it's alright and it's coming on.
We gotta get right back to where we started from.
MAXINE NIGHTINGALE, "Right Back Where We Started From"
(written by Pierre Tubbs and J. Vincent Edwards)

All life is a circle.
ROLLING THUNDER, Cherokee

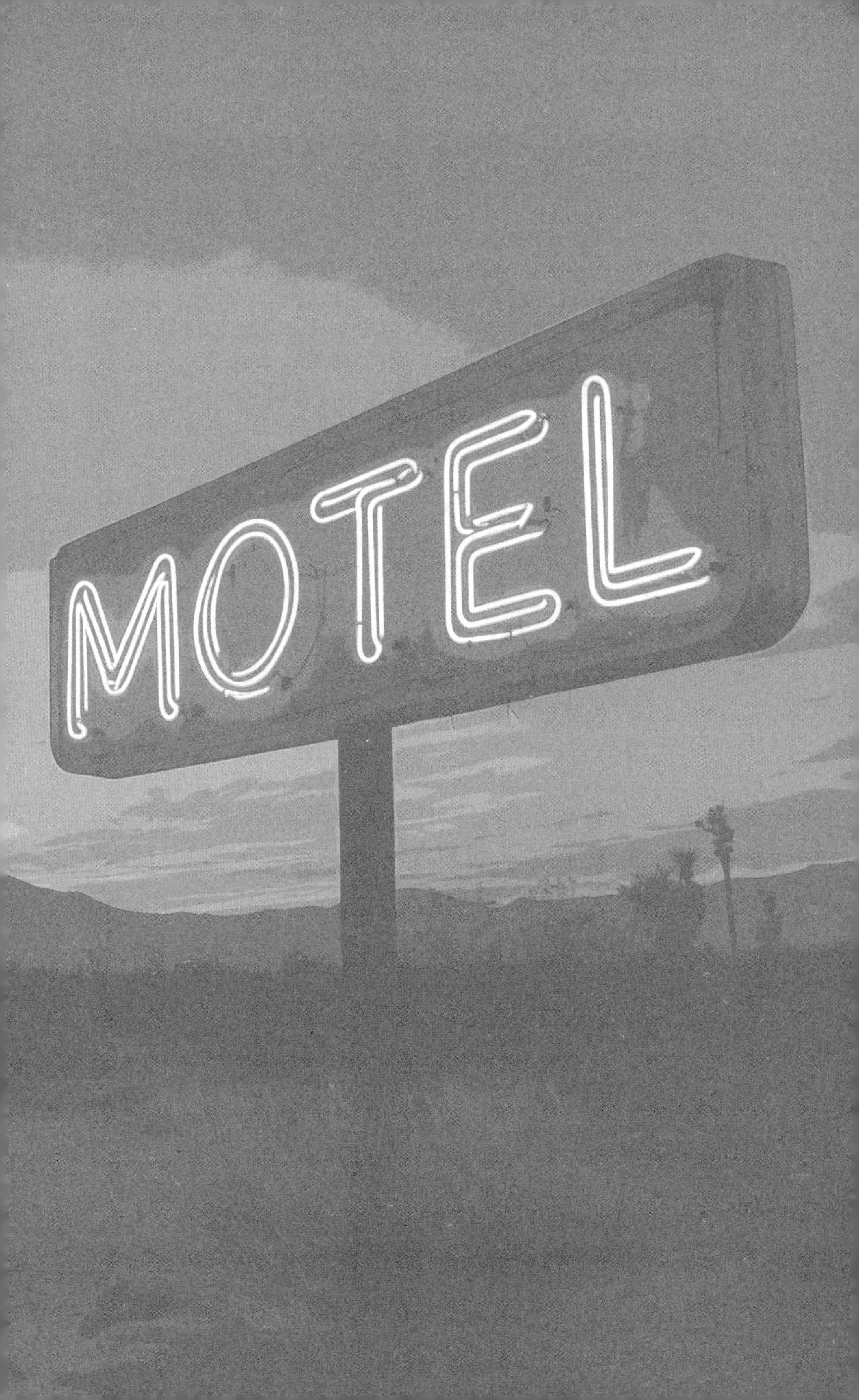
MOTEL

Part I

DÉJÀ VU

LEAVING

They left town at dawn. They left behind his brother's body on the couch upstairs and most of his brother's brain matter clinging to the ceiling. They left behind the shotgun his brother had used to kill himself. Years ago, Ethan had demanded that their mother buy him a Remington 12-gauge for his birthday so he could be like all the other boys in town. After much debate, their mother had bought two guns. She'd given one of them to Carter. "Keep an eye on him, won't you?" she'd said.

Even then, when they were barely more than boys, Carter suspected that his mother, like himself, had known that his brother Ethan wasn't going to die of old age.

Now, on a cold night a decade later, Carter had been downstairs playing a Nintendo game with Hunter. Carter was hardly a gamer, and the Nintendo was ancient and hopelessly outdated, but Hunter had taken to it instantly. Hunter had never touched a console before the boys met. It was the same with movies, books, TV. "My dad kept me too busy," Hunter said. "And then I was on the road." Hunter got restless with most things, but he took to video games with a child's glee that Ethan always found touching. There was an innocence to Hunter, buried under all the scars and fangs and razor blades.

"When you die, you get to start over and you know what's coming," Hunter said of the game on their TV. "Can you imagine?"

Which is when they heard the shot: Carter's brother, spraying brain matter across the room upstairs. Even before its echo faded, Hunter had the game turned off and a plot in place. "We can use this," Hunter said with a cough, and spat a bloody wad of phlegm.

"No one knows your brother came home last night," Hunter continued. "The shotgun took care of his face. They won't bother with the expense of tracking down dental records if they don't have to. We'll take your brother's truck. People will assume I left, just walked back out of town. They'll think you killed yourself for it. They'll think you couldn't stand another day of this."

Carter, getting over his shock, said, "What about DNA? Fingerprints?"

"The fire will take care of those."

The boys got up. They got busy.

"Grab the bag your brother brought," Hunter said. "Don't take any of your own clothes."

"He didn't bring a jacket. It's freezing outside."

"It won't be freezing in California."

Hunter had unlocked the door to the shop's engine bays, dug out a spare can of kerosene. He said to Carter, "Take your brother's wallet. Take his ID. Memorize the date of birth. Don't think. Don't hesitate. Don't even think of yourself by your old name anymore. Not even in your head."

They left behind the house, the shop, the street where he and his brother had played Cowboys and Indians until well after dark. They left behind the only life he had ever known. He already wondered, deep down, why he had been so willing to accept such a radical plan, to run away with a man he'd only known for six weeks, but he tossed the question out the window, pretended he'd never asked it at all. They were heading west, into the rising sun, and as they slipped onto the highway, they could see a cloud of smoke rising in their truck's mirror as it all went up in flames.

"Carter Cross," Hunter said. "I now pronounce you Ethan."

They were driving to California. Everyone started their lives over in California.

In spite of his brother's example, Carter—Ethan—still believed that it was possible to start your life over.

THE SILVER GLARE

FERNANDA

4:00 p.m.

She had been driving for as long as she could remember. Driving and driving and driving. In all that time, nothing had changed outside the stolen Malibu. The same blue-white sky. The same gold-brown desert scrub. The same straight ribbon of road. The Malibu's motor had thrummed at the same pitch for hours, the tires moaning against the blacktop. The Sierra Madres—or any other sign of the border—were still nowhere in sight.

Nothing had changed except the needle of the fuel gauge, sinking and sinking toward the red.

An unnumbered highway. The Dust Road. There were faster ways to Mexico, but when the girls had edged past the parking lot of the diner in Turner—past all the cruisers gathered there, lights flashing—Fernanda had chosen this route because Frank never sent his men down here. Frank feared the Dust Road, and for good reason. His mother had apparently disappeared at some motel somewhere out here. He used to wake up screaming in his bed, tormented by nightmares. Frank said his mother was still there, at the motel, calling to him.

A monstrous man, reduced to an infant weeping for his mami.

Those tears had been Fernanda's salvation. Just like she used to do with her brother, she would say to the weeping Frank O'Shea, "Have you heard the story about the bear that swallowed a princess?"

"The bird who built a city?"

"The little god that made new friends?"

It was pathetic, really, how easily Frank could be soothed. Until this morning, of course, when Frank had caught her in his office with a camera in her hand.

Kyla stirred in the Malibu's passenger seat, just in time for the two girls to watch a strange flash of silver light pass over the desert's sky. A mountain rose into view a moment later. A solitary mountain.

Fernanda felt a cold rash of gooseflesh spread over her arms. She told herself it was absurd to fear a mountain, whatever dreams Frank might have had. No time for fear. Fernanda's brother was waiting for her, down in Mexico. He needed her.

That was all that had kept Fernanda going these last awful months. Miguel needed her.

Kyla rubbed her forehead with a groan. "I just got the worst headache."

The girl leaned forward, unzipped the green backpack at her feet, fished out the roll of film inside buried under all the cash. "It's still here."

"Did you think we had forgotten it back in Stockton?" Fernanda said.

After a long hesitation and another rub of her temples, Kyla said, "I forgot *something*. I just can't remember what."

Kyla was restless, twitchy. Terrified. Who could blame her? On top of everything else, the fuel gauge of the Malibu let out a soft warning *ding*. Another thing to feel terrible about, another mess into which Fernanda had dragged this girl she barely knew: they were on the run from a very bad man, in the middle of nowhere, about to run out of gas.

Fernanda said, "Have you heard the story of the rabbit who met the pirate king?"

"No stories. I feel like I'm already living in one of the awful ones."

A sign for a motel appeared on the road ahead. A rusted pickup truck was abandoned by the side of the road. The sight of the sign sent the gooseflesh spreading to Fernanda's shoulders. Its paint was fresh, the wood new. Someone must have renovated the motel, put out a fresh sign. A terrible location, but they had probably bought the land for a song. Fernanda wondered how they could have kept the construction secret from Frank. He might not send his men down the Dust Road, but there was not much in west Texas he did not hear of.

BRAKE INN MOTEL
GAS—FOOD—WARM BEDS
HIKE SCENIC MT APACHE
5 MI THIS WAY

Fernanda must be thinking about a different place. Because if this was the motel of Frank's nightmares, he would never have allowed anyone to reopen it. He would have burned it to the ground first, and with the new owners inside.

RYAN

The Honda Odyssey appeared on the road ahead. Ryan Phan almost didn't believe his eyes. He crept forward just enough to make out the dumpy shape of the van's back frame and its lethally drab paint and its thick tires. There was no doubt about it.

Ryan's friend on the border patrol hadn't been lying. Stanley Holiday was indeed traveling the Dust Road. And according to that same friend, Stanley had Penelope with him.

The last two days had been strange for Ryan, even by the standards of his very strange life. Ryan wasn't religious—not even his father's placid Buddhism had ever stuck—but he'd always had a soft spot for the prodigal son of the Gospels. Who wouldn't root for a man fated by God to let down his family and squander all his opportunities and fail at just about everything he put his mind to? *Literally me*, Penelope would say.

The girl had no idea what failure was.

Ryan was a forty-five-year-old fuckup with a bad shoulder and a freshly broken nose and a life full of crazy stories that all added up to nothing. He'd gotten sober (twice), been to prison (twice), caught syphilis and Montezuma's revenge and a prize mackerel and another man's rap. He'd saved a life, taken another, had the scars to prove them both.

But there was one thing that Ryan had only ever done once in his life.

He'd made a promise.

Ryan had spent most of his life alone. People demanded consistency, follow-through, patience. They demanded all the things Ryan knew he lacked. He'd discovered, in his latest round of prison therapy, that his greatest fear was to be needed by another. To risk letting people down. So he never made promises. He never guaranteed anything except his own inconstancy.

Except three years ago, a few nights before the arrest that would land him in the Huntsville Correctional Unit, Ryan had made the sole, single, stupid promise of his life. He'd promised a beautiful woman that he wouldn't let a pair of girls languish in Fort Stockton if anything went wrong.

Are you afraid something will *go wrong?* Ryan, in Jessica's bed, pressed against Jessica's back.

Jessica was silent for a long time. *Just promise you'll get Polly and Adeline out of here.*

Ryan hadn't been able to save Adeline Holiday, as it turned out. He hadn't been able to save Jessica either. Ryan had been in lockup when some goons came to Jessica's house and placed bullets into the skulls of all the women sleeping inside. A pair of meth-heads robbing the wrong house. If Stan Holiday hadn't gotten Ryan chucked into Huntsville a few months before (a bogus charge, for the record), Ryan had no doubt the big man would have found a way to pin the murders on him, Ryan, the man who'd stolen the heart of Stanley's daughter.

If that had happened, Ryan wouldn't have faced a nickel for possession. He'd be on death row.

And if a passing neighbor hadn't come across Penelope stumbling down the road outside her house, bleeding from a hole in her forehead, the girl would have been even deader.

But they'd both dodged the scythe, Penelope and Ryan. Penelope had been rushed to a hospital. Her survival was declared a miracle, a one-in-a-million parabellum trajectory, and it meant that Ryan could keep the single solitary promise he'd ever made in his life. The minute they let him out of Huntsville last week, he'd gathered some gear and picked up a vehicle and headed back to Fort Stockton. He'd pulled up outside Penelope's school, met her eye through the window. He'd patted the back seat of his bike. The girl had slipped outside without drawing much notice. Penelope could sneak with the best of them, when she needed to.

She could also scare the shit out of him when she was bored. More than once on the long ride, Ryan had been certain he heard Franklin O'Shea on the back of his bike, berating his men for failing to make their numbers. "Enough of The Game," Ryan had said.

Ryan had thought that Mexico City would have been far enough from west Texas to escape Stanley Holiday's eyes—or, to be more exact, the eyes of Mister Frank O'Shea—but Ryan was never correct about much. Stanley had not only known the hotel where Ryan was staying with Penelope: he'd known the fucking room number.

Stanley had crushed Ryan's nose with the butt of a massive Desert Eagle magnum yesterday morning. If Penelope hadn't started crying, Stanley would have probably done much worse.

But was that enough to stop Ryan Phan?

Now, as a funny flash of silver light passed over the Texas sky, Ryan Phan was behind Stanley Holiday's minivan because he was an idiot with something to prove, if only to himself. Ryan was going to keep the promise he'd made to Penelope's mother. He was going to get the girl out of here, whatever it took.

Not that he had any idea how to do that. Stanley was no doubt still armed with that Desert Eagle. Ryan wasn't carrying any sort of weapon, not even a knife. He'd crossed the border with a fake passport and a pocketful of cash and bag of decent cocaine in case he needed to grease any noses. Thankfully, he'd found a friend at the Border Patrol station—one of the few men around here who wasn't a fan of Franklin O'Shea or any part of his entourage.

Still, his friend on the BP didn't like Ryan enough to give him a gun. And he'd taken the cocaine. Ryan was armed with nothing but his wits and his tongue and his temperamental luck. Ryan had no plan, no idea what he would do when he and that Honda Odyssey finally stopped moving. But when had that ever stopped him?

Ryan blew a clot of blood from his broken nose, let it whip away into the wind. Maybe he wouldn't just get Penelope back tonight.

Maybe he could get some revenge.

Blood for blood. It's the law of the desert. That's what Jessica Holiday used to say. And she'd probably say it went double for her father.

THE TWINS

Moments before the girls in the Malibu arrived, Tabitha stepped out from behind the desk.

Thomas paled. "What are you doing?"

Tabitha said nothing. She hurried into the cold, down the front porch, and stepped into room 5. The room that would soon house Kyla and Fernanda.

Tabitha heard the creak of Thomas's step on the boards behind her. He called her name. She didn't stop.

He caught up with her in the bathroom, just in time to see Tabitha bundle up the stack of towels Thomas had left on the vanity when they'd prepared the motel for another night's work. He said again, "What are you doing?"

"Repeating what we did yesterday."

"Yesterday was a mistake."

"But the mirror cracked again today."

"It was a fluke. It wasn't like the first night. Put them back."

"Maybe the first night was the real mistake."

The twins studied the mirror of room 5's bathroom. Again, today, a crack had spread down the glass a moment after the clock struck four. It was identical to the crack from yesterday, though perhaps that wasn't quite true. This crack might have been a hair wider. It was hard to say. Their memory wasn't what it used to be.

The twins were the only ones who remembered last night. Every night. They'd long ago acknowledged that the human mind wasn't designed to function under these conditions. How was a person supposed to remember a hundred identical nights? (Was it even a hundred? Could it be more?) All of those memories melted together, each lodged in the same place inside the brain. They were like layers of sediment over an archaeological record, slowly crushing themselves into dust.

Thomas sometimes wondered how many more nights of this their brains could handle.

Tabitha sometimes wondered if they'd already gone too far.

Her brother reached for the towels in her hands. "You'll ruin everything. We have our instructions."

"I don't care."

"You read what Father wrote."

"You don't even know what it means."

" 'Death sustains it.' That seems pretty unambiguous."

"You never were good with primary texts."

She pushed past him. Actually pushed him, hard, and carried the towels to the room's front door. Tabitha didn't have time for doubt. When she'd awoken in her bed this morning, alive and unbutchered despite the events of last night, she'd felt a shift in the air, a fragility. Everything in the motel felt *off* today. Hollow. Like it might crumble with one good kick.

Something had changed last night. Things were finally starting to shift.

Her brother, she knew, felt the same way. He wasn't half as excited about this change as she was, but then they'd never agreed on the particulars of what they were supposed to be doing here.

Tabitha carried the towels out of room 5. She wasn't entirely certain how, but when the twins forgot to leave towels in room 5's bathroom yesterday—when the crack in the mirror had distracted them from their usual routine—last night had been different. The guests had *done something* for the first time in ages. They hadn't hunkered down in their rooms. They hadn't all been slaughtered the instant the lights died.

Instead, they'd tried to understand Sarah's death. They'd formed a team.

And not a minute too soon, as far as Tabitha was concerned. Whatever Thomas might want to believe, she was under no illusions. Things were breaking down. The generator seemed to be getting weaker and weaker by the night. The Guardians of the mountain were growing more raucous. She sometimes thought they might be afraid.

Maybe the ceremony would hold for another hundred nights. Maybe even a thousand. But eventually things would crack. The seal would loosen. Whatever their father and the old Chief had locked away, it would be free again, and Tabitha had her doubts about whether another seal could be put in place in time to keep it contained.

So why not give the guests the chance to work together? To answer some questions of their own?

As Tabitha opened the door to the supply room that waited under the porch's covered walkway, she caught a glint of light from the old house that stood behind the motel. She looked up just in time to see Sarah Powers fiddling with her camera in the window of a room upstairs.

Tabitha had many questions about Sarah Powers, a cousin who had somehow been born decades after the twins, but was almost fifteen years their senior.

Thomas caught up with Tabitha in the supply room. He grabbed her by the arm, tried to pull her backward, as if he could rewind time and return these stupid towels to the precise spot he'd left them.

But then he heard a sound behind him. He went stiff.

Tabitha smiled. She'd timed this perfectly.

The rumble of the Malibu's motor reached them from up the road. Tabitha dropped the towels to the floor of the supply room and pulled her arm free of her brother's grip. He had nothing more to fear from her. This was the only thing she would do to interfere with the evening's proceedings. She would let the guests arrive in their due time: Kyla and Fernanda, Ethan and Hunter, Stanley and Penelope. The furtive Ryan Phan, so easily forgotten.

Soon, Tabitha would help her brother slash Stanley's tires. Stan Holiday was the only guest who had stopped here voluntarily and parked within range of the lights, meaning he was the only person at the motel with gas in his tank and easy access to his vehicle. He was the only person the twins had feared, on the first night, might leave before the ceremony could begin. The twins would dispose of the knife beneath the front porch. They would switch on the motel's sign in the moments after Hunter and Ryan, concealed against the wall facing the road, lit up a pair of menthol cigarettes.

Things could proceed however they wanted after that. An experiment, like every other night. Tabitha had simply adjusted a few control parameters.

She pushed back her hair. She smiled at her brother. She said, "Let's go greet our guests."

THE WOMAN IN ROOM FOUR

ETHAN

7:30 p.m.

He hadn't felt like himself for hours. Earlier this evening, not long after the truck ran out of gas, a strange silver light had passed over the sky, so bright it had almost blinded him. The light had given both Hunter and him a monstrous headache. Hunter's headache had seemed painful enough, but Ethan's temples had throbbed so hard he'd found it almost impossible to reach the motel. Every step across the desert seemed to twist a screwdriver behind his eyes. By the time he dropped their battered old gas can at the pump outside and stepped into the office, Ethan was almost afraid there was something seriously wrong with his brain.

It wasn't just the pain in his head. An awful sense of déjà vu, sticky as the residue of a nightmare, seemed to be leeching through his skull. The feeling had only grown worse in the time Ethan spent in the office, spent in his room, spent with Hunter on his bed.

The feeling was more than just mere anxiety, the dread of all that had happened in the little town of Turner. When Ethan looked back on that diner now, his horror didn't seem to come from what Hunter had done to the fry cook: the depths of violence Hunter had revealed, the danger it had placed them in. *Frank is going to kill you faggots!*

Ethan's horror, in retrospect, all grew out of the conversation he'd had while Hunter was in the diner's bathroom, well before the chaos had broken out. A man in a gabardine suit. A bubble of frozen time that seemed to last for an eternity.

Nine empty rooms. Twelve cold beds.

See you soon, Mister Cross.

Ethan forced his aching head back to the present, back to the problems that had come up in this motel. He'd come to dinner tonight because he needed to speak to Sarah Powers, the woman he'd met earlier in the motel's office. Ethan needed to understand something, desperately. He knew he should ask Sarah not to reveal his presence here to some man in Fort Stockton named Frank O'Shea, seeing as Sarah worked for Frank and the fry cook at the diner worked for Frank and Frank wouldn't look too kindly on Ethan and Hunter hurting one of his men and blah blah blah.

But for some reason, Ethan didn't feel especially frightened of Frank. If there was anyone he was scared to meet again, it was the man in the gabardine suit, but what were the odds of that?

See you soon, Mister Cross.

No. When Ethan and Hunter stepped into the motel's cafe, Ethan walked right past where Thomas stood at the bar, looking ready to mix him a drink. Ethan went down the motel's hall, toward the sounds of banging metal, and pushed open a swinging wooden door to the cafe's kitchen. He found Tabitha pouring mashed potatoes into an enormous silver serving dish. Her head snapped up, her face startled.

Ethan didn't bother saying hello. He turned back to a bewildered Hunter. Ethan said, "I just wanted to be sure it was really her making all that noise in there."

"Why?"

Ethan walked back into the cafe in a haze. "I really don't know."

Hunter seemed agitated, clearly anxious about Ethan's condition. "We should go back to our room. I can come get us some food later."

"No. No. I need to speak to Sarah."

"Who?"

"The woman from the office. The one with the camera." Ethan settled himself in the cafe's corner booth. "I want to know why she lied about meeting my mom. How . . ."

Ethan trailed off. The other question was even more unnerving. *How does Sarah know who I am?*

Watching the way Ethan rubbed his aching temples, Hunter made a little grunt of apology. "I wish I'd saved those cigarettes. They helped my head."

The clock above the bar struck 7:35. The bell over the cafe's door chimed. The Black girl from the Malibu, Kyla, stepped into the cafe, followed a few steps later by Penelope Holiday, the teenage girl from the Honda Odyssey. They scanned the room. They each looked distracted by their own problems.

Which is when something truly uncanny happened.

The clock above the bar struck 7:35. The bell over the cafe's door chimed. Kyla stepped inside, followed by Penelope Holiday, and with a rush of déjà vu, Ethan wondered if he was losing his mind. It was like he'd remembered this moment—had anticipated it—even though it had never happened to him before. He'd seen it coming a moment before it happened. Had recalled the moment before he'd lived it.

Ethan thought of camera film: double exposures, two images recorded over each other. He rubbed his head. Somehow the pain was getting worse.

Kyla made her way across the cafe. He'd only met her in the office a couple hours ago, when she and her aloof friend Fernanda had come looking for towels. Kyla and Ethan hadn't said much to each other then—really, all she did was apologize for leaving him and Hunter by the side of the road—but in a funny way, Ethan felt like he knew Kyla well, or at least well enough to see she wasn't faring much better than him. Her face was clouded, her mouth set in a grimace. She rubbed her head. She sat down across from Ethan and Hunter without a word, only to flinch, half stand, embarrassed by some mistake.

"Sorry," she said. "I don't know why I sat here."

"It's all right," Ethan said. "Sit. Where's your friend?"

"Fernanda? She went back to our room. I think her stomach's fucked up."

"Right." For some reason, Ethan didn't feel convinced by this story.

Down the cafe's hall, a pan struck the ground so loudly Ethan and Kyla both pressed their hands to their heads. Thomas watched them from behind the bar. He looked almost anxious. "Did y'all not want something to drink?"

The teenage girl, Penelope, said, "My sister says it's too late for that."

"Your sister?" Ethan said, only to hesitate when his mind caught up with him.

How did he know her name was Penelope?

"A drink is the last thing I need," Kyla said. Her hand was still pressed over her forehead. Ethan couldn't see her eyes.

He said, "You've got a headache?"

"From hell," Kyla said.

Hunter gave a little twitch in the seat next to Ethan. "Hold still," he said to Kyla. "You're bleeding everywhere."

He was right. A smear of red blood shined where Kyla's hand had touched her forehead. It was on her sleeve, on the table, on her cheek.

The blood was coming from the index finger of her right hand.

In that moment, Hunter revealed another flash of the strange new tenderness Ethan had experienced in their room. *Can I hold you for a minute? Just like this?* Here in the cafe, Hunter whipped open a roll of silverware to shake loose the cloth napkin. He tore the fabric down the middle, folded it lengthwise, grabbed Kyla's hand. He squeezed Kyla's first two fingers together until the wound closed, wrapped them in the makeshift bandage, tied it off with a tight knot.

Hunter didn't smile once during this entire process. Didn't say a word, showed no real sign of worrying for Kyla's well-being. Yet in his every move there was a soft, unassuming kindness, a firm care, that felt wildly out of place in a man so hard. You'd never think this was the same person who'd deep-fried someone not six hours ago.

Hunter tested the knot of the bandage. He released Kyla's hand with a soft squeeze.

"You probably could use some stitches," he said. "But it should clot eventually if you keep that tight."

Kyla stared at him. "Thanks. I'm surprised."

"Why's that?"

"To be honest, you look like you kill kids for a living."

Hunter went very still.

Kyla said, "Relax. It's a joke."

Another clang came from the kitchen. Ethan winced at the pain it sent through his head. He studied the bandage on Kyla's finger, feeling the strangest certainty that this had never happened before.

But of course it hadn't. He'd never been to this motel before. Had he?

"How did you cut yourself so bad?" Ethan said.

Kyla, too, was staring at her fingers. A bloom of red was spreading through the napkin, bright and insistent as a buried memory. Judging by the look in her eye, Kyla was deep in a world of her own.

"The mirror," she finally said. "The cracked mirror in our bathroom. It shattered."

KYLA

The mirror had looked strange from the moment she saw it. Standing next to her in the bathroom, shortly after they'd arrived at the motel, Fernanda said, "Did the twins not leave us any towels?"

Kyla could look at nothing but the mirror. "Was the crack in the glass that wide last time?"

Fernanda looked from Kyla to the seam in the mirror, back again. "Last time?"

Later, after the girls hurried back from the office—after meeting Ethan and Hunter, after encountering Sarah Powers and her camera, after watching Stan Holiday barrel his way toward the motel in a Honda Odyssey—Kyla realized just how differently she and Fernanda tackled their problems. Fernanda had grabbed one of the towels they'd taken from Tabitha as they'd passed the motel's maintenance closet on their return to their room. She'd cranked up the shower. "I need to think."

In a daze, Kyla had bolted their doors and sunk into a deep slumber, hoping it would clear her mind, or at least dissipate the awful headache that had hounded her since the road. It did neither.

Instead, Kyla dreamed of the dead city, just as she had in the Malibu. The silver streets were running with blood. The hot air thrummed with unstable energy. A voice echoed between the white buildings, across the empty plazas. A man's voice.

He was looking for her. He knew her name.

Oh no, Miss Hewitt.

It is I who shall have audience once more.

Kyla awoke a little after seven fifteen to the sound of a toilet flushing. Her heart was hammering, the pressure driving her headache to new heights. The pain was so bad she hardly noticed the way the toilet, after its flush, failed to refill its tank.

"I do not mean to worry you," Fernanda said, stepping into the main room. "But I believe the motel might be running low on water."

Without thinking, Kyla said, "He wants to control it."

"Who? Frank? Control what?"

"Frank O'Shea is the least of our problems."

Fernanda tilted her head, blinked like she, too, was coming out of a daze. "What are you talking about?"

Kyla had no idea what she meant. No idea why she'd said it either. No idea why she would have sworn she heard a tight smile echoing through the silent air of their room: those teeth, grinding together like stones.

Are you ready to play again, Miss Hewitt?

Kyla gave her whole body a jerk. She was forgetting something, something hugely important, but she had no idea what.

Get your head in the game, she thought. Kyla rose and pushed back the mattress of her bed. The green backpack was still there, exactly where she'd left it before she dozed off. Unzipping the backpack, digging through the wads of money, she found the prize inside.

Fernanda hurried to the front window to make sure the curtains were closed. "Careful. The cartel won't raise a finger to help us without that film."

Kyla only nodded. In her hand was a roll of Kodak Gold camera film, thirty-six exposures, stolen this afternoon from the Fort Stockton safe house where Fernanda had been taken to die. The girls had killed a man for this film. Granted, Lance had been sent to the safe house to kill Fernanda, so Kyla supposed it was fair game. You live by the sword, you die by the sword.

Lance hadn't seemed like such a bad guy, despite his line of work. And it wasn't like Kyla could talk. She'd spent the better part of the last six months serving steaks to men who'd made a small fortune shuffling all sorts of contraband back and forth across the border. Guns. Drugs. People. Kyla could have gone to the FBI ages ago with what she knew. She could have probably saved lives.

But why think about the past? Time didn't go backward. Kyla turned the film canister in the light, marveling that with all the blood that had been spilled for it, all the violence it contained, the yellow of its casing could still look so pristine.

If Kyla could help Fernanda get this film across the border and into the right hands, she could ensure that at least two lives had been saved: Fernanda's, and Fernanda's brother's.

She dropped the yellow canister back into the bag and tugged up the zipper and did her best to drag the mattress back into place. She stepped into the bathroom and closed the door, hoping to wash her face, but when she turned the tap, only a thin trickle ran from the sink's faucet. Fernanda had been right. The motel really was running out of water.

A soft breath of air brushed her cheek. A warm draft.

Kyla looked up. Call her crazy, but it almost felt like the draft had come from the crack in the mirror.

The moment the thought occurred to her, the crack expanded an inch, right before her eyes, with a soft tinkling chime like a wash of bells. A great black gulf loomed within the seam, and even with the light burning directly above her head, Kyla saw nothing inside the mirror but darkness.

Another draft touched her cheek. The air of the draft was warm and dry. It seemed to tingle on her skin with a latent power.

Where had Kyla felt air like that before?

A man whispered in her ear, just behind her shoulder.

"Touch it."

Kyla whipped around, her heart hammering, vision dilating, certain she would see the man from her dream standing right behind her, but there was no one. She exhaled a long breath. She scratched her neck.

She turned back to the mirror, to the great black crack. It had grown again.

The man whispered in her ear again. "Touch it, Kyla. Hurry."

She'd been wrong: that wasn't the voice of the man in her dream. This man was someone else. She hadn't met this man before, she was certain of it, yet he felt oddly familiar. When this new man spoke, a strange itch writhed along the back of her neck, but her headache seemed to abate. A strange trade. A porous seam in the weave.

Call her crazy, but this new man sounded almost—but not quite—like her father.

Kyla raised a finger to the crack in the mirror. Brought her hand close. Shivered.

There was no mistaking it: the crack was leaking hot air.

"Touch it, Kyla," the voice said. "Touch it and see."

Kyla told herself she was going crazy. Told herself she had so much more she needed to worry about. Told herself to get back to the bedroom and figure out some plan for the disaster of her night.

"Trust me, Kyla. It's important."

As gently as she knew how, she touched the mirror.

It shattered, and Kyla saw the city on the other side.

The sight didn't last long: a few seconds, the span of a long gasp. Kyla saw the white towers and the silver streets. She saw the everblack sky. She saw the column of silver light in the distance, rising from the city's heart.

The column released a pulse of light, a blinding flash. It sent a fresh wave of pain slicing through her head, it blinded her, and when Kyla could see again, the city was gone.

There was nothing behind the glass but a cinder block wall.

Fernanda was at the door. "Are you all right?"

Kyla took a step back, studying the glass that had fallen into the sink. She'd cut her finger. She sucked blood from the wound, wrapped it in a wad of toilet paper. When she spoke, her voice didn't sound like her own. "I'm fine."

The voice from over her shoulder was silent. It was no use pretending she'd hallucinated the sound or imagined the sight of the city; whatever going insane felt like, she doubted it felt like this. She'd seen what she'd seen. She'd heard what she'd heard.

Something very, very strange was going on here. But what?

When she opened the bathroom door, Fernanda shook her head at the shattered glass. "I hope the twins do not expect us to pay for that."

"We'll burn that bridge when we get to it. I'm starving."

"I'm not sure I want to go to the cafe. The two boys from earlier went that way a moment ago—I heard them on the porch."

"We'll be fine. Let's go. We still need to speak to Sarah Powers."

Fernanda hesitated. "Sarah was speaking to a man in her room a moment ago. It sounded like they were having an argument."

Kyla looked at the clock on the nightstand. It was almost 7:35. "We need to get to dinner."

"But why? Would we not be safer here?"

It's important, Kyla wanted to say, but she had no idea why that was so. She just grabbed her gun and shrugged on her coat and plucked up the key to their room. After a long hesitation, Fernanda followed her out onto the back porch. Penelope came up the porch from the direction of Stanley's room. Kyla watched as Fernanda took the key from her hand and stepped back into their room. "I'm sorry," Fernanda said. "I need the toilet."

Penelope tilted her head when she caught up with Kyla. "My sister says you look crazy tonight."

Now, a few minutes later, Kyla stared at the bandage Hunter had wrapped around her fingers, watched the blood seep through. All of the pain and trouble they'd left behind in Fort Stockton, the fear and anxiety of what awaited them in Mexico—it seemed so pointless now. So small.

That man whispered again, just behind her ear. The man who sounded almost like her father.

"You can't let him reach the city, Kyla."

Can't let who? she almost said, but didn't bother. Somehow—and this sounded crazier than anything—Kyla knew what the man meant without knowing it.

She passed time in the booth with the boys, all of them lost to their own silence. Ethan kept rubbing his head, sipping his water. He looked even worse than she felt, if that was possible.

Penelope sat alone in the booth near the buffet, clearly lost in her own anxieties. She whispered, "Why are you so upset? It's just a headache."

Kyla and Ethan both looked up, glanced around the cafe. Ethan said, "Who are you talking to?"

Penelope chewed her lip. "I've been trying to figure that out all night."

A few minutes after seven forty-five, the bell above the cafe's door chimed. Fernanda came inside. She joined Kyla at the booth, looking uneasy, flustered, and clearly not excited to be sharing a booth with two men she didn't know. Kyla ignored her. In the kitchen, Tabitha was banging pots and pans.

A little while after that, Stan Holiday arrived: sweat on his brow, a busted lip. He'd had a scrap with someone.

The big man grabbed Penelope by the arm. "Get up. You're coming back to the room."

"Back?" the girl said.

"To the room. Now."

"Why?"

"To keep you safe."

"Safe from what?"

Stanley hesitated, just a moment. The time was almost eight o'clock. "That bastard's here. He cut our tires."

That got everyone in the cafe sitting up a little straighter.

"Who did?" Penelope said.

"Ryan. Ryan Fucking Phan."

Tabitha appeared, pushing a trolley full of food. Thomas said, "Don't forget, Miss Powers asked that you bring a plate to her room."

Penelope and Stan kept talking about some man named Ryan. Kyla experienced a strange tingle in her mind: she knew the name, and yet she didn't.

Stanley said, "Frank can deal with Ryan when he gets here. You're coming with me. *Now.*"

Fernanda went very tense. Without even thinking about it, Kyla murmured, "Don't worry. Frank isn't coming."

Stanley whipped around to stare at her. "Excuse me?"

Kyla blinked. She wasn't entirely sure what she'd just said.

And then, outside, Tabitha started screaming.

THE ULTIMATUM

ETHAN

8:15 p.m.

That awful fog of déjà vu was growing thicker by the minute. It made Ethan feel strangely divorced from the horror of what he'd just seen: Sarah Powers face down on her bed, her pants around her knees, her head and neck hidden beneath a pair of bloody pillows. Ethan would swear he saw it all a moment before he and Hunter had followed Tabitha's screams into room 4. Ethan had passed through the door, gone down the hall, seen the body, turned and seen the face of a strange man watching him from the back porch—and then he'd done it all again.

Another double exposure. An aching overflow. It almost felt like his mind was trying to record two memories in the same place at the same time.

Those double exposures persisted, here, in the motel's office. He could hardly concentrate on what the twins were saying. Thank God he heard it twice, then.

"A grave crime has been committed on our land," Thomas said.

"Against our family," Tabitha said.

"Against our blood."

"We will see justice done," Tabitha said.

"Even if it means watching all of you die."

Ethan heard it, then heard it again. His head throbbed. He had to sit down. Fernanda stood near the door. Stanley sat in the office's other chair, his head in his hands, quivering like a child. A child with an enormous handgun strapped to his hip.

Kyla was near the fireplace, examining some sort of carved stone she'd plucked from the mantel. She didn't seem to be paying the twins any mind at all. Hunter appeared out of the shadows to crouch at Ethan's side. He murmured in Ethan's ear, "What's wrong?"

Ethan didn't know where to start.

"At midnight," Thomas said, "three things will happen."

"The door will open," Tabitha said.

"The lights will go out."

"And anyone who's not with us will—"

It started over again, their little speech, but before the twins could finish, Ethan raised his throbbing head, looked from Thomas to Tabitha, and said, "You're lying."

Thomas couldn't have looked more shocked. After an agonized silence, he said, "Excuse me?"

"You're lying. You don't have a place to hide us. You'll die at midnight if the lights go out, just like everyone else."

Stanley stared at Ethan, at the twins. "What are any of you people *talking* about?"

"I—" Ethan broke off. "I don't know."

Was he crazy, or did Tabitha have to suppress a small smile?

When they lapsed into silence again, Thomas said, cautiously:

"We'll make you a deal."

"An ultimatum."

"Tell us who killed our cousin, and . . ." He faltered. "And we'll take the innocent to safety."

Stanley scowled. "That boy just said you're lying."

"You want us to solve a murder? With what tools?" Fernanda crossed the office to toss a log on the fire. In the new light, she studied the twins. "How can you be serious? We are not detectives."

She looked to Kyla, probably for backup, but the girl's attention was still riveted to the egg-shaped rock in her hand. Kyla's thumb navigated the grooves that whorled its surface. Her lips were moving, silent.

A terrible *BANG* shook the walnut door in the back of the office. A furious clawing came from the other side, a *SHRIEK* like the scream of a massive owl that made the hairs on Ethan's neck rise.

Stanley recoiled in his seat. "What the fuck is in there?"

Thomas said, "The same as the things that are out there."

Tabitha raised a finger to the desert outside. Glints of yellow eyes, dark feathers in the black, more *SHRIEKS* echoing through the void.

And then Ethan heard it all again.

Thomas said, "We have a hiding place. Somewhere safe from the creatures of the dark."

"A place we use, on nights like this," Tabitha said.

Fernanda shook her head, pointed at Ethan. "How many times must we say it? You are lying. Where would you even keep such a place here? Why could we not just find your hiding spot for ourselves?"

Thomas gawped at her. He reminded Ethan of nothing so much as an actor whose performance has gone radically off-script.

It was Tabitha who improvised. "Let me put it a different way. If you want any hope of seeing tomorrow, you'll learn who killed our cousin. You have until midnight."

Ethan met her eye. The woman didn't look away. She was clearly expecting something from him, but before he could begin to guess what it could be, the office's front door opened, letting in a rush of cold air and the smell of menthol cigarettes. A man stepped inside, a familiar face. He was in his forties, Asian, dark hair, a splinted nose, a bright sneer. He wore leather riding boots. Ethan found himself staring a long time at those boots.

It was Ryan Phan, the man Ethan had seen staring into room 4 from the back porch.

But how did Ethan know his name?

"I think we can clear all of this up right now," Ryan said, his sneer widening. "Can't we, Stanley?"

KYLA

She didn't look up from the stone egg, not even when the door opened and this new man stepped inside. Kyla's thumb ran again and again along the grooves of the pale rock. She wasn't stupid. She wasn't crazy. She knew where she'd seen stones like this before, where she'd seen carvings just like this.

This pattern was everywhere in her dreams, in the bathroom's broken mirror. The walls of the dead city were hewn from this same pale rock. They were grooved, all over, in these same fine whorls.

Kyla's lips were moving, over and over, though no sound came. It was a single thought, repeating without beginning or end, just like the grooves in the egg.

the stone is from the city the stone is from the city the stone is from the city.

That voice—that *almost*-familiar voice—wouldn't let her go. "You have to remember, Kyla. You have to."

Elsewhere in the office, a whole drama was playing out. The man who'd just walked inside said he had information on Stanley that would incriminate the big man. Something about the Terra Vista Motel out in Fort Stockton. The new man said he would stay silent if Stanley let him take Penelope back to Mexico. Kyla, distantly, knew the man's knowledge wasn't so secret. That it proved nothing.

But she didn't care. She just stared at the egg.

Hunter said to Stanley, "You were the last person to come to dinner tonight. You had the best opportunity to kill Sarah."

Stanley said, "I was asleep in my room."

"Is that where you busted your lip?" Hunter said.

Stanley said nothing.

Ryan said, "Sarah put up a fight, huh, Stanley?"

"You're insane. I never even *met* Sarah before tonight," Stanley said.

Kyla turned to him, blinking, struggling to keep her head clear. "That's a lie, Mister Holiday. You've been having dinner with her at the steakhouse for the last six weeks."

The drama resumed. The pain in Kyla's head was growing worse by the second, but that pain finally felt productive somehow. It reminded Kyla of the way her baby teeth ached the more she used to loosen them. She remembered her tongue prodding at the gap between the tooth and the gum. The piercing, expectant agony as the root began to pull away.

The same thing was happening in Kyla's mind. Something was coming loose. Something was trying to come back to her.

Stanley was starting to sound frantic. Ryan and Hunter pressed the attack. Fernanda said simply, "I heard a man arguing with Sarah in her room at seven thirty."

"Did he sound like Stanley?" Ryan said.

Fernanda said carefully, "I am not sure. He might have."

"That's a lie!" Stanley said. "I don't care what pictures you have— that's a lie and you know it."

Ethan, Kyla noticed, had yet to say a word.

At the edge of her vision, Kyla saw Hunter nod to Ryan. "Let's take him somewhere quiet. We can get the truth out of him before midnight."

Hunter took a step forward, bumping into Kyla. The motion jostled the stone egg and sent it slipping out of her bandaged fingers. The stone struck the wooden floor with a dull crack: a warning shot.

The moment she heard that sound, the block in Kyla's mind came free with a wet rip, like a tooth tearing free.

All at once, Kyla remembered. She remembered everything.

Stanley started marching toward the door of the office, a vein *thump-thump-thump*ing in his throat. Ryan stepped in Stanley's way, said, "Where do you think you're going?"

Stanley pushed the man back with his left hand.

Ryan came right back, fists up now, looking like he was ready to coldcock a man fifty pounds heavier and a good four inches taller.

Stanley reached for the massive Desert Eagle on his hip.

Ryan didn't have time to react.

Kyla did. She was already in motion. She knew what was about to happen.

And she knew she needed to stop it.

Kyla lunged across the office, landing against Stanley the moment he got the gun free. Stanley might have been twice Kyla's size, but she had the advantage of surprise. She hit him full force in the side, got a foot hooked around his knee. Together they went plummeting to the floor.

As he fell, Stanley squeezed off two shots, just like he had last night, but Kyla's tackle had twisted him around. The shots missed their intended target. As she fell with Stanley, Kyla saw Ryan Phan take a step backward, startled but very much alive. Kyla saw Fernanda reaching for something near the fire. Saw the woman flinch as a bullet whizzed past her ear and buried itself in the wall with a poof of sawdust.

Kyla landed on top of Stanley. With a roar of anger, he heaved her into the air. Kyla was flying.

She landed, hard, against the office's desk. Her head struck the wood with a force she felt in the root of her tongue. The world started to spin. To go dark. Considering how hard her head had hit the desk, she wondered if she'd ever get back up.

And as her vision faded, she saw Hunter staring down at his chest. Staring at a massive circle of blood that had bloomed on his shirt.

"No," Ethan said, stumbling from his chair, rushing to Hunter's side. "No."

Hunter sank to his knees. Blood was pumping fast out of the wound Stanley's second bullet had created. Hunter opened his mouth to speak. A red bubble swelled where words should be. He struggled to stand. Fell. Reached out a hand for the side of the nearby chair, slipped.

Hunter came to rest near Ethan's feet. He didn't move again.

Stanley Holiday, too, tried to rise. Fernanda struck him across the skull with a fire poker. Hard.

Ethan was on the floor, shaking Hunter, saying again and again, "No. No. No."

Behind Kyla's ear, that almost-familiar voice sounded shocked. "This has never happened before."

And then Kyla's world went dark.

UNCHARTED TERRITORY

RYAN

8:45 p.m.

He could have carried the Black girl on his own, but her friend insisted on helping. "I will take her feet," the tall chick said. "You take her shoulders."

"Where to?" Ryan said.

"Our room. I want nothing to do with this."

Ryan nodded, but not because he had any intention of letting this tall Latina idle away the night in her room. She'd just shown herself to be handy with a fire poker. He'd find a use for her.

Ryan could be persuasive when he needed to be. It was why Frank O'Shea had first hired him, all those years ago.

Before they got to work, however, Ryan said, "What's your name, ma'am?"

"Fernanda."

"All right. Wait just a second, Fernanda."

Thomas and Tabitha still stood behind the office's desk, both of them looking shocked on some existential level. Stanley Holiday was blacked out. Considering the sound Fernanda's fire poker had made when it connected with his skull, Ryan marveled the big man was even breathing at all.

Penelope was nowhere to be seen. Ryan needed to find her, on top of everything else that had just landed on his plate. He couldn't let a teenage girl spend too much time alone in a place like this.

He'd made a promise. Etcetera, etcetera.

Ryan picked up the gun Stanley had dropped and carried it to where the tall boy, Ethan, was quaking on the floor next to the bleeding corpse that had once been the Hunter of Huntsville. Ryan almost couldn't believe it himself. In the years they'd been cellmates, Hunter had always seemed more like a force of nature than a mere man, a compact mass of muscle and violence fueled by some private black fire. It didn't seem possible that he could ever die.

But dead he was, face down on the hardwood floor. A great crimson circle was spreading from his corpse. Ryan touched the boy Ethan on the shoulder. "You might want to move, kid. You're going to get blood all over those jeans."

Ethan didn't answer him. Didn't give any indication he'd heard.

Ryan sighed. In the weak firelight, he saw a familiar shape poking from the hem of Hunter's shirt. Reaching carefully over the pool of blood, Ryan found a Colt Python tucked in the waistband of Hunter's pants. "Here," he said to Ethan, prodding the boy with the butt of the gun. "Hold on to this."

Still Ethan didn't move. Ryan left him there for a moment. He placed both guns on the office's desk, tugged loose the empty leather holster around Stanley's waist, and strapped it onto himself. The belt was built for much wider hips than Ryan's, but he was able to get it snug enough to stow Stanley's heavy magnum.

He carried the Python back to Ethan, crouched at the boy's side. Together, they looked at Hunter's corpse. A log popped in the fire.

"He cared for you," Ryan said to Ethan. "He told me so himself."

Finally, Ethan turned to look at Ryan. "When?"

"We smoked a cigarette together, earlier this evening."

"You knew him?"

"Like, before tonight? No," Ryan lied. He didn't hesitate. This was another promise he'd made, the second of his life. "I never met him before tonight. He noticed me checking in this evening, saw me light up a smoke. He said he had a headache. He hoped the nicotine would help."

"When . . . when was this?"

Ryan told the truth. "Maybe a quarter after six. Not long after I got here. Your man seemed like a decent guy. You're all he talked about. He spoke highly of you."

Ethan didn't respond.

"He said you were the best thing that ever happened to him," Ryan said.

Ethan started to shake again. Ryan patted his shoulder: firm, but kind.

"I'm sorry, kid. Really. I'll leave you alone for the rest of the evening, but I need you to do something for me, just for a few minutes. Do you think that's possible?"

Ethan didn't speak, but at least he looked Ryan in the eye.

"I need you to keep tabs on our friend Stanley here in case he wakes up," Ryan said. "Don't shoot him. Just make sure he doesn't go anywhere. I have some questions I need to ask him."

Ryan offered the Python again. Ethan stared at it. "How do you know I won't just kill him?"

"Because you're not that kind of guy. Hunter said you're the best man he'd ever met." This, again, was the truth.

Ethan's eyes clouded. "I'm not a good person. Hunter and I held up a diner before we got here. I watched him shove a man's hand in oil. I . . . I enjoyed it."

"Did the other guy have it coming?"

"I guess."

"Don't take this the wrong way, kid, but I have a feeling you've been pushed around a lot in your life. It's normal to want a little payback." Even as he spoke, Ryan felt the pain in his nose where Stanley had crushed it yesterday in Mexico City. He'd been smelling his own broken cartilage for the better part of two days.

Blood for blood. It's the law of the desert.

"I'm not a good person," Ethan said again. "A good person would have stopped Hunter from hurting anyone. Even if the other guy was shit."

"This is a tough part of Texas. You can't always make the right call. Doesn't mean you're evil." Ryan shrugged. "I don't trust a man who hasn't had to face how ugly he can be. So it sounds like I can trust you."

"I don't follow."

"You don't have to. Just take the gun."

Ethan looked Ryan in the eye. Looked at the gun. Without another word, he took it.

"Thanks, kid." Ryan nodded at Stanley. "Don't let him go anywhere."

It took most of the way to room 5 before Ryan could persuade Fernanda to share the name of the girl they were carrying. Kyla. He'd never met a Kyla he didn't like.

Fernanda was a different story. She was chilly, vaguely haughty, spoke from behind a thick shell of superiority, the kind only rich girls can grow. Ryan suspected it was a defense mechanism, and he also got the feeling Fernanda really, really didn't like him, and even though he had no idea why that could be, she was clearly in no hurry to share. The woman seemed determined not to say a word more to Ryan than necessary, but he wasn't daunted.

Before he and Fernanda left the office, Ryan had cleared up one thing with the twins. "Were you serious earlier? That if we want to see tomorrow, we need to figure out what happened to your cousin?"

Thomas had struggled to speak. "We have a place, a place to—"

Ryan waved this off. "You don't have anywhere to hide. If you did, you'd be there already. You just want to know who killed the girl. I can't blame you."

One of those awful *SHRIEKS* had echoed across the desert, set off all sorts of alarm bells in Ryan's mind. He'd never heard anything like that in all the time he'd lived in this part of Texas. He'd never heard anything like that in his *life*, full stop, and he didn't care for it. Not one bit.

Tabitha had said carefully, "The situation here is . . . worse than you think."

"You mean worse than the fact someone's murdered your cousin?"

"Yes," Tabitha said.

"In what way?"

"It's . . . hard to explain."

Another *SHRIEK*, this one from behind the door in the back of the office. Ryan had flinched. "You trap those things in your spare time?"

"Not exactly."

"Why did you say we have until midnight to figure this out?"

Thomas had finally cut in. He sounded angry. He sounded scared. "No more questions. Either help us or don't. The night's already ruined."

Everyone in the office had peered at him, even Ethan. Ryan said, "Ruined?"

Thomas had clammed up tight. When Tabitha had tried to speak, he gave her a sharp hiss. The woman hadn't seemed thrilled about it, but she'd held her tongue. Ryan had frowned. He'd come back to these two.

Now, in room 5, he helped Fernanda settle Kyla onto the bed closer to the wardrobe, the bed whose mattress was slightly askew. Before the moment could linger, Ryan said, "I used to work for Frank's operation, you know."

Fernanda reached a hand under Kyla's back. She withdrew it, now, to reveal a standard-issue, nine-millimeter Glock, the type all of Frank's thugs carried around.

Fernanda pointed the gun Ryan's way. "Get out."

"I was quitting the outfit when I got arrested. That was around the time they started trafficking people." Ryan held very still. "The guns and the drugs—whatever, someone was going to move them across the border. But people? Slaves? No. I couldn't handle that. I refused to work for them after that."

"I said get out of my room."

"I wanted to stop the trafficking. Truly. I was dating Stanley's daughter at the time. She felt the same way."

"I won't tell you again."

Ryan said, "How long you been in the States?"

Fernanda hesitated. She said, "That is no concern of yours."

"Judging by your accent and your attitude, I assume you came from a little money. Enough money to get the right papers to enter the US, but not quite enough for a plane ticket. You and a bunch of other good-looking kids got on a bus. You needed a cheap ticket for some reason, but who doesn't at your age? Y'all thought you were safe. You and the other kids didn't realize you were in trouble until the bus went off-road and started pulling up to the Rio."

The gun trembled in Fernanda's hand. She said nothing.

"You're lucky you got away before they sent you to Atlanta. Dallas. LA. They've got hubs all over, clearing houses for beauties like you."

Finally, in a small voice, Fernanda said, "Frank took me for himself."

Even Ryan, cynical bastard that he was, had been worried about that. The girl was, indeed, Frank's type to a T. "I am so sorry."

Fernanda said nothing.

Ryan said, "How long's it been?"

"Three months."

"Frank O'Shea normally burns through two girls in a week. Just like Stanley." Ryan felt himself shudder. "You must be special."

Fernanda said, "You have no idea."

Something about her stare sent the willies climbing up Ryan's arms. He looked at Kyla, the girl breathing slowly on the bed. "So you girls are on the run from Frank?"

Fernanda said nothing.

"I'm not trying to turn you in. I'm just curious about one thing. When I met that guy Hunter on a smoke break, he said that Sarah Powers was apparently *working* for Frank. Should I be worried about that?"

"You mean did I kill her? No. Did you?"

Ryan shook his head. It was the God's honest truth: he hadn't laid a hand on Sarah Powers tonight. He hadn't even spoken to her.

He'd tried, but he hadn't had the chance.

"It's like I told Stanley in the office earlier," Ryan said. "I was asleep until the screaming started. I went straight back to my room after that smoke break and dozed off."

Fernanda pulled back the hammer of the gun. Its *click* cut straight through the air of the room. "That is a lie. I heard a man speaking with Sarah in her room next door at seven thirty. It was you."

Ryan blinked. He said, truthfully, "It wasn't. I never said a word to Sarah all night. It must have been Stanley you heard."

Fernanda leveled the gun at Ryan's face. "It was not, and I know it for a fact. It also could not have been Ethan or Hunter or Thomas. That only leaves one person."

"Hold up—"

Her finger started to tighten on the trigger. "I think it is lucky you are still alive right now. Would you like to change this?"

Fernanda closed the door in his face. Ryan was losing his touch.

A bitter wind sliced across the motel. A SHRIEK rose in the dark. Ryan felt an awful certainty that something was wrong, that it was staring him in the face. He looked at his watch and found the time was 9:25. That didn't feel possible; he thought for sure the mechanism was running fast, but when he stepped into room 4 and looked at the alarm clock, he found the same time on display.

He also found Sarah Powers, but that wasn't exactly the right way to put it. He'd been in this room once already this evening (but again—and he couldn't stress this enough—he hadn't killed her). That had been at 7:50, shortly before all the screaming started, and Sarah looked now exactly the way she had then. Nothing about the room had changed except for a plate of food that had fallen, face down, from Tabitha's hands. Everything else here was exactly as Ryan had last seen it.

Again, he hadn't killed Sarah. He'd had no interest in doing so. But he *had* wanted to talk to Sarah, earlier in the night. Had *needed* to talk to her. For the last six weeks, Ryan had been haunted by a memory that refused to be ignored. An old Native dude used to sleep alone in the cell next door to Ryan and Hunter, back in the penitentiary. Everyone around Huntsville had called the old man The Chief. Ryan used to think this was racist, but The Chief only shrugged. *I'm the last man left of my tribe,* The Chief used to say. *I guess that makes me chief by default.*

Ryan couldn't think of anything sadder.

The night he died, The Chief had said some very strange—

terrifying shit your pants scary

—things. Had made some very strange requests. He'd urged Hunter to pass along a message to the beautiful young woman who'd lately taken to visiting the old man every few weeks.

You have to tell her. You have to tell her!

Tell her what? Hunter had said through the bars of the cell.

Tell Sarah, the mountain—

Here, in room 4, Ryan looked at the sprawled corpse of Sarah Powers and shook his head. He searched the room quickly, unimpressed by what he found. There were some ashes in a dinner plate on the corner table with bits of burned film poking out. Under the ash, he found a curious silver substance melted to the plate's surface, brilliant as liquid chrome. He didn't know what to make of that. He wasn't a chemist.

In the bathroom, he found where the burned pictures must have come from. A roll of film was tucked away in a black plastic cylinder on Sarah's bathroom vanity, right next to a fancy-looking camera.

He held the pictures to the light, found where the last six shots had been sliced away neatly. A pair of nail scissors rested next to the sink. Probably their work.

Stowing the film in his pocket, Ryan searched the room once more, stood back, shook his head at the chaos. Sarah's unbuttoned pants, the tossed luggage: child's play.

Instead, to Sarah's corpse, he said aloud the question he'd come here to ask earlier in the evening, just to get it off his chest. " 'The mountain is getting restless.' What the fuck was that supposed to mean?"

As if in response, the motel's generator stuttered. The lights dimmed down to nearly nothing, dark washing over the motel. The SHRIEKS came from very, very close by.

Ryan stood completely still, his back against the door, his heart in his throat. It sounded like those things were in the parking lot.

The generator came back. The things dispersed, shrieking all the way.

Ryan looked at the bulb burning over his head. He wasn't stupid. They'd be lucky if they made it until midnight.

Back in the office, he found Stanley Holiday still unconscious. The boy, Ethan, had moved from the floor to a chair, the Colt Python still in his hand. The pool of blood around Hunter's corpse had stopped spreading right at the edge of Ethan's boots. The grooved rock that Kyla had dropped earlier still rested in the gore. Hunter was still very dead.

The twins were still standing behind the desk, stone-faced. Ryan said, "You guys have any fuel for that generator?"

They said nothing.

He ignored them. Crossing the room, he said to Ethan, "Do you think you could do one more thing for me? There's a supply room down the porch. I'd like to get us some privacy, Stanley and I."

Ethan blinked. He rubbed his head like he was fighting off a hell of a migraine. "What are you going to do to him?"

"Just talk. What? You think I was going to work him over?"

Ethan studied him. Ryan had the uncanniest impression the boy was measuring the dimensions of his heart.

Ethan said, "You look like the kind of man who could."

Ryan said, "Torture's more trouble than it's worth. People lie the minute you start hurting them. It takes days to get anything useful."

"You still sound like you know a lot about it."

"I've known some pretty bad people in my life. I'm not one of them."

Before he'd returned to the office, Ryan had found a sturdy chair in the cafe and taken the liberty of relocating it to the supply room. He'd also taken the liberty of wiping away some bootprints he'd left, earlier in the night, on the room's dusty floor. Anyone with half a brain could figure out Ryan had been lying when he said he'd been asleep from the time he'd finished his cigarette with Hunter to the moment Tabitha had started screaming, but he also didn't see a reason to make it easy to figure out what he *had* been up to.

Old habits die hard.

From a shelf of gardening supplies, he'd dug out a length of old rope and brought it with him to the office, where he laid it, now, along the front desk. Ignoring the twins, he reached over the desk to pluck a pair of scissors out of a cup of pens. He measured lengths of rope against his forearm. He made some cuts.

Ryan said, "Keep the gun trained on Stanley, would you? Careful you don't aim it at me."

Ethan did as he was told, holding the gun level as Ryan took two lengths of rope and tied Stanley's wrists and ankles.

Ethan said, "What were you talking about earlier? Some motel in Fort Stockton Stanley wouldn't want people to know about?"

"Stanley takes women there. He likes to rough them up. Sometimes badly. He's got a nasty streak, Mister Holiday."

"But everyone knows that. He pays those girls. It doesn't mean he killed Sarah Powers."

Ryan's head snapped up. "How do *you* know that?"

Ethan blinked. "I-I'm not sure."

Ryan finished tying knots. He left a few more lengths dangling over his neck, ready for use once they got the big man moved. He didn't know what to make of this kid, he really didn't.

He asked Ethan, "You want his arms or his legs?"

■ ■ ■

In the supply room, Ethan helped Ryan ease Stanley into the chair. Stanley snorted, coughed: he was starting to wake up. Ryan worked quickly, undoing the knots he'd made earlier, pulling Stanley's arms behind his back, tying his hands and ankles to the legs of the chair.

While Ryan worked, Ethan said, "Where's that girl, Penelope?"

Ryan didn't look up from his work. "A fantastic question."

"Aren't you worried about her?"

"I'm worried about everything."

"I'm surprised you're bothering with this jerk when you could be looking for her. Who cares who killed Sarah? There's worse going on here than just a murder."

That made Ryan glance over his shoulder. "Like what?"

Ethan touched his forehead. "I don't know. It's just . . . this feeling I've got."

"Yeah. I feel it too."

"So why don't you find your stepdaughter and get somewhere safe?"

"Because I don't think there *is* anywhere safe."

Ethan said nothing. Ryan wondered if the boy had picked up the tension in his voice, the way he didn't quite want to meet the question. In truth, Ryan wasn't looking for Penelope because he wanted to keep her out of this mess as much as possible. The longer Ryan considered the timeline of the night's events, the more he suspected that Penelope might be more involved than he would ever want to admit.

Ryan changed tack. He asked Ethan, "How's your head?"

"It hurts."

"You want a cigarette? They helped your man."

"I'm good." He hesitated. "I guess I'll just go back to my room."

Ryan gestured to Stanley. He grinned. "Want to get in a few punches before you go? It's only fair."

A *SHRIEK* cut through the desert. Ethan shivered. He looked, suddenly, exhausted.

"Knock yourself out," he said, and headed out the door.

■ ■ ■

Alone at last with Stanley Holiday, Ryan propped himself against one of the supply room's shelves and pulled his menthols from the pocket of his jacket. He clicked his Zippo, caught the paper, took a drag. He studied the big man in front of him, the man who'd cost Ryan three years of his life to the worst prison in Texas. He watched the way Stanley's face twitched in the light.

Ryan thought of Jessica, pressed against his chest. *Promise you'll take care of the girls if anything goes wrong.*

Are you afraid something will go wrong?

Just promise you'll get Polly and Adeline out of here.

For three long years, Ryan had thought about that conversation. Thought about all that it could mean.

Stanley, at last, opened his eyes. He sniffed the air, made a show of coughing. "Christ—you're still smoking those things?"

"You knew she was going to the feds, didn't you?"

Stanley hesitated, just for a moment. He pulled against his ropes, made a face, but he didn't seem terribly surprised by the question. "Of course she was. According to her, she's been taking photographs for weeks."

Ryan smoked casually, but he was very curious at the tense Stanley had used. "Who was?"

"Fernanda. Who else? She told me all about it when she came to my room."

Now *that* was interesting. "Fernanda came to your room tonight?"

"What do you care?"

"I'm trying to help you, Stanley. The sooner I clear you of suspicion for killing Sarah, the sooner we can get you out of that chair."

"You seriously expect me to believe you'll let me go? It sounded like you and Hunter were going to beat a confession out of me a minute ago, back in the office."

Something about this felt off, sent alarm bells ringing. "You knew Hunter?"

A dark grin crossed Stanley's face. "I knew his type."

Ryan tapped ash onto a stack of dinner plates. He didn't like the implications of this. "So let's go back to Fernanda. You said she came to your room this evening?"

Stanley sighed, like he really couldn't believe they were going to bother with all this. "Yes. At seven thirty. Maybe a hair after. I was sound asleep, and that girl came flying through the door. Had a gun. Looked insane."

"And why would Fernanda do that?"

Stanley tried to stay quiet, but with a little patience Ryan was able to get a consistent story out of the man. He walked Stan through it once, twice, checking to see if the big guy would trip himself up, but eventually Ryan felt satisfied.

Finally, Ryan said, "And you went along with Fernanda's plan? Why not just kill her? Take the film yourself?"

"Because I'm not a bad man, Phan. I'm not a murderer."

"You shot Hunter in the office. Shot him dead."

Stanley's mouth twisted down. It looked like genuine disgust. "That wasn't intentional, what happened to Hunter. If that girl from the steakhouse hadn't tackled me, none of this would have happened."

"It almost looked like you wanted to shoot *me*."

"A warning shot. I just wanted to get you out of my way."

"What were you going to do? Drive back to Stockton and cry to Frank?"

Stanley said nothing.

Ryan was tempted to bring up the things Penelope had told him about Stanley on the ride down to Mexico—*He takes women to some place called the Terra Vista. He hurts them*—but what was the point? If even someone as out of the loop as Ethan knew those stories, it wasn't like they'd give Ryan much leverage.

Instead, Ryan burned down his cigarette and started up another. "What kind of work was Sarah Powers doing for the outfit?"

"You seriously expect me to tell you that?"

Ryan leaned down, blew smoke into Stanley's face. "Back in the office, the Black chick said you'd spent the last six weeks having dinner at the steakhouse with Sarah. That sounds like pretty serious work."

Stanley rolled his eyes. Ryan smoked, said nothing, curious if Stanley would fill in the gap.

Instead, one of those hair-raising SHRIEKS came from the desert, very close by.

Stanley flinched. "What the hell *is* that?"

"Let's not get distracted. How long was Fernanda in your room this evening?"

"Let me go and I'll tell you."

"What was Sarah doing for the operation?"

"Go fuck yourself, Phan. Let me go."

"We made a deal, Stanley. You help me clear your name from suspicion in Sarah's murder, and I'll set you free."

"I never signed up for that deal."

"And you also haven't cleared your name, so I'm wondering why you'd bother asking to leave."

Stanley closed his eyes, let out a long breath. "Fernanda was in my room for five minutes at the most."

"Meaning she was out of there by, what, seven forty? Seven forty-five at the latest?"

"Sounds about right, Mister Holmes."

"That's the funny thing—I didn't see you go into the motel's cafe until seven fifty-five. That's a ten-minute gap. What was happening in the meantime?"

"I saw *you* for one thing. Skulking around the side of the motel when I came out onto the front porch. Where did you even go?"

Ryan wasn't about to answer that question. He said nothing.

"I know you cut my tires, Phan," Stanley said.

This was a genuine surprise. "I did what?"

"Don't play dumb," Stanley said. "Go look at them yourself. They've all got a nice big hole in the side. Not that it'll make much difference. That van's part of the work fleet. Those tires are run-flats."

Ryan took another hit of his cigarette. "I don't think they'd get you very far if you tried to leave tonight. You'd be risking a run-in with the local wildlife."

"You think I'd ever leave this place without Penelope?"

"I think you *still* haven't answered my questions," Ryan said.

"I'm not going to talk about Sarah. Go get that fire poker Fernanda used on my head. See how far that gets you."

"Then what were you doing before dinner? Fernanda left your room at seven forty, maybe seven forty-five. You came to dinner at five minutes 'til eight. That gave you plenty of time to head over to

Sarah's room and have your way with her. It makes you, quite frankly, the prime suspect here."

Ryan flicked the cap of his Zippo up and down, up, down: *click-clack*.

Click-clack.

Click-clack.

Stanley finally blinked, like he realized Ryan sincerely expected an answer. The big man scowled, then looked briefly puzzled, almost like he himself wasn't entirely certain what he *had* been up to. He blinked again, squirmed in his chair, his brain clearly struggling to bring something back.

And then a look of absolute terror came over Stanley Holiday, a fear unlike anything Ryan had seen in a long, long time. The big man froze. He turned pale.

"You still with us?" Ryan said. "Stanley?"

"I . . . I don't remember," Stanley said, though it was clear from his voice this was a lie. He'd clearly recalled something in that moment, something he'd blissfully forgotten until now. He stared at Ryan. He stared *through* Ryan, through the walls of the room, through the desert. "I don't remember."

Ryan kept trying for a while, but it was no good. Stan Holiday was lost in his mind, deep in a memory, trembling at what he'd found there.

NOT LIKE THE LAST ONES

ETHAN

11:00 p.m.

This place was trying to torture him. For the past hour, the generator had gone down and up, down and up, bringing with every pocket of darkness a new wave of *SHRIEKS* followed by a strange half-light: a gloaming of mercury vapor, the power struggling to return. Familiar faces had appeared to Ethan in that half-light. Shades that dissipated like smoke when the lamps hummed back up.

Once, in the half-light, Ethan had seen the man from the diner in Turner, the one in the gabardine suit, peering into the room's wardrobe.

He'd seen Hunter stepping, stark naked, from the shower.

He'd seen the two men, both unaware of each other's presence, as they stood side by side at the window, peering out into the night. The sight had made Ethan almost double over in grief.

Everything was ruined. Everything. This time last night, he and Hunter had been in Ellersby, playing a video game on the couch. Upstairs, unbeknownst to them, Ethan's brother had been loading his shotgun. This time last night, Ethan had been happy. He'd thought that Hunter was a tough man, a little rough around the edges, but fundamentally decent. He'd thought things could last forever.

Bang.

Mark my words. This man is going to get you into the sort of trouble you cain't never get out of.

Here, at the Brake Inn Motel, there was a knock at Ethan's door. The strange man, Ryan, called his name. "Ethan, can I talk to you?"

Ethan wasn't sure he trusted Ryan Phan. When they'd spoken earlier in the office, the guy never quite met Ethan's eye, never seemed able to sit still. He had a shifty way of walking, a sort of scuttling quickstep—never in a straight line—that made Ethan think of a fox.

Sly, Ethan's mother would have said. *Never will give you the whole truth, no matter how many times he comes clean. Just like my daddy used to be.*

"Ethan?" Ryan called from outside.

Ethan sighed. With Hunter gone and the girl Kyla in her room— *Was she even still alive?*—the night wasn't exactly overflowing with friends. He rose. He unlocked the door. He found Ryan Phan standing with a fist raised, ready to knock again.

"I'm sorry to bother you," the little man said. "But we're in even more trouble than we thought."

FERNANDA

"But the little god underestimated the girl from the water. When the god's back was turned, the girl grabbed up the talking stone the god had thrown in the fire and tossed it to the bear because his thick paws didn't mind the heat. The stone was relieved, and promised to tell the girl where the little god hid—"

A terrible sound fell over the motel: a new sound, somehow even worse than the shrieking cries of the monsters in the dark. It was a strange, deafening bellow, like a foghorn or the wail of some massive beast, and when the sound rolled across the motel, Fernanda felt the earth shake. The glass of their window rattled against its bars. Her teeth vibrated in her mouth.

The sound had come from the mountain.

The shock of the noise made Fernanda hesitate, and hesitation was the death of a good story. The thread snapped. The story wouldn't return. She had been weaving a new one on the fly, a twist on a tall tale her grandmother used to tell when Fernanda was a girl—but then so were all of Fernanda's stories.

She was losing her touch. The last twenty-four hours had worn her down. Even just a few nights ago, Fernanda could have gone on and on forever, one story into another, the "Scheherazade of the Sierras," as Frank used to call her. Frank O'Shea: a sharpened stick of a man with a black heart and bloody hands, haunted by terrors in his dreams. Frank had lost his mother as a little boy—the most frightening thing that can happen to a child—and he believed that by inflicting fear on others he might somehow dilute the fear that lived inside him.

Frank was a fool, in other words. But a lethal one.

The man with the broken nose, Ryan Phan—he'd been correct when he'd guessed how Fernanda had entered into Frank's operation. She had indeed been picked up by his crew when she tried to cross (legally) into Los Estados Unidos. Last summer, Fernanda had returned from college in Connecticut to discover her life in Monterey in ruins. Her father's chain of camera stores had been going under for years. Apparently, he'd done some foolish things with his taxes to try to keep them afloat. The Mexican government is a strange beast, often corrupt to the point of uselessness, but it can still bite. Fernanda's father had been arrested while Fernanda was in the air. Her mother had already vanished with what money she could get her hands on. By the time Fernanda's taxi reached the house, the government was there, stripping the place to the studs.

Stepping inside, the first thing she'd heard was an endless scream from upstairs. She found her brother Miguel alone in an unfurnished room, screaming and rocking next to a broken sewing machine and a box of burned-out flashbulbs like any other piece of junk.

"It's good you came," one of the tax men told her. "We were worried we'd have to put him away somewhere."

Fernanda would never let that happen. Even in her shock—even as she realized that her fortunes had been obliterated—Fernanda's first priority had been Miguel. It was always Miguel. He was autistic, deeply so, and Fernanda had learned a long time ago that when he got like this—when his mind seemed to collapse in absolute free fall—the only thing that could calm him down was a story.

So she had sat on the bare floor in the upstairs room, careful to give him space, and said through the screams, "Have you heard the one about the baby wolf that ate the moon?"

By the end of the story, Miguel was quiet. The men from the tax office were long gone. She sat with her brother in the long sunset of a Monterey summer, watching the light seep over the bare walls like honeyed blood. Her life, hemorrhaging before her eyes.

But at least her brother stopped screaming.

In his tiny, tiny, tiny voice, Miguel said, "Nanda." His name for her. The only word she'd ever heard him speak.

"Nanda."

The stories were a trick Fernanda's grandmother had taught her back when Miguel's challenges had first become obvious. You get a good hook, a problem right in the first sentence, and all the rest comes easy. *Be surprising and familiar at the same time*, her grandmother used to say. *Not really* surprising: *life's bad enough with those already. Give the listener the sort of surprise they think they should have seen coming. Give them a magic trick.*

Fernanda often wondered just how much of her stories Miguel really took in, but they always calmed him down.

In the end, Fernanda had found a frosty aunt who agreed to take in Miguel, but only when Fernanda handed over the last of the money she'd been able to scrounge together from her family's devastated accounts. She didn't exactly trust her aunt to be a perfect caretaker for Miguel, but it only needed to last a year. Fernanda herself was going to return to Connecticut to complete her schooling. A bilingual woman with a prestigious finance degree—there wouldn't be much limit on what she could do.

Fernanda should have known, when she booked a bus back to the US, that the fare was too cheap. She had climbed aboard to discover a coach full of surprisingly good-looking young people heading north, passports in hand, only to watch in dread as they took a sudden detour into the desert. The fat driver and his wife up front had pulled a black curtain over the plastic partition, like an executioner draping a handkerchief over the face of a convict bracing for the axe.

The girl in the seat next to Fernanda started to weep. Fernanda said, "Have you heard the story about the cat that talked to the ocean?"

A reflex, really. But somehow, it always worked.

The rest was a blur. The bus stopped near the Rio. A pontoon bridge was already set up, waiting for them. Several men and dark SUVs waited on the other side. When the passengers saw the words on the sides of the SUVs, they were foolish enough to think, for a while, that they were safe.

Fernanda had no such illusions. When their hands were zip-tied and their documents seized, she held her head down and kept walking. Already, one thought and one thought alone dominated her mind.

She was going back to her brother. Some way. Somehow.

And then the tallest of the men at the border, the one who was clearly in charge, hooked a finger under her chin and lifted her head to study her eyes. "I'll take this one," he said. Like she was a dog at the market.

The name on his shirt read O'SHEA.

It didn't bear repeating what Frank had wanted from her. What he'd done to her when he'd taken her back to his massive home and his massive bed. What mattered was what came after. That first night, Frank O'Shea had dozed off on top of Fernanda, only to awaken a few moments later with a scream in the small hours. He shook with fear. He didn't know where he was. Who *Fernanda* was. Before he could collect himself, Frank whispered, "Mother?"

Fernanda knew an opportunity when she saw one. She forced down a wave of nausea and gently guided his head back down to her chest. "Have you heard the story of the wolf that met the falling star?"

It was absurd, it was humiliating, but it had calmed him down. The next day, he said, almost a little sheepish, "That's the best I've slept in years."

Frank didn't release her back to Mexico, of course. But he didn't sell her down the river either.

Here, in the Brake Inn Motel, the motel's generator stuttered yet again. Outside, the toe-curling *SHRIEKS*, like something from the worst of her grandmother's stories, came closer.

Through it all, Fernanda watched Kyla sleep. When Kyla had tackled Stanley Holiday back in the office, the big man had thrown her against the desk so hard Fernanda had feared the girl might not wake up. Probably no danger of that. Kyla seemed to be breathing steadily, deep in slumber, but her dreams had clearly troubled her. Her mouth twitched and scowled, twisted with fear.

Another of those deafening moans echoed over the motel, and this time Fernanda realized something terribly sad. There was a pain in the sound, an obvious agony, and it sent a bubble of tears swelling in Fernanda's throat. In a way that was hard to explain, the sound from the mountain made Fernanda think of nothing so much as the wail of her brother in free fall.

And then, when the sound faded again, Fernanda looked down. Kyla's eyes were open.

The girl sat up with a gasp, blinking in the light, wiping her mouth with the back of her hand. Without a word, the girl started to move. She rolled to the other side of the bed and struggled to stand.

Fernanda rushed to her. "Wait. Slow down. You hit your head. Hard."

Kyla sank back to the bed, but just enough to gather her strength. "I'm fine. What time is it?"

Fernanda looked at their alarm clock. "Just past eleven fifty, but I believe that clock is fast."

"It's not. Shit."

Kyla rose again, pushing past Fernanda. She grabbed her jacket from where Fernanda had draped it on the other bed, grabbed Lance's gun off the nightstand. Kyla wobbled with every step. She shook her head, popped her jaw. She didn't stop moving. She unlocked their door. She went out into the cold, Fernanda on her heels.

The wind was picking up. Fernanda had to shout over the noise. "Where are you going?"

"There's no time. He'll be here any minute."

RYAN

"Someone's fucking with us," Ryan said. "They have been from the start."

It was a little while earlier. He was in room 9, pacing, while Ethan sat in the corner chair and rubbed his forehead. The boy's migraine was clearly murdering him, but at least he was listening.

Ryan said, "Do you remember earlier in the office, the way Fernanda mentioned she heard a man speaking to Sarah in room four at seven thirty tonight?"

Ethan nodded.

"I heard the same thing."

"I thought you said you were asleep until eight?"

Ryan gave the boy his best *aw, shucks* smile. "I'm afraid I wasn't . . . thoroughly honest. I did sleep a long time, basically from the minute I got back to my room—"

"You mean after that smoke break with Hunter?"

Ryan told the truth. "Yes, exactly. I passed out quick when I got to my room, but I wasn't asleep for long. I woke up at seven thirty because I heard that same conversation in room four. I was in room three, sharing a wall with Sarah, and I heard the same exact argument that Fernanda did. It scared the shit out of me, to be honest with you."

"Why did it scare you?"

"Because for a second, I would have sworn it was Frank O'Shea I heard talking in there."

Ethan raised an eyebrow, looking curious almost in spite of himself. "Sarah said she had a satellite phone. Could it have been a call you heard? Like, on a speaker?"

"Not really. Those phones have terrible connections. The sound quality is atrocious. This sounded like Frank was *in the room*. But obviously that's impossible. We would have heard him arrive, Frank and his whole entourage. We would know they were here. O'Shea isn't exactly subtle."

"And it was dark by seven thirty." Ethan looked out his window. "I don't think anyone would have made it past those things outside."

As if to confirm this, a *SHRIEK* sliced through the room. Ryan had the uncanny feeling that the local wildlife—whatever the fuck they were—could hear them. He rubbed his hands together, suddenly cold.

"Right," Ryan said. "Ergo, Frank wasn't the man talking to Sarah at seven thirty. So who was it?

"Stanley Holiday, I guess. Or you, if you're still not being *thoroughly honest*."

"It wasn't me."

"I'm going to have to take that on faith, aren't I?"

Now Ryan gave Ethan his most honest look. He didn't have much practice with this expression: it was rare for him to tell the full truth about something, but he was doing it now. "You're also going to have to take it on faith it wasn't me, just like you're going to have to take it on faith that I didn't kill the girl. Because I didn't. I never spoke with her either. Not at seven thirty or before or any other time. I never got the chance."

Ethan wouldn't meet his eye. "You could be investigating all this for show. Finding a way to pin it on someone else."

"I'm not that smart, kid." Ryan smiled. "If I was, I wouldn't have let an idiot like Stan Holiday get me thrown in Huntsville."

Ethan chewed on this for a second, gave a little uncommitted shrug. "How's Stanley doing?"

"Alive and unmolested, fret not. But this gets us to the interesting part. Again, let's go back. If it wasn't Frank O'Shea talking to Sarah Powers at seven thirty, and if it wasn't me, who does that leave?"

"Just Stanley. It couldn't have been me or Hunter. We were already in the cafe by seven thirty. Thomas was already there, too, waiting for us. That doesn't leave many options."

A sudden, awful sound came over the motel then: a roaring moan, so loud and strange Ethan and Ryan both clapped their hands over their ears until it passed. The earth shook under their feet. Every nerve in Ryan's body lit up with fear.

Nothing good could make a noise like that.

Ryan looked at the clock. It was already past eleven thirty. They needed to hurry.

"Here's the problem—it couldn't have been Stanley in room four either. He *was* actually asleep at seven thirty. He didn't wake up until a few minutes later, when Fernanda went into his room with a gun."

Ethan blinked. "When Fernanda did what?"

"I've only heard Stanley's side of this story, but I think it's safe to believe the broad strokes. According to him, Fernanda turned up a few minutes after seven thirty waving a gun around. Scared the shit out of him, obviously. For a second, he thought the girl was trying to kill him, but she just wanted to make a deal. According to Stanley, Fernanda and her friend Kyla are making a run for the border. They have some camera film in their possession that's going to ruin Frank O'Shea's operation, and by extension Stan Holiday. Stanley's been Frank's accountant for decades. He knows where all the bodies are buried."

"And?"

"And so Fernanda promised she could keep Stan safe when shit hits the fan. There are apparently some shots on the girls' film that implicate him. Shots that Fernanda promised to slice out before handing the film over to the cartel."

"Wouldn't that look suspicious?"

"It's the desert, kid. Everything's suspicious."

"And do you believe her?"

"I do," Ryan said. "I went to room seven a few minutes ago, the room where Stanley and Penelope were staying. No sign of Penn, but I did find a long black hair next to Stanley's bed along with some blood on the nightstand. The hair looks like one of Fernanda's."

Ethan's eyes were still closed, his thumb and finger trying to rub some relief into his head. "So that explains why Fernanda came to dinner a few minutes after Kyla, looking all flustered. She'd just finished trying to put the fear of God into Mister Holiday."

"And it explains why Stanley's got a busted lip. Fernanda gave him a good thwack with her gun when he tried to talk shit."

"Why didn't Fernanda take his gun while she had the chance?"

"He probably had it stashed somewhere and she didn't have time to look for it. Remember, Penelope was sleeping in that same room.

Stanley's a thug, but he wouldn't want to leave a Deagle laying around where a kid could just grab it."

"And what did Stanley get up to after that? It was another ten minutes before he came to dinner."

"I . . . asked him that myself." Ryan chewed his lip. "Whatever it was, he's afraid to talk about it. He hasn't said a word since I asked him."

"Isn't *that* suspicious?"

"We'll get back to it. Here's the first important point: there isn't a single man unaccounted for tonight. No one who could have been in room four arguing with Sarah Powers at seven thirty. It wasn't me, it wasn't you or Hunter, it wasn't Thomas, it wasn't Stanley. I don't think the motel is haunted, or breaking the rules of Newtonian physics—"

Ethan shook his head, eyes still closed. "I wouldn't be so sure about that. *Something* is off about this place. About tonight."

"I agree with you there. But I think we have an easier explanation, at least in regards to the conversation at seven thirty. There's someone who wasn't in their room and who hasn't been accounted for."

Ethan finally caught on to what Ryan was saying. He opened his eyes, blinked, stared. "You don't think it was . . ."

Now that Ethan was looking at him, Ryan couldn't look back. Here was a fact he'd been avoiding all night, a question he'd been desperate not to answer. There was no escaping it. The answer, really, had been staring at him since Mexico.

"Penelope," Ryan said. "I think Penelope was in Sarah's room at seven thirty."

ETHAN

"Penelope has always been good with voices. Like, uncanny good," Ryan said. "When she was a kid, her sister, Adeline, used to come up with people for her to imitate. You know—the lunch lady at school, Stanley after a bad day, Uncle Frank complaining about the weather. The girls called it The Game. It was their favorite thing. It was like if Penelope had ever met anyone, even just the one time, she could imitate their voice almost perfectly. It's where we got our nickname for her. Polly. Like a parrot. 'Polly want a cracker.' Get it?"

Ethan still didn't trust this guy Ryan. Who would? But Ethan found himself growing convinced about this if nothing else. He had the strangest memory of a time he'd heard Stanley's voice rolling in out of the black desert, here and gone, like the stray broadcasts of a twitchy radio. The voice had sounded out of place. Wrong.

And then, the longer Ethan thought about the memory, the more he wondered when exactly he'd *heard* this voice. Ethan seemed to remember he'd been on the motel's back porch at the time, Kyla by his side. She'd heard it too. They'd both been confused.

But that had never happened tonight. Ethan hadn't stood on the back porch with Kyla. He hadn't seen the girl since Stanley knocked her unconscious in the office.

It was another of those strange double exposures.

"Penelope scared the shit out of me more than once in Mexico," Ryan said. "We'd be on the bike, or at our hotel, or out grabbing food, and I'd suddenly hear Frank O'Shea talking behind me, or Stanley, or both of them having a whole conversation. Penelope asked me if I had any requests, like Adeline used to do. 'For you to stop,' I said."

Ryan grinned at his own joke, in spite of everything. Ethan said nothing.

"Tough crowd." Ryan rubbed a spot on his jacket.

Ethan's head was hurting too much to smile. "What exactly are you saying? That Penelope went to Sarah's room at seven thirty and had some sort of fake conversation with her? She pretended to be Frank O'Shea just to scare us?"

"I think that was Penelope we heard at seven thirty, yes."

"Does it follow, then, that Penelope must have been the one who killed Sarah Powers?"

"No. Or at least not necessarily. Because by seven thirty, I think Sarah was already—"

Another of those horrible booming moans struck the motel like a heavy tide. It was somehow even louder than the last one. Every time Ethan thought the pain in his head couldn't grow any worse, something like this showed up to surprise him.

Through the pain, he felt his teeth chattering, his hands shaking. Outside, the wind was picking up. A terrible sense of finality suddenly struck Ethan, the crushing certainty of disaster. It was like seeing a car coming too fast to brake, a match suspended inches from kerosene.

A man with a hand to the bullet in his heart.

The time was 11:52. Ethan had no doubt the twins had been lying when they'd said they had some special place of safety, but when he saw the way the room's lights were flickering, he wondered if they hadn't been telling the truth about one thing:

Midnight was not going to be good for them.

And then he heard it all again, felt it all again: another double exposure. Déjà vu.

There was a knock on Ethan's door. Somehow he knew, even before he opened it, who would be waiting for him.

It was Kyla.

"I need your shotgun," she said. "Hurry."

Ethan said, "How do you know I have a shotgun?"

"There's no time. Please. We need to get to the office. It'll be midnight any second."

"But what do you want to do with my shotgun in the office?"

Fernanda stood behind Kyla on the porch, shivering against the relentless wind.

Ryan said, "If you want to scare the twins into revealing their hiding spot, don't bother—they don't have one."

Kyla snapped, "I know that. We figured that out last night."

"Last . . . night?" Ethan said.

"You haven't remembered yet, have you? That we've done this before a million times already?"

"Done this before?" Ethan said.

"A million times already?" Ryan said.

"Jesus, y'all sound like the twins." Kyla looked ready to punch someone. She pointed to Ryan. "You and Hunter met in Huntsville. You were cellmates."

Ethan turned to Ryan, a new cold coming through him. "Huntsville?"

"And you," Kyla said to Ethan. "Your name isn't Ethan. It's Carter. You took your brother's name after he killed himself, so you could start over somewhere else."

Ryan stared at Ethan. "You what?"

Ethan ignored him. He studied Kyla, knowing full well there was no way she could have figured that out herself. He and Hunter had brought no evidence with them. Hadn't slipped up all night.

Behind her, the generator was still struggling to keep the motel lit. The circle of light around them was shrinking. One of the mercury lamps fizzled into nothing.

SHRIEKS. Everywhere, the shrieks.

Kyla said, "Please. You have to believe me. We have to get ready. He'll be here any minute."

Ethan didn't remember the night she was talking about, didn't know who "he" might be, but the dread in the pit of his stomach hadn't abated. He'd ask for more answers later.

For now, he looked Kyla full in the face. He said, "I'll bring the spare shells too."

THE MIDNIGHT KNOCK
KYLA

12:00 a.m.

A new moan rolled down the mountain, and this time it didn't stop. The sound grew louder, louder, matched only by the *SHRIEKS* of the things in the night. A wild wind buffeted the motel. The generator sputtered, struggled: a lamp died outside, another. The circle of light was weakening. Shrinking. The guests stood in the cold office, lit only by the lamp with the green glass shade. Hunter's corpse was still sprawled across the floor. The twins stared at Kyla from behind the counter.

Stanley was locked away somewhere. Penelope was nowhere to be seen.

11:57.

11:58.

11:59.

The thing in the mountain: it sounded like it was screaming.

12:00.

The moment the clock struck midnight, the noise cut out. All of it, at once, just like that: the bellowing from the mountain, the *SHRIEKS* from the desert. The wind died down to a mournful breeze. It played across the porch and the parking lot: the last desperate breaths of the past.

In the silence, in the cold, they heard a new sound in the desert.

It was the whisper of tires on a gravel road.

Headlights washed through the windows of the office. A car pulled to a slow stop outside. The headlights went dark. The engine cut out.

A metal door whined open.

A foot stepped into the gravel outside. Another joined it. The car door swung closed. The feet crunched across the parking lot, thumped up the steps of the porch, creaked across its wooden boards. The feet came to a stop on the other side of the office's front door. A long, long silence stretched.

And then someone *knock*

Knock

Knocked.

No one moved to answer the knock. Kyla didn't bother. After a polite pause, the door opened, and a man stepped inside. A tall, slim man, dressed in a gray gabardine suit with a matching hat in his hand. No one wore suits like that anymore. It was a little faded, a little worn around the edges, utterly unmistakable.

The man had small, dark eyes. A lopsided hook of a smile. The index finger of his right hand ended at the second knuckle. A mass of scar tissue was seared to the joint.

The man spoke with a soft twang. An eerie formality.

"Evening, folks," the man said. "Room for one—"

Jack Allen broke off when he finally saw the shotgun braced against Kyla's shoulder.

She pumped a round into the chamber: *chunk-SHUNK*.

"Fuck off," Kyla said.

She fired.

The contents of Jack Allen's head scattered over the front porch. His gray gabardine hat flew away into the night. An awful smell of rot—of absolute decay—flooded everyone's noses.

A strange creeping itch, like the tickle of a million small fingers, played along the back of Kyla's neck. Through the echo of the shotgun's blast, the wet spatter of brain matter and pulverized bone, she heard a voice whisper just beside her ear.

"Well played, Miss Hewitt. Well played."

The sensation left her. Kyla ignored it all. She turned the shotgun to the front desk, pumped another round into the barrel.

She said to the twins, "You fuckers have some explaining to do."

TABITHA'S STORY
ETHAN

12:01 a.m.

He wasn't sure what he'd been expecting, but it hadn't been that. He told himself he should be horrified by what Kyla had just done, that he should try to disarm her, that the girl had just murdered some poor stranger wandering in from the cold—but he didn't.

The pain in Ethan's head didn't dissipate. He couldn't shake an awful feeling, like he was forgetting the most important thing of his life.

But he recalled the way this man in the gabardine suit, Jack Allen, had spoken to him in the diner in the little town of Turner earlier that afternoon. Ethan remembered the fear he'd felt in his presence, the dread, the way he'd been unable to move once the gabardine man had trained his eyes on Ethan.

Had the man introduced himself as Jack Allen at the diner? Ethan couldn't recall, but he'd given up wondering how he knew these people's names.

Fernanda didn't seem half so sanguine. A hand to her mouth, nausea gurgling her voice, she said, "What have you done?"

Ryan took a step forward to look at the corpse, picking his way over the blood and bits of bone. Of all things, he studied the pattern of the suit's cloth. "Is that called gabardine?"

Ethan blinked. "I think so. Why?"

Ryan chewed his cheek. He looked, for a moment, very afraid. "How did he get past those things outside? I had a feeling it would be a bad idea to head into the dark."

"It would be," Kyla said. She still had the shotgun trained on the twins. They looked petrified beyond words, the both of them. Glancing over her shoulder, Kyla said to Ethan, "Do you believe me yet? That we've done all of this before?"

Ethan studied Kyla. He didn't see madness in her eyes, didn't see desperation or panic or delusion in the muscles of her hands, the pulse of her veins, the movements around her mouth. When Ethan looked at Kyla, he saw only a woman with a purpose who desperately needed him to believe her. Her claim wasn't exactly easy to swallow, but he wasn't stupid. Kyla had somehow known that Ethan's name wasn't even Ethan. She'd also known that Hunter and Ryan Phan had apparently shared a cell in Huntsville prison, something that certainly explained why a loner like Hunter would leave their room to go smoke with a stranger (even if it raised plenty of other unsettling questions).

If Kyla was telling the truth—if they had done this a million times before—could it possibly explain these double exposures Ethan had been feeling all night, the persistent sensation of déjà vu? Could they be his mind's way of struggling to record the same memory in the same place?

Could they be lost memories somehow breaking through?

Ethan wasn't sure, but he didn't need to know everything at once. He said, "What should we do?"

Kyla said, "Someone check Jack Allen's pockets. You'll find a key. It unlocks the door in the back of the office—"

The thing behind that walnut door, quiet these last few moments, starting SHRIEKING again, clawing at the wood.

"—But you might want to take my word on that," Kyla said.

The gabardine pattern of Jack Allen's suit was rapidly melting into a single sheet of crimson. Ryan didn't seem especially bothered by the blood. From the pocket of Jack Allen's pants, he did indeed find a simple brass key.

And from the inner pocket of the suit's jacket, Ryan found a plain leather wallet. He flipped it open, frowned at something inside, flipped it closed. Digging deeper into the pocket, he removed a small, grooved stone, the size and shape of an egg.

The sight of the stone stirred a memory in Ethan. Ever since stepping into the office a few minutes ago, he'd avoided looking anywhere near the fireplace. At the lake of blood that had spread there. At Hunter's corpse, stretched like an oblong island in the lake's heart.

He looked now, though. And from the lake, he plucked another stone egg from the place Kyla had dropped it earlier this evening. Blood had congealed in the stone's grooves. A familiar weight seemed to anchor the egg in Ethan's fingers.

Ethan stepped closer to Jack Allen's corpse and wiped the blood on a clean patch of gabardine. He looked at the mess that remained of the man's head. He sniffed the air. That stench of rottenness—stale air, decay—still seeped, thick as engine oil, from the crumpled corpse. It didn't smell like death, like blood: Ethan had smelled that already, back home in Ellersby.

No. This stench was something else entirely. This stench was *wrong*.

Whatever was going on here, Kyla had been right to kill the man.

"There is another stone like that." Fernanda plucked a third grooved rock from the fire's mantel. She weighed it in her hand. "It is heavier than it looks."

"Gives me the creeps, if I'm being honest with you," Ryan said, and passed the stone he'd taken from Jack Allen's pocket to Kyla.

Ethan didn't feel so bothered by it. He slipped the egg in his hand into the pocket of his jeans. It felt familiar there, somehow. Comfortable. *Right*.

Kyla lowered the shotgun to look at the egg. She said to the twins, "What are these rocks for? And why did Jack Allen unlock that door last night?"

The twins still stared at her, struck dumb. Ethan thought, *This has never happened to them before*.

"Answer me," Kyla dropped the egg in her hand into the pocket of her jacket. She raised the shotgun again. "I said, *Answer me*."

Thomas looked like he would rather swallow a mouthful of buckshot than comply. Tabitha, however, raised her hands from the desk in a slow show of surrender. She eased sideways, away from her brother. She stepped around the desk.

"What are you doing?" Thomas hissed. "*What are you doing?*"

Tabitha ignored him. Nodding to Jack Allen's corpse, she said, "Could somebody move him out of the doorway? We need to refuel the generator."

Indeed, as Ethan and Ryan grabbed an ankle apiece and dragged Jack Allen toward the fire, the lights died down to almost nothing and took ages to return. The mountain, silent these last few minutes, moaned again. The creatures outside swept over the motel. They were right outside that same door.

There was a careful sound, a *scritch-scritch-scritch* at the window by the fireplace. Ethan saw a massive shape in the dark. A talon creeping on the glass, wondering if it was time to break in.

Scritch-scritch-scritch.

The lights returned but they were hazy, flickery, liable to fall again at any moment. Ethan knew the sign of a dying motor when he saw one.

"This way," Tabitha said. "Hurry."

KYLA

They left Thomas standing behind the counter, the man looking lost. Terrified. He said nothing as they filed out the door. He
seemed so scared, Kyla worried his brain might have shut down
entirely.

They had bigger problems.

A sleek black boat of a car—"A '54 Roadmaster," Ethan mur-
mured, clearly awed—was parked outside the office. Jack Allen's car.
Ryan swung open the driver's door, said, "The keys are in the ignition."
He cranked the engine, only to kill it a moment later. "The tank's dry."

"No surprise," Tabitha said.

Kyla hardly paid any attention. Her eye was drawn to the old
house behind the motel, its dark shape barely visible at the foot of
the mountain.

If not for the strange silver light glowing in the upstairs window,
she might have forgotten the house was there at all.

Ethan followed her gaze. He said, "There's something important
over there."

"Do you remember what?"

"No. But it's waiting for us."

They followed Tabitha down the front porch, the lights of the
motel guttering like candles in a strong wind. Speaking of wind, the
gale that had hammered the motel near midnight had died, but in its
place was an awful stillness, a tension like a wire between Kyla's ears.
She could feel those creatures out there, moving through the night.
She remembered the shape of them from yesterday. She remembered
their feathers and their scales and their terrible strength.

She remembered the way the one locked up in the office had torn
Tabitha's head from her body and heaved it against the window as
Kyla ran for her life.

Kyla remembered everything, not that it explained very much.
Her headache might have been gone, but her mind was still a blur.

Tabitha stopped outside room 1, the next door down from the

office, and dug a hand into her pocket. Kyla remembered that she and
Ethan had come to this room last night in their search for clues and
found this door locked. As Tabitha slid a key into the bolt and swung
open the door, Kyla saw that inside was a simple room like all the
others, only this one had clearly been lived in for some time. The two
twin beds were unmade. The open wardrobe was hung with clothes.

An unframed photograph was propped against the lamp on the
nightstand: Thomas and Tabitha and a thin, severe, black-haired man
who could only be their father. The three stood in some desert, all
three of them dressed in jeans and boots, each holding a spade in one
hand and a brush in the other. Only Tabitha was smiling.

Tabitha herself was hurrying down the room. From the other
side of the long dresser, she produced a series of heavy metal cans.

The first two were blue metal. "Can someone carry these? I believe the motel is out of water."

"Thank God," Ryan said. "I've been thirsty for an hour."

Tabitha dragged out another metal canister, this one painted red.
"Gasoline," she said.

"Music to my ears," Kyla said. With a nod, Ethan hefted the can.

Lastly, Tabitha's fingers hesitated over a piece of folded paper
waiting atop the dresser. After a long moment's deliberation, she
plucked it up and tucked it in her pocket.

"Let's take the back porch," she said. "It'll save a few seconds."

They stepped out of room 1's back door. A lamp died over Kyla's
head as they made their way down the side of the motel. The ring
of light that surrounded them was flickering, growing weaker and
weaker. The edge of the light had drawn so close, Kyla could have
reached out her hand and brushed its edge.

Probably lost a finger in the process. A *SHRIEK* came from mere
feet away.

That got them running.

At the far end of the motel, they found a massive metal engine,
Army green, rumbling on concrete blocks. The generator. Tabitha
unscrewed a cap in the engine's side. As Ethan emptied the sloshing
can of gas into its guts, a smile came over Tabitha. It looked like the
most profound relief Kyla had ever seen.

"We didn't get the chance to do this the first night," she said. "And so we've never done it since."

Kyla would wonder about this later. "How long will that fuel last?"

The generator weakened, then surged back to life, the lights around the motel shining so bright everyone had to cover their eyes. The engine practically purred with gratitude.

Ethan didn't seem as happy as the rest of them. "That wasn't much fuel, considering how much power this place is pulling."

Tabitha opened a door set into the wall nearby. "This way. I'll explain as quickly as I can."

As Kyla followed Tabitha inside, her eye caught the old house behind the motel. A single silver light was glowing in the window upstairs. Kyla murmured to Ethan, "Something's waiting for us in that house."

"If we can just find a way to get there," he said.

The door led into the motel's kitchen. Filthy cookware was piled in the sink, scattered over long gas ranges. Kyla found it almost as disturbing as the violence of the past two nights: after an aimless decade of working waitstaff, a dirty kitchen was one of her greatest anxieties.

But of course they had bigger problems. Even with Jack Allen dead and the lights back to full strength, she knew this was only a reprieve. Another moan from the mountain shook the motel. Whatever was making that sound, she doubted a shotgun and a few stolen pistols would do them much good.

Speaking of the shotgun, it was practically as tall as Kyla herself. Its weight was starting to drag on her. When they came around the corner of the cafe's hall, she settled the gun on the bar, something that appeared to give Tabitha even more relief. The woman was clearly eager to talk, even without the threat of getting her head taken off.

"You should get some food. All of you," Tabitha said. "I make it every night and it's never been eaten. I would like that to change."

"I'm not exactly hungry," Kyla said.

"You might as well get up your strength. This will take a few minutes to explain. If our father's to be believed, what's happening tonight has been going on for centuries."

ETHAN

"You've probably already worked it out by now, but the last time this motel accepted guests, the year was 1955."

They gathered new plates of food as Tabitha spoke. Ethan poured water from the jugs they'd brought from Tabitha's room, shot nervous glances into the dark outside. Once, twice, Ethan would have sworn he saw a hazy shape—a *man* shape—looming at the cafe's window.

But whenever he looked again, the shape was gone.

Ethan said, "That guy in the gray suit—he told me a story about this place."

Ryan raised an eyebrow. "You met him before?"

"At a shithole diner earlier today. He was there when me and Hunter pulled into town—just sitting there, drinking a coffee. He told me that twelve people disappeared from this place back in '55." Ethan rubbed his temples, wincing at his stubborn headache. *Nine empty rooms. Twelve cold beds.* "Jack Allen said this place has been abandoned ever since, but when me and Hunter got here and everything seemed normal, I just figured . . . I don't know, that he was pulling my chain."

Fernanda said, "Frank O'Shea told me the same story. I thought the twins must have somehow renovated this place behind his back. The land would be cheap, I assumed."

Ryan said, "Stanley had the same problem. His daughter told me all about it. Stan's mother and Frank's mother both vanished on the same night. The two women sold makeup together. They were driving back from a cosmetics conference in New Mexico and stopped somewhere in the area for the night. No one ever saw them again."

"Why would they stop here?" Kyla said. "Stockton's not two hours away."

"The ladies were an item. Not that anyone says that part out loud." Ryan chewed a piece of okra. "Frank and Stanley like to make out like their moms were kidnapped or murdered, but I'd always assumed those two girls had just run off to Mexico together."

"No. They didn't. I met them last night." Tabitha's face strained at a thought. "Or rather, not *last* last night. English isn't really built for this kind of paradox. Or maybe the brain isn't."

"Let's not get hung up on details." Kyla sat at the bar, pulling loose a handgun from behind her back and placing it near the shotgun. Ethan did the same with his Python, Fernanda with her own pistol. It was a relief to sit without chunks of metal digging into their backsides.

Tabitha said, "It's a shame Sarah isn't alive. She could probably explain this better than I can. She was a physicist. A very good one, at that."

Ethan said, "Sarah Powers was a scientist? I thought she worked for Frank."

"She was a tenured professor from Austin." A small, sad smile crossed Tabitha's face. "My brother and I were so proud when we learned that today. It's strange—we felt rather paternal about her, proud of our little cousin, when she was almost a decade older than us. Depending on how you count."

"What the hell was a tenured professor of physics doing working for Frank O'Shea?" Ryan said.

Kyla said, "One thing at a time. Twelve people checked into this place in 1955, right? And let me guess—they got stuck living the same night over and over again, just like us."

"I believe they did, yes," Tabitha said. "We don't exactly have a way of checking. There were eight guests that evening. A pair of newlyweds, the two women selling makeup, two young hikers, an insurance salesman, and a professional Negro."

The woman really is *from 1955*, Ethan thought. Everyone blinked at the word.

Everyone except Kyla. When an awkward pause threatened the cafe, she twirled two fingers in the air, the universal sign for *keep it moving*. "Eight guests. Plus you and your brother. And I assume your dad was here?"

"Yes. It had been Father's idea to buy this place."

"That makes eleven," Kyla said. "Who was the twelfth person?"

"Our father's business partner. A strange man. He must have told us his real name at one point, but I forgot it ages ago. We always called him The Chief."

RYAN

The Chief. The name sent alarms ringing up and down Ryan's mind.

"Tall Native dude?" Ryan said, interrupting Tabitha. "Long gray hair? Turkey feather necklace?"

Tabitha seemed surprised at the question. "Yes. We met him when Father came to buy this place."

"Did he happen to have a kid? A son?"

"I think he mentioned one, yes. There was some difficulty in the family. He wasn't able to see the boy often."

Ryan shuddered. This whole night had been loaded with fucking coincidences: What was one more? But judging by the way the others were studying him, it looked like he needed to give some sort of explanation.

He shrugged to Ethan. "I'm sorry, kid, but Kyla was right, earlier in your room. Me and your man were cellmates back in Huntsville. He was a friend. *Just* a friend, before you give me that look. When he and I bumped into each other tonight for that smoke, Hunter asked that I not mention anything about his time in prison. He didn't want you to think less of him."

Kyla said, "You know what he was in prison for, don't you?"

Ryan saw a look of blank horror cross Ethan's face. The boy clearly didn't want to know, and Ryan didn't see how it would help them. "Let's talk about that later. I only mention it because of the guy who slept in the cell next door to me and Hunter. He was an old Native dude who mostly kept to himself. He said he was the last man standing of his tribe. Everyone around the prison used to call him The Chief."

"What are the fucking odds?" Kyla said, though she almost didn't sound surprised. Tabitha blinked at her language.

"It gets weirder. A few months ago, Sarah Powers—yes, *this* Sarah Powers—turned up at Huntsville and paid The Chief—our Chief, the man who slept next to me and Hunter—a visit."

"Sarah visited Huntsville?" Ethan said. "Does that mean Hunter knew her too?"

"Not much better than me, I don't think. I never saw Sarah in the flesh until today. The guards at the prison pulled pictures of her from the surveillance footage, of course, showed them around. No one could believe it. The Chief was just some old man spending thirty years on a big counterfeit charge, minding his own business, and suddenly this beauty with long hair and longer legs comes striding up to the visitor center asking to see him. We thought she was one of those weird girls who get obsessed with guys behind bars, but The Chief swore it was nothing like that. He said he'd been wrong— apparently, he *did* have some tribe left in this world. That girl, Sarah Powers, was a distant relation. But that's all he ever really told us. Me and Hunter both were curious why she kept coming to see him, but The Chief just said that he and Sarah were catching up on old family business. And before we could learn more, The Chief died. I'd thought that was the last we'd ever hear of Sarah." Ryan felt a tingle on his arms: he was skirting, very carefully, around something he really—*really*—did not want to talk about.

"When was this exactly?" Kyla said. "When The Chief died?"

"Maybe six or seven weeks ago. Why?"

"That's around the time Sarah turned up at the steakhouse and started having those dinners with Stanley and Frank. Again, totally out of the blue," Kyla said. "Whatever work Sarah was doing with those guys, it started after your friend The Chief died."

"Is that another coincidence?" Fernanda said. "Or could the two events be connected?"

Ryan said nothing. That tingle crept up his arms. It wasn't guilt he felt, or fear of being found out. He really hadn't done much tonight to hide, at least nothing very serious. He hadn't killed anyone. He hadn't helped cover up the murder.

He just didn't want to think about the reason he'd gone to see Sarah Powers, earlier in the evening. It scared the shit out of him, thinking about the things The Chief had said the night the old man died.

The mountain—

Tell Sarah, the mountain—

"I know you killed her," Kyla said to Ryan: flat, thoroughly unbothered. "I'd just like to know why."

That jerked him out of the past. "You what?"

"You have no real alibi. You went to Sarah's room at some point before eight o'clock this evening. You even stole a roll of film from her. Considering the scraps of burned-up photo negatives we found in Sarah's room yesterday, I'm going to go out on a limb and say she took a picture of you that she shouldn't have. You aren't supposed to be here. You wanted to make sure there was no trace you'd ever come by."

Ryan's head was spinning, mostly because he was impressed. Not because he'd killed Sarah, of course, but because very few people could stitch together so many clues so wrongly.

"If you'd just admit it, we can move on to bigger problems," Kyla said. "Like how the hell we get out of this place alive."

Ryan took a sip of water. This was going to take some work.

"I did go to Sarah's room before eight o'clock, yes, but not to kill her. And I went back an hour ago and found the burned film you're talking about. I assume it came from this."

Reaching into the pocket of his jacket, Ryan removed the rolled-up length of camera film he'd retrieved from a strange black cylinder in Sarah's bathroom. He rested the roll of negatives on the bar. "I don't think those burned pictures were as exciting as you want them to be. Look at how neat and clean the cut at the end of the film is. A killer jacked up on adrenaline wouldn't have made such a clean slice."

Ethan said, "So if the killer didn't burn the pictures, who did?"

"Sarah, obviously. The film is flawed—there's weird gray smudges all over it. Sarah probably decided the last few shots just weren't worth keeping."

"But why would she burn them?" Ethan said. "Why not just throw them in the trash?"

Ryan shrugged. Fernanda plucked up the roll of film and held it to the light.

Kyla just stared at Ryan until he kept talking.

"I didn't kill Sarah," he said. "Yes, I did go to her room. That was around seven fifty. I went because I wanted to talk to her about something. I slipped through the front door while everyone was at dinner, but it didn't do me any good. Sarah was already dead."

"How convenient," Kyla said.

"You can believe me or not." Ryan stared Kyla in the eye. He was telling her the truth. "I didn't hurt her. And I didn't steal any film from her either."

Kyla didn't look impressed. "So Sarah was dead by seven fifty?"

"Yes. Very. She looked exactly the way she did when Tabitha found the body a few minutes later. I'd slipped back out of the room by then. Stanley must have caught a glimpse of me around that time, but I got into the supply closet without much attention. That's where I was, trying to figure out what the hell was going on here, and then all the screaming started."

"There's more, though, isn't there? Because you said in my room that you thought Sarah was already dead by seven thirty."

Fernanda looked away from the film in her hands. "That's impossible. I told you earlier that I heard Sarah speaking to a man in her room at—"

"I'm sorry to interrupt, but could this wait?" Tabitha said. "Time isn't slowing down, and we still have a lot to cover."

KYLA

Kyla felt it too. The clock on the wall showed 1:10. A lamp above the bar flickered. Was it a bad bulb, or was the generator already starting to fail again?

Tabitha said, "By 1955, this motel was bankrupt. It had been built by a fool entrepreneur who'd made a little money on an oil well in Odessa. This mountain never really had a name, so he started calling it 'Mount Apache' and tried to make it into a tourist destination. Which is foolish on its face. The Apache never lived here. In fact, they told terrible stories about this place."

Outside, the wind was picking up again. Kyla recalled a similar story from Jack Allen last night, shortly before he reached a hand into his gabardine pocket and removed that shining brass key.

As night came, as darkness rolled over the mountain, the braves died, one by one, until only a single young man was left behind to warn his tribe of the hell he'd seen.

"My whole family, we're archaeologists," Tabitha said. "Thomas and I, we grew up on dig sites. We used to joke that dirt's in our blood. Father's specialty was Indian history. That was in our blood, too, seeing as our family is descended from those very same Apache. They were one of the largest tribes to live in this area, and Father made the start of a brilliant career excavating some of their old encampments. Indigenous people and archaeologists have a long history with one another. A bad history. Father wanted to change that. I won't bore you with the technicalities. Just know that he was a reasonable man. A true scholar. In light of what came later, you might think him . . . a sensationalist."

Tabitha found a shot glass, a bottle of whiskey from the shelf behind her, poured an impressive measure. The glass chittered against her teeth. "A few years ago—a few years before '55, I mean—Father fell out of the scholarly mainstream. He found a few relics in this region that were much, much older than they should have been. Much stranger. Like nothing else we'd ever seen. Father became convinced that they were relics of a tribe that predated the Apache's arrival in Texas. This isn't especially novel. There are several branches of Apache, and we know that all of them absorbed dozens of smaller tribes as they settled across the southwest. Some of those tribes were brought in as a consequence of warfare, or famine, or simple convenience. This area can be a harsh place to live. Many small groups decided there was strength in numbers." Tabitha hesitated, a hand on the bar as if to stabilize herself, her story. "Things became strange, however, when Father convinced himself that these relics he'd discovered—these traces of a tribe that predated the Apache—that they belonged to our family. That *we* were descended from that precursor tribe. And as its descendants, we had inherited a sacred duty. An obligation to keep a great evil at bay."

"That's a hell of a jump from a few dusty rocks," Kyla said.

Tabitha said, "Me and my brother . . . we thought the same. Apparently, when he was a boy, our father had a grandfather who told him stories about our precursor tribe, our original tribe, the tribe our family belonged to before the Apache came. His father said that, according to *his* grandfather, our tribe used to live in a mountain, in a grand city concealed from the outside world. The precursor tribe believed the mountain had a special power. They said it ensured things always worked out the way they were meant to. That power, the stories said, kept us safe. We prospered thanks to the mountain, but one day a curious little boy strayed from the city. The child wandered into the caves of the mountain, deeper and deeper, and at the mountain's heart he discovered something . . . terrible."

Oh no, Miss Hewitt.

It is I who shall have audience once more.

Behind the motel, the mountain moaned, shaking the cafe so hard Kyla's fork skipped across her plate. Everyone's eyes, even Fernanda's, were riveted now to Tabitha's face.

Tabitha said, "According to the stories, the little boy had discovered an ancient creature, something almost as old as the mountain itself. They called it—"

Kyla spoke, almost without thinking: the name from the dream. "Te'lo'hi."

Tabitha stared at her for a long, long time. "Yes. That's one of the few words we still have from the precursor tribe's language. Te'lo'hi. It was a hungry force, a being of pure destruction. According to the stories, Te'lo'hi had slept for thousands of years, but now that the little boy had disturbed it, the god was beginning to stir. The tribe's Elders knew that if it woke up, nothing could stop the destruction it would unleash. Their city would be doomed. Maybe even the world. So they devised a ceremony that would harness some of Te'lo'hi's own power. According to the story, the ceremony sealed the god away, but in the process, they had to seal away their home as well. The city. Our people left the mountain and were banished into the desert, where they were soon absorbed by the Apache and began to forget their true history."

The clock was racing forward. 1:22. Ryan Phan was getting jumpy. "Can you pour me a shot? And hurry to the part where this concerns *us*?"

"I was getting to that." Tabitha frowned, her unease making her peevish. She sloshed whiskey into another little glass, pushed it his way. "According to the stories our father grew up with, our precursor tribe knew that the ceremony they'd performed to seal away the god wouldn't last forever. At some point, it would have to be repeated, or else Te'lo'hi would awaken at last. This idea began to haunt our father. He became . . . obsessed with it. There are plenty of similar stories in many tribes—people living in caves or underground, dangerous beings lurking in darkness—but Father didn't believe this one was a mere story. He feared that hundreds of years ago, our tribe had indeed forestalled disaster. If the ceremony wasn't performed again, soon, calamity would break free. He started . . ." Tabitha trembled. "He started having dreams. Nightmares. Visions of the world ending. We all did. Me and my brother and—"

Another moan came from the mountain, so loud Kyla would swear she saw the air itself tremble.

Kyla remembered being in her bathroom last night, shortly before Jack Allen killed her, when the mirror in her bathroom had shattered and they'd both seen the city of her dreams spread out on the other side. Kyla had seen it again, earlier this evening, when her mirror had broken before dinner. She looked at the bandage Hunter had knotted around her fingers to staunch the wound left behind by the shattered glass.

She said, "The stories are true. There is a city in the mountain. I've seen it."

Tabitha stared at her. "Seen it? How?"

"I'll tell you later," Kyla said. "All I know is that Jack Allen wants to go there. He wants to have audience with the god inside."

Ethan said carefully, "If Te'lo'hi is so dangerous, why would anyone want that?"

"I don't know. But *this* is the ceremony, isn't it?" Kyla said to Tabitha. She patted the bar, her chest, held out a hand to take in everything around them. "*All* of this. I'm just firing in the dark here, but I guess it makes a sort of sense. The same night repeating over and over—you people have us trapped here, but it's also trapped Te'lo'hi. You're keeping it from waking up. You did the same thing to the people in 1955. You trapped them, now you've trapped us, maybe down the road you'll trap some more people, right? It's a fucking curse for us, but if we try to break free, the world will end. Or am I just talking out of my ass?"

Tabitha said nothing.

Ethan said, "It's not that simple, is it?"

THOMAS

He couldn't remember the last time he'd been alone. For as long as he could remember—which was a *very* long time by some measures—Thomas and his sister had always been at each other's sides. Once, years ago, their father had taken Thomas aside and asked, in as few words as possible, if he should *be concerned*. If the twins' intimacy might not have *gone too far*.

Thomas had been shocked. Their father was so hopeless at human connection, he apparently couldn't imagine any chaste reason a man might want to stay close to his sister. Thomas's connection to Tabitha wasn't like that. The world simply made *sense* when she was around. Thomas sometimes felt like they viewed it through each other's eyes. A competitive advantage. A wider perspective.

Without Tabitha, Thomas felt vulnerable in a way he never had in his life. Afraid. If Tabitha was doing what Thomas thought she was doing, it could be the end of everything. Of them. The motel. The entire world.

Truly, the world.

"Then why don't you do something about it?"

The voice came from behind Thomas, just over his shoulder. He felt a tingle on the back of his neck, a chilly itch like the creeping of a hundred tiny legs. He flinched, turned—and found nothing.

The voice came again. Again, just behind his shoulder. Again, whispering in his ear.

"You can stop her, Thomas," the voice said. It was a man's voice. A familiar voice.

Thomas looked at the corpse in the gabardine suit that lay sprawled near the door. He said, very softly, "How are you talking to me?"

"Don't act so surprised. You know I don't play by the rules." The tingle on the back of Thomas's neck grew stronger. "You need to hurry, son. If she tells them *everything*—well. That might just be the end."

Thomas closed his eyes. He told himself he should cover his ears.

"Haven't I been a friend to you before, Thomas? Haven't we done everything we needed to do to keep this place safe? To cull the chaff?" Jack Allen was smiling. Even without a face, Thomas could hear the man smiling. "It'll all start again tomorrow, right?"

"If she . . . if she hasn't ruined it already."

"Then tick-tock, Thomas. Tick-tock."

KYLA

Tabitha said, "There is a great point of contention between my brother and myself. Our father left us sorely uninformed. Back in 1955, he decided that this mountain—Mount Apache, for lack of a better name—was the mountain from which our ancestors had come. He wanted to hike it, explore, maybe do a few digs. He said it was the mountain he saw in his dreams, and Thomas and I believed him. The moment we arrived, we recognized it, all of us."

She went on. "Our first night here, at the motel, it was obvious the business was going under. The entrepreneur who'd built this place was almost shocked to see guests. He spent most of the night drinking at this very bar. Our father joined him at dinner. It was just the four of us, alone way out here in the desert." Tabitha stared at the gleam of the bar's wood, like she could still see the night reflected there. "And then, through that door, a man arrived. The man we called The Chief."

Ryan pushed his empty shot glass around, clearly debating another. Ethan rubbed his forehead, his migraine obvious. Kyla felt a twinge of sympathy: even after getting slammed into the office's desk, her own head had been clear and light ever since she'd awoken in her room.

Then she looked at the clock.

"I don't want to rush you, babe," she said. "But you really need to pick up the pace here."

Tabitha nodded. "We're nearly done. You've probably noticed by now the way coincidences multiply around the mountain. Here was ours: The Chief had been doing research of his own into the precursor tribe, trying to reconcile the stories he'd grown up hearing with the true history of his people. *Our* people. He'd been having terrible dreams of his own, and his journey had brought him here, to this motel, on the very same night as us."

Ryan said, "He was one of them, too, wasn't he? Another member of that precursor tribe."

"Yes. We'd thought we were the only ones left, but here was another."

"My Chief, the one in Huntsville, said the same thing." Ryan rubbed his swollen nose. "And then along came Sarah Powers."

"A cycle. A wheel. Its pull is . . . extraordinary."

Tabitha forced down a gulp of water.

"That night in '55, The Chief and our father quickly realized that they were both here for the same reason. And as luck would have it, the entrepreneur had something to tell them. He'd apparently purchased this land sight unseen, and there had been no mention of any existing structures in the deed of sale. When he arrived, however, he found the old house standing at the foot of the mountain that you still see today. The house had a strange effect on him. He said it felt as if it had always been here."

Kyla thought of the strange two-story Victorian that had lurked in the background of this place from the moment she arrived. Just remembering the house made her uneasy: even looking at it from the outside, everything about the place just felt *off*.

Jack Allen had been right, in the office last night: only an idiot would stick around if they found a mysterious house waiting for them on a plot of land that was meant to be empty.

Tabitha said, "The house made the entrepreneur uneasy. He hardly stepped inside it for the first several months he was here. But without much business to keep him occupied, the entrepreneur decided to finally take a proper inventory of the place. And then he found it."

The woman trailed off, almost like she was afraid of what she needed to say.

Ethan said, "He found a door, didn't he? A locked door."

"He did find a door, yes. But it wasn't locked at the time. Father did that later, Father and The Chief, because that door leads to a basement, and in that basement is something incredibly dangerous. Incredibly old."

"What, exactly?" Kyla was getting nervy, impatient. The wind outside was growing stronger.

"I don't know. Truly," Tabitha said. "Whatever it was, the entrepreneur agreed to show it to my father and The Chief that very night. My brother and I were told to wait here. Even then, I think The Chief and Father realized they were playing with fire. Whatever the entrepreneur showed them in that basement, it was enough to convince the men to pool their money and purchase this place together. Then and there."

Kyla said, "But they never intended to make a dime from this motel."

"That's right. All Father and The Chief did was hang a few missing shingles and replace a water tank that had been badly installed. They spent most of their time studying the thing in the basement, comparing it to an object The Chief had brought with him. It was a relic of his own, but again they kept it concealed from my brother and me. All I know is that it bore words—carved writing—and I think that with the help of my father's scholarship the two men were finally able to decode it. If I had to guess, The Chief's relic laid out the steps of the ceremony they needed to perform to keep the mountain—the thing in the mountain—sealed away."

The ground trembled, the air, as a new moan, the loudest yet, washed over them.

"Father and The Chief grew strange in the months after they bought the motel. Our dreams grew worse. We all knew that something terrible was coming, but Thomas and I had no idea what the men had planned. It clearly frightened them. It's like they didn't want to poison us with their knowledge. Finally, one morning, they told us everything was ready. They were to reopen the hotel that night."

Kyla said, "And everyone came."

"Yes. It defied belief, how quickly this lonely little place suddenly filled with people. Father and The Chief seemed . . . maybe not happy, but relieved."

"Frank's mother was one of those guests, wasn't she?" Fernanda said, glancing away from the film that had fascinated her all this time. "And Stanley's?"

"Yes. All the people I described earlier. The newlyweds, the hikers, the—"

An idea struck Kyla, another memory from last night.

Your grandfather was always kind to me.

"The Black guy who checked in, what was his name?" Kyla said.

Tabitha looked suddenly ashamed, faintly found out. "I forget."

"No, you don't. It was Hewitt, wasn't it?"

But before Tabitha could nod, Kyla again heard that whisper behind her ear that had haunted her since she arrived last night. She realized, now, why the voice was almost familiar.

It sounded almost—but not quite—like her father.

The voice whispered, just behind her ear. "Who else did you think it could be?"

ETHAN

Kyla shook her head. "My grandfather was an engineer for the power companies. He traveled all over the country working on dams and shit. I didn't find out until I was grown, but apparently, he committed suicide somewhere out here, coming back from a work project. Just wandered into the desert and never came back. Or at least that's what my dad told me. Are you telling me my grandfather checked into this place that night? That he got trapped here, the same as us?"

Tabitha said, "I am so sorry. Our father and The Chief were playing with a power I don't think either of them understood. There were . . . consequences."

Ethan said to Kyla, "Is that why you moved here? You were looking for answers into his disappearance?"

Kyla said nothing. She studied her hands, her face completely empty. Ethan would have guessed, in that way he sometimes could, that the girl might have initially come out here to west Texas in a very bad frame of mind. Might have even had a strange, morbid desire to follow in her grandfather's footsteps.

Or maybe he was imagining things. His head was throbbing. How was the pain getting worse with time, not better? He said to Tabitha, "So what exactly happened that night? After everyone checked in, what did your father do?"

"More importantly," Ryan said, "what do *we* need to do?"

"I don't know." A blast of wind shook the back of the cafe. Tabitha's nerve seemed to be failing her. "Father and The Chief kept us in the dark, right until the end. I served our guests dinner that night. Thomas poured drinks. We cleaned up. Father and The Chief gathered everyone together for a commemorative photograph, our grand reopening, and that was the last we saw of them. Father took Thomas and I to our room. He told us to bolt the door and not open it, whatever happened. Whatever we might hear outside. Father said that if all went well, we would wake up tomorrow, us and him and The Chief, like nothing was the matter. But then he gave us something strange. Two pieces of a silver material. Like metal, but softer. I know how odd this sounds, but he told us to swallow them. And when the silver touched our tongue, it dissolved like water."

"What was it?" Kyla said.

"I have no idea. He said that it was a precaution in case anything were to go wrong."

Outside, in the dark, a familiar sound came: one *SHRIEK*, three, a wave. Ryan said, "Those fuckers are getting restless."

"We heard them that night too," Tabitha said. "We call them the Guardians. They had never come out until that night. During all the months we spent preparing to reopen the motel, the desert was silent. The mountain—"

As if it heard its name, the mountain moaned.

"That night in '55, the mountain grew noisome too. The sounds outside were . . . awful. Thomas and I were terrified. We thought my father and The Chief had acted too late. That the seal had already broken. It sounded like the world was ending. But then, a little after four o'clock, between one moment and the next, things just . . . broke off. I don't know how else to explain it. We didn't remember falling asleep, but we woke up in our beds. It was morning. Everything was quiet. Normal. Except we were the only two people here."

"Nine empty rooms," Ethan said. "Twelve cold beds."

"I think that's how it looked from the outside, yes, back in '55. Thomas and I didn't know yet, but we'd awoken *today*. Now. In your time. We didn't know, that first morning, how many decades had passed while we were asleep. We found the motel just as we'd left it the day before, like it had been preserved in amber. Only a few things were different. We found a letter and a pair of stone eggs in the office. They were—they were the only real clue Father left us."

Tabitha faltered there at the end. Ethan knew, in an instant, there was something she'd chosen not to tell them. Seemingly trying to cover the slip, Tabitha reached into her pocket and pulled free the folded piece of paper she'd taken earlier from her room. She unfolded the paper and passed it to Ethan, who laid it out on the bar between Kyla and himself. The writing was sloppy, clearly done in a rush, and the pain in Ethan's head made deciphering it almost impossible.

Kyla did the honors. She read aloud,

" 'T and T. If you're reading this, the ceremony has failed. I'm sorry I didn't explain more—no time for it at this point. You two are now the stewards of this place. If we're lucky, someone will come today, someone who has been brought here to continue the ceremony, and you must help them in whatever way they ask. In the meantime, you must prepare this place. Clean out the rooms and the luggage. Use the gas we set aside to fuel up the cars left behind by last night's guests and drive them around the mountain, out of view. Be prepared. Things will probably be uglier for you than they were for us. That's entropy. But everything depends on you. Maybe life itself. Don't give anyone a chance to escape. Don't deviate from any instructions you are given. And if you awaken tomorrow and things are the same, then that means the ceremony has succeeded. Life is safe.' " The next part was underlined. " 'If that's happened, you must repeat everything you did the night before. Repeat every moment as perfectly as you can. You CANNOT risk letting it break.' "

Ryan said, "The person who came today to repeat the ceremony—that was Sarah Powers, wasn't it?"

Tabitha nodded. "Yes. Sarah came in the early afternoon, though she didn't tell us much either. I think she was terrified. We all were. All Sarah wanted was a dinner plate and a box of matches, and she asked that I bring her some food around eight o'clock. Then she went to the old house out back. She was there until five thirty, when Mister Cross and Hunter walked in from the road." Tabitha looked between Ethan and Kyla. "That first night, and all the nights that followed, you two never met, not really. In all the original nights, Miss Hewitt and Fernanda arrived in their Malibu and shut themselves up inside their room. Mister Cross and Hunter came much later and did the same. Everyone came running when I found the body and lost my head. Everyone came to the office, and Thomas and I—we made a rash decision."

Ryan said, "Y'all wanted to find out who killed her. You made up some bullshit story about having a place to hide when really you just wanted revenge. Or at least some sort of satisfaction."

Of all things, Tabitha smiled. It was clearly a relief, after God knew how long, to come clean.

"Yes. In many ways, it was Thomas's idea. He was indignant.

A crime had been committed on our land. I was just frightened. I thought that with Sarah dead, the ceremony would never take place. I thought we'd failed. That none of it mattered because the world would end that night. So Thomas decided we should get revenge, like you say. He wanted to torment the killer. Scare them. We invented the ultimatum about having a place of safety, for all the good it did us. That first night and the nights that followed, nothing seemed to change. You all did the rational thing and barricaded yourselves in your rooms." Tabitha hesitated. "For all the good it did *you*."

Kyla said, "Jack Allen came that night, didn't he? At midnight on the dot?"

"Yes. Originally, I think Thomas came up with the idea of making midnight the ultimatum's deadline out of a . . . a dramatic flourish. Something to unsettle you all. Unnerve you. We had no idea that Jack Allen would come that night. We had no idea *how* he could have come, seeing as we'd left him in 1955. And even though he hadn't aged more than a day in the intervening years, something had happened to him. He was different. He'd gone mad."

"And he killed everyone when he got here," Kyla said. "Just like he did last night."

"I'm not sure." Tabitha swallowed. "Thomas and I were the first to go."

The light flickered over their heads again. Once more, at the edge of his vision, Ethan imagined he saw the shape of a man watching him from the cafe's window.

He refused to look.

Kyla said, "But why? What does Jack Allen gain from killing all of us?"

"I don't know. Truly. Just like I don't know how he went from 1955 to now without aging a day. But he's come every night since, at midnight on the dot. And just like us, he's done the same thing over and over and over again."

"Because of this letter from your dad," Kyla said. "Even though it means you and your brother had to die every night, you've repeated everything as precisely as you can."

"Yes. *Something* about it clearly worked. We awoke the next day and found the motel just the same. And so we did it again. And again.

And again." Tabitha swallowed as another moan shook the cafe. "We went rather out of our heads for a while there, I think. Even with all the blood, it seemed like the right course of action. Look at what Father wrote at the bottom of the page."

Ethan and Kyla scanned the letter again. There, written in a cramped hand near the bottom corner, was a short line, written even faster than the rest.

Kyla read it aloud, " 'Remember: death sustains it.' "

Ethan went very still. Ryan rose from his stool, anxious like a schoolboy stuck too long at a desk. He said, "The fuck is that supposed to mean?"

"That line is the great point of contention between my brother and myself. Thomas believes 'it' refers to ceremony. He thinks that the death—all of this death, from Sarah to us, and yourselves—he believes it necessary to sustain the ceremony. Thomas thinks that Sarah Powers isn't the person Father referred to in his letter, the person who will come to continue the ceremony. Thomas thinks the person responsible for continuing the loop, perpetuating the ceremony—he thinks Father was referring to Jack Allen himself."

"But that's crazy," Kyla said.

"Is it?" Tabitha said. "*Something* clearly worked that first night. And whatever our disagreements, Thomas and I do concur on one point: this cycle, this horrible night that repeats again and again, is serving to keep Te'lo'hi sealed away."

"So where's the contention?" Ethan said.

" 'Death sustains it.' I don't believe Father's last line is an instruction. I think it's a warning." Tabitha looked at the letter herself. "These last few nights, I've come to fear that 'it' refers not to the ceremony, but to Te'lo'hi. I don't think Jack Allen is a component of the ceremony: I think he's a scourge. A danger. He seems to have devices of his own, and he's clearly insane. I fear that death—all of this death, this endless violence—might be somehow *feeding* Te'lo'hi, night after night. And I think it's working. The ceremony is breaking down. Te'lo'hi is gaining the power to resist it."

"Like the crack in our bathroom's mirror," Kyla said.

"Yes. And the sheer fact that you've remembered last night— that's never happened before. I'm afraid Te'lo'hi is growing stronger with every night of slaughter. And the longer we let the cycle of carnage repeat, it will simply *continue* to grow stronger until it's able to break the ceremony entirely."

"So we need to figure out a way to stop the violence," Kyla said.

Ethan stared at the wall of liquor behind Tabitha, not seeing it. He felt something stir at the bottom of his mind. He saw a flash of silver light. For a moment, the pain in his head abated.

He recalled—

he recalls the feeling of a wooden floor beneath his knees. Recalls the sensation of a sleeve against the back of his neck. He recalls that man, Jack Allen, staring with him at the thing concealed under the sheet.

He recalls Jack Allen saying,

Everything proceeds from her death. Like a river from a wound in the earth.

Ethan said, "I think I remember something from last night. Something Jack Allen told me before the end."

As Ethan spoke, Fernanda reached down the counter, past Kyla and Ethan, to pluck up Ryan's empty shot glass. No one paid her much mind.

"I don't know what the ceremony is or how it works. But Sarah Powers is still the key. Her death is the source of everything."

"Meaning what?" Ryan said.

"Meaning that maybe the twins were onto something in the first place when they made their BS ultimatum. If we could figure out who killed Sarah, maybe we could stop the ceremony from starting in the first place. I—what's wrong?"

Fernanda had stiffened. Ethan turned and saw that she was staring at the film in her hand through the bottom of the shot glass. When he leaned over to see what it was she'd found there, Fernanda lowered her hands. She stood, stuffing the film in her pocket. To Kyla, she said, "Where is the other roll of film? The one stolen from Sarah's room?"

"Ask him," Kyla said, nodding to Ryan. "What's the matter?"

"We might have time to develop it if we're quick. I need to see what Sarah saw."

Ryan clearly had his own misgivings. "That roll of film is in the supply closet. I'll go with you. Stanley's in there too—I don't want him trying anything funny. Just . . . don't get your hopes up."

Ethan said, "What's that supposed to mean?"

"I'll explain later. I need to check on Stanley anyway. He's a crafty bastard—I didn't mean to leave him alone for this long."

The lights of the cafe stuttered, briefly threatening to go down. They survived, but the warning was obvious.

Ethan said, "Be careful. We don't know how long the generator will last."

Ryan plucked up Stanley's Desert Eagle. He checked the magazine, motioned for Fernanda, started for the door. "We'll be right back."

Kyla shook her head. "We'll be fine here. Take the film straight to Sarah's room—there's chemicals in her bathtub, you can use them to develop the negatives. Just hurry."

Fernanda said nothing. She picked up the other handgun and stuffed it down the waistband of her jeans. She had her head down, her hands in her pockets, the amber thread of film jutting from near her wrist.

Ethan said to Tabitha. "Didn't you say that the first night, the night in '55, ended a little after four o'clock?"

"Yes."

He looked at his watch, the clock above the bar. The time was already 2:37.

STANLEY

"Wake up, Stanley."

"Wake up."

"Wake *up*!"

Stanley felt an eerie tingle on the back of his neck, like the creeping of a frozen insect. It woke him, though he hadn't realized he'd dozed off. The supply room was bitter cold. His arms ached from being tied to this wooden fucking chair and his feet were numb, and had they all forgotten about him? Abandoned Stanley to *freeze* to death? They would regret that. They would regret that very fucking hard. Stanley knew things about the people here—about the boy who'd stolen his brother's name, about the waitress who thought she was being so clever, about Fernanda and Ryan and all these fucking people—Stanley knew things they wouldn't *begin* to understand. He'd studied them. He and Sarah had spent the last weeks learning everything there was to know about them.

And this was how it turned out?

Sarah Powers had first wandered into Stockton Steaks on a night like any other night. She was tall, beautiful, an angel in thigh-high boots. That first night she'd arrived, Sarah had walked straight up to Frank's table and sat down without being invited and looked between Frank and Stanley and said simply, "I can help y'all find your mothers."

And look what that had come to.

"Stanley, you're embarrassing yourself."

The voice came from over his shoulder: a man's voice, vaguely familiar, whispering in Stanley's ear. The voice brought with it another itch on the back of his neck, that cold creeping of insect feet, long nails, sharp fingers. Stanley shuddered against the ropes that held him—why had Ryan Fucking Phan just *left* him like this?—and he turned his head, following the voice.

There was no one back there.

"Don't waste time, Stanley," the voice whispered in his other ear now, and Stanley realized where he'd heard it before.

A moment ago, Stanley had thought the supply room was cold. He thought he'd known what cold was. He thought he'd known fear.

Ha. Ha. Ha.

Earlier tonight, Fernanda had come barging through the door of Stanley's room with a gun and a pissy attitude and awoken Stanley from a deep slumber. She'd laid out in very clear terms that she was running away from Frank, she was getting her revenge on Frank, and by God if Stanley wanted to keep clear of trouble, then he wouldn't try to stop her.

I have photographs that implicate you in many crimes, Fernanda had said. *If you want those photos to disappear, then you will stay out of my way.*

Stanley had been too tired after his trip to Mexico City to give much of a shit. He'd nodded along to Fernanda's terms, hardly bothering to listen. Frank was due to arrive at some point this evening. Sarah Powers had already made sure of that. Sarah had called both Frank and Stanley this morning and said simply, *It's time.*

Fernanda could have all the pictures she'd like; it wasn't as if Frank wouldn't get them right back the minute he arrived.

But when all this was over, Stanley and his old buddy Frank would need to have a nice hard talk about the way Frank had sampled the wares. Stan had warned Frank, time and time again, that the man was a fool to keep Fernanda at his house like some goddamn princess under ransom. Fernanda was smart—dangerous smart—with a retard brother in Mexico she thought Stanley and Frank didn't know about. Women like Fernanda lose their heads over brothers like that. She was bound to try a stunt like this.

All Stanley had said to Fernanda tonight, however, was, "You didn't kill Frank on your way out of Stockton, did you?"

"No. We killed Lance."

That had made Stanley arch an eyebrow. "Lance got in your way? Kyla Hewitt's boyfriend? I thought y'all were going to the cartel."

Fernanda had hesitated. "We are."

"And Lance tried to stop you? I was starting to think he was working for *them* more than he was working for—"

Fernanda's face had gone dark. Was it fear there, or anger, or shame?

The result was the same. She'd hit him—*hit him*—with the butt of her fucking gun. Busted Stanley's lip wide open. She'd stood over him, panting, as Stanley dabbed blood from his chin.

He'd looked up. He'd seen tears in her eyes.

"He was trying to help you, wasn't he?" Stanley said. "Lance was trying to help and you made a bad, bad call."

Stanley had thought Fernanda would hit him again. She turned on her heel and left without a word.

He hadn't given this much thought. It wouldn't matter, would it, when Frank came? Stanley hadn't realized until that moment that Penelope wasn't there, in the room's other bed, and he told himself he should be more worried about this. Even after all he'd done to get Penelope back from that reprobate Ryan Fucking Phan, in all honesty Stanley couldn't actually stand being around his granddaughter.

Even if the girl didn't have the attitude of a colt (and the same tendency to bolt), the guilt Stanley felt every time he saw the scar on her forehead would have defeated ten better men than him.

But then, back in his room earlier this evening, as he rubbed his busted lip and glanced over his shoulder at Penelope's empty bed, his eye had settled on the mirror inside his wardrobe's open door. His heart had plummeted into his stomach. His mind had briefly shut down.

In the reflection of the glass, Stanley had seen a man—*imagined* he'd seen a man—standing behind him at the side of the bed. A man in a gray gabardine suit.

"Stanley."

That voice—that man—was whispering in his ear. Here in the supply room. Here in the cold. "I just want to give you a warning."

"You're not real," Stanley's anxious voice echoed off the concrete floor, the concrete cladding of his mind.

"I don't really *need* to warn you, of course, but it seemed like the polite thing to do."

"You're not real! I imagined you! She'd hit me in the head!"

"*Imagined* me?" The man whispering in his ear—the *imaginary* man, the man who couldn't really be here, who couldn't fucking *be here*—sounded almost hurt. "But Stanley, I warned you all of this was going to happen, didn't I? Earlier tonight, back in your room, I warned you that Sarah was already dead."

No. No. Stanley didn't want to remember. He didn't like being scared.

Stanley didn't behave well when he was scared.

"Fine, Stanley. Have it your way. Pretend that *wasn't* me you saw in your wardrobe's mirror. Me in my best suit. Me with my hand on your shoulder. Me whispering into your ear. Pretend I was lying when I said Sarah Powers was a fool meddling with forces she didn't understand. Pretend I was lying when I said that *I* knew your mother, that *I* could bring you to see her again."

It was no good. Remember or not, Stanley was very, very afraid. He screwed his eyes shut. He thrashed in the chair, desperate to escape this creeping, insinuating *voice* crawling into his ears into his skull into his *mind*.

"Pretend you didn't glance over your shoulder when Fernanda left your room. Pretend you didn't see me there, Stanley. Waiting for you. Smiling in your mirror, so keen to speak with you at last."

"Go away. Go *away*."

"Was I so terrifying, Stanley? You haven't even seen me in my splendor. You haven't seen what this place can *do* to a man."

That creeping sensation on the back of Stanley's neck had climbed to his scalp. It had become colder, sharper. It started to prickle along the flesh of his head. It started to *scrape*.

"What are you doing to me?" Stanley said, pulling at the ropes with all his strength. "That hurts. That hurts!"

"It won't for long."

"Stop! *Stop!*"

"I really don't need your permission, Stanley. Maybe if you'd listened to me before dinner we wouldn't be in this situation."

"You told me . . ." Stanley didn't want to remember what the man in the gray suit had told him, back in his room, back before dinner. He didn't want to remember, but as the scraping sensation along the back of his head grew stronger, he found he couldn't think of anything else.

"You told me . . . to kill everyone." Stanley could barely bring himself to say it. "You told me to kill *Penelope*."

"Because she's always hidden herself by the time I arrive. Something *keeps* me from finding her. If you'd killed her when you had the chance, you wouldn't be in this chair. You wouldn't feel what's about to happen."

"What are you doing? *What are you doing?*"

"What am I doing?" Stanley heard a smile in the voice. "This."

That awful burning cold: it pierced Stanley's skin. It pierced Stanley's skull. The sensation was so horrible and strange all he could do, all Stanley could do, was moan.

He found he couldn't move his lips. He moaned again, the sound leaking out of him, bringing with it a ribbon of drool that eased down his chin and piddled in his lap. He twitched, like a fish on a dock. He mumbled, "Hurts. Hurts."

And Stanley felt fingers—long, sharp fingers—burrow into the deepest recess of his brain. Felt them close around his mind. Felt them squeeze.

Whatever essence made up Stanley Holiday, whatever calcified detritus formed his soul: it broke in that moment. Broke and flowed away, like splinters of shattered ice dissolving into water. When the door of the supply room opened a few minutes later and a friend stepped inside, it wasn't Stanley they found lashed to that chair. Not really.

Stanley's eyes opened, but another man gazed out.

"Did you bring it?"

The new arrival shivered in the cold, shivered at what he saw before him. He was clearly terrified. Ashamed.

But resolved. He knew what was at stake, even if he was too stupid to realize its consequences.

The new arrival stepped into the supply closet, carrying with him the knife he'd thrown under the porch earlier in the evening, when he'd cut the Odyssey's tires. Most nights, Jack Allen retrieved this blade himself after kicking off the fun in the office, but tonight—tonight was a new story.

At last.

The arrival cuts Stanley's ropes. Blood flowed into the feet and hands. The new arrival passed over another item, this one stolen from the junk in Sarah Powers's room: a grooved stone egg.

"Well done, Thomas," Stanley said, though of course he was Stanley no longer. He pocketed the egg, took the knife.

Not-Stanley said, "Now go finish the job."

FERNANDA

Fernanda had learned to tell stories from her grandmother. The little boy who found a city in his trunk. The coyote who tricked the eagle to carry him to the moon. The ocean princess who came to land looking for friends. Again and again and again, one story following the next from her grandmother's lips with grace and endless style: *there* was the real master.

The trick? Her grandmother actually *believed* the stories, or believed pieces of them, or maybe just believed the stories as she told them. Her grandmother believed in a lot. Spirits and wards, crosses and smoke. She never passed a cemetery without blessing herself and pressing a hand over her navel. She never came home from a long trip without saging her house.

She never approved of her son, Fernanda's father, growing wealthy on camera stores. Never approved of Fernanda's interest in photography, for that matter. "Cameras and mirrors—you have to be careful with both," the old woman said. "They catch pieces of the soul."

Fernanda had always written this off as superstition. She was a rational woman. Well traveled. An economics major.

But as Tabitha told her story about the way this motel had apparently become stuck in time, Fernanda found herself thinking of her grandmother. Realized, almost to her surprise, that she wasn't at all incredulous of what this could mean. It felt like the sort of story her grandmother would tell, one of the wilder ones. *Have you heard the story about the travelers who became trapped in the desert to seal away a god?*

Fernanda wouldn't say she exactly believed *everything* Tabitha was telling them, but she *did* believe her eyes. She'd spent ages studying the film Ryan Phan had brought from Sarah's room, the amber roll with its last six shots sliced away. In each of the surviving frames, Fernanda had found a single dark gray smudge.

Ryan had called the smudges defects in the film, but that didn't seem right to Fernanda. If the smudges were a flaw in the film, they would appear in the same position within each frame, but no. They moved from shot to shot: left side, right side, upper corner, lower edge. The smudges grew and shrank, almost seemed to blur or sharpen, like an object obscured by distance or lack of focus.

For reasons she couldn't quite explain, Fernanda had found herself fascinated by these little black smudges. Finally, she'd had the idea to use Ryan's shot glass as a magnifier, like a jeweler's loupe. She'd tipped up the shot glass, allowing a last thread of whiskey to drain free, and held it to the light with one hand. She'd threaded the film between the finger and thumb of her other hand and brought it, too, to the light. She'd peered at the film through the thick glass.

It worked.

The first shot Fernanda studied was a photograph of the wooden house behind the motel. The photograph grew large under magnification, and clear enough to make out the shape of the house's porch, its door, the bottom frame of an upstairs window.

And there, on the porch, was one of those strange smudges. Fernanda brought the film closer to the glass. She squinted.

Magnified, the dark smudge took on the shape of a man. A tall man. He wore a suit and a hat and a smile. Yes, even with his face blurred, his expression shaded, Fernanda could see a wide, wide smile on the man's face.

That smile was *wrong*. It was too wide. Too tight. Even in the quiet cafe, even as Tabitha talked, Fernanda had imagined she could hear the smile's teeth grinding together like stones.

This man in the suit: he was the dark smudge in every photograph.

Here he was at the end of the long front porch. Here he was in a photograph of what looked like Sarah's room in the motel, standing near the dresser. The last frame on the film was a photograph of the motel and its parking lot, shot from behind and at some elevation and there, in the parking lot, the man was staring up at the camera— up at Sarah—with a tight, tight smile and a hand raised in greeting.

Fernanda didn't understand how it could be possible, but she knew where she'd seen that man before. He had stepped into the motel's office at midnight this evening, scaring the absolute hell out of everyone, and eaten a mouthful of buckshot from the shotgun Kyla had brought with her from Ethan's room.

But these pictures had been taken *before* the man's arrival tonight, hadn't they? Of course they had. Because look, here in the left edge of the last photograph, at the shot of the motel taken from behind and above: there, that sliver of a car's hood on the road, about to make the turn into the parking lot. It was the Malibu.

Sarah Powers had taken their photograph, had snapped Fernanda and Kyla as they arrived a little after four o'clock this afternoon.

And the man in the gabardine suit had already been here, smiling and waving to anyone who could see.

Cameras and mirrors.

They catch pieces of the soul.

Fernanda had gone stiff then. Ethan had finally noticed her tension, turned to see what about the film had so fascinated her. Fernanda had lowered the glass, risen, and stuffed the film in her pocket before he could get the chance.

She said to Kyla, "Where is the other roll of film? The one stolen from Sarah's room?"

Fernanda needed to see that film. Develop it. She felt a sudden sick fascination with what she'd just discovered. It frightened her in a way that was hard to describe.

She needed to know how the gabardine man could do this. How he could be in every frame of this motel. It felt important, somehow. Vital.

Ryan Phan, too, seemed restless. He rose and grabbed a gun, which made Fernanda figure she should take one for herself. She tucked the Glock down the back of her jeans and stuffed her hands in her pockets, burying the film further. She did not want to frighten the others with this information yet. She wanted to see *all* the photographs Sarah had taken, get the full picture of what was happening. Pardon the pun.

Ethan said to Tabitha. "Didn't you say that the first night, the night in '55, ended a little after four o'clock?"

"Yes."

Fernanda looked at the time. It was 2:37.

Ryan led the way outside. The cold was a shock after so long in the cafe. Ryan jumped like he'd just been kicked. "Jesus," he said, then looked at her funny. "You all right?"

"I will survive."

They started down the porch. Fernanda realized, as she walked, just how tired she was. Her feet were heavy, her mind getting slow. She'd lived too much for one day. She'd awoken before dawn to snap photographs of Frank's office. She'd been caught. She'd been chained to a pipe in the operation's safe house by noon. Kyla's boyfriend, Lance, one of Frank's better thugs, had arrived at two o'clock. He had been sent to kill her because Frank did not have the stomach for it.

But Lance had had other ideas. Maybe. Or maybe he had just been trying to calm Fernanda down so she would not struggle.

Fernanda had wondered about this all day. Because Lance hadn't called her a fool, or threatened her, or gone silently about his work. He had said, *It's all right. I'm getting you out of here.*

If Fernanda had remembered the rest of the story, she would have stopped, right here, and collapsed under the guilt. She did not have time for guilt. Fernanda was going to survive this night. She was going across the border. She was going home to her brother.

The lamps sputtered momentarily, freezing Fernanda and Ryan to their places. Outside, the creatures of the desert let out a *SHRIEK*.

When the lights recovered, Ryan seemed to make up his mind. "Hey, about this film we're going to get—you . . . well, you already know what's on it."

But Fernanda hardly heard him. A strange sensation had stirred in her pocket. Earlier, in the office, she had plucked an object from the mantel of the fireplace: a grooved piece of stone, the size and shape of an egg. As the night got busy and their little party had left the office with Tabitha, Fernanda had placed the stone into her jacket, hardly giving it a thought.

But now—now she withdrew the stone. She held it beneath one of the porch's lights. She stared.

The stone was trembling, very faintly. The tremor in the rock was rhythmic, almost like the pulse of a heart.

"Is it me," she said, "or is this stone shaking?"

Ryan held out a hand. "May I?"

The sensation of the stone unnerved her. She was almost relieved to get rid of it. Relieved, too, when Ryan clearly felt the same thing she had. At least Fernanda was not losing her mind.

Ryan said, "What in the hell?"

He walked more slowly now, his attention riveted on the stone egg. He swung open a door under the motel's covered walkway. Over Ryan's shoulder, Fernanda saw your average storage room. Concrete floors. Metal shelves along the walls.

A bare bulb dangled from the ceiling, beneath which stood an empty chair.

An empty chair.

Ryan's mind was clearly on the stone egg. Fernanda's mind had returned to the dark smudges on Sarah's film. Neither of them registered danger until a moment too late.

Fernanda felt a thump in her back, like a heavy punch. She staggered forward, into Ryan, who stumbled himself and nearly dropped the egg. Fernanda felt a hand grab the collar of her jacket, holding her in place, while another hand reached into the waistband of her jeans and pulled free the gun she'd stuffed there.

Things were moving too fast. Her mind couldn't keep up. Pain was radiating from the punch in her back, and when she tried to turn, she stumbled again, striking the wall, and agony spread through her. She didn't realize she was screaming.

She realized that something was jutting from her back, right between her shoulder blades. Something long and sharp, buried to the hilt.

A knife.

She turned enough to see that Stan Holiday was behind her, but it wasn't Stanley. Not really. The lights of the porch sputtered again, nearly went out, and when they struggled back up Fernanda saw another man's face over Stanley's. Superimposed. Like two men occupying the same space in a shot.

The other man, the superimposed man, was the same man she'd seen in each of Sarah's photographs. He smiled at her now, as he had in Sarah's film. He opened his mouth to speak.

Whatever she might have expected him to say, it wasn't this.

"I know you think you've hidden him away, but Frank's operation is well aware of your brother. There are men watching his house right now. Miguel will be dead the minute you cross the border."

Fernanda hardly had time to register the horror. Stanley—the gabardine man—raised the gun in his hand. A loose, lazy gesture, almost an afterthought.

The flash of the muzzle blinded her.

Funny, the thing that crossed her mind then. She didn't think of her brother, or of Kyla's boyfriend Lance saying, *I work for the cartel. You're safe*. She didn't think of Kyla.

She thought of herself. Fernanda saw herself as a girl, sitting on her grandmother's lap, asking, "Where did you learn all these stories?"

"El otro mundo." *The other world*. "It's like our world, but better."

The afterlife, hell, the depths of space? Fernanda's young mind boggled. "Then how did you hear them?"

"I got them from my little sister. She and her friend went to hike a mountain and never came back. A tall, tall mountain with a city inside it."

Fernanda thought this was just another story. Maybe part of it was. Maybe none of it.

"My sister still sends me postcards with all the stories she hears over there," her grandmother said. "Postales del otro mundo."

Here, on the porch of the Brake Inn Motel, Fernanda didn't hear the gunshot. She heard a wet spatter that she realized was the back of her head bursting across the wall.

Then nothing.

ETHAN

Minutes before the gunshot, Ethan and Kyla were still seated at the bar, trying to devise a plan. "You said that Sarah Powers spent time today at the old house out back, right?" he said.

Tabitha nodded. "It's where she was when you first arrived."

Ethan said to Kyla, "If we want to figure out what happened to Sarah, that seems like the best place to start."

Outside, the lamps sputtered. A wave of *SHRIEKS* from the dark. Those things out there refused to be forgotten.

Kyla leaned to look out the window, peering in the direction of the old house. Following her gaze, Ethan saw a familiar sight: the upstairs window was glowing with a silver light.

Kyla said, "There's a lot of dark between here and there. I don't think we'd make it five steps. I want to see what's on that film Ryan stole from Sarah's room. Maybe if we're lucky, the woman took pictures of whatever she found in that house, and we won't even have to go there."

Ethan hesitated, massaging the pain in his head. With every minute that passed the pain grew worse, worse: but not absolute. Here and there, fragments—images, sounds, words—had begun to shoot through his mind, fast as stars, and while they traveled, the headache seemed to leave him.

It happened again now. He felt a moment of pure adrenaline, saw himself running

running through the dark, running for the house, running through the night.

He sees himself heave open the house's door.

He turns, expecting to see Hunter right behind him and seeing only

Ethan blinked. The memory left, the pain flooded back in, but he knew what he'd seen. He wasn't stupid. He was seeing a fragment from yesterday.

"Last night, I think we made it to the house," he said. "At least . . . I made it. There *is* a way to do it."

"And that is?"

"I—" Ethan pressed his fingers to his temples, willing his mind to go back. He felt like this was vital, desperately important.

But it wouldn't come.

Kyla turned her attention back to Tabitha. "How do you and Thomas remember this every day? Why don't *you* lose your memories like we did?"

"I suspect it has something to do with the strange metal our father gave us in 1955. But I don't know why you've regained yours."

Ethan saw something else:

the office in the dark, midnight approaching, Tabitha says, "You still haven't figured out the purpose of the

"The eggs," Ethan said, feeling the weight in his pocket. "What's the point of the grooved stone eggs?"

"I'm not sure. I have a theory—"

A sound reached them from the back of the cafe: a faint *ding* of metal. It came from the kitchen. Ethan barely heard it, but Tabitha straightened up.

"Give me a moment."

She disappeared around the corner of the cafe's hall. The hall stood open to Ethan's left, just past the end of the bar, though he was too distracted to think much of it. He pulled the stone egg from his pocket, studying it in the light. One half of the egg was still a dull red from where it had sat in the lake of blood on the office's floor.

Ethan swallowed. He rubbed his thumb along a red groove, felt a little of it flake off onto the skin. This was Hunter's blood.

Kyla took out the egg that she, too, had taken from the office. She said, "Jack Allen had this in his pocket. Remember?"

"I know. I feel like I've seen another one—"

A scream tore through the night. It was a sound of pure pain, pure fear. It came from the direction of the supply room.

Kyla was on her feet. "That's Fernanda."

Ethan rose as well, hesitating when he realized something strange. The egg in his hand: it was trembling.

He'd felt a tremble like this before.

No time to remember where, however. No time for anything.

The lights sputtered, died down to almost nothing. The Guardians of the mountain seemed overjoyed at the sight. They *SHRIEKED*. And as Kyla reached for the shotgun on the bar, another scream came, this one from very close by.

It was Tabitha.

"Stop!" the woman screamed. "STOP!"

Ethan smelled gas.

They didn't hear the first explosion. Ethan remembered the kitchen they'd passed through earlier on the way inside. He remembered the long stretch of gas cooking ranges. It wasn't hard to guess what was happening. What was coming next.

He grabbed Kyla by the arm and wrenched her backward, out of the path of the hallway's mouth. A moment later there was a great rush of heat.

Fire flowed down the hall. It swept over the bar, engulfing the wood in flame, and Ethan kept pulling Kyla back, back, back. The boom of the gas ranges deafened them for a moment. All Ethan could hear was a high, high whine.

As they backed themselves against the wall of the cafe, his hearing returned in time to hear another explosion, much more powerful than the first. The force of it tossed Ethan and Kyla off their feet. For a moment, Ethan thought it was the mountain—the thing in the mountain—bursting free.

And then the lights died, and he realized it was the generator that had exploded.

Ethan and Kyla landed, hard, on their backs. He saw something white rolling away under one of the booths: the egg that had been in Kyla's hand. He heard pops outside, gunfire, men screaming, and then more pops closer by; the guns on the cafe's flaming bar had just exploded. A chunk of metal whizzed past Ethan's head, missing it by an inch.

Darkness swept over the motel. The flames in the cafe did little to stop it.

Glass shattered behind the bar as the wall of liquor exploded. Kyla screamed. In the firelight, Ethan saw blood running down the back of her arm where she'd lifted it to cover her face.

Tabitha, too, was screaming. The woman crawled into the cafe from the mouth of the burning hall. She was on fire. She was a wailing ember. It was in her hair, in her skin, in her eyes.

"Thomas," she said. "He . . . Thomas . . . he—"

The fire crept into her mouth. She stopped moving. She stopped everything.

The shock of this hadn't even settled before a new sound, worse than all the others, burst over them.

The cafe's front window shattered as something very large and very dark barreled its way inside. It seemed undaunted by the flames. It turned, lit by the fire, and Ethan remembered last night, remembered

the things that encircle him and Hunter outside the old house. They stand on two long legs like a man. They have two long arms, with claws that end in bright black talons. Their limbs and chests are blanketed with black feathers, the same feathers that coat the enormous pair of wings sprouting from their backs. The things

"Oh my god," Kyla said. Here in the cafe, she tried to crawl backward, tried to get away, but there was nowhere left to go.

The thing in the cafe studied them in the firelight. The Guardian of the mountain. Where its head should be, Ethan and Kyla saw scales and a long curving neck and the head of a great black serpent. Yellow eyes. White fangs.

It raised its wings wide. It opened its mouth. It *SHRIEKED*.

And it rushed their way.

ENDGAME REDUX

ETHAN

2:45 a.m.

Should he be afraid? He was about to die, it was going to hurt for a second—hurt pretty bad if he had to guess—but then he was going to wake up tomorrow, same as ever, wasn't he? He wouldn't remember tonight. Wouldn't remember all that he'd learned.

Wouldn't be any closer to getting free of this place. But he'd be alive. Right?

The creature from the desert moved faster than anything on two legs should be able to move. The feathers of its wings hissed through the air. And as it came nearer, Ethan felt an unfamiliar emotion rising in his chest. It wasn't fear.

It was rage.

Twenty-four years he'd been trapped in a shithole town, chained to a dying car shop. Twenty-four years he'd been beholden to a mother with brilliant technical skills and no business sense, always in the shadow of a useless brother who seemed determined to break all their hearts. Twenty-four years and Ethan had finally gotten a break, a chance to escape.

Twenty-four years, and *this* is what it came to? Being trapped, yet again, in a hell of someone else's making?

Ethan did something he'd never done before.

He opened his mouth. He screamed at the creature bearing down on him. He screamed in absolute, impotent fury.

And then the thing stopped.

The Guardian loomed above Ethan and Kyla, mere feet away, but it didn't move any closer. Ethan's first thought was that he'd startled the thing into submission, maybe stopped time itself with the sheer force of his anger. Hardly. The Guardian blinked, regarded him impassively. Its feathered chest rose and fell. Its scaly head bobbed, softly, on its serpentine neck.

The creature let out a low hiss. It almost sounded like a question.

Ethan became aware of a pulse in his hand. He opened the fingers of his clenched fist and revealed the grooved stone egg he'd taken from his pocket a moment ago. The egg was trembling on his palm.

The Guardian peered at the stone and gave a soft bob of the head. It seemed satisfied.

Kyla realized what this meant. She didn't waste time. She scrambled sideways, reaching under a nearby booth to pluck up the egg she'd dropped when they'd fallen to the floor. She thrust the stone in the creature's direction, panting hard, and after a moment's regard, the Guardian took a step back. Another. It closed its talons. It turned its scaly head to study the fire rapidly approaching them from the kitchen.

The creature held out one arm and one wing in the direction of the cafe's broken window. It didn't move, even as the fire crept closer.

Ethan rose to his feet, knees shaking with surplus adrenaline. He helped Kyla stand. Smoke was filling the room, choking them both, doing *wonders* for his headache. His heart hammered. The human body wasn't designed to stand this close to a creature this terrifying. He didn't have the fortitude to look at it for more than a second at a time. He said to Kyla, "I think it's waiting for us to leave."

Kyla looked at the grooved stone still trembling in her hand. "I guess we figured out what these are for."

Outside, a man screamed. The Guardian remained motionless as Ethan and Kyla picked their way through the cafe's shattered window and out onto the porch. Ryan Phan was on the porch, pounding their way, a pair of Guardians *SHRIEKING* on his heels.

Ryan held a gun in one hand. In the other, Ethan saw something pale and white.

"The stone!" Ethan shouted. "Show them the stone!"

Ryan looked at him, clearly bewildered by the instruction, and his foot caught a loose board in the porch. He fell to his knees with a shout. He tried to tumble away from the approaching creatures— but they were on him already. There was no escape.

Except they hesitated, inches from his body. When Ryan rolled onto his back, he was holding up the egg.

With a low hiss, the Guardians registered this. They nodded. They stepped away.

Ryan looked at the egg, at the creatures, at Ethan. "What in the fuck?"

"Fernanda," Kyla said. "Where is she?"

Ryan's face fell.

With a grunt of pain, he rose to his feet. There was something wrong with his shoulder. In the moonlight, Ethan saw the black leather of his jacket was wet.

Ryan was bleeding, badly.

"Something happened, didn't it?" Ethan said.

Ryan let out a slow breath. "Follow me."

The Guardians stepped out of their way as Ethan and Kyla followed Ryan down the porch. He led them to the covered walkway, where two corpses waited for them. Fernanda was slumped against the wall near the supply room's door, a long streak of blood and hair spread along the wall above her. She had fallen forward enough for Ethan to see the hilt of a knife sticking from her back.

Fernanda's eyes were wide with sadness. Fear.

Stanley Holiday was across the porch from her, sprawled on his back through room 3's open side door. Two red craters had opened in the man's chest. Fernanda's gun was in his hand.

"I'm sorry," Ryan said to Kyla. Nodding to Fernanda and the wound to his own shoulder, he said, "Stanley got loose somehow. He got the jump on us."

Ethan said, "Thomas, probably. It sounds like he blew up the kitchen and the generator while he was at it. Tabitha was right—he's scared of changing *anything*."

"It may not have been entirely his idea," Ryan said. "I swear, for a second when I turned around, it wasn't like I saw Stanley standing here, but that other guy. The weird fucker who showed up at midnight."

"Jack Allen," Kyla said. She took a deep breath, and Ethan could hear the tears in it. She crouched down near Fernanda, shut the woman's eyes. "I thought I could save her tonight."

"There's always tomorrow, yeah?" Ryan said.

"Hopefully. Unless Thomas is right, and we've already ruined the ceremony."

Behind them, the mountain moaned and shook the earth. Ryan shivered. "In that case, there won't be a tomorrow for anybody, right? Sort of consoling."

Kyla stood, shaking her head. She looked at Stanley's corpse, bent down to take the gun from his hand. "I still don't get it. I don't get why Jack Allen is so set on killing all of us. He said last night that we were standing in his way. But standing in the way of *what*?"

Ryan said, "He's just fucking crazy. He got stuck here back in the fifties, right? That'll break anyone. I saw it all the time in Huntsville: keep a man trapped for long enough and they'll lose themselves in a hurry."

"It feels more complicated than that," Ethan said. He saw another flash of a memory,

feels himself on the floor of the old house. Hears Jack Allen say,

"I will be granted audience once more."

Ethan rubbed his head. The memory was gone, but he knew what it meant. "Kyla's right. Jack Allen's got some kind of agenda. He's getting something by killing all of us. He might even be strengthening the thing in the mountain, just like Tabitha thought."

The mountain moaned again, the sound almost trampling them.

Kyla said, "I don't want to know what a man like Jack Allen could do with a thing like *that*."

"And somehow, Sarah's death is the key to all of it."

"If we don't figure out a way to expose that film, I don't think we'll ever know what happened to her," Kyla said. "And if we don't figure *that* out, we might be stuck here—"

Ryan gave her his best sly smile. It was almost impressive, considering how much pain he was clearly in. He nodded to the supply room. "I really need to talk to you about the film you found hidden in here last night."

A great *pop* and crash echoed from the cafe behind them. A

tongue of flame lapped through its shattered window. Ethan said, "Let's talk about it somewhere else."

The fire was growing: they could hear it spreading through the cafe, a hot roar. As Ethan led them to the end of the porch, he studied the motel's roof, the wooden railings of the porch. He thought of the shop in Ellersby, the sun climbing over the highway, the smoke in his rearview mirror as his whole life went up in flames. He thought of the resolve he'd felt. The certainty that he was about to start his life over.

He felt it again now.

Ethan led the way into the motel's office. It was pitch-dark, the air thick with the warning smell of smoke. Ryan pulled a Zippo lighter from his pocket and gave it a click. Surrounded by a little bubble of light, the three of them stepped over Jack Allen's corpse. Over the lake of blood around Hunter. Over Hunter.

In the back of the office, they found the walnut door that had loomed there from the beginning. It was still locked. Ethan could hear scratching and shuffling from the other side. To Kyla again, he said, "Did you say Jack Allen opened this door last night?"

"Yeah. One of those things is on the other side. It killed Thomas and Tabitha."

To Ryan, Ethan said, "Do you still have the key you took from his pocket?"

Ryan dug around in the pockets of his jacket and produced a shiny brass key. Before he handed it over, he said, "Why do you want to open this door? We got lucky with the other Guardians. Are we sure the stone eggs will work with this one?"

Ethan felt another memory flit through his mind. When it passed, he nodded. "Jack Allen had one of the eggs in his pocket, remember? It kept him safe."

"But still . . ."

"He unlocked this door for a reason. I think I know why."

Another hesitation, and Ryan passed over the key.

The three of them pulled the eggs from their pockets before Ethan slipped the key in the lock. The creature on the other side went quiet at the sound. From the direction of the cafe, the fire caved in a wall.

Ethan turned the key.

He pushed open the door and took a rapid step back. Sure enough, a Guardian was waiting there, its wings and talons stretched wide, but the moment it saw the stone eggs in the glow of Ryan's lighter, it went calm, just as the others had. It regarded them, regarded the office, and stepped out of the sealed room. A tongue darted from its serpent mouth, tasting the air.

The creature stayed in the office with them. It stood near the window, watching the trio with what almost looked like concern.

"I almost liked it better when they were trying to kill me," Ryan said.

Ethan took the Zippo from Ryan's hand and examined the room on the other side of the walnut door. It held a single twin bed, a desk, a short dresser. The walls were covered with maps and diagrams and index cards bearing symbols Ethan didn't recognize. A chunk of grooved white stone, like a broken piece of wall, stood on the desk, near smaller fragments of rock. When Ethan touched it, he felt a strange warm energy leak from the stone and stir his blood, like a latent charge of electricity.

As he searched, Kyla and Ryan stayed in the office. In the near-total darkness, a strange honesty seemed to come over the older man. It reminded Ethan of the way he himself had lain next to Hunter—and admitted something he'd kept hidden his entire life, even to himself. He'd admitted he wanted something more than Ellersby.

Ryan said to Kyla, "That film you found in the supply closet—I stole it from y'all's room."

"You *what*?"

"Earlier tonight, before I went to try and talk to Sarah, I heard you and Penelope going down the back porch. I was in room three. I watched through the peephole as y'all went into the cafe. A few minutes later, I saw Fernanda doing the same. She didn't kill Sarah, don't worry. She just went to rough up Stanley, probably because with Penelope out of their room, she knew she'd find Stanley alone."

Kyla said nothing.

Ryan went on. "I had a smoke with Hunter when I first got here—we happened to catch each other's eye across the parking lot. He told me the situation. He said that you two girls seemed to be on the run from Frank, and I figured that might have made y'all and myself . . . allies, of a sort. But I wanted to do some reconnaissance, just to be sure. I was trying to keep my presence here as secret as possible. I didn't want to spoil that for nothing. So I went to y'all's room when I knew the coast was clear. Fernanda had left the front door unlocked. I let myself in. I poked around. One of the mattresses was a little off-center, so of course I had to see what was under it."

Kyla's silence was growing lethal. Ethan found a bookcase in the dim room, flipped through a few volumes.

"There was a green backpack under the mattress," Ryan said. "It had a lot of money inside, but I didn't care about that. There was a roll of yellow Kodak film hidden at the bottom. *That* got me curious."

"So you *stole* it?"

"I was curious what sort of chips I could get on the board, you know? Thought maybe the three of us could use it as some sort of leverage, a way for me to get Penelope away from Stanley. But then I went next door and found Sarah Powers more than a little murdered. I figured it would look very bad to be found with a roll of stolen film on my person in case things went sideways, but before I could put it back in y'all's room I saw Stanley coming out of *his*. Your back door was locked, so I had to keep moving. I found the supply room and stuck the film there. I figured I'd come back once the coast was clear and get the lay of the land, but I was still in the supply room when Tabitha found the body. One thing led to another. You know how it goes." Ryan let out another grunt of pain, no doubt thanks to the wound in his shoulder. "Sarah used the same brand of film as y'all, but you probably figured that out by now. I guess it's not much of a coincidence. Everything's going digital. There can't be many companies still out there selling actual camera film, right?"

Kyla said nothing.

The smell of smoke grew thicker. From nearby, Ethan could hear the crackle of flames.

And then, in the nightstand of the little room, he found what he was looking for. Stepping out into the office, he showed it to the others.

"Another key?" Kyla said.

Indeed. A long silver key that looked like it belonged to a serious lock.

Ethan had a feeling he knew where that lock was.

Without any further warning, the fire reached them: in the span of a second, the whole ceiling burned to life. The Guardian they'd released a moment ago, still standing to one side of the office, let out a *SHRIEK* of alarm. With one long arm, it shattered one of the windows near the fireplace. It *SHRIEKED* again.

"It wants us to move," Kyla said.

"Gladly." With a kick of his foot to dislodge some more glass and then another grunt of pain, Ryan heaved himself over the sill and out into the dark. Kyla regarded the Guardian carefully as she made her way past it. The creature kept its head bowed, almost out of respect, just like the one in the cafe.

Ethan shot one last look around the office. He hurried out the window when a roof beam collapsed, crushing the desk and setting the floor alight.

Outside, the desert was colder than ever. The hard wind from the mountain was growing stronger and stronger, goading the flames that had crowned the motel. The fire was so bright it threw out a halo of illumination all its own, stranger and more fickle than the mercury glow of the motel's lamps, closer than anything to the flicker of a campfire in the primal night.

The Guardian from the office clearly didn't like being so visible. The creature leapt through the window the moment Ethan was clear and barreled into the dark.

The three guests crossed the parking lot. They had to go slow: Ryan's steps were getting sluggish. Ethan realized, in that moment, just how much blood Ryan had lost.

Realized, also, he had no idea how to help the man.

Instead, he asked a question that had bothered him all night. "You came to my room a little before midnight tonight. You said that Penelope was good with voices."

Ryan hesitated, as perturbed by the thought as he had been earlier. "Yeah. She can imitate just about anyone she's had a conversation with. Stanley. Frank. You or me, probably."

"And because none of the men here were unaccounted for, you think it was *Penelope* you heard at seven thirty in room four. It was Penelope using a man's voice."

"That's . . . the gist of it."

They neared the side of the motel. Kyla said, "Why the hell would Penelope go to Sarah's room and argue with the woman in someone else's voice?"

Ryan bit his lip. He pushed harder against his shoulder. "I think she was doing both sides of the conversation."

Kyla's eyes widened. "You mean she was playing both Sarah *and* the mystery man?"

Ryan said, "I think . . . I think . . ."

He was struggling to speak, but Ethan got the gist. "You think Sarah was already dead."

Ryan nodded. "Her blood, on the pillow of her room . . . when I went in to speak with Sarah at seven fifty, it was almost . . . almost completely dry."

"So if Sarah had died at seven thirty—if Penelope had killed her when she went to have that fake conversation—the blood would still be damp?" Kyla said.

Ryan nodded again.

Ethan said. "How long would it take blood to get that dry?"

"I'm not an expert." Ryan swallowed hard. His skin was getting pale in the firelight. "But I read a lot in prison. I'd guess . . . an hour. Give or take."

"An *hour*?" Kyla said. "Meaning Sarah was dead by—holy shit."

"Yeah," Ethan said. "What was Fernanda doing at six thirty?"

Kyla hesitated. "I was sound asleep. To be honest, I was more concerned about her not stealing the backpack and running off without me. I knew if I slept on top of the mattress, she'd have no choice but to stay."

"Is it possible she could have left y'all's room while you were out?"

"And gone to make sure Sarah couldn't rat us out to Frank?" Kyla met his eye in the firelight. "Of course it is. She was in the shower when I woke up."

"Meaning she could have been washing off the evidence."

Ryan said, "She certainly seemed keen to keep y'all from investigating the crime."

Kyla considered this. She didn't deny it, but she had a question of her own. Frowning to Ryan, she said, "You still haven't explained something."

With a grunt of pain, he said, "Shoot."

"Why did you go to Sarah's room in the first place tonight?"

"Because I wanted to know what The Chief's message meant." Ryan let out a grunt of pain. " 'The mountain is getting restless.' I wanted . . . I wanted . . ."

He broke off as the trio rounded the side of the motel and saw what was waiting between them and the old house.

The Guardians were standing in the moonlight. They'd assembled themselves in two parallel lines—their eyes down, their wings extended tip-to-tip—forming a tunnel through the desert just wide enough for Ethan and Kyla and Ryan to walk through. It felt ceremonious, deferential. It made Ethan think of a military battalion offering an honor guard.

The creatures were silent as the trio crossed the dark to the old house. Feathers rustled in a soft breeze. The tunnel of bodies seemed to breathe around them, in and out, with a slow steady hiss.

The mountain had grown massive, its silhouette seeming to swallow the sky. The house with its strange angles and its bright silver window was ready for them. Through the crackle of the fire, Ethan heard a familiar voice coming from the darkness of the desert.

"You're the best thing that ever happened to me."

It sounded like Hunter.

Ethan kept walking. He looked at his watch. It was 3:09.

"You know what else has been bothering me?" Kyla said, turning her attention to Ethan. "When you first got here, Sarah Powers somehow knew who you were, but she still told that lie about meeting your mom when her car broke down. Remember? Something about an engine fan?"

Yes. Ethan remembered.

"If Sarah knew you, she would know you worked on cars. She'd know you'd see through the lie sooner or later." Kyla chewed her lip. They had to walk even slower: Ryan could barely handle a step at a time. "And then Sarah told me and Fernanda about how she had a satellite phone, how she was going to talk to Frank O'Shea, even though she must have seen how jumpy we got when his name came up. She would have known we wouldn't have wanted her to have that chance."

Ethan said, "And to top it all off, she told us all that her doors would be unlocked. That y'all should drop in whenever to look at her photographs."

Through chattering teeth, Ryan said, "It sounds like she wanted to put a target on her back."

Another voice came through the desert, this one a woman's.

"I will destroy that man."

It sounded like Fernanda.

At the end of the line, they encountered a Guardian that stood a solid foot taller than the rest. It watched them approach, its feathered arms crossed across its chest, clearly unimpressed.

"Is it just me," Kyla said. "Or do these things almost seem like people?"

Ethan held out the stone egg in his pocket. The largest of the Guardians regarded it, regarded Ethan, and stepped aside.

They climbed the steps of the old house. As they neared the door, Ryan came to a stop. He leaned against the wall and slid slowly down, coming to rest on the porch's boards. His shoulder left a trail of blood along the house's paint. His teeth chattered hard.

"Y'all go ahead," he said. "All this stuff is getting . . . over my pay grade."

"You shouldn't stay out in the cold," Kyla said.

"Just . . . find Penelope for me, yeah? Make sure . . . make sure she's all right."

"At least come inside—" Kyla began, but Ethan touched her arm. Ryan's eyes had already gone cloudy.

The man let out a long, long breath. He didn't draw in another.

Ethan stepped past him to open the front door. He said, "See you tomorrow."

KYLA

The front room of the house had no light, no windows, but the air seemed to glow with a strange latent illumination. The room was bare, the ceiling tall, the walls somehow longer than they should have been. To her right, she saw a photograph of the mountain behind the motel. The photograph bore a small plaque.

IT SLEEPS

On the other wall, she saw the stars and planets and a great black void in the heart of a familiar solar system.

IT WAKES

Dead ahead, there was a tall door held shut with a massive silver padlock.

Ethan withdrew the silver key he'd taken from the locked room in the back of the motel's office. A twist, and the padlock popped free. The door seemed to ease itself open, leading to a set of stairs that went down and down and down, disappearing into a well of perfect dark.

Kyla traded frowns with Ethan. A weird electric heat came up out of that darkness, brushed her cheek. She'd felt that heat before.

"I think I know what's down there," she said.

Kyla wasn't afraid of the dark, but the void under the house was something entirely different. The strange light that filled the front room seemed to stop at the head of the stairs. With nothing to guide them but the tiny flicker of the Zippo lighter, they started down—Ethan first, then Kyla—into a black that felt deeper than nothing. The flame was barely strong enough to reveal one step on the staircase, and then the next, and then the next. There were no railings on the stairs, and no walls.

Just empty air in all directions.

Empty air, growing hotter by the second.

Kyla's heart was beating so hard she was afraid it would somehow make her stumble. A few steps down, the mountain started to moan again, and this time the sound had a weight—a desperation—that told Kyla they were near the end. The sound rattled the stairs, rattled their teeth. It came and went, came and went, like a siren, a wailing animal. A warning.

It was coming from below them.

At last, the stairs ended at a rough dirt floor. To the left, to the right, an unfinished basement seemed to stretch away toward a black infinity. Ahead was what they'd come for. A wall of white stone stood in front of them, its surface covered with fine, whorling grooves. The pattern was like those of the eggs in their pockets: loops like finger-prints, galaxies, waves. The wall was dizzying, in a way. Lovely.

Familiar. Kyla had seen walls just like it in her dreams.

Unlike the eggs, the pale stone wall had a seam in its grooves. The outline of a tall rectangle stood in the wall's center. It was clearly a door.

Kyla pressed her hand to the stone. It radiated that weird heat.

"The city," she said. "The city in the mountain. It's on the other side."

The door trembled with another moan from whatever the old tribe had sealed away. She gave the door a push, but it didn't budge. There were no handles. No knobs. The groove in the stone was de-ceptive: she couldn't even fit a fingernail in the gap.

"I guess we know what convinced the twins' father and the old Chief to buy this place when they saw it," Ethan said.

"This door is part of the seal, isn't it? The seal the ceremony cre-ated," Kyla said. "The old tribe locked away the city when they left. They sealed it behind here."

"Sounds like a decent guess to me."

"Does that mean that if the ceremony were to break, the door would open? That anyone could go to the dead city?"

"I guess so. But why would anyone want to do that?"

Kyla swallowed. "So they could have audience once more."

Ethan shuddered, rubbed his head. "Let's get back upstairs. Some-thing's waiting for us."

ETHAN

The fragmented memories were coming quickly now. When he and Kyla emerged from the basement, they found another set of stairs waiting for them. Stairs leading up. These stairs hadn't been there when they arrived at the house and yet somehow Ethan felt they had *always* been there. The stairs

he remembers climbing the old wooden stairs on his way to the house's second floor. He remembers this long hall where he walks in a daze, the boards creaking beneath him. He recalls this single, unlocked door. He recalls this room, dead center of the house: a long room with one window, no furniture, something waiting against the far wall, something tall and square and shrouded by a black sheet.

He remembers voices whispering from behind the sheet. He remembers

Here, tonight, the whispers cut out as Ethan approached the shrouded shape that waited in the long room. He pulled loose the sheet, just as he had last night, took a glance at what waited beneath, but he knew not to stare at it, not yet. If he started staring now, he might never look away.

It was Kyla who stared instead.

For his part, Ethan returned to the window that stood dead center in the house's front wall. The window that had glowed with a silver light all night, beckoning to them. Outside, he saw the burning motel, the stars, and—where the road should be—an enormous black void, a field of pure nothingness, even worse than the darkness of the basement. That void was the edge of the ceremony, he thought. The place where this little pocket of time was sealed away from the rest of reality.

Three objects rested inside on the window's sill. One was a simple leather pouch with a jute drawstring. The other was a black circle of plastic with the word *Nikon* printed on it: the lens cap of Sarah's camera.

The third was a folded piece of paper. A letter, written in a man's hand.

Sarah,

Don't try to steer the wind. The ceremony is drawing them together all on its own. It wants to be repaired. You'll know when it's time to check into the motel. There won't be any mistaking it. And when it's time to check in, here's what you must do.

I am so sorry.

The instructions that followed were simple, clear-cut. They read less like an occult rite and more like the repair guide for a foreign engine. Ethan found himself nodding along. Understanding.

Remember, Sarah: <u>suicide will not work.</u>

The substance of my father's mirror is like no other material on our planet. Which makes sense; he always said it was glazed with a little piece of Te'lo'hi itself, back when the creature first fell to the earth. A fragment of the mirror can break away easily, and even though it seems to be metal, Dad swore the material can burn like wood.

The bottom of the note was a final line:

And if anything goes wrong, if you need protection from the ceremony's power, he said it can be drunk like water, whatever that means.

The letter was signed,

The Chief

Ethan folded up the letter. He crossed the room and stared at what had been concealed beneath the black sheet. It was a tall, rectangular mirror glazed with a quicksilver substance, like chrome. The silver should be reflective, but when Ethan neared the mirror, he didn't see Kyla in its surface. He didn't see the room around them.

Instead, Ethan saw himself and Hunter leaving Ellersby. He saw the fire starting in the shop. He saw them checking into this motel. He saw Hunter coated in blood. He saw himself screaming.

He saw himself and Hunter lying on the bed of their room:

Hunter naked, fresh from the shower, curled up against the small of Ethan's back.

He heard Hunter whisper, "Can I hold you for a minute? Just like this?"

More images came, too fast to make sense of them, but it was enough. With a strange, wet, tearing sensation—like a baby tooth coming free—Ethan felt the block in his mind loosen and release. The pain in his head disappeared.

He remembered last night.

Ethan remembered what Jack Allen had told him about Hunter. *He killed families, Mister Cross. It was a specialty for Hunter.* He remembered headaches, the smell of menthols, pain. He remembered everything.

Ethan understood what had happened to Sarah Powers.

Kyla was still staring at the mirror. In a dazed voice, she said, "You're not seeing the same things I'm seeing, are you?"

"I doubt it."

"It's beautiful. And awful. And sad."

"It's life."

Ethan came nearer to the mirror. He held the Zippo into the crack between the mirror's back and the wall it leaned against. The lighter finally sputtered, died, but not before Ethan found words carved there in a language he didn't know. He'd seen those characters before, though: words like this were all over the little room that had been locked away in the back of the motel's office.

"This mirror is what The Chief's father brought with him to the motel. It has the instructions to the ceremony. He probably needed the twins' father to help him decode the language."

Kyla only nodded. She couldn't take her eyes from the mirror's surface.

Ethan saw several places around the mirror's edge where shards of the strange silver substance had been broken away. Two more pieces came away easily in his hand. He handed one to Kyla. She pulled her eyes away from the mirror with an obvious effort.

"What is this?"

"I think it's the secret to fixing everything. I think it will let us remember everything when we wake up tomorrow."

"Remember tonight, you mean?"

"Yeah. Like the twins can. We won't have long to stop the ceremony, but maybe this will give us a chance."

All this time, that plaintive moaning from the mountain had gone on and on. Kyla tilted her head toward it now. "Are you sure that's what we want? To let *that* break loose?"

"It doesn't sound dangerous to me." Ethan frowned. "It almost sounds sad."

"Sad people do terrible things."

Ethan studied the shard of silver in his hand. He let out a long breath.

"I spent my whole life trapped in a shithole. I'm not going to spend eternity stuck in another."

He carried the silver fragment in one hand and the stone egg in the other. Back out of the room. Back down the stairs.

Kyla followed him, clearly reluctant, out into the night. "Where are you going?"

He didn't answer her right away. The Guardians still stood where they'd left them, stationed in two parallel rows, but their heads had lifted, turned, to stare at the mountain.

Above the house, at the mountain's peak, a silver light was beginning to shine.

A moan came, and the light trembled. The whole earth seemed to shake with it.

Ethan looked at his watch. 3:47.

Around the side of the old house, he found a large spigot set into the ground. Near the spigot was a heavy metal lid, almost like a manhole cover, and beneath the lid was a hole just wide enough a slim person could slip inside. In the starlight, he saw a metal tank resting beneath the hole. A massive crack had split the tank's bottom half. Ruined it, no doubt.

"Some kind of septic system?" Kyla said.

"There's probably one of those around here too." Ethan rose, brushed his hands on his jeans, started back for the motel. "But no. Mom told me stories about when she used to live out this way. Every house had a tank like this. A big truck came once a week and filled it up with fresh water. She had a neighbor who drowned in one. They stopped making tanks like this—with wide lids like this—ages ago."

"Didn't Tabitha mention something about how her father and The Chief—the older Chief—had to install a new water tank when they bought the motel?"

Ethan smiled. "They did indeed."

A tremor started in the earth, violent enough Ethan and Kyla had to pick their way carefully back to the motel. He shouted over the noise, "Did your headache go away when you remembered everything?"

Kyla touched her forehead. "Yes, actually. I don't think I really noticed it in the office, but I know when I woke up the pain was totally gone. Why?"

Ethan nodded to himself, though it broke his heart. "Because my memories came back, and I'm clear as a bell."

By the time they reached the motel, the noise from the mountain and the shaking in the earth were so loud Ethan had to shout into Kyla's ear. "Look for a hatch in the ground. It'll probably be buried in dirt after all this wind."

The motel had burned down to cinders. Behind the place the cafe had stood, they found a blasted chunk of metal: all that remained of the generator. In the ruins of the kitchen, they saw several blackened chunks of a man. The remains of Thomas, no doubt, after he blew it all to pieces.

And there, maybe a yard from the kitchen's back door, Kyla kicked away a patch of dirt to reveal a metal hatch with a recessed handle set into the ground. She gave the hatch a pull. It lifted easily.

Beneath the hatch was another water tank, but it wasn't empty. A bedraggled face stared up at them from deep in the hole.

It was Penelope Holiday.

The girl was wrapped in blankets, seated on a stack of cushions in a thin puddle of water. A blocky black shape—Sarah's satellite phone, if Ethan had to guess—was at her side, along with a few empty bags of chips and a candy bar. The girl had clearly come prepared to ride out the night.

But she wasn't alone.

Another girl, much younger than Penelope, was crouched behind her. The younger girl was strange, somehow both here and not: her skin and hair were vaporous and pale, her whole body cast with a soft silver pallor. After everything that had happened, Ethan wasn't particularly surprised to realize he was looking at a spirit. A shade. What was Penelope's sister's name? Her *dead* sister?

Adeline.

"NO!" the younger girl screamed, loud enough to be heard over the mountain. "We've been safe! We've been safe here every night. Now he'll know where to find us. HE'LL KNOW!"

Ethan felt an icy tingle along the back of his neck. It climbed into his scalp.

Jack Allen's voice whispered in his ear.

"Thank you, Mister Cross. I've wondered for ages where these girls have been hiding."

Glancing after the voice, he saw a familiar face looming near his ear. Blank eyes. Sharp cheeks. A tight, tight smile. It was Jack Allen, thin and silver and vaporous as the shade of the girl in the water tank.

The man smiled wider. His eyes were inches from Ethan's own.

"What?" the man said. "Did you think I could ever really *die*?"

The little girl in the water tank was still screaming at Ethan. "WHY ARE YOU RUINING IT? *WHY ARE YOU RUINING IT?*"

Ethan held Jack Allen's gaze. "Why are you doing this? Why do you want to kill us?"

Jack Allen started to laugh. His mouth this close, Ethan could smell the staleness on him: time, rot, a man who'd lingered too long in the dark.

Jack Allen said, "Don't be afraid, Mister Cross. It's for a good cause. I will build a grand world atop these corpses. I will create a future unbound by consequence and fear."

A deafening *BOOM* came from the mountain, followed by a shock wave that knocked Ethan and Kyla to their knees.

Jack Allen whispered in his ear, "See you tomorrow, Mister Cross."

The scrap of silver material Ethan had taken from the house dropped from his hand. It shivered across the quaking dirt, dancing right at the edge of the water tank's hole.

It started to fall.

Ethan snatched it from the air.

Kyla still had hold of her own silver fragment. "What are we supposed to do?"

Ethan glanced over his shoulder: Jack Allen had dissipated, and judging by the way the ground was shaking, they had more immediate problems. Ethan thought back to Tabitha's story in the cafe. He thought of the note The Chief had written to Sarah Powers. Before he could talk himself out of it, Ethan opened his mouth and dropped the shard of silver metal on his tongue.

Sure enough, it melted like water. Warm, tingling water.

Ethan swallowed.

Kyla watched him, nodded, said, "Bottoms up."

She dropped the silver shard into her mouth. Her eyes opened wide—surprise, no doubt, as it dissolved—and she swallowed.

"Do you feel any different?" she shouted.

"I don't know."

No time for more questions. A new sound came, a great crash of breaking stone. It was the last sound the planet would ever know.

Ethan took Kyla's hand. In the final silence—in this new, absolute hush—a great silver explosion tore free from the crown of the mountain, followed by a shock wave that flattened them to the earth. There was a blast of silver light, hot and pure, and it blinded them a moment before the heat vaporized everything in its wake. The last thing Ethan thought was:

How many people get to see the end of the

THE MIDNIGHT KNOCK

A NOVEL

JOHN FRAM

ATRIA BOOKS

NEW YORK AMSTERDAM/ANTWERP LONDON
TORONTO SYDNEY/MELBOURNE NEW DELHI

You know when people change
They gain a piece, but they lose one too.
FUTURE ISLANDS, "Seasons (Waiting on You)"

Anywhere on earth can be the center of the universe.
BLACK ELK, Oglala Lakota

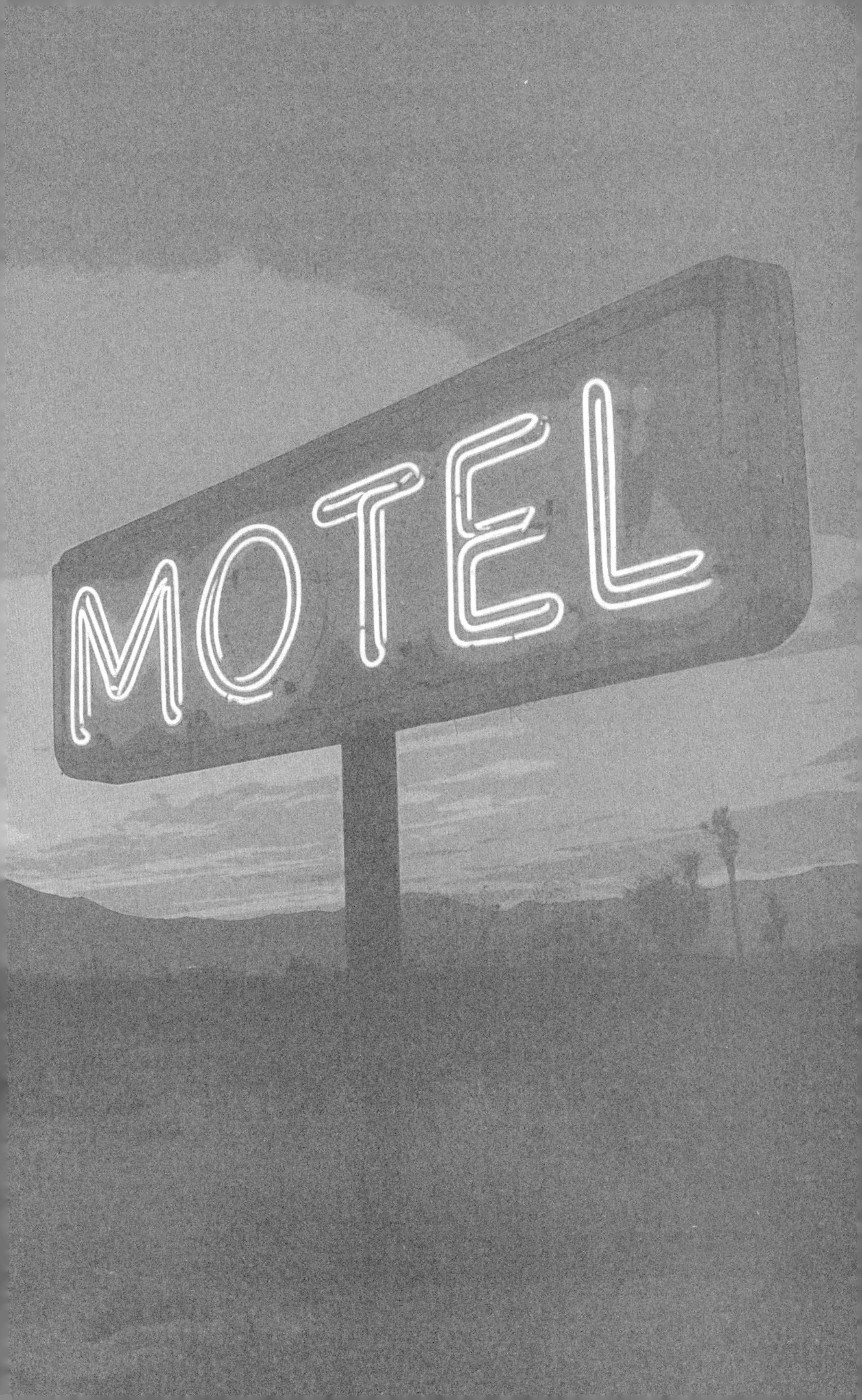
MOTEL

Part I

DÉJÀ VU

LEAVING

They left town at dawn. They left behind his brother, the fires in the engine bays, the only life Ethan had ever known.

Finally.

Before they left, he took a look into the spare room, at the remains of his brother. He walked downstairs, one foot in front of the other. He stood at a wall of photographs his mother had created for them, years ago. Ethan and Carter, aged seven, dressed up as cowboys. Their picture stood next to a faded photo of their mother. Aged seven, same getup. Little Miss Annie Oakley.

How could any children have grown into the people they'd become?

Earlier in the evening, a tedious repair in the shop had occupied Carter—Ethan—for more than an hour. In that time, Hunter and his brother had been alone together, here in the house. They'd spoken about something, and at length. Ethan had heard the rumble of their voices through the wall, though he couldn't make out what they'd said.

Now, Hunter descended the steps behind him. He looked at the wall of photographs.

Ethan said, "You didn't give him this idea, did you?"

Hunter pressed a hand to his chest. The smoke was kicking up his lungs. "Let's get moving."

Ethan told himself he was imagining things. He knew better but pretended he didn't.

The boys drove west, into the rising sun. They were driving to California. Everyone started their lives over in California. Ethan still believed it was possible then, to start your life over.

He knew better now.

Something was changed in Ethan. He watched all of this—all of the choices and breaks and self-deceptions that had led to this moment—and saw them honestly for the first time. Had he known that Hunter was dangerous before they left Ellersby? Yes. There had been times, these last six weeks, when folks around town had been fool enough to disrespect Hunter—or worse, disrespect Ethan—and a black fire had flared to life in Hunter's eyes, the unmistakable signal of violence ready to break free. Once, when Ethan was on his way back from a solo trip to Walmart, Sheriff Powell had pulled him over. *Wanted to give you a chance to talk one-on-one*, the sheriff said. *Just in case you've got yourself in a bind with a man you can't handle.*

Ethan had waved this away. Ethan had told himself that Hunter wasn't a bad man, but of course, deep down, Ethan knew this was a lie. He knew it was a lie, and he hadn't cared. That morning when they left Ellersby, Ethan hadn't seen Hunter hurt anyone (not yet), but he'd always known that it could be done.

Ethan had also known *this*, even if he never admitted it: the shop wasn't sustainable. The bank would reclaim it eventually. There was nothing left for him in Ellersby. He'd known for years that he would need to leave, and the thought had filled him with such fear he'd never once considered it possible. He'd held on. He'd scraped by. He'd put off the inevitable for as long as he could.

And then, when Hunter laid out his plan, Ethan realized he had his way out. That he wouldn't be alone. He was ready, all at once, to burn it all down, whatever the cost.

Whatever the cost.

He killed families, Mister Cross. It was a specialty for Hunter.

Now, after swallowing the shard of the silver mirror, Ethan saw without delusion. His choices—his willful ignorance—are what got him into this mess. Looking at them honestly was probably the only way he was going to get out of it alive. Ethan watched himself watch the fire burning in the truck's mirror. He accepted it all. He started to plan what he would do when they reached the motel.

Ethan watched himself, in the past, watching Hunter watch the sun. Ethan felt the roil of love and desire and fear that he suspected would always define the time he'd spent with this man. Ethan was so scared that first morning they left town, so thrilled at all the potential suddenly unfolding in his life, so desperate to pretend he hadn't made an enormous error. Ethan had felt so young that first morning, in all the best ways and in all the worst.

Ethan reached out a hand for Hunter. "Promise you'll always watch out for me?"

Hunter looked him in the eye. Gave his hand a squeeze. "'Til the end of time."

THE BORDERLANDS

It all fell apart in west Texas, just like his mother always warned him it would.

Lola's Den, the same as it ever was. The sign outside: DEEP-FRIED HAPPINESS. Inside, a smell of biscuits and warm grease. A little rat-faced fry cook scowling at Ethan and Hunter as the boys stepped in out of the cold. The booths all empty. The time on the clock showing 2:02.

The man in the gabardine suit seated at the bar, stirring his coffee with a silver spoon.

Ethan watched himself watch Hunter as Hunter said, "I need a piss." Hunter headed for the restroom. Ethan watched himself standing at the cash register at the end of the bar, uncertain whether to seat himself. He felt Jack Allen's presence at his elbow.

But then something new happened.

Jack Allen said, "Good job last night. You and the girl accomplished more than I ever did."

Ethan turned his head. Jack Allen was smiling at him, but unlike the first time Ethan came to this cafe, he didn't feel himself trapped in the man's thrall. Ethan could look away, could look at the clock behind the bar. It was still 2:02.

"Don't worry, I can't hurt you," Jack Allen said. "We can't change anything about these early hours. Until the silver light strikes at four, you're just living in the past. But we can make a little time for ourselves, I think. Now that you're a little more like me."

So, Ethan thought, and recalled the sensation of silver turning to water on his tongue. *This is the power of The Chief's mirror.*

"Why should I talk to you?" Ethan said.

"Because you've changed, Mister Cross. You seem . . . tougher. Clearer. Like you've finally decided to grow up."

Ethan said nothing.

"And you're curious. You want to know why this is happening.

Why I do the things I do. Why I am the way that I am." Jack Allen sipped his coffee. "Tell me—do you think I was surprised when Miss Hewitt blew off my head with your shotgun?"

Ethan thought of the way this man's spectral form had clung to his shoulder last night shortly before the mountain exploded. The way he'd seen a glimpse of Jack Allen standing in the parking lot of the motel, two nights ago, when the power had stuttered. The way Ryan Phan had sworn he'd seen Jack Allen's face superimposed over Stan Holiday last night, when the big man had killed Fernanda and tried to kill Ryan himself.

Ethan said, "No. You're always there, aren't you? Like a ghost or something."

"Or something, yes. I exist in a state even I still struggle to understand. Here and not. Alive and dead. At midnight, my body is given corporeal form and I can undertake my work. Until then, however, I can only bear witness."

"But if you're some kind of all-seeing spirit, how come you never found where Penelope was hiding until last night?"

A frown crossed Jack Allen's face. He looked at the clock, seeming almost embarrassed. "She was . . . well concealed."

"It's like she knew you were coming. Her, or that little girl who was with her."

"What little girl?"

Ethan grinned. "So you can't see *everything*."

"It doesn't matter." Jack Allen's smile returned, though it didn't light up his eyes. "Penelope has eluded me for an eternity, but now I know where to find her, thanks to you and Miss Hewitt. I knew I was right to let Kyla kill me. To let you people think you were safe. You found what I never could, and now I can complete my work."

Outside, the world was frozen in the middle of a breeze. Scrub grass was bent back in surprise. A veil of dirt hung over the hood of a glossy black Buick Roadmaster.

Jack Allen was right: Ethan did have questions. "And what *is* your work?"

"Let me ask you a question first. Do you understand what you saw last night? That silver energy bursting from the mountain?"

"The end of the world."

"I'm sure that's what Tabitha told you. She's a weak-minded woman, almost worse than her brother and her father and their loathsome Chief. All of them lacked imagination, just like their ancestors before them. What you witnessed last night at four o'clock was the fulmination of a power beyond our comprehension. You saw the awakening of Te'lo'hi. You saw a god in truth."

It sleeps.

It wakes.

Jack Allen said, "Te'lo'hi radiates enough power to fuel the ceremony in which we are all ensnared. Hundreds of years ago, the old tribe of the mountain, the twins' ancestors, used the god's power to seal it away on this, the night of its full awakening. The tribe was terrified of what the god might do. They couldn't fathom the potential of its power."

Ethan remembered the brilliance, the terror, of that silver light. "Maybe they had the right idea."

Jack Allen grinned. "Oh, come on, son. Don't have second thoughts now. Last night you were so eager to break the ceremony. To be free."

Ethan said nothing.

"Let me tell you a story. One cold night in 1955—almost fifty years ago to the day, come to think of it—a group of strangers checked into the Brake Inn Motel. They never checked back out. As the night grew colder, they listened in horror as the mountain moaned. They saw the Guardians circling at the edge of the light, the creatures that ensured none could leave the ceremony once it began. The guests watched in horror as the silver light burst from the mountain. They watched the end of the world."

A look of genuine unease passed over Jack Allen: the memory still haunted him.

"And then it started all over again, not that we realized that at first. We lived through the same nightmare, night after night after night. It worked, until it didn't. There was one glaring problem with the plan the twins' father and the old Chief had devised. The souls ensnared by the ceremony must *want* to be there. It's the reason the first ceremony, the one undertaken by the old tribe, lasted for hundreds of years before *our* ceremony was required: the Natives had *agreed* to be

trapped. But in '55, we were ignorant, unwilling, unwitting participants. And over time, the ceremony started to collapse because of it."

Ethan said, "You realized what was happening. Just like we have."

"Precisely. *I* began to realize it, along with Miss Hewitt's grandfather, but there were problems. You've probably figured it out by
now, but a death is required for this to work. For Te'lo'hi's power
to be harnessed. In your time, that death belongs to Sarah Powers.
In ours, it was The Chief, the elder Chief, who had his throat slit by
the twins' father, there in the bathtub of room five. For some reason,
the ceremony has to be performed afresh every night, but me and
Miss Hewitt's grandfather could never regain our memories in time
to stop The Chief's death from taking place. We learned the purpose
of the eggs, but we had no idea what to make of the mirror we found
in the old house. We found ourselves trapped once more, only now
with the knowledge that we *were* trapped. The elder Mister Hewitt
found a way to maintain his dignity. I was . . ." Jack Allen's smile:
those teeth grinding together like stones. "I was less fortunate. I'm
sorry to say, but I went rather off my head."

Ethan looked at the clock. 2:02.

He said, "You killed them, didn't you?"

"Am I truly that predictable?" Jack Allen acted shocked. "Why
yes, I'm afraid I did. I killed them all, one by one: the newlyweds, the
backpackers, the twins, their father, the lady lovebirds. I killed them
all. And wouldn't you know it, when everyone but me was dead, I
heard a noise coming from the old house. Past the locked door, down
in the basement, I discovered the stone door standing open. The seal
had broken. The city in the mountain—it awaited me."

Ethan thought of the hot white stone wall in the basement of the
house, the pale grooves broken by the shape of a tall rectangle. Kyla
had been right: the city *did* wait on the other side.

Jack Allen said, "Te'lo'hi, the god of the mountain, rests in the
city's heart. I saw it, Mister Cross. I was granted audience with a
being beyond space, beyond time. I beheld its grandeur. I took a sip
of its power. I tried to take more, and see what it did."

Jack Allen held up his scarred finger, the one that ended at the
second joint.

"I only had a few moments with Te'lo'hi. Because when four

o'clock arrived, to my surprise, things started over again, although now I took the shaded form you saw last night. I discovered that I'd broken one ceremony, only to be dragged into another. Because time had been passing *outside* the ceremony, of course, and somehow Sarah Powers realized that a new one was required, or that the existing one needed repair. It's probably why . . ."

Jack Allen trailed off, seemingly lost in a new thought.

Ethan shook his head. "So you're trying to kill us all again so that you have 'audience once more.' Are you insane? A creature that powerful—do you want to lose your whole hand this time?"

"No. I understand it better now. What Tabitha and the others never grasped is that Te'lo'hi is a *young* god. It is . . . pliable. Frightened, even. It's why it makes those horrible noises—those bellowing moans—as it begins to awaken. The god is powerful and it is *afraid*. Nothing is easier to control than a frightened child, believe you me."

Ethan stared at Jack Allen.

"You see where this is going, Mister Cross. You've known all along. I will become a god in truth. When I am granted audience with Te'lo'hi, I know what to do this time. I will drink deep of The Lake That Travels. I will *ascend*. I will use the power of my godhood to remake this world in my image. I will bend time to suit my whims. I will be king over death and consequence. I will have my family back, Mister Cross. I will have the life that was taken from me, and I will have my revenge on those who stole it." Fury leaked through the cracks in Jack Allen's smile. "Mine will be a world of precision and elegance. Mine will be a world free from doubt."

"How in the hell is that supposed to work?"

"It will work wonderfully for *me*. Who cares about the other billions of fools on this rock? They've had millennia to ascend to something higher. This whole world is a scam. This whole *life*. There's never enough money. Never enough time. Never enough love. I will transcend all of that, Mister Cross. I am the one man on this earth brave enough to grab the sun. But maybe . . . maybe I can bring you with me."

Something in the man's tone—a faint trace of worry, or hope—gave Ethan pause. "How do I enter into this? You have to kill everyone but yourself to break the seal of the ceremony. Including me."

"Maybe. Maybe not. I suspect we might be able to . . . bend the rules a little."

Jack Allen reached his maimed hand into the pocket of his suit jacket. He removed a leather wallet, the same wallet Ryan Phan had removed last night when they'd searched Jack Allen's corpse. Now, Jack Allen flipped the wallet open, fished out a photograph, slid it across the bar. "Take a look at this, why don't you?"

Like he was in a dream, Ethan felt a sudden flood of fear with no obvious source. Something about the idea of looking at that photograph filled him with more dread than all the horrors of the desert and the mountain and the cursed motel. He wanted to look anywhere but there.

The clock. 2:02.

Ethan said, "Why bother? I'm going to stop you. I have a plan."

"Just do me a favor, son. One tiny peek."

Ethan tried to resist, but his curiosity got the better of him. He looked down at the photograph. He blinked, trying to look away, but it was no good. He stared.

"My daughter," Jack Allen says. "Precious, isn't she?"

In the photograph was a young girl, aged seven, dressed like a cowgirl: hat and boots, spurs, a pellet gun. A little Annie Oakley.

Ethan had seen this picture before. He'd seen it earlier this morning, hanging on the wall of his house.

The girl in the picture was Ethan's mother.

"What did she tell you?" Jack Allen's voice was suddenly soft. Almost vulnerable. "Did she say I ran out on the family? Did she say your grandfather was a deadbeat good-for-nothing? She was wrong. I never meant to leave them. It wasn't my choice. All this time, I've been right here."

Ethan looked from the photograph to Jack Allen and back. "You . . . you . . ."

"She never even told you my name, did she? I figured as much. Otherwise you would have put together our resemblance sooner. We're not exactly *restarting* the ceremony, son. We're *repairing* the last one. You, Miss Hewitt, Fernanda, you're all descendants of the last participants. Even your man Hunter, those newlyweds who left a bastard baby at home . . . well. You've all been gathered here.

Brought together to repair the damage I inflicted on the last ceremony in 1955. And I think that gives you and I a glorious opportunity. If we work together, if we clear out the trash, the two of us might *both* be granted audience. We're the same blood, after all. Maybe the ceremony will see us the same way."

Ethan couldn't speak. He could hardly think.

Jack Allen said, "You've been trapped all of your life. More trapped than you ever thought. The power of the mountain, of the ceremony, has bent your fate, the course of your steps, day by day, to its own dread purpose. You've been nothing but chattel. Meat for the sacrificial fire. You want something new. You want to break free. I can smell it on you. Can you imagine the sort of *freedom* we would have together? The freedom of gods?"

Ethan realized his hands were shaking. He thought of that explosion of silver light. He saw the shape of the fry cook in the kitchen here in Lola's Den, thought of the cruelty that lay in store for him after this.

The fry cook's cruelty, far outmatched by Hunter's own.

Now every time you touch yourself, you'll think of me.

Mark my words. This man is going to get you into the sort of trouble you cain't never get out of.

All Ethan's life, he'd been scrawny. Vulnerable. Until Hunter came along, he'd never had anyone to defend him, and look at the consequences of *that*. And even if they did somehow escape this nightmare—even if Ethan's plan succeeded—Ethan would still have to keep living. He'd committed arson back in Ellersby and broken God knows what laws to do with a corpse. Ethan would have to live with that always on his heels. He would be chased by all the mistakes that brought him here.

For one delirious moment, Ethan allowed himself to imagine what real power—real freedom—might feel like.

And then he realized his madness.

Ethan pushed the photograph away. He said, "You're right. My mother never said your name. She still had the scars from where you used to hit her."

Jack Allen's face darkened.

"My mother didn't hate you because you ran out on them. She and my grandmother were grateful. When you didn't come back from that trip, it gave them the courage to finally leave west Texas. They ran away before you could get back." Now Ethan had a brutal little smile of his own. "Mom said you were a tiny man with a tiny mind and an ego the size of a house. She said you were a tyrant who couldn't hold down a job. She said you were a fool who wasn't smart enough to realize how hard he'd wasted his life. She said you were the most loathsome bastard to walk the face of the earth. She was *happy* you disappeared."

"That's a lie. A *lie*." But Jack Allen wouldn't meet his gaze. Ethan realized he'd cut the man in a place his grandfather didn't even know could still be wounded.

"You? A god?" Ethan said. "You wouldn't be any better than what you are now. What you've always been. You'd just be a petty man in a faded suit who thinks he can make the world lick his fucking shoes."

Jack Allen said nothing.

Ethan put a hand on the man's shoulder. "I know who killed Sarah Powers. I'm going to stop them. I'm going to stop all of this bullshit, once and for all. I'm going to break the ceremony before it has a chance to start. I'm not even going to give you a chance to turn up at midnight."

Jack Allen tilted his head. His face grew darker. "Are you sure about that, son? You realize that with the ceremony broken, there won't be any coming back. No tomorrow. Anyone who dies tonight, they'll stay dead. You'll be playing for keeps. And with Te'lo'hi unfettered and no one to control him, it'll just be a matter of time before this planet itself ceases to exist."

"When the ceremony breaks, so will the seal on the city. I'll go talk to this god myself. *I* will have audience."

"And do what? Ask a being from beyond the stars to please not destroy the world?"

"I don't know. Maybe I won't be able to stop it. Maybe the world is *meant* to end tonight." Ethan shrugged. "Or maybe *I'll* be the one to ascend. I'm not sure. But I can't imagine the sort of hell a man like you would make with that kind of power." Ethan gave Jack Allen's shoulder a squeeze. "I don't care who you are. I don't care if we're kin. You're a piece of shit. And there's no way in hell I'm going to let you get away with this."

Very, very slowly, Jack Allen wrapped his scarred fingers around Ethan's wrist. He pulled Ethan's hand away. He tightened his grip.

Ethan didn't flinch.

Jack Allen finally met his eye. There was nothing inside him. Nothing. "My boy, I promise you this. You will witness true horror. When I am a god, I will peel the flesh from your bones. I will let creatures beyond imagination feast on your heart as you scream. I will make it last. I will spend lifetimes watching the blood pump from your open veins. I will make you wish, for days upon years upon *eons*, that you could go back, to this very second, and beg me for forgiveness."

Jack Allen released Ethan's hand. The man climbed from his stool, vibrating with rage, but he placed his hat on his head with his usual lazy aplomb. He made his way to the door of the cafe. He turned back to give Ethan a final tight smile.

He said, "See you soon, Mister Cross."

THE SILVER GLARE

KYLA

4:00 p.m.

Even in her dream, she remembered. She remembered this afternoon, Lance's house, her boyfriend getting the call from Frank about Fernanda: *She's been taking pictures. She's been taking pictures of everything.* Kyla remembered the trouble on Lance's face.

Take care of Fernanda, Lance. I can't do it myself.

Take care of her.

Kyla remembered Lance leaving his house, making up some excuse. She remembered standing in their bedroom, her keys in one hand, her shoes in the other.

For the last six months, Kyla had lived and worked in Fort Stockton—worked for the worst man in town, lived with one of his finest soldiers—and she had done nothing. Kyla knew the sort of work these men did. She knew that they moved people across the border like cattle. She knew that Frank O'Shea ruined lives on a weekly basis and made more money than God in the process.

Kyla knew all of this and had done nothing. First, she had blamed her grief: she'd arrived in Stockton a shell of a woman, her father barely buried in his grave. Kyla had wandered into this desolate corner of Texas where her grandfather had vanished and half hoped to do the same thing to herself. As the grief had worn off and her senses returned, Kyla had blamed her inaction on the corruption and duplicity rampant in the borderlands. To whom could she report Frank's crimes? How did she know whom to trust?

Then, as Kyla had grown more accustomed to the glances and signals of the steakhouse and the bars, she had come to know the good cops from the bad. She had identified the people trying to bring down the operation, and she had known she could help them.

But by then, she had convinced herself she'd been here—in Fort Stockton, in Lance's house, in Lance's bed—too long to make a difference. To scrub the dirt from her soul. To escape, if the outfit decided to come after her. Kyla had told herself there was no point in being a hero. She'd trapped herself here, an orphan girl alone at the sharp end of Texas, and one day soon she would wake up like any of the other flinty waitresses and housekeepers and barkeeps in this desolate town and feel nothing at all. Like them, her guilt would build up over her, layer by layer, a lacquer, until it had completely separated her from her own heart.

Take care of Fernanda, Lance.

Take care of her.

Kyla saw all of this through the windows of the dead city. In her dream, she walked the silver streets, peering into the towers and houses, crossing the empty plazas, beneath the everblack sky. Kyla saw herself, through a window, hesitate for a moment longer in Lance's house, knowing that she had seconds—mere seconds—to make up her mind. Kyla didn't know Fernanda terribly well, had only spent a few awkward afternoons with her in Frank's house under the eye of his housekeeper, but Kyla knew this: the woman deserved better. She didn't deserve to die here.

And if Fernanda had been taking pictures, maybe Fernanda and Kyla could do something about this operation—all this violence and pain—after all.

Here, in the dead city, Kyla took a turn. She saw, at last, that the streets of this place were paved with the same strange silver substance as the mirror that she and Ethan had discovered in the old house last night. Beneath the streets, threads of silver light—silver energy—pulsed under her feet like a beating heart.

That energy was growing dangerously unstable. The air almost hissed with it. Everywhere she went, Kyla tasted it on her tongue, felt it burning her nose with a smell like hot ozone.

Kyla passed a long, low building of grooved white stone. It might once have been a market, a restaurant, a cafe. The building's front window stretched far enough for Kyla to see herself in a single, unbroken shot as she walked by.

She saw herself pull on her shoes in Lance's house. Pull on her jacket. Squeeze her keys tight. She saw herself step outside, into her car, and follow Lance to the safe house at the edge of town.

The safe house's door was unlocked. The sound of Lance's voice came from the back.

A spare gun had been left on the kitchen counter. Loaded.

Kyla saw herself arrive in the room in the back where Lance was reaching for the cuffs on Fernanda's wrists. Fernanda was lashed to an exposed pipe in the wall. She was terrified. Lance was murmuring something in Fernanda's ear. He sounded like a man trying to calm a horse.

Fernanda saw Kyla over Lance's shoulder. She gasped.

Lance turned.

Time stopped.

In the window, Kyla stepped past the end of the window, the end of the building, just in time to hear Fernanda whisper, *Help me.*

The shot echoed out behind her. Kyla could almost smell the gun smoking in her hand.

Kyla kept walking. She saw—she knew, at last—that the past is the past is the past. She rounded a final bend in the silver street. She was almost there.

Up ahead, the column of silver light released a sound almost like a scream of fear, maybe a moan of pain, or maybe just the future waiting to be born. A shock wave pounded the air. The buildings trembled. A great crack climbed the grooved stone wall beside her. The energy in the air burned hotter.

"It's the home stretch, Miss Hewitt."

Jack Allen, the gabardine man, stood before the archway that awaited them all. His smile was so tight she could hear those teeth, grinding together like stones.

The light was wailing behind Jack Allen. Behind Kyla, she heard a great crash as the first of the city's stone towers began to fall.

Blood dripped from the blade in Jack Allen's hand.

Drip.

Drip.

Drip.

"I hope you're ready, Miss Hewitt," Jack Allen said. "Tonight, we play for keeps."

■ ■ ■

Kyla awoke at four o'clock in Lance's Malibu, just in time to watch
the silver glare pass over the desert sky. The light was brilliant, it was
everywhere, and when it passed, she realized that her body was her
own again. That the ceremony had restarted once more.

Maybe for the last time.

In the driver's seat of the Malibu, Fernanda said, "How did you
sleep?"

Kyla reached down to touch the gun in her door's pocket, to
unzip the green backpack they'd taken from the safe house this afternoon. She found the roll of camera film they'd stashed at the bottom:
their ticket out of this mess.

If they survived the night.

Kyla said, "I'll live."

Fernanda rubbed her temples, clearly in pain.

"Are you all right?" Kyla said.

"Just a headache."

Kyla didn't know what to think of that.

Up ahead, the great dark shape of the mountain sprang up on the
horizon. Fernanda said, "Do you want to hear a story?"

On all the other days, Kyla had said, *No stories. I feel like I'm already
living in one of the awful ones.*

Now, though, she suspected this might be her last chance to hear a
story in a long, long time. Kyla tried to smile. She said, "Tell me one
I've never heard before."

THE TWINS

The end of the day is just the beginning. It was one of the few things their father used to say about running this motel, back in the months when he and The Chief prepared for their grand reopening. Not that the men had any intention of running the motel like an actual business. Not that their father ever cared about the place. Like so much else, their father never really explained what he was trying to say, almost like he didn't trust his children to understand him.

Had their father known, even then, that Thomas really wasn't cut out for this kind of thing? Tabitha had always had the keener mind; Father had never forgiven her for it.

Tabitha watched herself and her brother empty the motel of the last guests' belongings, the guests from the fifties, the guests from the grand reopening. In Mister Hewitt's room, Tabitha and Thomas gathered up shoes and pants and a letter to his son (Kyla Hewitt's father, no doubt) that would never be mailed. From the dresser of Jack Allen Cross, they removed a small diamond necklace and a card that read simply, *Sorry. Again.* In the room shared by Mrs. Holiday and Mrs. O'Shea, the twins discovered that only one of the room's two beds has been slept in. Tabitha hoped the women had found satisfaction last night, or at least a warm presence at their side as the world ended.

All of these people had once had hopes, lives, futures. Just like Thomas and Tabitha themselves.

No more.

In 1955, their guests had stopped here because they'd run out of gas. The gas pump outside had been empty by the time they'd arrived—The Chief had seen to that, but thankfully Father had left a few cans stockpiled in the twins' room. It had been enough for Thomas and Tabitha to load up the guests' cars with their suitcases and bags and drive the vehicles into the desert, around the side of the mountain, out of view of the road. Thomas and Tabitha walked back together, silent.

This was what they had done the first day. This was nothing Tabitha could change.

Thomas and Tabitha stripped the beds, cleaned the windows, scrubbed out the blood left behind in the bathtub of room 5. But as Tabitha watched the events of the day play out, she thought also about last night, the most recent last night, the night in which Kyla Hewitt regained her memories and killed Jack Allen before he could begin his midnight rampage. For all the good it did them. Not three hours later, when Tabitha had wrapped up her story, as Ryan Phan and Fernanda went to check on Stanley Holiday and Kyla and Ethan asked more questions, Tabitha had smelled danger. She'd stepped into the cafe's kitchen and discovered Thomas standing in a rainbow haze, the stoves all pouring gas, a book of matches in his hand.

I have to stop you, Thomas said, tears in his eyes. *He says that if I don't stop you, everything will break.*

Tabitha remembered the spark as Thomas struck the match. The next thing she knew, she was here, waking up again, just like always. She was observing her own memories like a woman watching a film.

She'd never had patience for the movies. Her mind always wandered. Now, for instance, as Tabitha watched herself fix the linens on room 5's bed, she wondered if Jack Allen Cross was even more dangerous than she'd once thought.

She wondered if maybe, after these endless nights of death and pain, her brother might have finally lost his mind.

And then, at four o'clock, the silver glare passed over the sky, and once again the world was in motion.

There was so much Tabitha still didn't understand about their father's ceremony, but she knew that the silver light signaled the moment when a new loop properly began. Without deliberate intervention, things would repeat as they always did—an object in motion, after all, will remain in motion—but after the silver glare faded from the sky, anything was possible, at least theoretically. At least for the next twelve hours.

Tabitha never did get used to that thought.

Here in room 5, she tossed pillows onto a bed, where they landed at just the right angle to look dense and inviting. She heard a familiar *tink* of glass: that crack, the one that changed everything, spreading again over the bathroom's mirror.

What she did *not* hear was the steady scrubbing of Thomas's brush on the porcelain of the bathtub.

Instead, Tabitha heard only silence in the bathroom. The hairs rose on the back of her neck. The first twitches of anxiety spread in her belly. That silence was new. That silence might be bad.

Better safe than sorry, she thought. Tabitha eased a hand behind the nightstand. She unplugged the cord of the room's heavy brass lamp, just in case.

The air shifted behind her, and Tabitha knew she'd been right to be afraid.

Tabitha wrapped both hands around the lamp, gripping it like a cudgel, and began to turn, but she was too late. Before she could even get her momentum going, something wrapped itself around her neck and jerked Tabitha backward, away from the nightstand. The lamp slipped through her hands, landing hard on her foot, but she didn't feel the pain.

She was too busy clawing at her throat. She tried to scream but found she lacked the air.

For his part, Thomas was trying not to cry. In his fists he held the two ends of a tightly wound towel. It served as a decent garrote, just as Jack Allen had promised him it would. Tabitha was not the only one who'd taken stock of last night's events as the twins had watched the earlier, immutable part of their day play out. And when the silver glare set the world into motion again, she was not the only one who'd known that something drastic might need to happen.

The only difference? Thomas wasn't entirely alone.

"It's fine, son. It's fine." Jack Allen's whisper was soothing in his ear, paternal. "She's not really dying, you know. The two of you will start over again together tomorrow, right as rain."

Tabitha fought. Thomas wept.

"You're doing the right thing, son," Jack Allen said. "You're saving the world."

At long last—much, much longer than Thomas would have thought possible—Tabitha finally stopped struggling. Her face had turned blue. Her eyes bulged hideously from their sockets. Thomas eased her to the floor, his chest heaving, and pressed a finger to his sister's throat. He found no pulse.

"It's fine, son," Jack Allen whispered again. "It's fine. You'll see her again tomorrow. She just needs to calm down a little."

There was a knock at the adjoining door that connected this room to room 4. Sarah Powers said, "Is everything okay?"

Thomas caught his breath. He forced himself to smile. "Just dropped a lamp. Nothing to worry about."

There was a pause, their cousin clearly not entirely convinced, but in the end, she said simply, "I'm going to the house out back. I'll see y'all when it's time."

"Good luck over there."

Thomas heard steps across the back porch. The faint whisper as Sarah's boots crossed the dirt.

He rose. He replaced the lamp his sister had dropped. Plugged it back in. Tried to smooth a dent the fall had made in the lampshade and gave up. He hooked his hands under Tabitha's shoulders and started dragging her toward the front door. He'd get her into the supply closet. She'd be fine there for the night.

She's not really dead, Thomas told himself. *She's not really dead.*

There wasn't time for more thinking. The guests would be here any minute, and Jack Allen had so many instructions.

WHAT ARE THE ODDS?

ETHAN

5:15 p.m.

"It's good the Malibu didn't stop for us," Hunter said, rubbing his temples. "Those girls were armed."

They walked the Dust Road: Ethan's fingers numb around the handle of their gas can, his mind in the past. He thought of what Jack Allen had told him today in that little pocket of suspended time they'd shared at the diner in Turner. He thought of a scar his mother had shown him once. Two scars to be exact, a pair of small circles like a snakebite in the flesh of her thigh. *Daddy did this to me with a barbecue fork*, his mother had told Ethan. *Can you blame Mama for running the second she could?*

Ethan remembered the night his mother had died. The *moment* she'd died. She'd passed in her sleep, in her little bedroom behind the shop. Ethan had been in his own bed upstairs, directly above her, and he'd awoken a few minutes before dawn to feel an electric tingle in the air, a creeping sensation on the back of his neck. Something seemed to vibrate for a long moment in the room, tense and melancholy as an unanswered question.

Ethan had known, even before he found the courage to go down and check her pulse, that he'd just felt his mother's soul move from one place to the next.

He remembered the crushing weight of the debts she'd left him. He remembered the tinkle of the bell over the shop's door when Hunter had stepped inside, a few months later, and asked for a job. Ethan remembered the letter he'd found addressed to Sarah Powers in the old house behind the Brake Inn Motel last night, shortly before the end of the world.

Don't try to steer the wind. The ceremony is drawing them together all on its own.

Ethan wondered if there had ever been a moment, in all his life, when he hadn't been trapped in a plan not of his own design. Just as Jack Allen had said.

You will witness true horror.

Up ahead, the mountain grew closer. Ethan thought of what Tabitha had said in the cafe last night.

The old tribe believed the mountain had a special power. They said it ensured things always worked out the way they were meant to.

But at what cost?

He saw the motel come into view. An hour ago, when the Malibu had passed Ethan and Hunter on the road, time had seemed to dilate for a moment when Kyla's face passed near Ethan's own. There had been a question in her eyes so obvious, Ethan could almost hear her voice in his head.

Do you remember?

Ethan had nodded. Somehow, when they'd swallowed the shards of the silver mirror last night, they'd finally broken free of the amnesia that had cursed them for who knew how long. Ethan had brought a finger to his lips. *Don't say a word.*

They couldn't risk Sarah's killer knowing something had changed. That this night wasn't like all the other nights. The killer might do something drastic. They might find a way to murder Sarah before Ethan and Kyla had the chance to stop them.

Kyla nodded in agreement, looking as if she understood all of this. The car crept along the road until the moment they lost sight of each other's eyes. All in a rush, time kept moving. The car rocketed away.

Hunter spat a wad of bloody phlegm into the desert. He thumped his chest. Ethan pulled his mind back to the present. He said, "What?"

As they neared the Brake Inn Motel, Hunter spotted the Malibu parked at the gas pump. He grew tense. He withdrew the Python they'd stolen in Turner from the back of Ethan's jeans, just as he did every night. Ethan saw a glint of light from an upstairs window in the old house behind the motel. The lens of Sarah's camera snapping their photograph. Just like always.

But through the window of the motel's office, Ethan saw his first surprise of the evening: Thomas was standing behind the front desk. Just Thomas. Alone.

Tabitha was nowhere to be seen when the boys made their way inside. Thomas smiled. "Good evening."

"Evening," Hunter said. "We need to pay for some gas."

"I'm so sorry. I'm afraid our pump is dry for the night. We've been told to expect a delivery—"

Hunter tilted his head. " 'We'?"

"Yes. My sister and my . . . myself." Thomas seemed anxious, his patter falling flat. His hand twitched across the desk. He toyed with the heavy fountain pen. "She's in her room. Not feeling well."

They heard footsteps on the porch. Kyla arrived, followed a moment later by Fernanda, and she gave Ethan a single alarmed look, a brief widening of the eyes.

Something else was wrong.

Thomas certainly seemed bothered. There was an edge in his voice as he said, "What is it?"

"We need some soap. There's none in our room."

"Of course there is. I left it with the towels not twenty minutes before you arrived."

Kyla shrugged. "I looked high and low. Can you just grab us some more?"

Thomas spent an age behind the desk, turning a scowl from Ethan to Kyla long enough for Ethan to fear the man might be about to spoil everything. Hunter watched it all with curiosity. So, too, did Fernanda.

Finally, Thomas said, "I'll just be a moment."

When the man headed out the door, Ethan turned to the fireplace and discovered a second surprise: the stone eggs that had rested on the fire's mantelpiece on every other evening were, now, nowhere to be seen.

Hunter said to the girls, "Thanks for the ride."

There was a hard flatness in his voice. A dangerous edge.

Kyla and Fernanda hesitated a moment near the door.

Hunter went on. "I'm surprised to still see y'all here. You were in an awful fucking hurry."

Fernanda said, "I apologize. We were dangerously low on fuel. We were afraid the car might not even make it this far."

"And look at all the good *that* did you."

"I get it," Ethan said, just as he had the first time they'd all met. "It's dangerous out here. There's no telling what kind of people could be looking for a ride."

Kyla came to warm herself near the fire. Near Ethan.

"For what it's worth, I felt bad about it. I'm sorry."

Their backs to the others, Kyla flashed Ethan a glimpse of something concealed in the pocket of her jacket: a bar of soap, no doubt swiped from her bathroom. Her eyes scanned the junk on the mantel. She was looking for the eggs, too, and no doubt trying to avoid the same frightening conclusions as Ethan.

"Is it true what the man said?" Ethan asked, trying not to sound robotic as his mind moved in a dozen other directions. "That the pump here's out of fuel?"

"I tried it myself," Kyla said casually, though that fear was back in her eyes. "An hour ago, when we got here, I didn't believe him. I went and squeezed the pump. It's bone-dry."

"Why didn't you believe him?" Hunter said.

"I don't know."

Ethan was worried for Tabitha. Whatever Thomas was doing here, his sister wouldn't have gone along with it. Not willingly.

Ethan remembered the explosion in the cafe last night.

He remembered Jack Allen saying, *I will become a god in truth.*

They didn't have time to be bothered for long. There was creak from the porch outside, the shape of a body passing by the frosted window, but it wasn't Thomas who stepped into the office. It was a woman in her late thirties, with tan skin and very dark hair tied back in a ponytail. She wore the kind of comfortable outerwear a well-off traveler would take on a camping trip: tall brown leather riding boots, gray cashmere sweater, black vest trimmed with fox fur. A camera hung around her neck. It looked expensive.

A large knife in a leather sheath rode on her hip.

It was Sarah Powers.

"Afternoon," she said. "Y'all out of gas too?"

Only Ethan replied. He nodded carefully toward the parking lot. He said, "That's your Rover?"

"It is. I can't believe I ran dry. I thought I'd left Stockton with a full tank."

Sarah took a few steps toward the coffee maker in the corner, rubbing her hands.

Ethan knew he only had a moment. While the others were distracted, he looked to Kyla, met her eyes, mouthed, *Wait for me.*

She nodded.

Sarah Powers hesitated in mid-step. She looked at Ethan as she walked past, looked at him again.

"I'm sorry," she said. "But is your last name Cross? This is going to sound crazy, but I think I knew your mother."

RYAN

Maybe it was the fumes of the road. Maybe it was his tight helmet, the rumble of the bike, the broken nose he'd gotten out of his fight with Stanley in Mexico City yesterday. Maybe it was the weird silver glare he'd half imagined he'd seen passing over the sky a couple hours back. Whatever the reason, Ryan had a headache that could fell a horse. The way he'd parked out of sight of the motel now seemed like a terrible idea: every step across the desert was like a knife through his skull.

The pain slowed him down. Slowed him down enough to notice, for the first time, the way the curtain of room 4's window flickered as he stepped into the motel's parking lot, the glint of what almost looked like a camera lens. It was gone before Ryan could even be sure it had been there at all—could it have been an illusion at the edge of his vision, like the aura of a migraine?—but it left an uneasy impression regardless.

Who would want to take his picture? Not Stanley Holiday, that was for sure. If the big man had seen Ryan coming, he would have shot him with a bullet, not celluloid.

But then a stranger question came to mind. Why had Ryan thought that this was *the first time* he'd spotted that glint of glass?

A dour man in a red uniform waited for him in the office. Ryan said, "Is it just you?"

The man studied him. "What makes you say that?"

Ryan was suddenly very confused. "I . . . I don't know."

A few minutes later, stepping back out into the parking lot, Ryan saw another curtain move. A familiar face frowned at him from the window of room 9. An impossible face. And yet somehow, with a surge of déjà vu—and another stab of pain in his head—Ryan was not surprised. The man motioned toward the end of the building, out of sight of the other windows, and Ryan nodded. By the time Ryan joined him, he almost felt like he'd done this a million times before.

"The Hunter of Huntsville," Ryan said. "Am I crazy, or do I smell trouble here?"

"You have no idea. Can I have a smoke? I've got a migraine like no other."

Ryan hesitated. What a coincidence. "All I got is menthols."

"Better than nothing."

Call him superstitious, call him deranged, but as Ryan clicked open his Zippo and lit up their cigarettes, he almost felt as if the pain in his head was trying to tell him something. To *warn* him of something. Somehow the pain was reminding him of six weeks ago, of Huntsville, of the night he and Hunter had awoken in their bunks to hear a horrible low moan leaking from the cell next door.

It had been midnight, and The Chief had been dying.

"*I see it. I see it,*" The Chief had wheezed. The old man let out a gasp of tears. "*The world purged in silver light. The time where all time stops. Twelve souls to begin again. A man in gabardine with blood on his blade.*"

In the dark of their own cell, Ryan had whispered to Hunter, "What the fuck is he talking about?"

Hunter had been silent, which was how Ryan had known the man was afraid.

No one called the guards. No one came to help.

The Chief said, "*It sleeps. It wakes.*"

"*It sleeps. It wakes.*"

"*IT SLEEPS. IT WAKES.*"

The Chief might have been Indigenous, but he never really talked about his heritage. He wore a feather around his neck, but it felt like more of an accessory than a symbol. He didn't pray to anything. He didn't talk about the past, or ancestral spirits, or tomahawks, but he did once punch the lights out of a dickhead in the yard for calling him a medicine man and prancing around with some bullshit war cries.

For a man pushing seventy, The Chief still had a good right hook.

Things changed. In the wake of the visits that a strange beauty named Sarah Powers had started paying him, The Chief had grown pensive. He'd dug out a leather pouch from his belongings and started carrying it around with him everywhere. Ryan and Hunter had always shared their meals with the man, but lately The Chief had become so distant they felt like they weren't eating with anyone at all.

But speaking of Sarah Powers, on the night The Chief died, in the middle of his delirium, the man had suddenly fallen into a silence that was worse than all the babble. Ryan had listened as The Chief dragged himself from his cot. As he'd made his way to the cell's barred door.

"Hunter," The Chief had whispered. "Hunter, please, I need you."

Ryan had watched from his own bunk as Hunter went to their door. "What is it?"

"I know you do favors for the guards. I know they do you favors in return." (*That's one way to put it*, Ryan had thought. Hunter had a skill for eliminating problems the prison had grown tired of. At least if the rumors were true. Which they were.) "Please, do this for me, Hunter. Sarah Powers is coming to see me tomorrow. Meet with her. Don't let them turn her away."

"Why would they turn her away?"

"Because I'm dying."

Hunter had said nothing.

"Make sure they give her this. Please. Sarah *has* to have it."

Hunter had reached through the bars to take something The Chief had offered. "A letter?"

"And this." Later, Ryan had found The Chief had passed Hunter his little leather pouch. "Hunter, tell her . . . tell Sarah the mountain—"

Ryan came back to the present as Hunter worked his way down his cigarette. The man was giving him the lay of the land. Apparently, Sarah Powers, of all fucking people, was here, at the Brake Inn Motel. She was working for Frank O'Shea, though Ryan felt like this should bother him more. It didn't. Somehow, for reasons he still couldn't explain, Ryan felt like Frank O'Shea was the least of his problems tonight.

The mercury lamps burst to life over their heads. A halo of light spread around the motel. Out in the dark, an owl let out a nerve-splitting *SHRIEK* that made every hair on Ryan's arms stand on end. It made Ryan want to get back inside.

Hunter wanted to know what Ryan was doing here, which was fair enough, but Ryan didn't go into much detail about Penelope or Stanley or the drive from Mexico City, and Hunter didn't pry. Ryan rubbed his throbbing skull. Why wasn't the nicotine helping this headache?

For his part, Hunter seemed just as distracted. Or maybe *haunted* was the better word. In a small voice, almost a frightened one, "Do you remember that last night with The Chief? The way he wanted me to pass a message to Sarah?"

Hunter was still just as unnerved by that night as Ryan.

Ryan replied, " 'The mountain is getting restless.' Did you ever figure out what he meant by that?"

Hunter grew still, his cigarette halfway to his mouth. He stared across all that desert past the edge of the motel's lights. All that dark.

He was silent so long, Ryan said, "You all right?"

In reply, Hunter turned to look down the back of the motel, and Ryan found himself following his gaze. They both saw the same thing, though Ryan struggled to believe his eyes.

"Am I crazy?" Ryan said. "Or does that mountain look bigger than it did a few minutes ago?"

Hunter looked away. He shook off some shivers. "You got another cigarette?"

"You can have the whole pack. They aren't helping."

"I just need the one."

Ryan handed it over, though he wished his friend wouldn't partake. Considering the wheeze in the man's lungs, the Hunter of Huntsville should probably quit while he was ahead.

"Can you do me one other favor?" Hunter said.

Ryan hesitated, a cigarette between his fingers. He was bad with promises. "I can try."

"I'm with a man. Ethan. Tall kid with a nice face." Hunter tucked the cigarette between his lips. "I don't know if you'd ever talk to him, but on the off chance . . . don't let him know how we met. He's the best thing that's ever happened to me. I don't deserve him. It would probably kill him to know who I am."

"Of course," Ryan said. It was the second promise of his life, but it was a hell of a lot easier than the first.

Flicking open his Zippo, sparking the flame, Ryan asked a final question. "The day after Sarah came to the prison for the last time—right after The Chief died—there was a fire in the woodshop. They said it had killed you, yet here you are."

Hunter lit up. "That was the deal. Remember the Aryan Brother-hood asshole, the one who hung himself in solitary?"

"That was you?"

"Light work. He was cutting into the warden's side business. Of-fice politics." Hunter spat. "She got me out when I did the deed. Smuggled me onto a laundry truck with all the confusion in the fire. Feels weird, honestly—on paper, I've been dead six weeks."

"I don't think anything could kill you, son."

Hunter said nothing.

Ryan looked at his watch. It was a few minutes shy of 6:25. "I'm going to grab some shut-eye. I might need your help later, getting Polly out of here."

"You know where to find me."

Ryan left Hunter and headed around the corner of the motel. He went around back, listening as the man took a long pull on his cigarette. Ryan walked in the dirt so the creaky boards of the porch didn't betray him. He needed sleep, badly.

He wasn't going to get it anytime soon.

The back door of room 9 opened without a sound. A tall boy with brown hair and deep eyes stood there, a shotgun braced against his shoulder and aimed at Ryan's head.

This must be Ethan. Somehow, Ryan knew that even though the boy was holding a gun, Ethan didn't want to hurt him. Instead of being afraid, Ryan pulled his eyes from the shotgun, back to his watch. Back to the time.

6:30.

The time, Ryan thought. Why was the time so—

And then he remembered. All in a rush, just like that: Ryan re-membered last night, and with a sensation like a loose tooth being pulled from the gum, his headache evaporated. He stood very still for what felt like forever, his mind reorganizing itself in a blur, and then he gave Ethan a nod. He knew the score.

Ethan lowered the shotgun, motioned for Ryan to come inside. He did, his feet silent as a cat's.

Ryan whispered, "She doesn't have much time left."

Ethan nodded. The boy was way, way ahead of him. "You need to do exactly as I say."

THE CEREMONY
SARAH

6:30 p.m.

The Chief had been disgusted by this entire process. Back in the Huntsville visitor's center, during one of their long talks before he died, the old man had said, "Trapping people against their will isn't a good way to make any sort of power work," he'd said. "It's probably why we're in this mess in the first place. My father said the Te'lo'hi ceremony should last for a few hundred years. It's barely been five decades."

"So we fix it. We know how, right?"

"Sarah, you don't understand. The ceremony, it requires a catalyst. It . . . it's not like the dances and sacred rituals of any tribe I know. It's darker. Barbaric. I'm not sure it's even Indigenous at all. Dad said the forefathers would have never come up with it on their own. He said it must have had an outside source."

"Like what?" Sarah had said. "Aliens?"

The Chief had fallen silent a long time. "That may not be as unrealistic as it sounds."

Sarah hadn't much cared about the forefathers. She was "Apache, sort of, I guess," as her mother once described it. The Chief was a distant relation, and his father had clearly been far more devoted to the old ways, the old world. In Sarah's branch of the family, the last people to take any real interest in the old world, were a distant uncle and some forgotten cousins—Thomas and Tabitha and their archaeologist father—all three of whom had vanished off the face of the earth one night in 1955. "And let that be a lesson," Sarah's mother had said. The lesson, apparently: marry a white man and forget the past, just like her mother had done.

Sarah hadn't cared about the past, the old tribes, the violence that had paved over them like the tiles of a great white reliquary. She hadn't had the fortitude to be that heartbroken by everything that had happened to her people. She would have been angry and devastated every minute of every day, and who had the time for that? What would it change?

In the visitor's center of Huntsville, she had said to The Chief, "Whatever's in that mountain, it's trying to get out. You know it. I know it. So what kind of catalyst are we talking about here?"

"Murder, Sarah. *Your* murder. Just like my father's before you." The Chief had held her gaze, sat very still. "Hence our disgust. The tribes of this continent, almost to a man, hated the idea of a human sacrifice. Any stories you heard about it north of Montezuma were almost always propaganda by the white man. But there's no getting around it. My father said it's what had to be done. And according to the journal you brought me last time, I'd say he was right. But think about it, really. Do you have any idea what you're signing up for?"

Sarah had studied the old man through the prison's perforated glass. They had a room to themselves, which was apparently a favor from the guards on behalf of The Chief, or some friend of The Chief's, she never understood. Prison politics were like border politics, as she'd quickly learned: money and power, mirrors and feints. On a table in front of her, Sarah had laid out a notebook, a felt-tip pen, and a small photograph.

She'd pressed the photograph to the glass. The Chief had studied it for a long time.

He'd said, "Are those your boys?"

Sarah had nodded. She'd tucked the picture away without looking at it for herself. She couldn't bear to, most days. Not if she wasn't planning to spend the next forty-eight hours obliterated. "They'll be seven and nine."

"What happened?"

"Custody court. I lost." It was a long story with a simple solution. She'd once been a ferocious drinker. She'd been blazed on chardonnay one summer afternoon, had gone to pick the boys up from a friend's house and crashed into a highway embankment. One broken arm. One sprained little neck. Two protective orders filed by their father. Granted. Sarah's life had been downhill ever since. Her tenure at the university, her home in Austin: all up in smoke.

And then, last month, she'd started having the dream. The same dream, every night. Every. Single. Night.

A mountain in the desert.

A little motel.

A beam of silver light, washing away the world.

And fear—fear like Sarah had never felt in her life. A sweaty cold horror in the morning. The serrated certainty that this destruction was coming—that this was *real*—digging through her heart.

Sarah had known that if she didn't do something about it, that silver light would kill everyone on this miserable fucking planet.

And, most importantly, her boys.

Sitting across from The Chief in the Huntsville Correctional Unit, Sarah had popped the cap on her felt-tip pen and opened the journal to a fresh page. "I don't care what it takes. I don't care what it costs. Just tell me what I need to do."

Now, at the Brake Inn Motel, Sarah unscrewed the cap of the black plastic cylinder in her bathroom. With a pair of tweezers, she pulled free the roll of film she'd snapped today. She wiped away the last of the exposure chemicals in which the film marinated, tossed the towel to the floor, held the film to the infernal red light bulb she'd installed above the sink. She'd been worried she hadn't given the chemicals enough time to soak, but she hadn't had the time to wait. The ceremony needed to start, *now*. Sarah knew it in her gut.

She'd learned to trust that, if nothing else.

Luck was on her side. Luck, or something else. The chemicals had done their job: the film was clear. This afternoon, from her vantage point in the upstairs window of the old house, Sarah had snapped a photograph of the two young women—Kyla Hewitt and someone else—climbing from the white Malibu. Later, Sarah caught a picture of the two boys, Ethan and Hunter, walking in from the road, moments before she went down to speak to them in the office for herself.

A few minutes after that, on her way out of the office, she'd snapped Stanley Holiday climbing out of his van, his granddaughter visible from the back seat.

And last of all, Sarah happened to glance outside—pure coincidence—in time to see a man in a motorcycle jacket steal across the motel's parking lot, almost invisible in the growing dark. Snap.

Sarah had first come to this motel six weeks ago, a few days after The Chief's death. She'd found nothing but a ruin: broken windows, a collapsed porch. She'd wandered the empty rooms, sat on a fallen wardrobe, and listened to the silence around her, the wind. She'd felt no strange power in this land, at the foot of this mountain, in the way the ancestors allegedly had. The power to ensure that things always work out the way they should. Sarah hadn't been sure what that would feel like, but she'd felt nothing but cold.

But when she'd closed her eyes, she'd seen the silver light.

That very night, she'd stepped into a steakhouse in Fort Stockton and sat down across from Frank O'Shea and Stanley Holiday and said, "I can help y'all find your mothers." To Sarah's absolute shock, the men hadn't batted an eye when Sarah had explained her theory that the men's moms had vanished during an ancient ritual designed to bend time and space. "I guess I always knew it must have been something . . . unorthodox," Frank O'Shea had said. "We've spent fifty years looking for them in all the normal ways."

Stanley had been almost desperate, childlike. "You really think they're still there, at the motel? That you could save them?"

"Yes. With y'all's help." A lie, of course. Sarah had had no idea if the men's mothers could be saved. She'd been hazy on the ceremony's details. She'd let the men believe that by helping her—by repairing the broken ceremony—they could free their mothers from the motel's grasp.

Sarah hadn't told the men that they would, in fact, be trapping themselves here. She'd had no idea what would happen after that. Maybe they could meet their mothers in whatever strange pocket dimension the ceremony would create. Maybe they'd spend eternity living the same night over and over, blissfully unaware. She hadn't known, and she hadn't cared.

Frank O'Shea was famous in Huntsville prison, apparently. After the stories The Chief had told her about the man, Sarah had felt no compunction about keeping O'Shea trapped here. She didn't believe in justice, but it was probably better for society to have two fewer men like Frank and Stanley on the loose.

Sarah had felt a bit worse for the others, though. Stanley had leapt at the opportunity to help Sarah track down the descendants of the folks who'd disappeared in 1955, or as many as they could find paperwork on. He'd made some calls. He'd put people under observation. He'd said over one of their many dinners at the steakhouse, "I've been having the strangest dreams."

And then they'd waited. *You'll know when it's time to check into the motel*, The Chief had written in his last letter, giving Sarah little to do but while away her life savings in a luxury motel in Marfa. Every morning she'd awaken from her terrible sleep in time to watch a band of golden sun give birth to the desert, again and again, drawing the world out of black nothing like the hero in an old legend.

Finally, this morning, things had changed. Her phone had dragged her from sleep. It had been a sheriff from some nowhere town in east Texas, a corrupt old man named Powell who Stanley had put on the payroll. "Just wanted to let you know those boys you got me watching lit out from town today," the sheriff had said. "They started a little arson out in Ellersby, but I let them go, seeing how keen y'all feel for them. I hope you'll remember that when it comes time for my compensation."

Sarah had said, "Where were they heading?"

"West. They're heading straight your way." The sheriff had hesitated. "Ethan's a good kid, but watch out for the other. He could poison a snake if he wanted to."

Sarah had hung up without a word. She'd called Stanley. She'd called Frank. She'd told them both the same thing. "Meet me at the motel. Tonight. It's time."

And what do you know, The Chief had been right. When Sarah had pulled up at the Brake Inn Motel a little before two o'clock this afternoon, she'd found a building that hadn't aged a day since 1955. She had found a pair of twins who were somehow in their early thirties and also decades older than Sarah herself. Cousins, long gone. A family legend here, now, in the flesh.

There had been clumsy introductions. The twins were ready and willing to help her, however she needed. They had some sort of instructions of their own. Sarah had made them pose for a photograph. She'd been so unnerved at all of this—so terrified to realize that this was really happening, that this was really *real*—the camera had trembled in her hands.

Looking now at the photo's negative, Thomas and Tabitha were so blurry they may as well have been ghosts.

It was almost six thirty, and Frank still wasn't here. Sarah decided she would have to start without him. *You should begin around dark*, The Chief had written in his letter. *My father always said the old powers were strongest at sundown.*

Again, in her gut, Sarah knew this was right.

In the bathroom, Sarah sliced away the last six photographs from the roll with a pair of nail scissors—the photos of the night's guests—and dropped the remainder of the film back in the development tank. She stepped into the main room. At the cluttered little corner table, she gathered the few tools she would need. Into a plain dinner plate, Sarah placed a shard of silver metal she'd broken away from the mirror in the eerie old house out back. She pulled a match from a matchbook printed with the motel's name. She struck a flame and eased it, carefully, to the shard of silver.

Even though it seems to be metal, Dad swore the material can burn like wood.

And so it did. The shard of the mirror caught the fire easily. It began to burn: smokeless, odorless, and intensely hot.

Something strange started to thrum in the air of the room the moment the fire got burning. It reminded her of the electric pulse of the powerful magnets she'd once used in her physics lab, but dialed up out of all proportion. A furious energy. It crackled on Sarah's skin, lifted the hair from her neck, sent her stomach somersaulting. She smelled hot ozone burning the inside of her nose.

Sarah knew—*knew*—that it was the power of the mountain, a sliver of the power of the thing *inside* the mountain, let free by the flame.

Te'lo'hi.

You know this is serious, Sarah, The Chief had written. *I really do believe the fate of the world hangs in the balance here.*

When Sarah felt that pulse in the air, the last of her doubts fell away. If a single shard of Te'lo'hi could expel this much energy, imagine the damage the full thing could unleash.

Sarah looked again at the film, the photographs of the night's guests. *All the old traditions say that photographs—real film photographs— capture pieces of the soul. Originally, the people participating in the Te'lo'hi ceremony would gather in person around the flame, but my father believed that their pictures should be enough.*

Thomas and Tabitha, the girls from the Malibu, the boys: all of them would be trapped here, maybe forever, and they'd done nothing to deserve it. But that was life, right? Bullshit happens for no fucking reason. Just ask the Apache.

But then something caught Sarah's eye. Looking again at the photograph of the twins, she saw something just past them, a strange gray shape like a flaw in the film. She saw it in the next shot, and the next, and the next. Sarah fished her bifocals from her bag, brought the negatives under a better light. Squinted.

At the edge of the photograph with Thomas and Tabitha, lurking in the corner of the office, was a man in a suit with a hand raised in greeting. He was smiling to Sarah. Smiling so hard she almost imagined she could hear the teeth—

She heard them now—she *really* heard them—grinding together like stones. The sound came from just over her shoulder. Right by her ear.

A sensation like a hundred little legs scuttled down the back of her neck. A man whispered, "Lovely to finally meet you, Miss Powers."

Sarah muffled a yelp and dropped the film into the fire.

She watched its ends curl up with flame. The energy thrumming through the room took on a new depth, a new urgency. The junk on the side table began to tremble. The strange, grooved stone that The Chief had left her when he died started to vibrate on the table, pulsing almost in time with the energy in the air.

This was it. There were no special words, no "medicine mumbo jumbo," as her mother would have called it. Sarah wasn't sure she would have been brave enough to say them. She had worked for long enough at the bleeding edge of quantum physics to know there were forces in this universe that the human mind had yet to fully comprehend. Might even be incapable of truly grasping. Sarah knew she was playing with one such force now. She could feel it in her bones. She knew what had to come next. She knew, and despite all her preparation, all her plans, it terrified her.

But her boys would be safe. Her sons, the ones who never wanted to see her again—whatever she did in this motel, she could die knowing her boys would never see that awful silver light.

Murder, Sarah. Your murder.

In his last letter, The Chief's handwriting grew shaky. *Suicide will not work. It's not just about death. It's about the act taking a life, removing the soul from the body by force. It's a terrible, powerful thing.*

> Someone will have to kill you.
>
> There. I wrote it. I wrote it and I hate it. I don't know how you'll do it, but you have to convince someone to take your life before the fire goes out. It's the only way. The only way.
>
> I am so sorry.

Sarah could only hope she'd done enough to make that happen, earlier tonight in the motel's office. That her lies had been good, but not *too* good.

They were.

At 6:31, the front door of her room eased open, and the Hunter of Huntsville slipped inside without a sound. He seemed ill at ease, almost distracted, glanced at the windows and the door and said, "Let's get this show on the road. We don't have much time."

Something was wrong. Penelope didn't understand how she knew this—just like she didn't understand how the heck her sister was speaking in her ear after being literally *dead* for three years—but whatever the reason, Penelope knew that things weren't working quite like they were supposed to. Adeline sounded scared. Petrified.

"They've ruined it," Addy said, more than once. "They've ruined everything."

"Ruined what?" Penelope had whispered.

"Just stay here. I need to figure out what to do."

And where was here? The shower of their room, of course. Penelope had been standing in the shower for ages, almost from the moment they'd checked in. It was amazing the water hadn't gone cold yet, but apparently cold was what Adeline was worried about. "We have to be sure there's no water left in the tank. Otherwise you might get hypothermia."

"Where did you learn about hypothermia?" Penelope said. "What tank?"

"Just be ready to go play The Game. We need to play The Game in room four and take the phone and . . . and . . ."

"Are you crying?" Penelope said.

"It doesn't matter. *It doesn't matter.* They ruined it last night. He knows about the water tank now. It was the only good hiding place, and they *ruined* it."

A sensation started on the back of Penelope's neck. It was a cold creeping itch, like the scuttle of a hundred little bug legs down her skin. She'd felt tingles like this before in the last three years, the strange itch that she wasn't quite alone, but it had never felt like this. The sensation had never felt this insistent. This *painful*.

Penelope scratched her skin. The sensation didn't go away.

"We have to check on them," Adeline said. "We have to make sure he made it to the room."

"Who did?"

"Hunter, who do you think? We have to make sure he's still following the plan. Things will be a million times worse if he doesn't— a *billion* times worse."

"Who's Hunter?"

"The man who shot us. Who do you think?" Adeline said it casually, like she was describing a classmate at school. "That's in the past. He's the only reason everything hasn't fallen apart a hundred times already."

Penelope shuddered. The itch on her neck wouldn't go away. It was climbing to her skull.

"What are you talking about?" she said. "Why are you even here? What is going *on*?"

She felt a stab of pain in the back of her head. It hurt so bad it made her see stars.

No, not stars: a brilliant silver light. A *familiar* silver light.

"I've always been here. Ever since that night," Adeline said. "I don't know why, but we got put together somehow. It was done for a reason. It was done for *this*, and they've ruined it."

Penelope clawed at the back of her neck. The back of her head. It felt like those little scuttling insect legs were probing her skin. Testing for weak spots.

Penelope said, "You're scaring me."

Adeline said, "Do you want to go back to Fort Stockton, Polly?"

"Of course I don't."

"And do you want to wake up tomorrow?"

Penelope hesitated. Shower water ran into her eyes. "Of course I want to wake up tomorrow."

"Then don't scream. It'll be easier if Stanley stays asleep."

"Why would I—"

But then Penelope felt it. All at once, those creeping little feet on her head stopped itching. They stopped for a long, long moment.

And then they started to *dig*.

There was no word for the sensation. With an awful burning cold, the hundred creeping feet seemed to solidify, forming up into five sharp points, and all at once Penelope had a vision of a hand with long, long nails—nails that had been left to grow and grow in the grave—that were sinking, now, through her skull. Sinking into her brain. *Burrowing.*

Penelope didn't care what Adeline said. She screamed. Or at least, she tried to scream and found she couldn't. She tried to fight. She couldn't. Penelope stood under the water of the shower, stock-still, as those five long nails sank deeper and deeper into her brain. Into her mind.

The nails found something inside her, something vital. They squeezed.

With a great shudder, Penelope sank to her knees beneath the shower's jet. She was there for a minute. Maybe more.

When Penelope rose, she wasn't Penelope anymore.

"It's safer if I do this part myself," Adeline whispered. "I'll see you tomorrow, Polly."

HUNTER

He opened Sarah's purse and found a wallet resting near the bottom where it always did, full of cash like it always was. Hunter scattered the bills along the long dresser, nice and distracting. He bent down to unzip Sarah's luggage, toss her clothes.

He plucked up the knife from the side table.

Sarah made no effort to stop him. She seemed too stunned to move. "Why are you doing that?"

"Keep your voice down. I'm making things look more complicated than they are. I'd rather Ethan not figure out that I'm doing this."

"Who's Ethan? Why would he—"

"Because the twins are going to try and scare everyone into investigating your death. They have no idea what the ceremony really entails. They're going to think someone's killed you before it can start and the world is going to end because of it. They're going to want revenge."

"You mean their father never told them what's going on here?"

"No. He was a piece of shit by the sound of things, and they're more than a little cracked themselves. I can usually convince Ethan and the others not to bother investigating, but I always cover my tracks. Just in case."

Sarah finally realized the full weight of what he was saying. "You mean the ceremony has really worked? We've done this before?"

"Yes. More times than I can count."

The mountain is getting restless.

Every night, every time he had a cigarette with Ryan, whenever Hunter heard those awful words of The Chief's, it all came back to him. With a sensation like a tooth being ripped out of his mouth—out of his mind—Hunter's migraine evaporated. He remembered. He remembered everything, from the first night they'd done this until now. All in a rush. Every time.

But tonight, Hunter hesitated. For the first time in a long time, things felt different. Off. Hunter could always smell trouble, and he smelled it now: Ethan and Kyla were acting strangely. Tabitha was nowhere to be seen. Last night, something had happened that had never happened before, and Hunter was still trying to grapple with its consequences.

Last night, Hunter had died, and he had no idea what had happened after that.

Now, in room 4, Hunter thumped his chest to clear a painful wad of phlegm. He plucked up Sarah's knife from where it rested on the corner table and tossed its sheath under the bed. He tested the edge of the blade against his thumb, just like his father had always told him to. Old habits.

He motioned Sarah toward the bed. "Get moving. Please."

"But I'm confused. If the ceremony works, why are we doing this at all? My death is supposed to be the catalyst that powers everything. Are you saying the ceremony restarts from a time *before* I die?"

"Yes. At four p.m. every afternoon, when the silver light passes over the sky, a new loop kicks in. Everything before then is just a memory. A vivid one, so strong people don't realize they're seeing stuff that actually happened ages ago."

"Four o'clock? By why would it start over so early?"

Hunter was getting twitchy. Normally, he could hear Fernanda in room 5 next door: opening a drawer, washing her hands. Could hear the soft, almost imperceptible creak of Ryan Phan's snore in room 3.

Not tonight. Tonight, the motel was silent. No sounds from the desert. The mountain. Not even a *SHRIEK* from the Guardians.

Silent.

"I don't know why the ceremony starts over so early. If I had to guess, it's some kind of fail-safe. Or maybe just a flaw in the whole operation," Hunter said. "I don't ask a lot of questions. I just need to get this done. Now."

He wanted to get back to his room. He wanted to get back to Ethan, and not just because the boy would grow more suspicious the longer he stayed here.

Hunter wanted to get back to his room because the best part of the night always came next. Hunter would return to their room. He would step directly into the bathroom, into the shower, unseen by

Ethan. He would scrub off any stray beads of Sarah's blood that have gotten on his skin. In his hair. He'd rinse out his clothes.

And then Hunter would step out of the shower and the steam wearing nothing, nothing between him and this kind, smart, gentle, clever, handsome man who deserved so, so much better than Hunter. Hunter would curl up next to this man and press himself to his back and say, *Can I hold you for a minute? Just like this?*

Sarah finally saw the frustration on Hunter's face. She said, "I'd heard stories about you from the guards in Huntsville. It's why I told those lies about knowing your boyfriend's mom in the office—I wanted you to come investigate. I wanted to get you here."

"I know."

"I wasn't sure if it would be both of y'all, or just you, but I heard that if I got you angry enough, you'd do something drastic. You seemed protective of Ethan in the office. I figured if I got you riled up enough you would . . . well."

"I know. You lay a good trap. The very first night, it worked."

The very first night. Hunter didn't want to think about the very first night. Things had gone very, very badly the very first night.

Sarah tried to smile. "Maybe I should have called back that CIA recruiter I met in undergrad."

Hunter had seen this a million times before, and not just from Sarah. People always babbled when they realized there was no escaping an imminent death. When they were right up against the wall of the hereafter.

He took control. "Get on the bed. Face down. Unzip your jeans. And hold still. It'll be a lot worse if you start wriggling."

"My jeans?"

"Don't give me that look. I just need things to look confusing. To kill time."

Sarah blinked. She stood near the bed and unzipped her jeans with an agonizing slowness, but at least she didn't try to argue. "Should I take off my boots?"

"It doesn't matter. Hand me those pillows. Lay face down."

She did, far slower than Hunter's nerves appreciated. On the corner table, the little smokeless fire was still burning. A weird energy thrummed in the air, making the grooved stone egg chitter and shake.

Somehow, after all these nights, it was that little pulsing egg that still gave Hunter the willies.

He eased himself on top of Sarah, a knee to either side of her waist. He guided her head, making sure her neck was stretched long. He picked up a pillow. He placed it over her neck.

She said in a small, small voice, "Will it hurt?"

"Only for a second. Trust me. I used to be a professional."

He covered her head with the second pillow. An old cartel trick. One of many he'd learned in his time working out this way. Hunter balanced the knife carefully in his left hand. He brought the tip of it to the pillow over Sarah's neck. He would drive it in with the heel of his other hand, sink the point of the blade straight into the aorta, and step back before the real hemorrhaging could kick in. She'd be dead in seconds. Quick and easy.

Hunter took a steadying breath. He balled his free hand into a fist. He brought it close to the butt of the blade's hilt.

He said to Sarah, "Hold still."

In his haste, Hunter had forgotten to lock the front door. He'd never bothered with it before. He was never interrupted before this, so why waste a second he didn't need to?

He wished he had now.

The room's front door swung open, and Ethan stepped inside, his shotgun braced against his shoulder. He had it aimed straight at Hunter's head.

Ethan said, "We're not doing this anymore."

ETHAN

It was the headache that did it. Rather, it was the way Ethan's headache had disappeared, last night, when his memories had returned. Yesterday, from the second he'd seen the silver glare at four p.m., a migraine had haunted Ethan until he'd stared at the strange mirror in the old house and felt the past come flooding back. Kyla had experienced the same thing earlier in the evening: when they'd recovered their memories, their headaches had left them. Just like that.

Last night, Ryan had explained that Penelope had an uncanny skill for voices. Ethan didn't believe for a second that Penelope was a murderer, but by coming to this room long after Sarah was dead and feigning an argument between Sarah and some mystery man, she could give the killer a perfect alibi. By seven thirty, every man at the motel was more or less accounted for. It created the perfect crime. Or at least an impossible one to solve.

But if Penelope was working with the real killer, when would the pair have had the time to create this plan?

We've been safe! We've been safe here every night.

And then Ethan had thought of Adeline, Penelope's strange specter of a sister. Last night, when he'd found the girls in the water tank shortly before the end, Ethan had realized that Adeline appeared to be immune to the amnesia that affected all the other guests when the ceremony began again. Maybe it was because the girl was some kind of spirit, a shade—a *revenant*, his mother might have called it—but Ethan suspected the girl simply went on, night after night, aware of everything that had ever happened to them here.

What a hell that would be.

Hell or not, it meant that if Adeline was immune to the ceremony's amnesia, she might have been able to enter into a conspiracy to protect Sarah's killer on *another* night. A previous night. By setting a plan in motion in the past, Adeline and the killer could then act independently of each other on all subsequent nights. Never meet in person. Never risk being seen together. Never risk betraying that there was a conspiracy at work at all.

But for that conspiracy to succeed, the killer would need to remember the past as well. And unless they were a shade themselves, they would have also suffered the same pain and relief as Ethan and Kyla had felt last night. The headache, and the sudden release when their memories returned.

If that was the case, there was one person here whose head had hurt, every night, until it didn't.

The waitress had been right, all the way back in Turner.

Mark my words. This man is going to get you into the sort of trouble you cain't never get out of.

Stepping into room 4, the shotgun braced against his shoulder, Ethan found Hunter right where he'd expected the man to be.

And of all the expressions Ethan had expected Hunter to wear, it wasn't this one: a soft smile, a sort of pleasant confusion. Pride.

Ethan ignored it. He said simply, "We're not doing this anymore."

Hunter didn't move right away. He remained poised over Sarah, her knife in his hand, his eyes locked onto Ethan's. He hardly blinked when Kyla came through the back door and down the short hallway, armed with her Glock.

Ethan locked eyes with Hunter. "I said drop it."

Hunter said, "Did you live long enough to see the world end last night? Have you realized what Jack Allen is like? Do you really know what's at stake here?"

"I'm not going to ask again."

"Then shoot me. I don't think it matters *who* dies. The ceremony will still keep going."

Ethan hadn't considered this. He suddenly felt very tired. "Please, Hunter. Just put down the knife."

Hunter watched his face a moment longer. "Do you have some kind of plan for how we deal with the mountain? Without the ceremony to seal it away, what are you going to do about whatever the fuck is trying to break free?"

It sleeps.

It wakes.

"I don't know," Ethan said. "But I'm not going to spend eternity trapped here."

Kyla spoke. "Besides, the loop is already breaking down. Jack Allen said it himself. This isn't sustainable. One way or another, it's going to end. Seems smarter to me that we break things on our terms before the whole thing falls apart."

"She's right," Ethan said. "And Jack Allen knows where to find Penelope and her sister now. There's nothing to stop him from killing us all and breaking the loop for himself. He thinks he can *merge* with whatever's in the mountain. Eat it or something. Use its power for himself."

Hunter hesitated a moment longer. "Jack Allen—you know he's your grandfather, right?"

Ethan didn't bother asking how Hunter knew this. "Yes. And my mother hated him so bad she never told me his name. Even if I hadn't seen the crazy in his eyes, that right there would have been enough to tell me I can't let him get away with this."

Hunter held his gaze. That look of pride never left him. "So you're sure? Positively sure?"

"Yes."

Hunter seemed to tote things up in his head. He nodded.

He stood up off the bed. He bent down, retrieved the knife's sheath from the floor, slid the blade away.

Hunter said, "Time for one last adventure, then."

Sarah was suddenly in motion. She pulled the pillows from her head and neck, sprang from the bed, and made a grab for the knife in Hunter's hand. When the man easily backed away from her, Sarah turned instead to Ethan.

The woman's face was all panic. "Listen to me—you can't do this. If the ceremony's been going for a long time, then stopping it now isn't just going to return things to normal. We've created a loop, a pocket dimension in the fabric of space-time. We've done things that shouldn't even be possible. If we were to prevent the ceremony from beginning again, that pocket would start to collapse in on itself. There's no telling what it would do."

Sarah's eyes caught something over Ethan's shoulder. He turned, just in time to see Penelope Holiday, her hair soaked with water, standing in the doorway of room 4 with Stanley's massive Desert Eagle in her hand. The gun was aimed at Ethan's head.

"We're not going back to Stockton," the girl said.

She didn't look quite like Penelope. There was a childish sort of fear on her face, the look of a kid far out of her depth. She held the gun clumsily, like she was startled by its weight. It took her three tries to cock the hammer.

Plenty of time for Ryan Phan to make his move.

Earlier in Ethan's room, when he'd motioned Ryan inside from the cold, he'd explained that he was worried Penelope—or more appropriately, Adeline—might do something desperate. Right on cue, Ethan heard Ryan pounding up the front porch. Ryan slammed into Penelope's side, a flying tackle. The gun went off with a deafening boom, and everyone, even Sarah, fell to the ground.

There was a gasp as a chunk of the back wall exploded near someone's shoulder. Ethan's head swiveled to the back hall. He hadn't even noticed Fernanda follow Kyla inside.

No time to worry about that. Springing to his feet and heading outside, Ethan found Penelope—or at least Penelope's body— kicking and flailing in the parking lot. The girl was bawling like an infant. "I don't want to go back! I DON'T WANT TO GO BACK!"

Ryan kept her pinned down easily. He shushed her. He seemed to know exactly which of the two girls he was dealing with. "It's all right, Addy. It's going to be all right."

"What in the *fuck* do you think you're doing?"

Stan Holiday was standing on the porch outside room 7, clad in a pair of basketball shorts and a white wifebeater, his eyes blurry from sleep. He looked ready to sprint across the parking lot. Maybe try to break Ryan's nose a few more times. He added, "What are you doing to her? How the fuck are you even *here*?"

Kyla took care of this problem. Stepping out of room 4, she raised the service pistol in her hand and fired, twice, at the window next to Stanley. One bullet pinged off a metal bar and ricocheted into the dark. The second shattered the glass, rooting Stanley to the ground.

"Turn around," Kyla said. "Go inside. You have no idea what you're dealing with here."

Stanley didn't seem convinced, however. It wasn't until Hunter followed Ethan into the parking lot that the big man got his act together.

Hunter said, "Go. Now."

Stanley went. He turned around, closed his door, and turned off the lights.

Ethan realized, in that moment, that Stanley knew exactly the sort of man Hunter was. That the big man—or the outfit—might have had reason to hire Hunter, once or twice.

And maybe, in the course of that business, Hunter might have met Penelope and Adeline before tonight.

Ethan never got the chance to ask. He heard rapid footsteps—running footsteps—coming from the direction of the office. Turning on his heel, raising the shotgun, he found Thomas barreling toward them with a fire poker in his hand and a look of pure horror in his eyes. He didn't speak. He didn't scream. He just ran in their direction, looking ready to cave in everyone's skulls.

Hunter withdrew the Colt .357 Python from where Ethan had tucked it in the back of his jeans. Casually, without even a beat to aim down the sights, he fired a round into Thomas's kneecap.

Thomas's leg seemed to detonate. He collapsed into the dirt—*now* he was screaming—and tried to cradle his knee to his chest. He screamed even harder when the joint let out an awful, wet *squelch* and bits of cartilage came away in his hands.

"Why?" Thomas screamed. "Why?"

Hunter crossed the parking lot. Kicked the fire poker away. Dug through the man's pockets even as Thomas still writhed and gasped and moaned. Hunter aimed the Python into the man's face. "What did you do to the eggs? The ones that were on the office's mantel?"

So, Ethan thought. Hunter had noticed their absence too.

Thomas said, "Couldn't . . . couldn't let you . . . They're gone. Threw them . . . threw them out into the dark."

Which was, of course, when the Guardians of the mountain let out one of their hair-raising chorus of *SHRIEKS*, as if to remind everyone they were still very much an ongoing concern. Ethan saw movement past the ring of the mercury lights. Saw dozens of yellow eyes.

"If the eggs are out there, we'll never find them," Kyla said.

"Sarah has one," Ethan said. "It's on the table. Someone could go take a look. They'd be safe."

"I don't think we'll have time for that," Hunter said, rising to his feet.

"But without the eggs, how can we reach the house?" Kyla said. "The door to the city's over there. And that's a lot of dark to cross with only one stone."

"We'll figure something out," Hunter said. He rose and looked back toward the motel.

Thomas moaned so hard he threw up a mouthful of bile into the dirt. There was another chorus of *SHRIEKS* from the dark. Ethan wondered if those things could smell blood.

A hand wrapped around Ethan's arm. With surprising strength, Sarah Powers dragged him back into room 4 and pointed at her side table. Her jaw was tight, her pupils wide, her hair swirling around her. You didn't have to be an empathetic genius to see the woman was scared—almost literally—out of her mind. "Please. You have to kill me before that fire goes out. *Please.*"

Ethan saw a flame burning in a dinner plate, there in the clutter of the table's junk. Two nights ago, he'd found that same plate coated with a strange silver substance. That silver had been a shard of the mirror from the old house, he realized now. *It can burn like wood.*

"If the fire burns out and nobody dies, that's it," Sarah said. "The ceremony's over and we risk destroying reality as we know it. Everything, everywhere, could collapse into this hole we've carved out of the universe."

Ethan looked to Hunter, who shrugged. "It's your call."

He turned to Kyla. There was fear in her eyes, just like he felt in his own: they hadn't planned on this contingency. The pair shared one of their silent consultations.

Are you sure? she seemed to say.

Ethan gave a cautious nod. *I think so.*

Outside, Ryan had finally calmed Penelope down, or at least calmed down the girl in Penelope's body. He brought her to her feet, took a few steps away to pluck up the Desert Eagle, and hurried back. "Go on inside," he murmured, rubbing the girl's back. "Come sit down." From the back door, Fernanda rubbed her head and asked, "Are you sure this is good idea?"

Sarah gave Ethan's arm a last, desperate squeeze. "Please."

The fire in the dish was starting to gutter and choke.

Sarah said, "*Please*."

Kyla said, "We've just been delaying the inevitable here."

"Yeah." Ethan pulled free of Sarah and stepped well out of her way. "Eventually you just have to face whatever's next."

"You idiots," Sarah said. "You fucking idiots."

Ethan watched the fire burn, feeling the pulse of energy that thrummed through the room. The pulse grew weaker as the flames died. Weaker.

And then the fire went out. The pulse weakened down to nothing. The grooved egg on Sarah's table gave a last faint shudder and went still.

A last, long silence came over the motel. A lonely wind, a breath from the past.

Sarah sat on the bed. She put her head in her hands. "What have you done?"

Penelope shuffled through the door, her eyes bright with tears. She whispered to herself, "How will I get her back now?"

Ryan stepped through the door behind her. He froze. He swallowed. "Would you look at the time?"

Ethan looked at his watch, the alarm clock on the nightstand, back again. Its hands were flying: 6:55.

8:22.

10:13.

Somewhere outside, from the direction of the road, Ethan heard a low rumble.

Hunter said, "Close the doors. Now."

Outside, on the horizon, Ethan saw two pinpricks of light from the direction of the road. Headlights. Coming this way.

He recognized the growing rumble for what it was: the approach of an engine.

Ethan said, "It's him."

10:52.

11:23.

11:45.

Ryan slammed the room's front door, bolted the chain, grabbed the cluttered side table and heaved its contents to the floor. The table was just wide enough to wedge it beneath the door's knob like a barricade. The fast-food bags and matches and ashes went everywhere. The grooved stone egg went rolling, bounced off the wall, came to rest near Sarah's boot. When she didn't move to take it, Ethan plucked up the stone and handed it to her. "The Chief gave this to you for a reason. Hold on to it."

At the edge of the room, Kyla was trying to shove the long dresser toward the back door. "A little help?"

11:47.

11:52.

11:55.

Outside, the mountain let out one of those booming moans, louder than a crack of thunder, and it was followed by a shake in the earth so powerful it knocked them all to their feet. Hunter was the first back up, dragging Sarah from the bed so he could pull the mattress free. With some help from Ryan, he heaved it against the window.

Ethan and Kyla rallied too. They dragged the long dresser to the hall and shoved it against the back door. Behind him, Ethan heard Hunter's chest rattle and wheeze. He glanced over his shoulder in time to see the man cough up a spray of blood onto the back of his hand and try to wipe it away before anyone saw.

The roar of Jack Allen's car filled the room. Headlights washed through a chink between the mattress and the window. Out in the dark, the Guardians were getting restless.

11:56.

11:57.

11:58.

The approaching car swerved into the parking lot, coming to a stop right outside their door. A familiar voice sounded just behind Ethan's ear. A grinding crunch of teeth.

"Oh, son. Now we're playing for keeps."

Jack Allen laughed.

He laughed and laughed and laughed as the time trembled at

11:59, the racing hands of the clock suddenly hesitating like they couldn't bear to allow this to happen. But there was no stopping it.

11:59 became midnight, and a horrible bellow of pain from the mountain knocked out the power. All of it, at once, just like that.

Room 4 sank into darkness, right along with the rest of the motel. A wave of *SHRIEKS* went up: the Guardians were on their way.

And from the front door, there came a courteous *knock*
Knock
Knock.

KYLA

Before anyone could answer the knock—as if anyone would—a Guardian *SLAMMED* into the room's back door. Kyla heard a furious splintering of wood. Heard talons clawing. Kyla had half wondered if maybe the creatures of the desert might have remembered the way they'd given her and Ethan and Ryan a veritable honor guard across the desert last night, but judging by the way those things descended on this room, she doubted it.

With the lights out, the motel was fair game. And anyone without a stone egg was in the shit.

Jack Allen knocked again at the front door. He jiggled the handle. "What are you so afraid of?" the man said, his voice seeming to echo in Kyla's head. "Would you deny a weary traveler some shelter and warmth?"

In the darkness, she could just make out the shape of Sarah Powers leaning against a wall nearby, trembling. "Who the fuck is that?"

Kyla said, "You really don't want to know."

From the window, Kyla heard a bright *TWANG* of metal as one of the chevroned bars was pulled away. Another. The glass shattered. Talons clawed at the mattress on the other side. More wood splintered from the back door.

Ryan had Penelope on the ground, crouched over her like a wolf prepared to take a bullet for its cub. Hunter was wheezing, his hand on his chest. Fernanda seemed just as confused as Sarah, but she'd grabbed the heavy brass lamp from the nightstand—a plausible weapon—although judging by the way it trembled in her hands, Kyla wondered how much good it would do them. Kyla had eight rounds left in Lance's Glock, plus another ten in the other gun they'd taken from the Fort Stockton safe house this afternoon. Between those firearms and the ones Ethan and Hunter carried, would it be enough ammunition to take down everything waiting for them outside?

Ha.

Kyla found Ethan's eyes in the gloom. Whatever plan the boy had devised for them, it clearly hadn't involved this.

What do we do?

I have . . . no idea.

A third bar came away from the window. A fourth. The mattress shuddered and quaked. It wouldn't hold much longer. Behind her, Kyla heard a crack and felt a rush of wind: a chunk of the back door, gone. The creature out there was getting through. Was nearly here.

Kyla realized she was about to lose control of her bowels. All of their hard work, all of their lucky breaks, all that Kyla had done to atone for the months she'd spent ignoring the evils of Fort Stockton—it was all going to end here, now, as she was torn to pieces by these fucking creatures of the night. With the ceremony ended, that would be the end of everything, wouldn't it? She was going to die for good this time.

Which is when a familiar voice whispered, just behind her ear.

"Kyla," a man said.

"Kyla, come here."

She knew that voice. It sounded almost like her father's.

Kyla turned toward the hall, watching as another chunk of the back door broke free and a yellow eye stared through. Stared at her. She stumbled when the earth shook, when the mountain let out another moan.

"This way. Hurry."

Kyla followed the voice, skirted the end of the long dresser, made her way to the bathroom.

The only illumination in the room was the faint starlight that managed to seep through the glass block in the shower's wall. It was just enough for Kyla to make out the shape of a man standing in the mirror. Even in the weak light, Kyla knew that she had seen this same man before, standing in the mirror of her own bathroom two nights ago.

Even in silhouette, Kyla would recognize him anywhere. He looked so much like her father.

A cool tingle spread down the back of her neck. The man was

in the mirror in front of her, but Kyla heard his voice coming from behind her, over her shoulder, right next to her ear.

"I can't help you much longer," her grandfather said. "Don't you dare waste this."

The man brought a dim finger to the mirror between them. He touched the glass from the other side. Almost before it happened, Kyla knew what he was doing.

"Thank you," she said.

"Get moving," he said. So like her father.

The moment the man touched the mirror, the glass shattered in a great burst of silver light. On the other side, Kyla saw the dead city: the pale spires, the grooved stone walls.

Unlike the first night she had seen the city through her mirror, this time the vision didn't disappear. The frame of the mirror, like the frame of a window, let out onto a familiar silver street.

"Over here!" Kyla shouted. "Hurry!"

Ethan was the first to arrive, followed a moment later by Hunter. The man gave the shattered mirror a single glance, seeming thoroughly unfazed by the sight of the city beyond.

"What are you waiting for?" he said. "Get the fuck out of here."

From the front door, there was a

Knock

Knock

Knock.

"Just where do you think you're going, Miss Hewitt?" Jack Allen said. It sounded like he was right behind her.

Ryan and Sarah and Fernanda and Penelope were crowding into the room's short hall. Ryan said, "Go!"

Broken glass coated the bathroom's vanity and the sink and the mirror's frame. Kyla grabbed one of the towels, gave the counter a single sweep to clear the worst of it away. Through the mirror, Kyla could see a pale statue, some sort of dry fountain: a plaza.

And in the distance, at the heart of the city, she saw that column of silver light. It had never burned so hot.

She felt Ethan grab her waist, help her up onto the counter. "I'll be right behind you," he said.

From the other side of the mirror, from the heart of the city, there came a great moan of pain.

Kyla thought, *I am awaited*.

To Ethan, Kyla just said, "Hurry." She planted her hands on the mirror's frame, judged the drop to the silver street from the other side, stuck her head through, and

Part II

ETHAN

He'd never seen the city before. Never seen a city, period. Ethan had grown up in a state with four major metroplexes and yet the largest place he'd ever been was Tyler, a flat little burg of a hundred thousand people that had housed his mother's oncologist. Ethan had thought the first real city he would ever see was Los Angeles: Hollywood at sunrise, taking shape in a haze of fantasy and glamour. It's not that Ethan had wanted to be in the movies. He just wanted to live somewhere magic could happen. Somewhere alive.

Instead, Ethan's first city was here, in the heart of the mountain. He emerged from a window in a low limestone building and found himself at the edge of a strange forest. He never would have expected this.

Stretching before him were oaks and pines and pale ash trees, all lit by tall stone spires that glowed with a spectral, silver-white light. Water bubbled in a lattice of narrow streams, feeding the trees. To his right, he saw what looked like fields of crops, all gone to seed. Looking up, he saw a black sky that had never known a star.

Ethan looked at the watch on his wrist. Its screen was shattered, the hands frozen at 2:02.

Where were the others? This wasn't the place he'd seen a moment ago. A moment ago, he had been standing in Sarah's bathroom as the barricades fell, the Guardians breaking through. He had looked into the shattered mirror's frame and seen some sort of white stone plaza, likely near the city's heart. He'd climbed inside, Hunter right behind him, thinking it would be a quick run to a column of silver light that had pulsed up ahead.

Now, however, Ethan was alone on the city's fringes. In a way, he was relieved that Hunter wasn't here, because Ethan had no idea what he would say to Hunter if they were alone together. No idea what to think. The man had trapped them all here, night after night, for God only knew what reason. Ethan highly doubted Hunter had been hoping to save the world, so why had he gone along with

Sarah's plans? Hunter didn't seem like the kind of person to welcome such an obligation willingly.

Turning away from the spectral forest, Ethan saw that the dead city sat in a basin. Here, on its edge, he could look down on its tall spires and rambling buildings and its spiral lattice of streets. He never could have imagined this place was so big. How many people could have lived here? How large had this tribe been?

A terrible energy thrummed through the air inside the mountain, a hundred times worse than the strange power that had coursed through room 4 as the fire had burned on Sarah's corner table. The energy here felt unstable. Ready to blow.

He smelled hot ozone. An unnerving tingle climbed the hair of his arms.

Dead ahead, in the city's heart, the column of silver light surged and trembled. One of those awful moans echoed over the city. Now that he was so close, Ethan could hear the pain in the noise, the fear. Te'lo'hi, the god in truth, was massive, it was hurting, and it was going to destroy the world. As that moan rumbled through the city, a crack spread across one of the white walls nearby. A fine rain of dirt and stones showered the city from the mountain's peak high above.

Ethan realized his Remington shotgun hadn't made it through the mirror with him. Had he left it in room 4, or had it simply disappeared in transit?

No matter. It wouldn't have helped him against what lay ahead.

Instead, Ethan hurried along the city's perimeter until he found a winding silver street that looked to lead toward the column of light. Te'lo'hi let out another awful moan, and in the distance a tall white spire began a long, slow fall. This place wasn't going to last long.

Run.

KYLA

Kyla found Sarah Powers seated in the street, her back against one of the pale grooved walls, staring at the stone egg in her hand. The silver surface of the road was so slippery that when Kyla stumbled to a halt, she nearly skidded onto her ass. She got the impression the city's streets hadn't been made for people who were ever in a hurry, people who ever needed much of anything at all.

"What are you doing?" Kyla said. "We need to move."

The woman looked up. Whatever she might have wanted to say was cut off by a deafening crash from somewhere up ahead. One of the city's great white spires had fallen.

As the sound faded, Sarah said, "Where should I go? I don't have anything left."

At the city's heart, the column of silver light let out a wail of pain that shook the earth. The wall behind Sarah groaned as a fissure—so like the arc in room 5's mirror—spread down its grooved surface. Sarah seemed not to notice. Or maybe she just didn't care.

Kyla wasn't sure what to make of Sarah Powers. What kind of person willingly signed up to die night after night, just to keep a group of strangers trapped in a motel from hell? Sure, the fate of the world had been on the line, but still—that kind of sacrifice took a special degree of self-loathing. Now, with her purpose failed, Sarah looked ready to just lie down and die.

Kyla didn't have time for that.

"Come with me," Kyla said. "We can't stay here—the whole city is going to collapse if this keeps up."

"Then let it." Sarah never took her eyes off the egg. "I've ruined my life. I've ruined everything."

"Join the fucking club." Kyla stuffed her dead boyfriend's pistol down the back of her jeans and grabbed Sarah by the arm. "Up. Now. We're going to need all the help we can get."

FERNANDA

Fernanda stood in a room with bare wooden floors, bare wooden walls. A single window looked out onto absolute darkness.

She knew, in some way, that she was in the old house at the foot of the mountain, but the Brake Inn Motel was gone. Outside this house was the void at the edge of reality. Outside the house was pure, utter nothing.

But here, inside the house, was a strange silver mirror.

In the mirror, Fernanda saw all that had been, maybe even all that could be. She saw herself on the bus that had brought her to Frank. She saw herself snapping photographs of Frank's office: furtive, one eye over her shoulder, still not enough. She saw herself in the safe house at Fort Stockton earlier today (or whenever *today* was, anymore) when Kyla's boyfriend, Lance, had come inside and said, "Don't worry, I'm not going to kill you. I work for the cartel."

Fernanda had not believed him. Why should she?

When Kyla herself appeared a moment later, Fernanda had done the only thing that seemed smart. She'd said, "Help me."

Judging by the panic in Lance's eyes after Kyla shot him—the shock, the betrayal—Fernanda realized he'd been telling the truth.

But already, the image in the mirror had faded, replaced by a vision of Fernanda leaving her brother behind in Monterey with the promise to be home before he could ever miss her. Had Miguel understood her? Did he even care? Who knew.

She heard what Stanley—or the man inside Stanley—had said last night before he killed her.

Frank's operation is well aware of your brother. There are men watching his house now. Miguel will be dead the minute you cross the border.

Fernanda stared and stared, searching the mirror, only to feel a gnawing realization take hold of her bones, a savage clarity.

And then a sound reached her from downstairs. Someone was weeping.

She turned from the mirror with both reluctance and relief. She knew, in her heart, that she was needed elsewhere. That she was here for a reason. That, just like in all her grandmother's stories, she served a purpose, right along with everyone else.

On her way down the house's stairs, she found postcards with blurry photographs littering every step. *Postcards.* Who had once told her about postcards?

The ground floor of the old house was as barren as the top. No furniture. No sign of habitation. The only difference was a terrible stench of blood that lingered in the air. Blood, and that urgent weeping.

Fernanda followed the sound of tears across the living room, past a padlocked door, and rounded a corner into what must have once been a dining room, though the thought of eating in this room nauseated her now. She'd found the source of the stench.

Bodies were stacked in piles around the room, strewn across the floor, slumped against the walls. Blood coated them, their eyes wide with horror. Their faces were horribly flat, like they'd been crushed in a massive press. Blood oozed from their pores. Gray matter had dried in the shells of their ears.

Worst of all, every corpse in this room belonged to the same person.

Penelope.

Penelope Holiday, again and again and again. The girl had died a hundred times and been left here to rot.

Sitting in the midst of the carnage, plopped right down in a pool of blood, was a young girl who couldn't have been more than eight. One look at her, and Fernanda could see the child was Penelope's sister—though, of course, on some level this made no sense.

Fernanda had picked up plenty by living at Frank's house. She knew that Penelope's mother and sister had been shot in their beds long ago. She even suspected that Frank (or someone in his operation) had hired the gunman, a specialist at these things, apparently. Penelope's mother, after all, had been planning to go to the FBI.

Dead or not, the little girl was here now, and she was wailing just like Miguel used to wail.

Adeline. The name came to Fernanda like a gift.

"Hello there." Fernanda crouched down, right into the blood. What did she care if she ruined her jeans? "Adeline, can you hear me?"

The girl kept wailing. Fernanda patted her hair. Adeline pulled away.

"She's dead," the child said. "She's dead, and I *killed* her."

Fernanda looked at the stacked corpses. She doubted she would ever fully understand the consequences of the ceremony in which they had all become ensnared, but after watching the mirror upstairs, she had seen so many things. She had seen the way time could be bent. She understood, on some instinctive level, what she was seeing in this room.

"You did not kill her, child," Fernanda said. "She died every night, right at the end, after you kept her safe for as long as you could. That is all you wanted to do, yes? To keep Penelope safe?"

Adeline blinked, her breath hitching. "I don't know why I'm here. I don't know why I'm not dead. I don't know why she is, and I'm not, and why is she *here*?"

Fernanda said, "I do not know much either, child. But I believe this house has served a purpose. It is the in-between space. It collects things. It shows things. And now that its purpose has been fulfilled, it is beginning to collapse."

As if to prove her point, Fernanda glanced over her shoulder. The door through which she had entered was gone. In its place yawned that black void of nothing.

They could not stay here.

Adeline, too, saw the nothing. She started to wail again. "It's over. I couldn't save her, and *it's over!*"

But it wasn't. Because when Fernanda looked past Adeline, she saw that something was trying to help them.

The silver mirror from upstairs had moved. It leaned, now, against an empty patch of wall between two stacks of corpses.

Fernanda took a slow, steady breath. She knew what she needed to do.

She smoothed Adeline's hair, brushed her cheek.

Then she said, "Have you heard the story about the little girl who met a fallen star?"

ETHAN

Ethan heard screaming.

As he sprinted around a soft bend in these endless silver streets—as another moan ripped through the air, sending fresh cracks spidering through the pale stone walls—he caught the sound of a man crying out in pain. In horror.

The screams were coming from a window at the base of a tall building up ahead. Peering inside, Ethan realized he was looking through one of the bathroom mirrors in the Brake Inn Motel. The door was open, giving him a clear view of the back hallway.

Stanley Holiday was there, in the hallway, trying to wrestle off one of the Guardians of the Mountain. The thing had a talon sunk deep into Stanley's eye. As Stanley screamed, he lost his grip on the creature's other arm and fell backward to the floor. A moment later, the Guardian buried another talon in his throat.

Stanley didn't scream for much longer after that.

"If there's any justice in this world, that one used to be his mother."

Ethan spun, heart hammering.

Ryan Phan emerged from another window across the road. Not that Ethan recognized him at first. This Ryan appeared to have aged by a decade, maybe more, in the few minutes since Ethan had last seen him, and he'd picked up the scars to prove it. The Ryan Phan standing here was missing an eye, an ear, a finger. His hair had faded to a dull gray. And his clothes—some kind of tunic and long pants in a material Ethan had never seen before—was somehow familiar.

"What happened to you?" Ethan said.

Ryan only nodded over Ethan's shoulder. "Have you figured it out yet?"

Through the window behind him, the Guardian ripped something flabby and pale from the floor. Stanley's arm.

Ethan said, "What did you mean, you hope it's his mother?"

"The ceremony doesn't just hold back time. It transforms the people it's trapped here. It creates its own Guardians."

"You're telling me that those things used to be . . . people?"

Ryan nodded. "They appear whenever the ceremony is active and the city could theoretically be reached. They protect this place. They slaughter anyone they find. The stone eggs were created to allow a few select individuals safe passage back home. Anyone else is fair game."

Through the window, the creature in Stanley's room was finished with its work. It rose and tore back out into the dark, *SHRIEKING* loud enough to make Ethan's mind stutter, even after hearing the sound so many times.

Ethan said, "You seem to know a lot about those things."

Ryan raised his right hand, revealing the strange implement he held. It was a staff—if you could call it that—with a wicked curved blade at its tip. Bone white. Vaguely organic.

The man flicked his wrist, and the long claw at the end of the weapon curved open wider, like a bird stretching its talons.

A faint echo seemed to come from the blade as it moved. A familiar *SHRIEK*.

"I've had some practice with them," Ryan said.

Ethan looked at Ryan's clothes, his scars, his blade. "You look like you've been to a war."

"I've been looking for Penelope." This wasn't, Ethan noticed, a denial. The man gestured to the streets, the rows of buildings with their blank windows. "You can go through one gap and come out another. Don't try it for yourself. You never know where you'll end up."

"How long have you been doing this?"

Ryan adjusted a strap on his strange garment, rubbed a finger on what looked like a bloodstain. His one eye seemed afraid to look at Ethan. "You really don't want to know."

At the city's center, the column of silver light let out another terrible moan. Ryan said casually, "Move." Ethan started running almost before he realized the danger he was in. The great building in which he'd just watched Stanley Holiday meet his maker collapsed behind him, releasing a nasty barrage of cracked stone. Ethan took a nick behind his ear.

That could have been much worse.

But when Ethan turned back to thank Ryan, the man was already standing at another building's window. A moment ago, Ethan would have sworn that window was nothing more than a plain hole in a stone wall. Now, through its stone frame, he saw a strange wasteland. A jagged ridge of bony mountains. A black sky. A single flame on the horizon—redder than any fire Ethan had ever known.

The sight scared Ethan in a way he could never explain. "Is that . . . the future?"

"A possible future. One of many, if you don't figure out how to deal with Te'lo'hi. Or Jack Allen." Ryan braced a hand on the window's frame, preparing to leave.

"Wait a second—come with me. I'll need your help. He—"

"I'll catch up with you later." Ryan nodded over Ethan's shoulder. "You should run."

Ethan turned back just in time to see the road on which he'd walked suddenly crack and split and cave in, crumbling away into a coursing stream of pale silver light. The energy in the air grew even hotter, sparking on his clothes, almost like his shirt was trying to ignite.

The road kept crumbling a few feet at a time, heading Ethan's way. No time to think. He turned, sprinted, and saw that Ryan was long gone, the window onto the lonely world with the bloodred fire now empty of anything at all.

KYLA

For the life of her, Kyla could not figure out Sarah Powers. A few minutes ago, the woman had been practically catatonic, only walking under duress and silent as a stone. Now, she was peering through the windows of these strange buildings and muttering, "They used cutlery. Who would have guessed?"

Kyla glanced through the window. The inside resembled a dining room: a low table sunk into the floor, scattered with square dishes and knives and, yes, something that looked like a fork.

"This civilization was centuries ahead of their time." Sarah pointed at a recessed point in the building's ceiling, which glowed with a faint silver light. "Hundreds upon hundreds of years old, but they had indoor lighting. Water. Architecture. Why would they just leave?"

Kyla sniffed the air; that thrumming pulse of energy was burning her nose. "You're the physicist. We're in a nuclear reactor that's trying to go critical. You think anyone could have survived in this place even if they'd wanted—"

Another moan came from the silver light, so loud Kyla and Sarah both fell to their knees and slapped their hands over their ears. The ground trembled, sending cracks rippling through the buildings around them. Chunks of rock rained down from the sky. As her hearing returned, Kyla heard the stone walls around them groan, like they were on the verge of collapsing.

The girls froze, barely daring to breath. This entire block—hell, half the city—seemed ready to crumble on top of them.

Then through the very window they'd just been staring at, Fernanda stepped out, clutching a child in her arms. She woman looked over her shoulder at the room she'd left behind—were those corpses Kyla saw, flattened and stacked like red Sheetrock?—and said, "The mirror let us through. Just as I thought."

Kyla had never seen Fernanda like this. For once, the woman didn't look poised and haughty and uptight. She didn't look anxious, or desperately proud, or scared. She was calm. She was ready for whatever was coming.

Kyla almost wondered if Fernanda *did* know what was coming.

Squeezing the child tighter to her chest, Fernanda nodded to the column of silver light. "We must hurry. He is almost there."

ETHAN

As the roads collapsed beneath him, as the moans from the column of light grew louder and faster and *LOUDER*, all Ethan could focus on was the heat—raw energy thrumming in the air. Sweat soaked his hair, slicked his palms. He didn't know where he was going, but the city seemed to be guiding him. Every road curved inward, always toward the mountain's wailing heart. A turn, another turn, and he'd be there.

"Let go, Mister Cross," Jack Allen's voice murmured in his ear. Ethan could feel him nearby, the man's presence crawling through his bones. "Submit to the primal current. Submit to me."

Ethan pushed forward, rounding yet another bend, rushing past windows glimpsing other times, other worlds: snowy landscapes, empty houses, a desert with two moons in its sky, a trench in the earth funneling blood into a gaping pit, a pale sun the color of ice.

And in so many windows, there was nothing. No life. No reality. Just a black void where reality itself had been burned away.

It sleeps.

It wakes.

"I will destroy all that divides and distinguishes." Jack Allen's teeth—that awful grinding. "I will create a world unlike any Te'lo'hi can dream."

Ethan rounded a final bend and found himself on a wide silver thoroughfare. There was a deafening boom of stone to his right: another great spire falling from the sky.

This wide road, at least, seemed more durable than the crumbling streets. Better yet, on the road's other side, Kyla and Sarah Powers and Fernanda all came sprinting around a bend of their own. Fernanda held a small girl to her chest. It looked like Adeline, Penelope's spectral sister.

She wasn't a specter any longer. This girl was solid. Real.

But where was Penelope?

Kyla gave Ethan a curt nod and pointed to the end of the wide road. It ended ten yards away at a tall stone archway, past which was a round courtyard that encircled the column of silver light. The light moaned and shuddered. The air warped and shimmered around it, like heat off a hot Texas road.

Jack Allen stood up ahead, beneath the stone archway, smiling at them all. He held a long knife in his hand. Its blade dripped with blood. When the man opened his mouth to speak, Ethan heard Jack Allen's voice coming from just behind his own shoulder.

"Mister Cross. Miss Hewitt. A shame you couldn't make it here any sooner. You might have had a chance."

Jack Allen moved his arm so fast, Ethan almost didn't realize it was in motion. With a grunt of recognition, Kyla grabbed Ethan by the wrist and pulled him to one side. Jack Allen's knife whizzed past Ethan, missing his chest by an inch, and left a ribbon of blood dribbling through the air.

Something small and white went flying back in the opposite direction. With a wicked overhand snap, Sarah Powers had heaved her grooved stone egg, the one Ethan handed the woman earlier in her room. The egg struck Jack Allen dead between the eyes. Even from this distance, Ethan could hear the *crack* as the egg broke through the bone.

Jack Allen fell backward. His hands twitched. Sarah might have killed him.

"Jesus," Kyla said.

"Softball scholarship," Sarah said simply.

"Look out!" shouted Adeline, still in Fernanda's arms.

Following the girl's finger, they turned back and saw men descending the road behind them, heading their way at a steady, unbothered pace. There were six men, all of them dressed in identical gabardine suits, all clutching identical bloody knives. Ethan had thought he was finished being surprised by this place, but clearly he'd been mistaken.

He stood a moment, staring in shock, at six smiling Jack Allens sprinting his way.

"You didn't think it would be that easy, did you?" Jack Allen whispered in his ear.

Kyla had apparently been able to hold on to her handgun on her way through the window, but it did little good. She fired three shots, knocking one of the Jack Allens down, only to stare as two more identical men clambered out a pair of nearby windows. All around them, Ethan heard that steady *knock*

Knock

Knock.

"This way!"

A new voice called from the heart of the city. As Ethan turned, the column of light let out a moan and a great flash of energy, so that when he saw Hunter, the man was backlit, surrounded by noise, standing beneath the stone archway, his face shrouded in shadow.

Ethan saw two glints of silver in the shadow. For a moment, he thought they were Hunter's eyes.

"Hurry!" Hunter shouted. Ethan heard running footsteps behind them. Jack Allen was coming.

That awful *knock*

Knock

Knock never stopped.

A bloody knife flew past Ethan's ear. Another grazed Sarah's arm. As Fernanda ran near Ethan's side, he heard the woman, through panted breath, whispering to the terrified child in her arms. "So the little girl—turned to the sun—and said—"

Nearing the archway, Ethan said to Hunter, "Where have you been?"

"No time."

Easy as breathing, Hunter pulled the Glock from Kyla's hand. The girl didn't protest. She probably knew he was a better shot. Hunter said, "Where's your other gun?"

"I lost it. I think it fell out of my jeans as I passed through the window."

"Here," said a new voice. Stepping through the window of a long house at the end of the silver thoroughfare, Ryan Phan—looking even older than before—tossed Hunter the pistol Ethan had once seen Fernanda carry. In his other hand, he still clutched that hideous hooked staff.

Hunter caught the gun in his left hand, nodded to everyone, said, "Get back."

He motioned the others closer, past the stone archway and into the courtyard that surrounded the column of light. The small army of grinning men was growing closer, but Ethan noticed there were no windows in this courtyard, only a tall round wall. No more portals for more Jack Allens to emerge from. A good place for a last stand.

Hunter stepped sideways, dodging a thrown blade, and glanced upward. He fired two rounds into a crack in the stone archway and brought the whole thing down with a great crash, blocking the road.

He said, "This won't hold him back for long. You need to go."

Ethan glanced over his shoulder. Now that he was so close—no more than ten yards away—he saw that the silver light was rising out of a round hole in the center of the courtyard. Kyla was already there. She shouted, "I see stairs!"

Ethan looked at Hunter. "What's down there?"

Hunter gave him a quick glance. Again, Ethan thought he saw a flash of silver in his eyes.

With a nasty cough, Hunter said, "He's waiting for you."

Kyla and Sarah were already on the way down the hole. Ryan stood near Fernanda, a hand on Adeline's cheek. The little girl said, "What happened to you?"

"I've been looking for your sister."

Tears stood out in Adeline's eyes. "She's dead. I killed her."

"I don't think it's that simple." Ryan gave the girl a scratch on the top of her head. It looked like an old touch of love. "There's a million worlds out there. I think Penelope's bound to be in one of them."

The column of light released a moan that almost shook him to his knees. A face appeared over the rubble of the stone archway. A smiling face. Hunter fired, striking Jack Allen between the eyes, but three more came crawling up beside him.

"Go on," Hunter said to Ethan. "I'll keep him busy."

"*We.*" Ryan stood next to Hunter, giving his hideous weapon a flick of the wrist.

Adeline said, "Aren't you coming with us?"

"Don't worry about me," Ryan spoke with a grin, and all at once the age and the scars fell away and he was the man Ethan remembered from the motel. "I still have a promise to keep."

Fernanda bumped her shoulder against Ethan's. "We must move. Now."

Hunter gave Ethan a single glance. He seemed to know what Ethan was thinking: there was so much to say, where could he even start?

Hunter nodded. Ethan nodded back.

Ethan turned and ran for the light.

KYLA

A set of wide, pale steps spiraled down into the earth, winding around the column of light. The steps didn't seem to be tethered to anything. They floated in the air, sturdy enough under her feet, but Kyla found herself desperate to reach the bottom. Even after everything she'd seen these past three days, these floating stairs—like the first sinking moments of a dream—unnerved her to the bone.

Kyla went down. Down. Down. Down.

The column of silver light radiated unbearable heat. One slip on these stairs, one brush with *that*, and all this would be over very fucking soon.

Down. Down. Down.

Above her, the city's collapse echoed: stone cracking, the last of the towers falling. Gunshots were fired. A man screamed in pain. Hunter and Ryan both seemed good in a fight, but from what she'd seen on the silver street, Jack Allen appeared to have an endless supply of bodies. He'd overwhelm the pair eventually. He'd get here sooner than later.

Down. Down. Down.

With no warning, the stairs ended. She found herself standing on a wide platform of pale stone that ringed the column of light. Like the stairs, the platform was suspended in space with no obvious tether. The moment her foot hit the stone, all the sounds from up above ceased. She heard the soft tap of her feet, the sound of her heart in her ears, the rustle of clothing as Sarah reached the platform behind her, followed by Fernanda and Adeline, Ethan bringing up the rear.

But that was it. As if the world outside this chamber had vanished entirely.

Adeline murmured, "Where are we?"

Good question. When Kyla came to the platform's edge and looked down, the motion below caught her eye—like the lapping of waves.

Whatever was down there was the source of the noise that had haunted them for days: a low moan of pain rose from the depths, echoing through the dark chamber.

And then, light.

The glow rose from beneath them, a diffuse starlight. Those were indeed waves Kyla saw lapping down there, far beneath the platform. The group was floating above a massive lake of the quicksilver material that also glazed the silver mirror in the old house. The lake stretched away, seemingly into infinity, letting off a faint illumination just strong enough to see the way its waves were growing stiller. Flatter.

The lake became motionless, and Kyla could see her face reflected back at her, far below. It was as if the lake itself was *watching* her.

Beside her, Ethan said, "Is that lake—"

Kyla nodded. "Te'lo'hi."

The silver liquid began to move again. It gathered itself together, and a moment later a long ribbon of silver, like a tendril, rose from the lake's surface, up and up, coming their way, before attaching itself to the edge near Kyla's feet. The tendril took on a new, grooved shape, solidified. Kyla inhaled in surprise. It had created a set of stairs.

Two figures emerged from the lake. They started up the steps.

One of the figures appeared to be a woman. She was plump and short, maybe in her forties, and the woman looked, like so many other people at the motel, faintly familiar.

The other figure was a child, a boy, but he wasn't like any child Kyla had ever seen. He climbed the stone steps with a limp, his whole frame tight with pain. His skin was alabaster white, his hair so long it came almost to his ankles. That hair was like a million silver filaments. They glowed with their own light.

When the boy reached the platform and came to stand a few feet away, Kyla saw that his eyes were the same bright silver as his hair. And they appeared to be weeping.

The boy opened his mouth, threw back his head, and released one of those moans of agony. How could such a small frame produce such a massive sound? Kyla and the others all recoiled in shock, hands over their ears.

Everyone but Sarah Powers. She was studying the plump woman

who'd come up the stairs with the child. This woman, too, had silver eyes and silver hair, but she seemed more solid, somehow. More human.

"I've seen a photograph of you before," Sarah said. "You're Laura O'Shea. Frank's mother."

The woman didn't seem surprised Sarah would know this. More likely she hadn't been surprised by much in a long, long time.

"We are, and we are not," the woman said. Her voice was strange, resonant, carrying its own echo. "We are many people. A legacy. We are the Attendant."

The boy let out another moan of pain. The Attendant placed a hand on the boy's silver hair, but he seemed not to take any comfort in it. The woman frowned. "He is in great pain. He is frightened."

Fernanda eased Adeline to the stone platform and shook out her arms. Of everyone, she seemed the least afraid of a wailing child. "What does a god have to be frightened of?"

The silver-eyed boy blinked. He looked from one face to the next. Without opening his mouth, he said

this

ETHAN

He didn't know how to describe the moment he heard the child in his head. Te'lo'hi could never be mistaken for human—it was obvious to Ethan that the creature was making an effort to *sound* like a boy—but there was no hiding the youth in its voice either. Or the pain.

i came from far away

the boy said.

> *my kind drift among stars*
> *that your kind have not even named*
> *we tell stories*
> *and watch stories*
> *and dream of futures never passed*

"His kind are outsiders in all senses of the word," said the woman, the Attendant. "They are a substance of great density. They require no air. No warmth. They are . . . difficult to explain."

Sarah seemed to have some idea what this could mean. "Are you saying he's some kind of—what—sentient metal?"

"Even that is inadequate, but it is a start. When they come to full maturity, Te'lo'hi's kind become so heavy and release so much energy that they can bend the weave of existence around them. When he is full-grown, Te'lo'hi will be able to cross between all the infinite overlapping universes that exist at any given moment. That is what 'Te'lo'hi' meant in our old language. He is The Lake That Travels."

Ethan said, "That's what the mirror in the old house was showing us. It was glazed from a piece of Te'lo'hi. It can see the future, the past, all the different ways things could be."

"So what happened?" Kyla said. "How the hell did you wind up here?"

The silver-eyed boy lowered his head. His long hair, when it rustled, made a sound like rain pinging from a zinc roof.

> there was an accident
> a mistake
> i fell through a gap in time
> coming here to this world
> i became separated from the others like me
> and i lacked the strength to go back
> i became trapped here
> in this story
> and i was alone
> i fell to this mountain
> and called out for friends

"Our people struggled to survive in a dangerous land. The desert is a cruel place, and it created cruel people. We were often at war," The Attendant said. "But we respected this mountain. Even before Te'lo'hi's arrival, we believed that it held great power. The power to ensure that all things in the world happened as they needed to happen. One night, we watched a falling star pierce the sky and land right in the mountain's heart. We began to dream of a grand city. A permanent home. A safe home. We came to this mountain and found things exactly as you have seen them here. The city had been created for us. We brought seeds and saplings and Te'lo'hi provided the rest. Warmth. Protection. He sealed the mountain, keeping us safe from the violence outside. For a long time, it was enough."

> until
> it was not

"When Te'lo'hi was separated from the others like him, he was not yet fully mature. He could exist in only this world, unable to travel between other realities—other stories—like the rest of his kind," the Attendant said. "However, after many hundreds of years living with us, he realized he was growing older. All beings like him experience a moment when their true strength is awakened. Their full power released. But this awakening would have a devastating effect on this planet."

Kyla said, "The silver light we saw bursting out of the mountain last night. The end of the world."

Ethan said, "It sleeps. It wakes."

"Precisely. The moment Te'lo'hi reached full maturity, the moment he awoke his full power, we understood it would destroy more than we could ever know. Te'lo'hi did what he could to delay this change, but it brought him great pain. At last, he created a ceremony that would seal him away and prevent the end of all life as we know it. By waiting until the night before his awakening—the night his power was at its strongest—we could bend the weave of time, as you've seen."

"You just had to kill someone to do it," Ethan said.

The Attendant hesitated. "Yes. Te'lo'hi knew the power of a sundered soul. Of taking a life. It was like a spark needed to start a fire."

"But the rest of you had to leave the city," Kyla said. "Te'lo'hi's power had grown too strong. Too unstable. It would be dangerous to live here."

"Yes. Twelve of our people volunteered to undertake the first ceremony. The rest of us left the city and encountered the real world for the first time, believing that we would be called back when the time came to repeat it. Te'lo'hi had warned us that there was conflict and pain outside, but we were not prepared for the violence that had swept this continent. The white men. The disease. The starvation. Our people were scattered and lost. Soon, we had forgotten our true history. Except for a few relics passed down from parents to children, nothing remained of the city for us. Nothing but legends."

the story was beautiful

Te'lo'hi said.

until it was not

Above them, Ethan couldn't hear any sounds of fighting, but he doubted Hunter and Ryan could hold out forever against Jack Allen. Ethan caught Kyla's eye, saw a nervous twitch in her lip.

They needed to hurry this up.

Sarah Powers, though, had other ideas.

KYLA

"You have got to be *shitting* me," Sarah said.

Kyla had never met a woman with more moods than Sarah Powers. Not half an hour ago, Sarah had been slumped in the street like a drunk, barely able to walk. Then she'd been pensive and curious like a lost dog. Now she stood tall and furious, striding across the stone platform without a trace of fear and thrusting a finger in the Attendant's ghostly face. "Your people just hid here, safe and sound? The world was falling apart outside, people were being slaughtered by the thousands, entire tribes disappearing, and you did *nothing*?"

The Attendant lowered her eyes. "There was . . . talk. But by the time Te'lo'hi told us how dire the world outside had become, it was too late. We needed to begin the ceremony. He couldn't constrain himself any longer."

Sarah's finger swung toward the little god-child. "But *you* knew all along, didn't you? You knew what was happening to the people of the continent. My ancestors lost our homes, our families, our entire existence. You could have stopped that. You could have changed everything."

Te'lo'hi studied Sarah with those silver eyes. The look of pain on its face was growing sharper by the minute.

> *i can see many stories*
> > *many futures*
> *but i have no way of knowing which story*
> > *will be the story that is told in this world*
> *random chance can still take hold*
> > *bad luck*
> *i saw futures full of death*
> > *futures where i killed men by the millions*
> *i was*
>
> > > *afraid*
> *i was*
>
> > *afraid i would be—*

Te'lo'hi broke off.

"That's your excuse?" Sarah said. "You're a being of infinite power and you were *afraid*?"

Kyla shook her head. "She's right. It doesn't matter if you're afraid. Knowing you could stop evil and sitting on your hands—that's a kind of evil all on its own. Trust me. I'd know."

Te'lo'hi tilted his head toward her, looking ready to speak another one of those same dream thoughts into her head, but a man's voice interrupted him. A grinding of teeth.

"I agree," Jack Allen said, and his voice came from right behind Kyla's ear. "I saw all this power and thought, *'What a* waste.'"

A door opened behind the Attendant. There was no other way to describe it. A wooden door, like all the doors they'd seen at the Brake Inn Motel, appeared out of nothing—literally from thin air—and swung open to reveal Jack Allen and his gabardine suit and his awful, awful smile.

His teeth had finally cracked from all that grinding. His smile was painted in blood.

The Attendant didn't realize what was happening until it was over. Jack Allen grabbed her silver hair and pulled back her neck and ran a knife across the veins. Brilliant silver blood jetted from the gash. The woman collapsed with a noise like a dog choking on a bone.

At the same moment, Sarah Powers let out a scream. Kyla saw another open door behind her, another Jack Allen emerge and bury a knife in Sarah's side.

A door opened behind Te'lo'hi, and Jack Allen emerged and laced his fingers through the boy's long silver hair and lifted the god-child from the platform. Jack Allen brought his knife to the boy's throat. He smiled to Kyla. To Ethan. "Last time, I drank just a few strands of hair and look what it did for me. Imagine what will happen when I drink from the source."

Kyla felt movement behind her and Ethan. She stepped forward, all instinct, and felt something sharp and fast slice through the air. Turning, she saw a pair of Jack Allens, knives at the ready. Not far away, Fernanda threw herself over Adeline as yet another gabardine man emerged from yet another door.

The men were everywhere, appearing all over the platform. There was no escape.

"Why struggle?" said the Jack Allen that held Te'lo'hi in the air. "I will create a new world entirely. I will free us all from pain and doubt. I will create a world full of love unending."

The blood on Jack Allen's teeth gleamed. Te'lo'hi was screaming

no!

   no!

      NO!

Kyla scrambled away from the gabardine men who had appeared behind her and Ethan, but there was nowhere to go: the Jack Allen who had killed the Attendant turned his attention toward them. Sarah Powers fell to the platform as Jack Allen sank his knife into her back.

"I will destroy all that divides and distinguishes," all of the Jack Allens said, all at once. "I will destroy time and fear and all that controls me. I—"

Which is when Kyla and Ethan, at the same time, seemed to notice something. Their eyes met: *Do you hear that?*

Kyla did. Te'lo'hi wasn't saying, "No! No! No!"

He was screaming

NOW!

ETHAN

The chaos stopped. All of it. At once. Just like that.

Time came to a halt on the stone platform. The grinning men pursuing Ethan and Kyla halted in mid-step. A knife hung in the air above Fernanda's back. The blade held to Te'lo'hi's neck went nowhere. Nothing moved.

Nothing except the man coming down the spiral stairs.

"Hey."

It was Hunter. He was bloodied and bruised: an eye scabbed shut, a great gash across his chest. He held a knife whose blade had broken off at the hilt. He seemed to notice it was broken at the same time as Ethan. He threw it aside.

Everyone else on the platform was frozen in place, but when Hunter came to a stop at the foot of the stairs, he hesitated, held out a hand, and Ethan realized he could walk. He took one step through this strange bubble of suspended time. Took another step. Another.

The moment he was in arm's reach, Hunter grabbed Ethan and pulled him close and squeezed him harder than he'd ever held Ethan in all the time they'd known each other. Ethan could feel Hunter's lungs rattle and scrape in his chest. He felt blood seeping through his shirt.

Ethan said carefully, "I figured when Jack Allen turned up here, it meant you were dead."

Hunter let Ethan go, wouldn't meet his eye. "Yeah. Funny story about that."

help!

Te'lo'hi was squirming in Jack Allen's grip, still held aloft by his silver hair. Hunter crossed the platform and pried the knife from Jack Allen's outstretched hand. Jack Allen let it go. It was obvious he could do nothing to stop this.

The widening shock in Jack Allen's eyes, however, proved he knew what was happening.

Hunter swung the knife against Jack Allen's other hand, the hand holding Te'lo'hi in the air. He swung at the wrist, specifically. Jack Allen stood, frozen, as Hunter struck the wrist with the knife again and again and again until the bone cracked and the tendons tore and the mangled hand ripped loose from Jack Allen's arm. Its fingers opened, and Te'lo'hi was free.

The little god-creature landed on his feet, silent as a cat. A few strands of his silver hair had come loose in the struggle and had melted into a silver puddle. When the boy kicked the water, the puddle sang softly with a sound like wind chimes.

Hunter finally looked in Ethan's face. His eyes glowed with a brilliant silver light.

"Can you guess where I turned up when we went through the mirror this evening?"

Ethan looked around at the platform. "Here?"

Hunter nodded.

"You drank a little bit of Te'lo'hi, didn't you? Just like Jack Allen did in '55."

It was Te'lo'hi that answered. Scowling at the half dozen Jack Allens still standing around the platform, the child said

> *this man was a fool*
> > *he thought he had stolen a piece of my power*
> *taken it by force*
> > *he never realized that i gave it to him willingly*
> *he was not the only one of his ceremony to learn what was happening*
> > *through time and study*
> > *they all realized they were trapped*
> *it is how this woman came to be my new Attendant*
> > *the way the engineer shattered the mirror for Kyla*
> *it was*
>
> > > > *a disaster*

"They spent too long trapped here against their will," Hunter said. "Even longer than us."

> *i decided to try something new*

i allowed Jack Allen to find me
      i gave him a sliver of my power
                but when the new ceremony began
      i concealed the dead child and her sister
               to ensure she was never found
every night Jack Allen would cull the rest of you
           thinking he could break the circle
        giving no one else the opportunity
to learn what was happening here
           no one
i thought
             would break the circle again

Ethan shuddered at the word *cull.* He thought of what Jack Allen had told him in the diner today about being unable to find Penelope and Adeline in all his many nights at the motel. He looked to where Fernanda had crouched over Adeline. He said to Te'lo'hi, "Are you the reason Penelope's sister was stuck to her like a shadow?"

yes
      i could see that in many stories
i would be unable to guide enough souls to the motel tonight
      the new ceremony would not have had the power it needed
so when Adeline died,
    i did not allow her soul to escape
    I bound her to her sister
slumbering
    until she awoke today

Hunter frowned at this, a look of sincere pain crossing his face. *He killed families, Mister Cross.*

Ethan said to Hunter, "Every night at six thirty, on that smoke break with Ryan, you always remembered what was happening, didn't you? You remembered that you killed Sarah the first night and got us all trapped here."

"Yes."

"Why? Why keep it going?"

"To save the world. Why else?"

"That's bullshit," Ethan said. "You and I both know you'd let the world burn before you let someone tell you what to do. Just give me the truth. Please."

The silver light in Hunter's eyes seemed to shiver. They produced a pair of silver tears. "Do you remember two nights ago, right before the end, when I said how meeting you had changed me?"

That was six weeks ago. People don't change in six weeks.

"Yes."

"I've known you a lot longer than six weeks, Mister Cross," Hunter said. He tried to laugh, but the scratch in his chest turned into a hacking cough. He spat out blood. It, too, gleamed like mercury. "I felt like every night with you made me a better man. Just sitting in our room for a few hours at a time. Talking to you. Being near you. My dad always told me to make the best of a shit situation, so I did. I just . . . never wanted it to end."

Ethan could think of a million things to say to that, but he supposed it all boiled down to the same question. "So what happens now?"

With the knife in his hand, Hunter began to walk around the platform, slitting throats. He cut the throat of the Jack Allen behind Sarah, the ones that had been pursuing Ethan and Kyla, the one that had killed the Attendant, the one threatening Fernanda and Adeline.

Hunter said, "Now, I do what I was brought here to do. I've got the same power in me as Jack Allen has in himself. I'm the only one who can take care of him."

Ethan said, "But?"

"But . . . let's just say that Jack Allen and I would have to cancel each other out."

A great weight settled in Ethan's chest. All the horror, all the pain, and still it came down to this: two young men looking at each other in a pale light, knowing it could never last.

"That bug in your chest is terminal anyway, isn't it?" Ethan said.

"Of course. Why do you think they let me out of Huntsville? It would have cost them a fortune to treat me." Hunter studied the blood on his palm that he'd hacked up from his lungs. "I'd hoped you and me could have a little more time together before the whole ceremony broke down, but that's life, right? You never get as much time as you think."

Out of nowhere, Te'lo'hi opened his mouth and released one of those awful moans of pain.

it hurts

IT HURTS

Hunter said to Ethan, "He can't hold out much longer. Y'all are going to have to figure something out."

there's nothing to do

nothing

"I hope there's a way you can save yourselves," Hunter said. "I really do."

it's over

it's all OVER

Through the noise, Hunter pulled Ethan close again. He said, "If anyone can figure this out, it's you."

"Me? What am *I* supposed to do?"

"You're good with people, Ethan. I don't think a god is all that different at the end of the day."

Hunter squeezed him tighter. For a brief, hideous moment, Ethan couldn't imagine ever letting go of this embrace.

The man went on. "I have money in California. A lot of it. If you make it out of this, you'll find instructions on where to get it. There'll be more than enough to get you started again."

"Do I want to know how you made that money?"

"Money is money, Ethan. Just use it wisely."

Te'lo'hi started to moan again, and this time he didn't seem able to stop. Ethan remembered this sound from last night: when the mountain had started to scream like this, uninterrupted, things were about to end.

Still, Hunter held him. "I'm going to go now."

Ethan said, "All right."

Hunter said, "I love you, Ethan Cross."

Ethan met his gaze. "I know."

Hunter closed his eyes for a moment, let out a small smile. He nodded, probably because this was the best he was going to get. He let go, stepped away, and raised the knife again. He approached the Jack Allen that been stupid enough to grab Te'lo'hi, to ever think he could control a god. There was a mangled stump on the man's arm where the hand had been hacked away. A look of horror in his dark eyes.

Even frozen in space, Jack Allen had changed. He looked small and outplayed, pathetic in a way that was almost painful to fathom. In that moment, Ethan felt something he'd have never thought possible.

He was grateful his mother had died. He was grateful she would never have to see what her father had become.

Hunter slashed open the man's other wrist. He ran the blade along Jack Allen's neck. He buried the blade in the man's weeping eyes and dug them out, one by one. He sank the knife into Jack Allen's chest, deep in his heart.

Hunter thumped his own chest with his fist. He was wheezing bad. He looked at Ethan one last time. He opened his mouth, thought better of it. He gave Ethan a nod.

Time surged forward, all at once. The Jack Allens around the platform fell to their knees, clutching their slit throats. The one to whom Hunter had given special attention was screaming, blood jetting from his wounds.

Hunter moved fast. He grabbed the man by the arm and heaved him forward, across the platform, and planted his shoulder against Jack Allen's back. The man in the gabardine suit was powerless to stop him as Hunter pushed them both right to the edge of the column of silver light. Even through his pain and his blindness, Jack Allen seemed to realize what was happening. He dug in his heels. He tried to stop it.

With a wheezing roar and the last of his strength, Hunter slammed himself against Jack Allen, hurling them both into the air.

When the two men struck the silver column, a boom ripped through the air. A boom, and a flash of light, and the echoes of two voices amidst the noise.

Jack Allen was saying, "Love me. Love me. Love me."

The other voice was calm. Grateful. Sad. "Thanks, Ethan. For everything."

There wasn't time for any sort of sentiment. With time moving again, Kyla was at Ethan's side, staring down at the wailing god, saying to Ethan, "What the hell just happened?"

"I'll tell you later."

there is no later

                         there is no tomorrow

THERE IS NO NOW

Sarah Powers lay in a pool of blood, struggling to stand. The Attendant was dead. The column of silver light was glowing brighter than ever.

And Te'lo'hi was screaming.

Kyla shot Ethan a panicked look. She said to the little god, "Why don't you just *leave?*"

The child looked at her.

                         leave?

"You can exist anywhere, right?"

i don't

                         i don't know

"She's right," Ethan said. "If your full power is awakening, then doesn't that mean you can travel anywhere now? Go find some corner of the galaxy where nobody lives. Just go and release all your energy there?"

        i

            i

                i can't

                    i CAN'T

Ethan studied the little god. He saw the way that even as Te'lo'hi wailed and wept, there was something else in those silver eyes, a strange sort of shudder in his pale flesh. Ethan felt a stirring of understanding. *If anyone can figure this out, it's you.*

Ethan said to Te'lo'hi, "You can't, or you won't?"

The moans of pain continued, but the god somehow seemed to hesitate. He lifted his silver eyes to stare at Ethan.

what?

Hunter had been right. As Ethan watched the way the silver eyes trembled, the twitch in Te'lo'hi's small fingers, the flicker of doubt at the corners of his mouth, Ethan realized that a god wasn't so different from a person. Or at least not a god who had spent so long with the human race.

Te'lo'hi had the same little tics and tremors as any person. The same clicks and rumbles of an engine, all betraying the motor of the heart.

Ethan said, "You're afraid to be alone."

Te'lo'hi's moaning softened. It didn't end, but it calmed enough for Ethan to know he'd touched a nerve.

i'm

what?

"You're afraid of being left alone. You already lost your own people. Now you're afraid of losing everyone. You're afraid to be by yourself in this big, empty universe. I can't blame you. I was too afraid to leave home by myself too."

Kyla looked from Te'lo'hi to Ethan and back again. "Is he right? Is it really that simple?"

Te'lo'hi said nothing, but the beam of light was growing more unstable by the second. A crack spread through the stone platform beneath their feet. Sarah Powers stirred in her pool of blood.

"Please. Do something. Don't kill my boys."

i don't want it

    i don't want it

        I DON'T WANT TO BE ALONE

Every time Ethan thought this creature couldn't get any louder, he was proven wrong. It released a sound that defied definition. Ethan and Kyla doubled over in pain. The column of silver light started to expand.

Sarah spoke. It sounded like it took the last of her strength. "Why don't . . . one of you . . . go with him?"

Ethan looked at Kyla. Kyla looked to Ethan.

"Go with him?" Kyla said.

Ethan looked at the corpse of Frank O'Shea's mother, the dead Attendant. He said, "I guess we could become like her."

Kyla didn't look any more thrilled by the idea, but she gritted her teeth, nodded to Te'lo'hi. "We could leave. We could take you away. We could make sure—"

"No."

The voice that spoke was calm. Dignified. Effortlessly in command.

Two figures rose from their place on the platform. One was Adeline, who approached the screaming god-child without a scrap of fear. She put a hand on his shoulder and gave him a shake. "Hush. You're being a baby."

Fernanda crouched down next to the girl with a smile. She looked Te'lo'hi in the eye. She said, "Have you heard the story about the little god who made new friends?"

KYLA

Fernanda had plenty of practice with this sort of thing. Kyla could see, in an instant, how she'd survived so long at Frank O'Shea's house. With just a handful of words, a gentle hand on the head, she had calmed Te'lo'hi. The awful noises of pain began to ease. The column of silver light stopped spreading. A few words more, and the light began to cool. To stabilize.

It was like watching a magic trick. A master at work.

"The little god realized that if he had friends, he could survive anything," Fernanda said. "That he could *do* anything. That he would never be alone. He realized that with good people at his side, he could go on adventures forever through the stars."

She stopped to smile. Te'lo'hi said cautiously,

what

what kind of adventures?

Fernanda looked back at Ethan and Kyla with the saddest smile Ethan had ever seen.

Kyla said, "Are you sure about this?"

Fernanda said, "I looked and I looked in the mirror, but there isn't a future where my brother and I are safe together. I never found a world where we were both happy."

"I see," Kyla said.

Adeline patted Fernanda on the arm. "It's okay."

Ethan said simply, "Thank you."

With a soft grin, Fernanda turned back to Te'lo'hi. "What adventures? Oh, mijo. We should go see for ourselves."

A few feet away from Kyla, something shifted. Sarah Powers had stopped moving, Jack Allen's knife still buried in her back. But above her, something odd began to rise—silver and diaphanous, like the vapor of a dream.

Kyla's breath caught in her throat. That might just be Sarah's soul.

Te'lo'hi saw it too. The god flicked a little hand up and over and around, conducting the invisible forces around them. The shimmering substance rose higher into the air before flying over the platform and plunging into the silver waves below. Beneath them, Kyla heard a metallic chime like a bell.

She said, "What did you just do?"

> *i sent her to another story*
>   *one where she could still convince*
> *me and the old tribe*
>   *to help the people of this world*

Kyla said, "And what about your people? The other beings like you, the ones you got separated from? Why can't you go find them?"

> *they are*
> *so far away*
>   *even with my power*
>   *it would be*
>   *a very long journey*

Kyla looked from Adeline to Fernanda and back to Te'lo'hi. "Don't be afraid. I think you'll have some friends for the road."

Ethan said, "You can't keep putting off the inevitable. Sooner or later, you have to move forward. You have to face the facts. Time only goes one direction, even for you."

Little Adeline gave Te'lo'hi's shoulder another firm pat. Fernanda placed a hand on the back of the little god's neck. She said, "I've always wanted to know what else was out there. As long as we do not suffocate in the vacuum of space."

> *there are*
>   *there are ways to make the journey*

"Then let us make it," Fernanda said. "There is no time like the present."

Te'lo'hi seemed to smile.

i have seen
              many ways this night could end
i never believed
                   not for a moment
                             that this was the story you would choose

The silver light began to expand again, taking on as it did a new, softer color. It started to grow over the platform, heading toward Ethan and Kyla. Softer or not, Kyla had a feeling it would still be a bad idea to touch that light.

Te'lo'hi said,

       will you two join us
                    or will you follow another story?

Kyla and Ethan traded glances. They didn't have to ask each other. They already knew.

"I want to stay in this world," Ethan said. "I want to live this life."

Kyla said, "I want to finish what I started before I came here."

                    very well

Te'lo'hi pointed a finger to the rim of the platform at their feet. Out of the lake, a long ribbon of quicksilver rose up and formed itself into a bridge that seemed to stretch away for eternity.

Fernanda looked to Kyla. "Get the film to the cartel. Make sure they take care of my brother. They made a deal."

Kyla said, "I will."

Ethan caught Adeline's eye. He said, "I'm sorry for . . . whatever he did to you."

With a startling wisdom, Adeline just said, "It's the past."

The column of light would overwhelm the platform soon. Te'lo'hi said,

       you should go

No need to tell Ethan and Kyla twice. Turning toward the silver bridge, they found they were holding each other's hands. They traded one more look. They looked over their shoulders. Adeline and Fernanda were already beginning to glow with their own silver light. Te'lo'hi's long hair was floating around them like a shroud.

"Bye," Kyla said.

Fernanda's voice was already growing strange, like it bore the sound of its own echo. "Good luck."

Kyla and Ethan were a step away from the silver bridge. He gave her hand a squeeze.

Here goes nothing.

As a metallic sound broke out behind them, almost like the chime of a thousand bells, Kyla and Ethan raised their feet at the same time. A quick breath. A final hesitation. They took a step forward and

Part III

KICKING OUT
THE FOOTLIGHTS

LEAVING

The motel is desolate, like seventy years have passed in a single night. Graffiti. Water stains. Rust. In room 5 they find a shattered mirror, a splintered wardrobe. Beneath the filthy mattress, they discover Kyla's green backpack—the money still inside, the roll of film, all miraculously untouched by time. In Ethan's room, they find his duffel bag, the one he took from Ellersby. Inside he finds an address in California, the combinations to four padlocks, and a note that reads, *Good luck out there. I love you.*

Beneath this, someone has added in a different hand, *Y'all got this—R.P.*

Ethan will never know how this note was placed in this bag.

Ethan and Kyla walk all the way to Turner. It's not so far, now that the power of the ceremony isn't stretching out the road. In Turner, they find the dregs of what must have been a very bad day. Lola's Den, the fateful diner, is surrounded by police tape. The parking lot is a crime scene: trucks and SUVs are scattered everywhere. Broken windshields, shell casings. Blood.

An old farmer in bald overalls is surveying the violence with a pleasant smile. He gives Ethan and Kyla a polite nod. "Run out of gas?"

Ethan says, "How'd you know?"

The farmer is cheery as he drives. They're in a rusted pickup truck that smells, not unpleasantly, of dog.

Ethan says, "You're in a good mood."

"Who wouldn't be? Frank O'Shea is finally dead."

Kyla turns from the window. "He's what?"

"Apparently, the bastard and his goons turned up yesterday to that diner in Turner. Some thug who worked there also worked for Frank. He was a cook or something, but he was also a snitch; we all knew it. Anyway, he got his arm deep-fried. They're saying the cartel did it."

Ethan says nothing.

"Frank turned up at the diner a couple hours later, like I said, but then so does the cartel, along with every law agency you can think of. The rumor is that someone done killed a man that the cartel had planted on the inside of Frank's operation, one of O'Shea's top troops, but that's a rumor, obviously."

Kyla says nothing.

"Turns out, most of all the boys working for Frank were ready to move on. Half of them was working for the feds and the other half for the cartel. When the chips came down, they knew a lost cause when they saw it. O'Shea saw the writing on the wall. He tried to run. One of them UBP thugs shot him straight in the back."

Ethan says, "What's the UBP?"

"Didn't you see the SUVs in the parking lot? The US Border Patrol, son. O'Shea was the captain around these parts. Crooked as the day is long. It's how he got away with moving people like he did. Just picked them up trying to cross the border and sold them right down the river. Or so they say."

Kyla says to Ethan, "You didn't know?"

"As of four o'clock yesterday afternoon, Frank O'Shea stopped being captain of anything. Maybe they'll let him boss some men around in hell."

Four o'clock yesterday. By the time they'd reached the Brake Inn Motel, Frank O'Shea had been long dead.

The farmer scratches a spot on the seat, somehow releasing a fresh whiff of dog. "Some new son of a bitch will take over his spot sooner than later, I'm sure. But for now, at least we'll have some calm. You wouldn't believe the stories of what that man did."

"No," Kyla says. "I bet we wouldn't."

The farmer lets them off at the intersection of two highways. North will eventually lead to I-10, which rolls all the way to California. South leads straight to the border. The farmer keeps heading west, presumably back to the dog.

In his duffel bag, Ethan has two bands of cash each worth ten thousand dollars. Kyla wanted to give him more, but this will get an old car up and moving.

"Are you sure you don't want to come with me?" Ethan says. "You can head to Mexico from California. There's money waiting for me. A lot, by the sounds of it. Plenty to share."

Kyla shakes her head. "I'll catch up with you later. The border will be chaos today with Frank dead. There won't be a better chance to slip over without being stopped."

"If Frank's dead, the men from the cartel may not even want that camera film. They may not want to help Fernanda's brother anymore."

"I can be pretty persuasive. And if they don't, I still have the cash. I'll make sure the kid's set up all right."

"Not the same thing as having a sister."

"That's life."

"Yeah." Ethan nods. "That's life."

Kyla looks back. She can just see the mountain in the distance. "Do you think it's true what the old tribe thought? That the mountain has the power to make sure things happen exactly like they're supposed to?"

"I hope not. I'd rather not imagine some mountain was responsible for wasting my whole life in Ellersby. For putting Hunter in prison for what he was in prison for."

"For keeping Fernanda trapped at Frank's house like some animal."

"Yet here we are."

"Yeah." Kyla nods. "Here we are."

Which is when Ethan realizes that he and Kyla have been speaking, all this time, without opening their mouths. Kyla is already some ways down the southern road. Ethan is well to the north.

He realizes that Te'lo'hi might have given them a piece of *his* power on their way out the door.

"Keep in touch, Mister Cross," Kyla says, and despite the distance, he hears her just fine.

"Same to you, Miss Hewitt."

They left the mountain at dawn. They left behind the city, their friends, The Lake That Travels. One moment, Ethan and Kyla took their first step on the long bridge. The next moment, they were at the mouth of the cave. Behind them was nothing but rubble. No bridge. No silver light. No dead city.

Ahead was the most astonishing view of the desert they would ever see. They watched the sun rise over a landscape so massive it seemed a galaxy itself. One by one, small trees appeared, thin creeks, mile after mile of bright gold potential. A bird sang. Another answered.

High in the sky, just at the limits of their vision, Kyla and Ethan saw a departing glint of silver light.

Kyla said, "What day is it?"

Ethan said, "Tomorrow."

"Oh, I dream a highway back to you, love
A winding ribbon with a band of gold
A silver vision come and arrest my soul.
I dream a highway back to you."
GILLIAN WELCH, "I Dream a Highway"

ACKNOWLEDGMENTS

First and foremost, this book would have never existed without the endless support of Melissa Danaczko, agent extraordinaire, and the entire staff at Stuart Krichevsky Literary Agency. Equally massive is the support of my editor, Loan Le, who guided this book from a Zoom pitch at my dining room table to the book you hold in your hands now. Enormous thanks to her, Elizabeth Hitti, Natalie Argentina, Holly Rice-Baturin, Aleaha Reneé, Liz Byer, and the entire staff at Atria and Simon & Schuster.

My heartfelt thanks as well to the incredible team of beta readers who read this book in various early forms and provided incalculable feedback: Stacey Armand, Aashay Dalvi, Caroline Reilly, Pablo Armendariz, Jessica McComas, Ian Carrico, Paul Leonard, Jordan Moblo, and Brad Summerville. All the good parts got better because of them. All of the bad parts were entirely on me. Deserving of special thanks are my parents, Rose and David, who listened to endless brainstorming sessions over the two years it took to write this novel and who read it in almost every form. I don't know if I would have had the fortitude to keep going without their support.

Finally, portions of this book were written, based, or researched on land that was originally home to the Wi-iko (Waco), Naishan Dene (Plains Apache), Ná-izhán (Lipan Apache), Suma, La Junta, Tapaxcolmeh (Concho), Xumani (Jumano), and Chiso peoples. A land acknowledgment feels like scant justice for the ongoing violence inflicted on the first residents of this continent, but at the very least it can serve to counter the amnesia that always follows in the wake of a genocide. I'd like to imagine that in another world the tribes of the first Americans are living in the future they deserved. In this world, all we can do is to help them fight for that future the old-fashioned way.

AUTHOR'S NOTE

While this novel's mythology was inspired by many sources—some Indigenous, some not—it was not drawn from the sacred stories of any singular tribe. I am deeply grateful to this book's sensitivity readers. Their thoughtful notes made the book infinitely better.

ABOUT THE AUTHOR

John Fram is the author of the critically acclaimed supernatural thrillers *The Bright Lands* and *No Road Home*. He has written for *The Atlantic*, *The New York Times*, and elsewhere. A native of Texas, he lives in Waco and Austin. Find out more at JohnFram.com.

ATRIA BOOKS, an imprint of Simon & Schuster, fosters an open environment where ideas flourish, bestselling authors soar to new heights, and tomorrow's finest voices are discovered and nurtured. Since its launch in 2002, Atria has published hundreds of bestsellers and extraordinary books, which would not have been possible without the invaluable support and expertise of its team and publishing partners. Thank you to the Atria Books colleagues who collaborated on *The Midnight Knock*, as well as to the hundreds of professionals in the Simon & Schuster advertising, audio, communications, design, ebook, finance, human resources, legal, marketing, operations, production, sales, supply chain, subsidiary rights, and warehouse departments who help Atria bring great books to light.

EDITORIAL
Loan Le
Natalie Argentina

JACKET DESIGN
Emma Van Deun
James Iacobelli

MARKETING
Aleaha Reneé

MANAGING EDITORIAL
Paige Lytle
Shelby Pumphrey
Lacee Burr
Sofia Echeverry

PRODUCTION
Liz Byer
Stacey Sakal
Fausto Bozza
Esther Paradelo
Hannah Lustyik

PUBLICITY
Holly Rice-Baturin

PUBLISHING OFFICE
Suzanne Donahue
Abby Velasco

SUBSIDIARY RIGHTS
Nicole Bond
Sara Bowne
Rebecca Justiniano

SENSITIVITY READER
Jessica Elm